A Green

Bough

A Green

Bough

John Ware

PAGE D'OR
MMXXII

Page d'Or is an imprint of Prosperity Education Limited
Registered offices: 58 Sherlock Close, Cambridge CB3 0HP,
United Kingdom

A catalogue record for this book is available from the British Library

ISBN: 978-1-913825-57-7

Typeset in Times New Roman and Garamond by ORP Cambridge
Cover designed by ORP Cambridge
Cover photo: Battle of the Somme. "Trenches corrected to 5-8-16."
"Ordnance Survey, 1916." Reproduced with permission from Lloyd Reeds
Map Collection, McMaster University Library.
Back-cover photo: Kilworth Army Tents, Fermoy, County Cork: Mounted
Infantry Camp. Reproduced with kind permission from Bill Power
Photography
Frontispiece: Royal Munster Fusilier cap badge. Image courtesy of
the National Army Museum, London.

For further information visit: www.pagedor.co.uk

Ad infinitum et ultra.

But the bridge it stands and the water runs

As red as yesterday,

And the Irish move to the sound of the guns

Like salmon to the sea.

—Rudyard Kipling, 'The Irish Guards'

EXPLANATORY NOTE

A battalion is a sub-unit of a regiment. A regiment is a body of regular troops sharing a common corporate identity. A battalion (meaning roughly 'battle formation') might number anywhere between five hundred and a thousand personnel, and there might be one or two, or three battalions to a regiment. It all depends on the time and the place.

In the United Kingdom of Great Britain and Ireland, in the last decade of its existence as such, there was a minimum of two battalions to each regiment, but it wasn't quite that simple. For a start, a British regiment was not a tactical unit, but a family united by shared insignia and tradition rather than by organisational structure.

The Royal Munster Fusiliers were one of fifteen Irish regiments in the British army at the beginning of the twentieth century. They called themselves the Dirty Shirts in memory of their years of Indian service when they had sweated off their red coats, and they still displayed the Bengal tiger on their cap badge. Although transferred from Bengal to Tralee in 1881, they maintained their tradition of imperial soldiering. Of the two battalions that made up the fighting force of the regiment, one was always overseas while the one that remained at home trained up the replacements that would be fed to the foreign garrisons. In 1914, overseas meant Rangoon, with the various companies scattered across Burma. Home, in this case, was Aldershot in Hampshire. The regiment's actual home address – the depot where recruits were properly enlisted – was in Tralee, where there lived alongside

3

the small administrative staff a nominal third battalion. This was the old Kerry Militia under a new name. Cork and Limerick boasted fourth and fifth battalions respectively, but they were understrength units which functioned as no more than military clubs for those who thought to play at soldiers for a few weeks of the year.

Perversely, the army was possibly the only institution in which the union of Great Britain and Ireland appeared to work. In general, the Irish might look on the redcoats as occupying forces and agents of English tyranny, but once in those red coats (or khaki for most duties), the Irish consistently demonstrated themselves dependable servants of the crown.

Again perversely, Irish service in the British army reached new heights just as the United Kingdom of Great Britain and Ireland was about to be broken apart.

For two generations, the campaign for independence had been championed by the Irish Parliamentary Party, the Home Rulers, who, under the leadership of John Redmond, had finally forced the British government to concede a large measure of self-government to Ireland. This did not come without opposition – not least from Irish Unionists.

As if there weren't enough uniformed men in Ireland, the troops already garrisoned on the island in 1914, and the additional units earmarked to reinforce them in case of unrest, were joined by various home-grown forces. In determined opposition to the prospect of Home Rule, the Unionists raised the Ulster Volunteer Force – eighty thousand strong, and trained and officered by veteran soldiers. In counterbalance, the nationalists mustered the Irish Volunteers – more numerous but more amateurishly organised and equipped.

The sectarian strife in Ireland and the clamorous debate in London were both silenced by the shots that felled the heir to the Austro-Hungarian throne in Sarajevo. When the war with

Germany began, one of the few decision-makers to believe that it would most certainly not be over by Christmas was the new Secretary of State for War. This was Field-Marshal Lord Kitchener, another of those Irish-born soldiers of long service in India and Africa. Within days of his taking office, his pointing finger was ordering men to the ranks in unprecedented numbers.

The Irish answered.

Unsurprisingly, the Unionists instantly demonstrated their loyalty to the crown, with the Ulster Volunteers providing the manpower for the 36th (Ulster) Division. But the nationalists weren't much slower in coming forward either. John Redmond hadn't been playing politics all his life for nothing. He persuaded the government that the kingdom need not fear the nationalists. He promised that they could be trusted not to take advantage of this crisis, and in return a relieved government granted the long-delayed Home Rule to come into effect once the war was over. So Irish Home Rule was now, at last, law if not fact, and Redmond, for so long a parliamentary troublemaker, was now Ireland's prime minister-in-waiting. A few weeks later, at Woodenbridge in Wicklow, Redmond, flushed with triumph, addressed the Irish Volunteers.

In a war, he said, 'undertaken in the defence of the highest principles of religion and morality and right', it was the duty of Irishmen to play their part. Although the Volunteers were divided on the issue of trusting the government, enough of them believed Redmond: enough to form the 16th (Irish) Division, which was to say twelve battalions of infantry, along with their supporting arms and services.*

Along with the 10th (Irish) Division, who had not waited for Redmond's appeal, these men constituted the first army that

---

* As it happened, the 16th Division was not to be wholly Irish. The division's artillery, instead of being made up of Irish recruits, was assigned to the Royal Artillery in England. Even in this time of apparent national harmony, it was deemed a step too far to give field guns to Irish nationalists.

Ireland had put into the field for more than two hundred years. Technically, they were soldiers of the king, but they were fighting for Ireland, commanded by Irishmen and displaying Irish insignia. For the first time the green flag was not a sign of sedition.

Before them lay a war that could grind down whole armies in a matter of days. Around them, often unseen, were those nationalist elements who had not answered the call, who saw the implementation of Home Rule deferred with every month the war lengthened, and who cared nothing for Redmond's promises, but chose to stay at home, watching for Ireland's opportunity.

I

KILLED, WOUNDED, MISSING

They fought as they revelled, fast, fiery, and true,

And, though victors, they left on the field not a few;

And they who survived fought and drank as of yore,

But the land of their heart's hope they never saw more;

For in far foreign fields, from Dunkirk to Belgrade,

Lie the soldiers and chiefs of the Irish Brigade.

—Thomas Davis, 'The Battle Eve of the Brigade'

1

'Stop your hand now,' he said, 'for that is enough for this time; and do not send me to my death yet awhile, and heal me of my wounds first.'

—Lady Augusta Gregory, *Gods and Fighting Men*

There was a break in the world. In appearance it was no more than an ugly strip of neglected land, somewhat battered and often waterlogged. It wasn't so wide that first winter that voices could not be heard across it on still nights, but it represented a gulf in understanding and a rift in human sympathy.

For example: a shell from a German 15-centimetre howitzer was fired a little before half-past ten, local time, on a November morning, spent little less than eight seconds in the air, but landed at roughly half-past nine, according to a different local time, on the British side of the line, where it was reported as being 5.9 inches in calibre. These were cultural differences with painful consequences.

The shell was fired in response to an irate telephone call from the front line where a working party was reported as having been fired on by a sniper. The sniper's location was approximated by the men in the line, and further approximated by the artillery officer using the improvised large-scale maps that were available. He furrowed his brow at all the variables to be calculated, took his best stab at it, and gave his instructions to the corporal in charge of one of the guns, who tacitly adjusted the range settings according to his own judgement. It wasn't as if there was a generous stock of ammunition to be throwing out every time the infantry got upset, and the front line should be grateful for the single round they were going to get. As luck would have it, the shell fell on, or at least close enough to its intended target, and the infantry was on the telephone again to congratulate the gunner officer, who was young and new enough to blush at the compliment and award a bottle of beer for each man on the gun crew – whenever beer might become available, that is. The men were pleased, but had already learned in this war that it didn't pay to get your hopes up. If promises came true, then they'd all have been in Paris months ago and back home in time for Christmas.

Things were less promising on the receiving end of the gunners' attentions. The shell did not kill any sniper, but it did cave in a forward post where two privates of the Royal Munster Fusiliers had alleviated the boredom by taking an innocent pot-shot at the enemy. One of the soldiers was more or less unscathed, and was at least able to make it to the aid post on his own two feet. To his undying disgust, the aid post sent him straight back to the line, with nothing more than aspirin and some sticking plaster for his pains. His comrade was given fuller treatment. He had been picked up and thrown down by the blast, and peppered by odd bits of debris for good measure. So, while Private Francis Moriarty soldiered on, grumbling, with little more than temporary deafness and ripening bruises, Private Daniel Wyndham left the trenches of St. Yvon flat on a stretcher, and was not expected to rise from his bed of pain any time soon.

Wyndham awoke in a field hospital, which is to say in a barn surrounded by tents. He was in no pain but was desperately cold and unable to move. Someone was murmuring in Latin. Wyndham opened one eye, which was all he could manage for some reason, and saw beside him an officer with a kindly face. A purple stole draped from the man's shoulders and a clerical collar above the khaki tunic told Wyndham all he needed to know. He was being given his last rites, and by a Roman Catholic chaplain at that. To die was upsetting enough, but to die in the wrong faith was too much.

It took effort, and Wyndham didn't want to give offence, but something had to be said.

He opened his mouth, but nothing much came out. He tried harder, but only succeeded in making himself cough. That was the first time he felt definite pain. The priest put a soothing hand on him.

'Go easy there, lad,' he said. 'You have a few broken bones on you.'

Wyndham, unable in his condition to pay proper respect to the man's rank or cloth, managed to grind out the words, 'Not Catholic', and the chaplain smiled and nodded.

'Do you know, but I didn't think you were. But I thought I'd say a prayer for you on the off chance. You've no identity tags and your small book is all gummed up. You got a nasty bit of a gash there and it bled all over, I'm afraid.'

Wyndham could feel it all of a sudden. His chest was broken. His body was wrecked. It made him feel infinitely sad.

'Will I die?' he whispered, and the weakness in his voice was not just from his injuries.

'Ah no,' said the priest. 'You're a bit knocked about, but you'll be grand. I'll talk to you again.'

And he patted Wyndham gently and was gone from his vision.

Wyndham lay awake in mourning for a while, and then it was some different time and he was somewhere else. Men came and gave him something to drink, and maybe someone else examined him, but that could have been a dream. The next time anyone spoke directly to him it was the priest again.

'Daniel Wyndham. Am I right?'

Wyndham's throat was too dry to work, and he was unwilling to try nodding his head. The priest had a clipboard and a pencil.

He was doing the nodding for both of them.

'2nd Battalion Royal Munster Fusiliers? Good. I have your small book here. One of the orderlies gave it a rinse for me. Religion – does that say Episcopalian? Well, now there's a thing. I'm helping out where I can. Everyone's rushed off their feet. Not as bad as a few weeks back, mind. Of course, I need hardly be telling the likes of you. Episcopalian, now. How does that happen, if you'll forgive me? There's a ward full of Sikhs over yonder, but I know how they got here of course. Ah! I see it here. Born in the United States. Parish of St. John's, in or near the town of Lowell, in the county of Middlesex, which apparently isn't the Middlesex we know at all but is apparently in Massachusetts. United States of America. Well, fancy.'

He beamed at Wyndham.

'So, we have you in order, then. I'd be fascinated to hear your story sometime. Goodbye for now, and God bless you.' And then he was gone. Wyndham never saw him again.

Well, fancy. How does it happen that a nice young Episcopalian from Massachusetts ends up fighting in a great war in Europe and, for all he knew, dying under wet canvas in bitter Belgium? How could that pleasant Wyndham boy become so misty-eyed by the allure of Irish heroic legend that he just had to go and see Ireland for himself, and fall in with low company like that same Private Moriarty who just now had so narrowly escaped serious injury? And how could it happen that, having learned the scandalous cost of drinking with soldiers in a public house in Tralee, the same Daniel Wyndham could be seduced by the paternal charm of old Major Hugh Fitzmullen-Brophy into actually joining up with the army, if only on an unofficial and strictly trial basis? And surely, all this having somehow come about, and war with Germany having been unexpectedly declared, the now-uniformed Private Wyndham should have had nothing whatever to do with Major

Fitzmullen-Brophy's harebrained scheme for getting into the war before it ended. Had Wyndham no sense? Had he forgotten that he was a citizen of the United States? That he had a mother at home in a respectable neighbourhood, who would be distressed beyond measure at her son's inconsiderate escapades?

But Wyndham had for some unaccountable reason taken a liking to the Royal Munster Fusiliers, the Dirty Shirts, and particularly to Major Fitzmullen-Brophy, and had followed the major to France out of curiosity and loyalty. It didn't work out as planned, of course. It couldn't have worked. The army found them out and ordered them all home in disgrace. But then everything had changed. The German army met the British and overwhelmed them, and by the time the British had gathered themselves after their long retreat, they were in no position to reject an eccentric Irish officer or his rag-tag company of half-trained militia.

And so Wyndham had found himself, with no military legitimacy and barely a notion of which end of a rifle to hold, in a trench south of the southern edge of the Ypres salient, and that was certainly not the time to mention to anyone that he was really no more than a tourist. He had come through the unsettling experience with a whole skin, and that was more than most men could have boasted, and in the relative lull that followed he had been waiting for the opportune moment to point out that his modest term of enlistment was up in December and that he wasn't a British subject in the first place, and, what with the war quietening down and enough fresh men arriving to see it through its final phase, he might suggest that he be excused.

And now he was sleepily running all this through his mind, rehearsing it in case he met the chaplain again, when unconsciousness took him. He woke up somewhere different again, somewhere cleaner, but still cold. There was a calm bustle about the place, and when he croaked for attention a busy young medical orderly told him to hold on a tick, and was back shortly with a mug of tea. He helped Wyndham take a few partly successful sips, addressed him as 'chum', and told him not to worry – he'd be in Blighty soon enough.

It occurred to Wyndham that he had heard mention of this Blighty before, but he did not know where or what it was. Old soldiers, their speech rich in Hindustani, Arabic and Afrikaans, had spoken of it. Blighty – a promised destination; a home to which time-expired men might return. It may in reality have been no more than a drab barracks in England or, given the funny parochialism of the empire's defenders, a pub in Portsmouth, but now Wyndham was seeing it as a mythical land of plenty, where old soldiers went at the end of their service: an otherworld reserved for the sweats and the swaddies, where the sergeants had no voices to shout with and where the beer was cheap. Heaven, Hell and Blighty.

Wyndham had got over his fear of dying for the moment. The fear took too much effort. But maybe that's what the orderly was really telling him. Daniel Wyndham had been a good soldier according to his lights, and now would be permitted to fade away into the west: to Fiddler's Green, to Tír na nÓg, to Blighty.

But he was not dying, and he would not die from these hurts. He had a broken collarbone, with a severe laceration above the break, and various lesser cuts and abrasions. He mercifully had no recollection of the smaller wounds being cleaned out (small stones, wood splinters and the odd, minute metal shard), but the first time he was awake for a change of dressing to his mangled shoulder, he was put in fear of any further attention, and thereafter dreaded every sound of approach to his cot. And even without that intensity of pain, there was the general pervasive pain that came in its own time and, once established, made Wyndham forget that he had ever been well and healthy. And besides the pain there was cold and nausea, and, when he was awake for longer stretches, anxiety.

He had been in a hospital before, but that had been in more civilised and considerate times. Here he didn't know what was happening or what would happen. There was the occasional offer of a sip of tea or the puff on a cigarette, but these were illicit kindnesses, and useless, for the thought of either made him feel ill. There was no gentleness here. Wyndham had no friends. They had taken his clothes at some point, and now, at any time without warning, brisk hands might be laid on him, and this borrowed shirt might be parted or lifted while medical procedures were performed. Sometimes he was spoken to, and sometimes the words were even kind, but it was with a tone used for horses or idiots, with no expectation of intelligent reply. And then it made sense to him: it was the tone used for soldiers. This is how soldiers were spoken to when they were not being harried and chivvied. Wyndham was still in the army.

2

...And I am certain that the water, the water of the seas and of the lakes and of mist and rain, has all but made the Irish after its image.

—W.B. Yeats, *The Celtic Twilight.*

In Festubert you couldn't stick a shovel into the ground without striking water. A trench more than eighteen inches deep was a flooded trench, and so the line that straggled across this waterlogged landscape was made up of low muddy banks fronting sodden ditches. It wasn't a line at all, but a makeshift alignment of sandbagged outposts – a dank archipelago.

There were places where the empty expanses between one island and the next were too wide: where the water pervaded beyond the endurance of men to hold their ground. Such gaps were an invitation to the enemy who, at this hopeless tail end of a failed year, might try to grasp even the smallest advantage in prospect of a better start to next year's campaign. Both sides were at the limits of their resources, but in this war every little bit helped. A wet field gained near Festubert in December could lead on – who knows? – to Paris in the summer.

A gap had opened up in the British line and the Germans could not be given a chance to exploit it.

Sent to plug the gap was the 2nd Battalion of the Royal Munster Fusiliers – what there was of it.

The story of the 2nd Munsters was an unhappily common one. In August they had constituted a body of first-class professional

16

fighting men – eager lads, trained to perfection, mixed with older reservists who had soldiered in Africa and India. By November they had been worn down almost to nothing, but the pitiful few that remained were valued because they were veterans, and because there was as yet too little to replace them in the line.

It was a common story, but the 2nd Munsters were more unfortunate than most. In their first proper fight they had been practically wiped out. Then the broken bits that were left had been shoved into the line here and there because there was nothing else, and those remnants had been worn down further, even as fast as the bewildered replacements had been arriving from home. The odds and ends had been collected together and reconstituted as a battalion just in time to be ground up at Ypres, but the war wasn't done with them yet.

GHQ must have felt that a little more could be squeezed out of the 2nd Munsters before they went on the scrap heap. Thus, in the week before Christmas 1914, they were marched for a day and a night through the lashing rain to a threadbare stretch of the Western Front near Festubert, and given the job – one more time – of plugging a gap before the Germans thought to exploit it.

It was like stopping up holes in the skirting board with wads of old newspaper. It only gave the rats something to chew on before they were through again.

'Moriarty! Moriarty, come on out of there!'

'Ah, for the love of God, leave me alone.' Moriarty's voice was muffled. He was curled up on a sort of a shelf, recessed in the trench wall a little above water level, and his back was to the world.

'Come on out of there!'

The response was a plaintive groan, barely distinct. 'For Christ's sake, I'm not well.'

'That's "For Christ's sake, Corporal," and you're grand.

There's nothing wrong with you, you lazy scut. I'm going to count to a very small number. Get your arse out of there. One.'

Corporal Sheehan didn't wait for two, but grabbed Moriarty's belt and heaved. Moriarty kicked and struggled free to keep from going backwards into the water that was knee-deep and bitter cold.

It was too early on a dark December morning, and the rain had been sweeping down for days. Back home they'd be saying that it wasn't fit for man or beast. Out here they reckoned it was fit for the 2nd Battalion of the Royal Munster Fusiliers – what there was of it.

The Munsters were to take the place of an Indian regiment. The Indians had not fared well in a French winter. They had wrapped themselves in their greatcoats and all their winter woollens, but had still shivered, and that was when they'd been mustered on the quayside in Marseilles. A month later, at Festubert, they still weren't used to the climate, but they'd been sent into the line anyway, and here the Indians stood against the Germans until there weren't enough fit men to carry the sick out.

The Indians were good soldiers, but this wasn't the sort of war for which they could have been prepared. It didn't take much for the Germans to break them.

And so the Munster Fusiliers – what there was of them – were called for again, only it was too much to ask of one of them at least.

Private Francis Moriarty could sympathise with the Indians. He had found this little bit of shelter when the battalion halted on the way up the line, and while it was anything but comfortable, and far from dry, it was out of the wind at least. It may only have been a hole scraped in the cold earth, but he was damned if he was going to forsake it and face another march like the one just endured. There was no tea, there was no rum, and somewhere the brigadier would be telling the colonel how they were to go about getting themselves all killed.

'I'm not well,' he told Sheehan again, and in truth he did not look well. Like almost all of them, Moriarty's uniform was filthy with months of rough living, and misshapen from all the layers worn underneath. His head was covered by a slovenly, knitted cap comforter instead of a soldierly cap. An untrimmed moustache drooped on an unshaven face. No man here looked smart, but Moriarty looked listless and spent, as if the last of the soldier in him had finally been wrung out.

Sheehan didn't care for Moriarty at all. Moriarty was a waster and a moaner. Back in Tralee Moriarty had been the old soldier, ill-inclined to pay too much respect to a new-made NCO like Sheehan who had never been out East. Out here in France he'd lost some of his strut. Out here the lessons of imperial service were meaning less and less every day. Even the men who had fought in South Africa were finding that experience increasingly irrelevant, and Moriarty hadn't been to South Africa. Moriarty, in short, was nothing special, but he was grousing like he deserved better treatment than the rest of them.

This past month, Sheehan had noticed, the grousing had tended more towards whining. Moriarty had gone from a skrimshanker to a skulker; not dodging out of distasteful tasks like a seasoned professional, but actively going into hiding and not even concocting excuses when he was caught.

Sheehan recollected the close shave that Moriarty had had a few weeks previously. That might well have been the start of the man's decline. The American, Wyndham, had been carted off on a stretcher, but Moriarty barely had a scratch. The MO had slapped on a plaster and sent him back on duty, but Moriarty's nerves had been badly shaken. That's what Sheehan now thought anyway. It didn't make him think any better of the wretched specimen in front of him, but he privately acknowledged that Moriarty's woes, even if they were all in his head, were a genuine trouble to the man and not just a self-indulgent pose.

Sheehan was a conscientious NCO. He wasn't going to let a man slide away into despair and uselessness.

'Go on, stand up, Moriarty. Have a smoke. You'll feel better,' and he pulled from deep in his clothing the remains of a packet of cigarettes that were just about the last dry things in his possession.

'Go on. Stand in out of the wind and I'll light it for you. You'll be grand.'

He watched Moriarty take a long shuddering draw and left him to it. The platoon sergeant was waving to him. They were moving forward again.

Sheehan looked back a little while later, searching out Moriarty, and was relieved to see that he had fallen in with the rest. The Munsters left the dubious shelter of the reserve trenches and, with the mud sucking at their feet with every step, they advanced into the dawn of another filthy winter's day.

3

The Munsters weren't going to be put out by 'a sup of water!'

—Lieutenant-Colonel H.S. Jervis, *The 2nd Munsters in France*

Moriarty was thinking about Private Dennehy – hadn't that been his name? Dennehy had been a gobshite who was always giving out, and he'd let them down badly at Armentières. When there was only a handful of the lads left and they'd been ordered to make another attack, hadn't Dennehy only gone and put a bullet through his hand. Moriarty hadn't actually seen it himself, but he was in no doubt at all. Dennehy had been talking about shirking beforehand, and then, when it was all over, hadn't he shown up with a nice clean wound in his left hand, and no one but him to say how he'd got it.

Moriarty was thinking about how a man might get such a wound without, say, blowing off most of everything below the wrist.

If – just for the sake of arguing, like – he were to shoot himself in the hand, he'd first have to be very careful in removing most of the charge from the cartridge, which wouldn't be so difficult if there was no one watching you. Then, to be on the safe side, and to keep from getting tell-tale burns around the wound, it would be a good idea to wrap a sterile field dressing around your hand. You'd have to take it off straight after, of course, and have another one handy. It would be tricky – no doubt about that – but if you miscalculated and lost a finger or two, or the wound got badly infected and you even lost the whole hand..., well. Moriarty had seen all manner of horrible wounds these last few months, and surely it would be better to lose a hand and get the hell out of this

21

awful business than it would be to hang around and get your face or both your legs blown off or something.

Not that he was going to commit a self-inflicted wounding, of course. That wasn't just a crime: it was a low act.

You might need pliers to get the bullet out of the cartridge, he was thinking. Hard to get a grip otherwise in this cold, with everything soaking wet.

Colonel Arthur Milton Bent, who had inherited the battalion in October, had striven to recreate from the collection of battle-scarred survivors and hastily recalled reservists a unit that could live up to the name of 2nd Munsters. He had done well, all things considered. He had nurtured and husbanded his command even as GHQ had seemed set on frittering it away. An undaunted loyalty to the regiment kept him at it. He carried on, no matter what. His reward was to lead his battalion into this desolation.

There had been no reconnaissance and no real preparation. The vile weather and the long march to the front meant that either the exhausted men could be sent floundering forward in hope of making sense of things, or they could be allowed a couple of hours to rest before their ordeal. Colonel Bent had reckoned that nothing useful could be gained by spending those hours slopping blindly forward. It was a humane decision, and possibly even the correct one. Maybe the destruction of the Munsters was foredoomed whatever happened.

The line had never been a coherent thing, so there was only a vague idea where the gap had been made, or where the enemy was, or where the Munsters were supposed to be.

At seven in the morning the battalion advanced into pelting sleet, and into nothingness. In poor visibility, and on a featureless and unfamiliar field, they pushed on until the Germans had them in range. Raked by machine-gun fire and pounded by artillery, the Munsters' battle lasted a mere ten minutes. After that they huddled in the wet earth and waited for the day to end. Those ten minutes had cost them half their number in killed and wounded.

Sometime during that bitter day, a message was sent back, asking for reinforcements. There were none to send. Instead, when darkness came down again, the shattered battalion was withdrawn. They recovered as many of their wounded as they could find, but it was no easy thing in the rain and the dark. They did find Colonel Bent because they were looking for him especially. He had been almost filleted by a shell – opened up practically from armpit to hip – and had lain through the day and into the night in freezing water, but he was still alive. Miraculously, he was to recover.

They didn't find Private Moriarty until later. His condition was far less dramatic, but it would be a good while before he would get much better.

Moriarty hadn't been wounded – not even by himself. In his wretchedness he was in no humour to be shot at all, whether it was with a German machine-gun bullet or a carefully doctored British cartridge. The past days had worn down what little courage he had left, and he felt every drop of rain like a slap. He was not up to adding to his discomforts with a bullet wound. That was just stupid. When the whistle blew and the companies extended into attack order, he went with them, his bayonet fixed and his heart in his boots. He went forward because it was easier than staying put. Staying put would have amounted to desertion in the face of the enemy, and he'd have had to become a fugitive, and that would have taken too much effort altogether.

So, forward he went, his soul numb.

Bereft of spirit and resigned to his fate he might have been, but this was Moriarty's third battle, and when the front erupted in jarring noise he knew enough to take cover and he knew not to be finicky about it. If there was a big, flooded shell hole right there beside you then into that big, flooded shell hole you went, and no dithering about it. It was a matter of urgency because new shell holes were suddenly being created and bullets were hammering into the mud all around. He didn't make a decision, and he certainly didn't wait for orders. Instinct sent him into the freezing water, and there he was going to stay for however long they kept on shooting up above.

He was shivering, and no wonder. It was late December and he hadn't a dry stitch on him, and there were men over there who'd kill him if he so much as raised his head. He heard someone fall close by. He didn't know who it was, but the man was shrieking in terror and pain. Moriarty could picture the unknown man clearly, desperately clawing his way towards shelter, dragging a shattered, useless leg behind him. Moriarty could reach out and drag the man in, but the man would die anyway. The shock and the blood loss would do for him in no time. There was no point in risking his own life.

Or he could hike himself up over the edge of the shell hole and see that it was too far to reach, and then he'd get hit himself, and then they'd both die. There was no point in that,

The wounded man was still crying out. There was nothing Moriarty could do for him.

A spiteful fusilade struck near the lip of the crater. Moriarty wanted to hunker down further, but if he did he'd slip down under the water. He'd help the wounded man, swear to God, only they'd both be killed. No point at all in that.

His teeth were beginning to chatter with the cold, and he was breathing so fast and shallow he was practically whimpering.

After a while he could no longer hear the wounded man.

A while after that and the firing tailed off. It seemed the Munster Fusiliers' battle – what there was of it – was over.

Moriarty stayed where he was.

He drove his rifle, bayonet first, down into the mud below his feet and that allowed him to lean forward, the upright rifle taking his weight, his hands resting on the butt and his chin on his hands. It meant that the rifle would get all clogged up with mud, but he didn't care. He wasn't fighting anyone anymore. He found that if he didn't move at all then he didn't feel the cold so badly. He was still freezing, mind, only he didn't feel it so badly.

Somewhere beyond, out there in the weather, he thought he heard shouting. Survivors getting organised, he supposed. It was all too far away to be any of his business. He wanted no more part in the fighting, or in the war, or anything at all. He wanted to be warm. He wanted to be sitting by a fire. He saw it all with perfect clarity. He wanted to be sitting by the fire in a pub, back in Cork. Not like a soldier, drinking aggressively, racing against the licensing hours and showing how he could handle his drink. No. He just wanted to be sitting quietly by the fire with his jar, reading the paper. Moriarty loved to read the papers. He'd sold papers when he was a kid, and he'd be reading them all he could and be telling people bits of news, and being a fella in the know. He wanted that back now. Sitting in the warm, all nice and quiet, and talking now and then to the barman about what was in the paper. *Did you see what they're saying here?*

And then he slipped forward a little and was wide awake again. In regaining his balance, he felt the wet clothes move on his skin and the last fragment of his illusory warmth was gone.

And he imagined that pub again, but he wasn't in the picture anymore. Now it was strangers, comfortable and uncaring.

Did you hear about that Francie Moriarty at all? Didn't he go and drown in a field in France? Drowned like a fool. Will we have another?

Moriarty vainly huddled into himself. Then he started crying.

When they found him and pulled him out of the hole, he couldn't walk. He couldn't speak either. They shook him gently and pulled and patted at his face like he was a dog, but they got no response out of him besides sniffles. Maybe he'd be alright after a rest and a cup of tea.

On Christmas Day he was in hospital, with the official diagnosis being exposure, but he remained unresponsive. They fed him beef tea, but they had to give it to him with a spoon. Some kindly soul gave him a bottle of stout, but it remained untouched on his bedside locker so they gave it to the man in the next bed, who was more appreciative of the spirit of the season.

When Moriarty was awake, he lay curled up, not making a sound and hardly even blinking. When he slept, he could be heard making little mewing noises.

By New Year's Day his strength had returned somewhat, as could be gauged by the tightness of his grip on the bedclothes. It took the brute strength of two orderlies to separate him from his blankets just so they could make his bed. When they finished, one of them brought him an extra blanket, tucked it around him and patted him on the shoulder. Moriarty started crying again. They took it as a sign of progress.

4

The Regiment did all, and more than all, that men could do; they played up splendidly. I have never known men do so much. I am very proud of them.

—Lt-Col G.J. Ryan, 2nd Royal Munster Fusiliers, killed at Givenchy

'What do we have here?'

'Private Moriarty, Munster Fusiliers.'

'What's wrong with him?'

'You tell me, old man.'

'Oh Christ, not another one?'

'Looks like.'

'Let's have a look at him.'

Moriarty, clean and presentable in hospital blue, was brought in. He could feed and dress himself now, and talk, but he was anything but talkative. When questioned he twitched and sniffed before giving a straight answer, and that was only when the question was simple and direct, and usually repeated more than once.

The two doctors cursorily examined him as if he were for sale.

'Neurasthenia?'

'Or shell shock.'

'I don't want to hear that term. You're not to use that term, do you hear?'

'All right then. Call it neurasthenia. Amounts to the same damn thing though.'

'Except that soldiers don't suffer from neurasthenia. Their sensibilities are too coarse.'

'You mean they don't have enough money.'

'Very funny.'

If they were to be perfectly honest, neither of the two Royal Army Medical Corps doctors was quite sure what neurasthenia was, only that it had something to do with the nerves and there was a lot of talk about it going round. Soldiers reduced to mental and emotional wrecks had been all too common a sight in the base hospitals that winter. Diagnostic guesses were being made and fancy names were being bandied about, but if the doctors who saw Moriarty had been interested in rooting out new ailments, they wouldn't have gone into the RAMC. Let the civilian specialists in Harley Street and the teaching hospitals do the academic stuff. These doctors were army officers first, and men of science somewhere farther down the line, after hunting and billiards perhaps. 'No bloody research' was the unofficial motto of the medical corps. But that was all very well until you went to war and found yourself having to deal with what were once perfectly sound soldiers reduced to idiocy or hysteria.

Some influential clever-clogs – no doubt one of those fellows who treated rich hypochondriacs and wrote for *The Lancet* – had termed it a nervous disorder, and thus the term neurasthenia had gained currency. It provided a label where one was needed and made the medicos look like they knew what they were talking about. Appearances aside, they still had no clue what they were dealing with.

Nobody remembered seeing such cases in South Africa, but then the medical corps had been young in those days and nobody had been looking too hard. If a soldier became deranged it was usually drink or sunstroke that was to blame, with the occasional case of syphilis thrown in for variety. But the men of the British Expeditionary Force, here at the dawn of 1915, had limited access to drink and hadn't seen the sun since October at the latest.

Moreover, none of the nervous cases had been found to suffer from an unmentionable disease.

It had been pointed out that what made this war different – to all the other campaigns that the army had soldiered through without any attacks of the vapours – was the new chemical explosives. An 18-pounder, high-explosive shell, for example, was about the size of a milk bottle, which on detonation instantly expanded into a ball of fiery gas about the size of a small drawing room. It stood to reason that this sudden and most violent expansion would have an adverse effect on whoever happened to be nearby. The theory was that the shock of the explosion physically disordered the victim's nervous system. He might be fortunate enough not to have a scratch on him, but the neurological damage was as real as any wound. Hence, 'shell shock'.

It was a neat explanation, but the army hated it. If a man were subject to the shock of artillery bombardment, and if this shell shock were a genuine medical condition, then he could legitimately report sick. Indeed, once the rank and file had got wind of the notion, soldiers had been remarkably quick to go absent or to slope off to the rear along with the rest of the wounded on the grounds that, since they'd been under fire, they were now shell-shocked. Naturally, this just wouldn't do. Let the Harley Street quacks and the Viennese mountebanks say what they liked: the army was having none of it. The army laid down that a man was either sick or well, wounded or mad. Pernicious modern theories were to be utterly disregarded. 'Shell shock' indeed.

But this firm definition did little to help the doctors endeavouring to dispose of the case of this Private Moriarty.

'All joking aside, old man, but if a fellow grows up in a bog in Ireland, then you can't expect delicacy and refinement. The man should be able to stand up to all sorts of hardship. Saying a fellow like that has a nervous disorder is just silly.'

'Fair point, but if his system has been knocked out of trim by shellfire, then why don't we have the whole blessed Expeditionary Force trooping through here, all palsied and drooling? I mean, the whole lot of them have been under fire since August and most of them seem to be bearing up reasonably well.'

'We've had this conversation before, you know. It doesn't get us anywhere as far as treating the patient is concerned.'

'Remind me what we did the last time.'

'Last time was different. Chap was suffering from paralysis. This one's just dull-witted.'

'Do you think he's shamming, this Moriarty?'

'Do you?'

'Hmm.'

'Look – here's the thing. If he's shamming then so are a lot of these cases, and beyond sticking them with pins there's not much we can do, just like there's not much we can do if they are truly suffering from some disease of the nerves. It's a waste of our time, if you can see what I'm getting at. If we start worrying about each and every case, we'll never get anything done. Let's just decide now.'

'Fair enough. Do we send him back to his unit?'

'They'll either send him straight back to us or they'll shoot him. I say we send him home. Let them deal with it. Send him back to his home depot. If he gets better, then all well and good. If he doesn't, then they can put him in hospital and he's someone else's pigeon.'

'Right-oh. So, what do we put down as a diagnosis?'

'Oh, just put "neurasthenia", I suppose. No one will have heard of it in Ireland, so they're hardly likely to object.'

5

'We would sooner death to bring ourselves away, than to see you with wounds upon your body, and with no physician to heal you.'

—Lady Augusta Gregory, *Gods and Fighting Men*

At the same time as the Munsters were slogging up to Festubert through the rain and the sleet, it was decided that Wyndham was to be sent home. Even though he was mild and obedient, he had displeased the medical authorities. His collar bone had refused to mend in a satisfactory manner, and the doctors were taking a dim view of a soldier who would not make the best of things and respond to their professional attentions.

Then the patient obstinately – almost wilfully – contracted pneumonia. That just wasn't good enough. The doctors looked at him as though he had let them down quite badly. As soon as they deemed him out of danger, they marked him for home. The army would be getting along quite well without the likes of Private Wyndham, D., Royal Munster Fusiliers.

The army's medical administration was efficient, but it had yet to become the awesome machine that could process casualties in their hundreds of thousands. Certainly, the army had been roughly handled these past months, but the army was small yet. The mutilated multitudes were still to come. The Royal Army Medical Corps was still learning, still finding its feet. This meant that awkward characters like Wyndham were not speedily dispatched across the Channel like second-class parcels. Things weren't running quite so smoothly just yet. Also, it was Christmas.

Wyndham spent Christmas Eve dozing on a stretcher in a draughty corridor. In a lucid moment he reflected on how the army existed either in a fug – an all-too human miasma of tightly packed soldiers – or in an excess of fresh air, where physical energy rather than warm clothing was expected to keep the chill out. His experience so far had convinced him that the army medics were fresh air fanatics. They couldn't leave their patients open to the elements, but they seemed bent on doing the next best thing. Hence the tents, the open windows, and now this corridor.

By rights he should have been in transit, but there had been some delay and it was hardly likely that they'd tell the likes of him what it was.

On Christmas morning he was woken up by two cheery stretcher bearers who wished him the compliments of the season, signed for him, and hoisted him into the back of a horse-drawn ambulance. After that first greeting they didn't speak to him again. They seemed like friendly types, but Wyndham was just a job to them, just a load to be carried, a delivery to be conveyed.

He was the only cargo that morning, besides a crate of beer that clanked merrily somewhere near his head as they rolled down the cobbled streets on their way to the docks.

Wyndham was too ill to do much besides clench his jaw against the shivering and hope to keep the next cough at bay. He listened to his keepers chatting to one another, with loud and merry asides to the driver thrown in from time to time, but he couldn't understand them. He supposed it might be his delirium, but in the end decided that it was their accents. This past half-year he had grown used to the Irish way of speaking, but here he was evidently cast among the English. It was odd, almost unfair. He had grown up an English speaker in New England. English was the only language he spoke well. And here he was among the offspring of the mother country and he was lost. He could pick up a word here and there, but could not grasp the sense of what was being said. He turned his head to read the lips of the man on one side of him. It was something to do, even if it was useless.

The man saw Wyndham's head move, and gave him his attention for the first time since he'd checked the luggage label to which Wyndham's identity had been reduced. He offered Wyndham a bottle of beer. Wyndham understood that. The tone was interrogative in a friendly way, was suffixed by the universal 'mate', and came with a bottle of beer pointed in his direction.

Wyndham's feeble croak couldn't be heard above the noise of the wheels, but it was obvious that wassailing was beyond him this morning. The man nodded in understanding and drank the beer himself, while his mate leaned forward and handed a bottle to the driver through the canvas flap.

It became clear that all aboard had been celebrating their saviour's birth for quite a while now – half a crate at least. One of the stretcher bearers precariously stood up and pissed off the tailboard, and the view he had of the street convinced him that the driver had taken a wrong turn. Wyndham clearly heard 'lost' as the operative word in an exchange that included wounded indignation from the driver and ribaldry from the men in the back. He could also make out the standard army obscenities that had been assailing his ears ever since he'd first unpacked his kit in the barracks in Tralee six months before. Here he was among the English, and they were mangling the language fit to make Milton and Shakespeare weep. Well, maybe not Shakespeare.

After some unknowable passage of time, they stopped and Wyndham was unloaded. He could smell salt water and coal smoke, and hear the thrumming and rattling of distant machinery and the screaming of seagulls. He was so cold it hurt. They nearly tumbled him out of his stretcher when they lifted him down. The strap across his chest that kept him secure felt as if it had done him an injury, but the stretcher bearers, though not unkind, treated the incident with brief hilarity. There was no point in berating your mate's clumsiness – not on Christmas Day at any rate.

A light rain was falling, but that didn't bother the stretcher bearers a bit. They had put Wyndham down and were having a smoke until someone came along that they could report to. When that happened, and the luggage label was checked and a clipboard was initialled, Wyndham was hoisted up once more for the journey across the quayside and up the gangplank.

He never did find out what happened, but somebody must have bumped into something, or somebody must have missed his footing, because near the bottom of the gangplank there was a cry of drunken alarm and the stretcher gave a lurch, and this time it did fall.

The last thing Wyndham saw was a bollard coming up to meet him.

6

'What is sharper than a sword?' 'The wit of a woman between two men.' 'What is quicker than the wind?' said Finn then. 'A woman's mind,' said Grania.

—Lady Augusta Gregory, *Gods and Fighting Men*

Because of his rank and his mature years, Major Hugh Fitz-mullen-Brophy had been tended to with greater consideration, and had been conveyed home from the front rather more smoothly than the men who had served under him.

Wyndham had suffered from a tiresome medley of footling wounds and illnesses, while Moriarty was the victim of something intangible and unheroic. Fitzmullen-Brophy's wound, on the other hand, had been more straightforward and more serious, and the medics, appreciating its no-nonsense nature, had been happy to give their best. He had taken a gunshot wound to the hip, which might have come with all manner of complications but luckily turned out to be something that could be mended, provided, of course, that the old boy looked after himself. That was the very phrase he'd overheard them use. He was the 'old boy', the superannuated duffer who'd pottered into the war and come a cropper, and now he was to be gently set to rights, and generally mothered, before being packed off home where he couldn't do himself any more harm.

That was what it sounded like to Fitzmullen-Brophy, and it was a hurt piled on top of a hurt.

He had suffered a wound in battle at the very moment of victory. He had led his men in a desperate charge, taken an enemy machine-gun post, driven a handful of Germans from their makeshift trench and regained a half-acre of dismal field near Armentières. It had been his triumph, and if the bullet that had laid him low had put an end to him it would have been a right and fitting end.

But here he was instead, a knocked-about old man in a hospital filled with men who had done as much as he had and had suffered as much if not more, and that was the least of it. He was past fifty and the army was a younger man's game. He'd had many years in which to come to terms with his ever-advancing age. By rights – and the attitude of heartless youth was perfectly justified here – he'd had no business being at the front. That being the case, he might have come round to the idea that his last adventure and his wound, honourably earned, were more than he could have reasonably asked for. But here in this hospital, with the damnable pain in his hip and the indignities of being an invalid, he was unable to see any of it as a last reward.

Instead, he dwelt on his guilt and his loss. He had been the author of his own misfortune, and worse than that. In his fear at missing out on this war he had hastened, unauthorised and unprepared, to France, and had brought with him many trusting young men who would be alive today if not for an old man's vainglorious deceit. He'd considered all of this before, but there'd been a battle to be fought then. He'd been in the whole of his health and the men were (mostly) still alive. Given those circumstances, it had been easy enough to shove the gnawing thoughts to one side. It didn't pay for a soldier to have too fine a conscience. But now there was pain and too much time to think. What this wounded, guilty old man thought most about was his lifelong friend, Tummy Belcher, who'd loyally followed him to war and met a soldier's death along with the younger men. Poor old Tummy – who could have stayed in the officers' mess in Tralee, dozing away his afternoons and deploring the wicked fads of the twentieth century – dead in the rain, somewhere between France and Belgium. And his foolish old pal, whose idea this had all been, would have to go limping home by himself, and live out however many years were left to him.

He wondered if the dreams would still be troubling him down all those years. Every time he slept, it seemed, he found himself alone and exposed on the parapet of that trench, and no one to be seen under the dark sky except the huddled bodies of his men.

When first he'd been wounded, he had been rapidly evacuated to Rouen and thence to a military hospital in England. There he spent the dark months of the year, and after that, when they were satisfied that they'd done as much for him as they could, he was returned home to Ireland. Initially they sent him to a convalescent hospital, but when he showed himself too crotchety and disagreeable he was discharged into the care of his wife. Technically he was on convalescent leave, but no one was too particular as to mention a date when he might return to duty. The retirement that had been a constant threat since he'd come home from India six years before seemed to have become fact at last.

Susan Fitzmullen-Brophy had been distressed to hear that her husband had been wounded, and the sight of him in that hospital outside Dublin did little to comfort her. He looked so reduced. Her husband, tall and energetic, buoyant and exasperating, now sitting in a wheelchair, wrapped in a rug, and feeling unutterably sorry for himself. Her pity, however, was more than outweighed by her relief that he was still alive and whole. Moreover, she was honest enough to admit that she was hardly surprised at how it had all turned out.

Sneaking off to war like that – like a schoolboy playing truant. Naturally it was all going to end in tears. Ridiculous to expect otherwise. One could only hope that Hugh had finally learned his lesson.

Like the good army wife she'd been for nearly twenty-five years, she knew better than to scold the fallen warrior. Just get him home, nurse him back to his old self and perhaps persuade him to take more time with the garden or something in future.

It was the wrong time of year for gardening, alas, or for doing anything much beyond sitting by the fire, and that was purgatory for a man who was not used to keeping still, and worse punishment for the wife who had to put up with him. His usual fussing and fidgeting had no outlet, and that made for an unhappy household.

There were visitors, of course, and well-wishers, but not from the regiment. All the officers who'd been there before the war had found employment, which usually came with promotion, and that did nothing to lift the broken-down major's spirits. Chaps were getting on, and commanding battalions, and here he was learning to walk again.

Susan Fitzmullen-Brophy was a woman of resource and decision, but she was at a loss when it came to their present trial. When the war came she had arranged the household's financial affairs as the experiences of India and South Africa had taught her. She'd mentally prepared to pack up the house and move if that was what events might require. She'd mobilised other wives and busied herself around the parish with patriotic funds and drives and the like. She'd sold the horse (an absurd expense) and bought a bicycle. All these things gave her something to keep from fretting about her husband, but they also broadened her horizon. Her wartime life so far – worries aside – had been one of capability and freedom.

And now Hugh was back, and an invalid, and she knew that she was in danger of being driven out of her wits by him, in all his irritability and mournfulness. There was nothing to distract him, nothing to take him out of himself. There was no use in giving him a book. His life was outdoors. His life was the regiment.

Their daughter Molly, loving and dutiful, was on hand, but love and duty only go so far when one is obliged to wait on a querulous parent and it's raining outside. Molly was engaged to be married. Molly wanted to be off with friends. She did her best, but after a week the tensions were becoming evident, and that was no good for either mother or daughter.

Until the weather improved and Hugh could walk unaided, she needed something.

And that was how she found Wyndham.

Susan knew all the business of her husband's command. He told her about it, whether she wanted him to or not, and she had learned that any time he wasn't telling her all about the ins and outs of military life he was usually hiding something from her. So she knew all about Wyndham.

The way Hugh told it, Wyndham was a perfectly splendid young American chap whom he'd saved from himself. Hugh had rescued him from some potentially disgraceful mishap and persuaded him to enlist in the army reserve for a spell. It would be the making of him. Without Hugh, young Wyndham would have wasted his life away. All through those summer weeks, before the war changed everything, Hugh had been full of how this Wyndham was getting on – straighter, fitter and altogether better. Didn't have his nose stuck in a bally book anymore. Hardly tell the chap was even American anymore. In short, Mrs. Fitzmullen-Brophy felt, Mr. Daniel Wyndham had been a tonic for Hugh, who had been growing stale in the regiment's reserve battalion, which meant that he had been becoming ever more of a nuisance at home.

She had never met this American prodigy, but all his things were still stored in their lumber room until, his term of enlistment complete, the new-made Mr. Wyndham, grown into the full potential of his manhood, should collect his bags and resume his travels. That had been the plan, but of course Wyndham had gone and joined in Hugh's adventure. Apparently, he had lived up to his early promise and Hugh spoke highly of his conduct in France.

She wondered if Mr. Wyndham were still alive. She considered the irregularity of his enlistment. She thought that if he'd had no real business being in the army in the first place, there was a possibility that he might have been discharged, and if that were so, perhaps he could be tempted to Tralee, to keep Hugh happy. But that was all too much to hope for. She knew that the inquiries of a mere reserve major's wife would hardly be attended to in a great war.

But then the letter came.

Wyndham was not only alive, but he was almost within reach. He was in a hospital in England, it transpired, and, as his letter explained, he had not been in any position to write before this. He was earnestly inquiring after the wellbeing of his commanding officer and patron.

What a dear young man, thought Mrs. Fitzmullen-Brophy, to think of Hugh when he himself had become a casualty. Such devotion should be repaid by providing the young man – so far from his own country – with a warm home where he could find peace and recover his strength. The other half of her mind acknowledged that such a nice young man would also be able to put up with Hugh's company for a month or two and give her some peace.

Wyndham's letter brought a smile to Hugh's face, but it had a positively galvanising effect on his wife. Susan Fitzmullen-Brophy knew the workings of the army. It would have been impossible for her to alter the fate of a fighting man. But an invalid?

She knew exactly who to talk to and exactly how to ask

favours. Within a few days she had not only arranged for Private Wyndham's transfer from England to Ireland, but she had set in train the process by which Wyndham would be formally and gratefully discharged from His Majesty's service. It troubled her not at all that the king would be deprived of an able-bodied volunteer at this time of grave crisis. Let the king put up with Hugh if that's how he felt about it.

7

I am a raven that has no home; I am a boat going from wave to wave; I am a ship that has lost its rudder; I am the apple left on the tree.

—Lady Augusta Gregory, *Cuchulain of Muirthemne*

It was the first time in months that Wyndham had seen a familiar face, and because it was the major's, he came perilously close to breaking down.

The major, the personification of the regiment, the rock of Armentières, looked pitiful. Leaning on a crutch he appeared smaller, and so very much older. Instead of the manly uniform there was a tweed suit of doubtful vintage. The man who had strode upon the parapet in France was now shuffling in carpet slippers.

The broken hero and the orphaned boy had parted on a battlefield. Now, in a perfectly ordinary house, the two survivors clasped each other in clumsy handshake, too overcome to speak.

The ladies were fussing and shooing them out of the cold hall, and two idiot brown dogs were bounding and barking, so it was easiest to show Wyndham upstairs where he could gather himself after his journey. Tea, Mrs. Fitzmullen-Brophy told him helpfully, would be ready whenever he chose to come down for it. And then, after the burst of noise and company, he was alone again.

He found his luggage waiting for him. He stared stupefied. After everything, after all he'd been through, his two neat suitcases were here, unchanged. He'd had them rooted out of the attic at home less than a year ago, and the Cunard Line had stuck labels on them and the customs officers and marked them with chalk and he'd thought he was a man of the world, embarked on a grand adventure. And the trappings of the adventurous man had stayed here, in peace and quiet, while he had gone and fought in the great European war. Now, when he discovered the suitcases empty, he reeled with loss and betrayal. His consternation was calmed, however, when a brief search revealed all his clothes neatly unpacked in wardrobe and chest of drawers, smelling of mothballs and lavender.

He'd been slipping out of the army ever since they'd cut his mud-encrusted uniform off him in hospital last November. Now all he had was a cap and greatcoat to show that he was a soldier, and they did not go with the ugly suit of hospital blue he'd been given. The suit was army issue, but it marked him as an invalid rather than a soldier. The cap was without a cap badge, so wearing it he was no fusilier. All the symbols of his service had been taken away. It was an easy thing to cast off these ugly remnants and put on civilian clothes again.

The clothes felt insubstantial. He had been too used to scratchy serge and heavy brass buttons. Also, he was disconcerted but a little proud to find that his suit didn't quite fit anymore. His trousers were too loose at the waist and his coat was too tight around the chest and shoulders.

He stood a long time before the mirror, seeing a man with a severe haircut and broken nose, and looking for that other man – the young innocent who'd first bought that suit.

Perhaps he'd see a glimpse of him again, given time, given the hospitality and domesticity of this house. Or perhaps that young man had died in Flanders.

8

'In your fate, O beautiful child, are wounds, and ill doings, and shedding of blood.'

—Lady Augusta Gregory, *Cuchulain of Muirthemne*

Diversions were few in Tralee, especially in February. The sad truth was that they weren't even in Tralee. The town was nearly an hour's walk away, and if you were to make that walk at this time of year then you might find little to reward you for your efforts.

Molly Fitzmullen-Brophy had friends scattered throughout the neighbourhood, and once in a while they would daringly meet in the most fashionable tearooms Tralee could boast, and perhaps do a little shopping, but that was about as much excitement as was on offer. So, after tea and gossip and a look at the shops there was nothing to do except go home again, and, since New Year, home meant looking after Daddy.

Molly loved her father, but longed for the day he would be up and about again and out from under their roof. Major Hugh Fitzmullen-Brophy was not a man suited to a life of inactivity indoors. He made for a poor invalid, and Molly's patience, like her mother's, had its limits. She loved her father, but this was the first time in all her twenty-one years that she'd been forced to put up with him.

In the beginning, of course, there'd been the regiment to consume his days. When Molly was very small the regiment had been stationed in Fermoy, and her father was like anyone's father, in that he went to work in the mornings and came back in the evenings, and everyone was happy. And then the day came when he didn't come home, and it had been explained to her that Daddy had gone away to South Africa. When next she saw him it was more than three years later, and that was in India. The regiment had been posted out to India and the womenfolk had gone trailing after. Then, after five years, it was back to Ireland again. For a fifteen-year-old girl who had been five years in India but had never really been to school, Tralee took some getting used to. In India she'd lived like she supposed minor royalty lived – idle, comfortable, but straitened. In Ireland, where the servants were fewer and money didn't go as far, she was merely a soldier's daughter.

She settled in. She made the best of things. She was a good daughter. She didn't dislike Tralee, but she wanted more.

Of course, India was not lost forever. After all, soldiers' daughters tended to marry soldiers, and soldiers were sent to India. On the other hand, soldiers' wives also followed their husbands to provincial Irish garrisons like Tralee, or Fermoy where she'd spent her earliest childhood. There was nothing at all wrong with a place like Fermoy – if you were a small child or if your horizons were happily limited to fox hunting and close-order drill. Molly Fitzmullen-Brophy wanted broader horizons than that. She wasn't yearning for the blinding splendours of the East, but would Dublin, say, be too much to ask for?

The year before last, after a long campaign of subtle agitation, it was decided that the family finances could stretch to a musical education in Dublin. Molly wasn't especially talented, but she applied herself. The idea was that she would stay with friends and learn a ladylike skill that would keep her occupied, perhaps as a piano teacher, until a husband came along. And one did.

Sidney Bryant was not particularly handsome, nor was he wealthy, but he could speak of things beyond the military or provincial. He read books. He went to the theatre. His work had even taken him to London, and, having been delighted by a year in Dublin, Molly was thrilled to think of a city even larger and more exciting. When she was out of sorts with him, she might think that Sidney could be as dull as anyone, but at least he was dull about interesting things. She would marry him, and live in a house with electric lights, and take the tram when she wanted to go shopping.

The war had dislocated everything. Her circle of friends broke up. Her studies seemed irrelevant. Sidney's work kept him busier. She came home. There was talk of packing up the house to follow her father's battalion to West Cork, but then her father had unexpectedly disappeared off to France with Tummy Belcher and sixty-odd men he'd no business in taking away from Tralee. Her mother, capable but anxious, was grateful for her daughter's company.

And now poor old Tummy – the irascible uncle she'd never particularly needed – was dead, and her father, much reduced in body and spirit, was home again. The neighbours spoke of his heroism and the local papers had even made favourable mention of him, but Molly knew that her father was under a cloud as far as the army was concerned, and in that house the opinion of the army was the only one that mattered.

She put her life to one side, but it did little good. She'd speak brightly to him, but mewed up in Kerry like this there was so little to talk about. She read to him, but he was never one for books, and the papers were full of war news that depressed him. He might remember to smile or pat her hand, but then he'd lapse into distraction. He spent the days fidgeting and grumbling, or staring morosely into the fire or out at the rain. When he started walking again he was even worse. Now he was still peevish but no longer confined to the sitting room. His ill humour could stump about wherever crutches could carry him. Nowhere was safe. It was all most trying. Molly, in desperate last resort, was wondering if jigsaw puzzles might be the answer when her mother had the brilliant idea of finding young Mr. Wyndham.

She had never met the mysterious American, but even without the stories surrounding him, he was a guest worth waiting for. It was all too easy to spend the grey hours counting down the day when Mr. Wyndham would come, and then there'd be someone to look after Daddy.

When he finally arrived – pale, thin and incongruously dressed – he did not appear much of a deliverer. He was, after all, something of an invalid himself, and so obviously lost and far from home. But Molly was not disappointed. She wasn't sure quite what she'd been expecting, but this young man with his battered face appeared to her as more than just someone to help with her father. Here was someone from the outside world. Here was someone who had seen the bright lights and travelled across the ocean. Here was someone she could talk to about something other than the weather.

9

I am an old man, in the 82nd year of my age, and have become very deaf and infirm, but I am still ready, if my services be accepted, to use my feeble arm in defence of my King and Country, having had the good fortune on former occasions to have been repeatedly successful in action against our perfidious enemies, on whom, I thank God, I never turned my back.

—Gen. John Reid, Colonel, 88th Regt, 1803

It was hard to tell what contributed more to Fitzmullen-Brophy's recovery. To be sure, Wyndham did all that was hoped for. He seemed to have an infinite capacity for patience. He sat with the major when sitting was required, and he accompanied the major on his increasingly ambitious walks around the house and the garden, and, as things progressed, ever farther afield. Quiet and diffident, he caused no trouble to anyone. Possessing the necessary social graces, he fitted nicely into the household. He was, in short, the perfect guest. His formal discharge from the army hadn't been quite finalised yet, but if the military police were to arrive before that time with orders to bring the errant Private Wyndham back to the regiment, the Fitzmullen-Brophy women would not have hesitated in hiding him under the stairs for however long it took. They were not letting Daniel go. Daniel was part of the family, at least until Hugh was fully mended.

But then came the summons that sent the major's spirits soaring and accelerated his restoration. On the face of it, it didn't seem like much.

Wyndham came down to breakfast to find the major in uproar, or at least to hear the major stumping around upstairs, shouting to his wife, shouting to the maid, and carrying on like the house had caught fire. Molly was in the dining room, grateful to be out of range.

'Daddy's been invited to appear before a medical board,' she explained. 'That's what's put him in a state.'

'Oh dear. Is it serious?'

'Oh no! It's tremendous good news. It means that the army hasn't forgotten about him. The medical board is to determine his fitness for duty. They'd hardly bother if they weren't thinking about giving him a job.'

'Ah, I see. That is good news.' Wyndham buttered a slice of toast. He had no idea what all this would mean for him.

'He's wonderfully bucked up. It's the shot in the arm he needed. Now, of course, he's rushing around like he's off on campaign again and driving Mummy mad.'

'I hope he doesn't over-exert himself.'

Molly looked at him sternly. 'That's something *you* must make sure of, Daniel. If he makes himself ill or has an accident, who knows how long it will take for him to get better. We would all be driven quite mad.'

Wyndham nodded, taking the matter most seriously. He'd have looked after the major no matter what, but now a young woman was entrusting him with her father's wellbeing. No young woman had ever asked him for anything important before.

There was a clattering on the stairs, which brought an 'Oh Lord!' from Molly and caused them both to rush out into the hall, the talk of accidents having conjured fearful visions in their minds.

But the major was upright and in full command. 'Oh, do let go of my arm, Susan. I can manage perfectly well. Wyndham! Did you hear? I've been summoned!'

'Yes, sir. Splendid news, sir.'

'Splendid indeed! Not much time. I have to make myself fit!'

He had forsaken his crutch and was negotiating the stairs with a stick. '*Please*, my dear. I must do this on my own.'

Wyndham never did gather what they'd been tearing around upstairs for. The major's boots? The necessary paperwork to submit to the medical authorities? Some patent elixir for joints made rheumy by German bullets? Everything was fuss fuss fuss. It was the army mobilisation of last August confined to a single house. The limping walks round the neighbourhood became route marches. The anecdotes about soldiering in India in the old days were recounted with emphatic decision, as though these campaigns were to be fought again, and soon.

When the time came to travel to Cork, Fitzmullen-Brophy was ready. He still leaned heavily on his stick, but he stood tall again, and was back in uniform. Wyndham saw the way the major's teeth were clenched on the stem of his pipe and was reminded of a shell-torn farmyard on the Belgian frontier, and the last minutes ticking away before the attack went in. Wyndham was to accompany the major on his journey but he knew that, no matter how many are with him, a man goes into battle alone.

The medical board was a success, or at least enough of a success insofar as Major Fitzmullen-Brophy was not dismissed from the service forthwith, and that was more than enough for him. In ordinary circumstances he'd have been put out to pasture, for whatever use was there for a man of his age who'd never been promoted higher than major – even if he would be able to walk without a stick in a month or two? But the war had changed everything. Field Marshal Lord Kitchener had changed everything. He had pointed his finger and fixed his pale eyes upon the manhood of the kingdom and they'd come in their hundreds of thousands. It was gratifying that so many had answered the call, but the army had increased fourfold in a matter of months, and there was an urgent need for experienced men to take charge of these legions of enthusiasts. With the men who'd usually take on this task off at the front, the job was passed onto the veterans, the invalids, and all the military oddments that the authority wouldn't normally have time for.

Major Hugh Fitzmullen-Brophy, 3rd Royal Munster Fusiliers (Special Reserve), might not have been the sort of man Kitchener had in mind when he'd created his new armies, but he was warm to the touch, could walk more or less unaided across a room, and had more than thirty years' experience of commanding men. In a pinch, he'd do.

Despite his age and his injury, despite the cloud he'd been under since he'd absconded from Tralee last August, Fitzmullen-Brophy was not to be consigned to the dust heap just yet. More than that, his name was now on a list.

10

Yet is the completion of my cure at thy hands lacking to me; when may it be that I shall have it?

—A.H. Leahy, 'The Courtship of Etain', *Heroic Romances of Ireland*

It had been stories that had brought Wyndham to Ireland in the first place. He'd been captivated by the romances of ancient Ireland as W.B. Yeats and Lady Gregory presented them, and he'd come to Ireland in hope of finding what lay at the root of it all. He'd found the Munster Fusiliers instead, but when he'd been beguiled into the regiment and had followed them to the war he still carried the stories in his heart (and a couple of the books in his pack), and, for want of any other diversion, he told them to his comrades. It wasn't that they wanted Irish myth and legend. What they wanted was America, and particularly the Wild West, which meant that Wyndham had to get creative, and that meant that he grew as a storyteller.

Molly Fitzmullen-Brophy wanted stories, too. The hero-tales of old Ireland meant nothing to her, but she was eager to hear about the United States. It didn't matter that Wyndham had led a quite constrained life in a small town in Massachusetts: to Molly America was as fabulous as the Tír na nÓg that also lay over the Western Sea. And Wyndham had seen Paris, too (if only briefly), and had had every intention of travelling further until events had derailed him last summer. To Molly, who missed Dublin, who was stuck in Tralee for who knew how long, Daniel Wyndham was a window on the grand sunlit world outside.

Twenty-odd years growing up in New England and a few weeks tramping across France weren't much to be building a store of traveller's tales on, but Wyndham had wit, and a deal of practice. He also valued Molly's attention more than she could have guessed. She was interested in him. She was interested in what he had to say. The last time he'd been asked to speak it had been by bored men stuck in a trench with damn all else to do. How could he give anything but his best for Miss Fitzmullen-Brophy?

He thought her pretty. From her devotion to her father he knew her to be kind. And she was kind to *him*, and more than kind. She respected him. She seemed to recognise in him a nobility that he'd never thought he had but had always wanted. The want was what had made him join the army. Now, in her eyes at least, the very act of joining, and of following her father to war, had made him more than other men. By himself he was just Daniel Wyndham, in unfamiliar surroundings and clothes that didn't quite fit, but with her he was the returned warrior, honourably scarred, who had seen far horizons and faced death in a glorious cause. And it was all true.

Wyndham had admired girls back home, and had been determined to pursue his admiration to more practical ends when he should get up the nerve. He had kissed girls in France, although it would have been fairer to say that they'd kissed him. The fact was they'd kissed everyone in the company, and stuck flowers in the men's caps and in the muzzles of their rifles on the triumphal march to war. When he'd overcome the shock and embarrassment of the French welcome, he'd decided that it was for a life such as this that he'd joined the army. This was him gaining wordly experience. Here was where he'd find the easy confidence it would take to cut a swathe through the fairer sex. He would come home from the war (sometime around Christmas) with an assurance amounting to swagger, and the young ladies would look at him with new eyes, and he'd pay no heed to the strictures of his mother or sister, or society at large for that matter, for he would have become a man.

11

'I cannot at this stage say what will be the limits of the forces required ... But if the war should be protracted, and if its fortunes should be varied or adverse, exertions and sacrifices beyond any which have been demanded will be required of the nation and Empire.'

—Field-Marshal Lord Kitchener, 25th August 1914.

In Parkgate, in Dublin, where the chains of command were being forged for the new armies, the councils of the great at last took note.

'Oh Christ. Not Fitzmullen-Brophy. The man's a bloody fusspot.'

'He's rather well-thought-of at the moment, sir. In some circles at any rate.'

'Really? Last I heard they were all for cashiering him. They should make up their damn minds. Hero or scoundrel? He's a bloody fusspot nonetheless. Dreadful type.'

'He did do rather well in Flanders, sir.'

'And he got himself shot, as did I, as did many another, and here am I buried beneath all this rot, having to sort out no end of bumf concerning appointments in Kitchener's bloody amateur recruits, while fools like Fitzmullen-Brophy are being praised to the heights by people who've never met the ass.'

'It's only a temporary appointment, sir.'

'True. True. A just reward for a gallant old warhorse who can always be quietly sent to the knacker's yard if need be. Very well. Approved. What's next?'

'Ah – before we move on, sir, there is another appointment for the 11th Munsters. Matter of fact, it's a recommendation of Major – ahem – Lieutenant-Colonel Fitzmullen-Brophy's.'

'Oh Christ.'

'A temporary commission is requested for one Daniel Wyndham, private, Special Reserve, Royal Munster Fusiliers.'

'Protégé of Fitzmullen-Brophy's?'

'Possibly, sir. An American anyway.'

'Who went along to the Continent on Fitzmullen-Brophy's outrageous little jaunt?'

'I imagine so, sir.'

'A regular fire-eater, no doubt. Very well. Considering the creatures we're already commissioning, I suppose an American adventurer won't be much out of place. Approved. Wild Bill Wyndham is now a probationary 2nd Lieutenant. Next.'

12

*Have **you** any women-folk worth defending?*

—Recruiting poster, 1914

'You've done *what*, sir?'

'Aren't you pleased, Wyndham? You're to be an officer. Don't think you haven't earned it, my boy.'

'It's not that, sir.'

'Don't think I didn't see your potential. You did very well in France. And you're the right sort, so it's only right that you should be an officer.'

The last thing that Wyndham wanted was to disappoint the old gentleman, but he shot an urgent look to Mrs. Fitzmullen-Brophy. She, after all, had assured him that he'd been delivered from the army. Evidently, she hadn't quite cleared it with her husband.

I've done my bit, was on the tip of his tongue, but then so had the major, and he was all fired up to go and do a bit more. He was aware that his mouth was making movements but no sounds.

He managed to stumble out something along the lines of home and family, but telling a man like Fitzmullen-Brophy that he wanted to go home to his mother was hardly going to go down well. But when he remembered the shells crashing down on the flooded trenches near Armentières, he really did want to go home to his mother.

He managed to stammer out something that he hoped sounded both grateful and non-committal, but could see from the look of dismay and confusion that it was not an answer that Fitzmullen-Brophy understood. He made an incoherent excuse and left the room before he made things worse.

He spent the next few hours avoiding everyone. In his mind he argued and pleaded.

He thought about waking up in barracks in Tralee last summer, and a genial old soldier fussing over him.

He thought about a bearded German soldier who'd tried to ram a bayonet into him in a slippery farmyard.

Molly sought him out.

'Daniel, whatever's the matter? Daddy's quite put out.'

The rain had stopped for the first time that day, so they went outside. They walked aimlessly about the garden, with the dogs frolicking barbarously and Wyndham trying to articulate his reluctance in a way that didn't sound craven or childish. Nothing of substance came out. After a little while they brushed the water off the garden seat and sat down. He tried again.

'Those stories I was telling you about: the stories of ancient Ireland.'

'Of course.' Molly knew them well. If there was one thing about Daniel that did not enchant her, it was the way a grown man could enthuse about fairy tales that managed to be both puzzling and dull.

'Before we went to France, I used to look at the men I was with and wonder how they'd measure up to the ancient heroes. I wondered if the war would be anything like The War of the Brown Bull, or some other tale of champions.'

She noticed how he was drumming his fingers nervously against his leg, steadfastly avoiding her look.

'It's nothing like that at all, Molly.'

'Oh.'

It's cold and wet and there are lice in your clothes and there are no bathrooms and there's blood and guts and horrible things and everything smells of shit.

And the food's bad.

And it's frightening as hell.
And the dirt! My God! The dirt!
And it's so damn cold.

'It's really most unpleasant. Quite squalid actually. Nothing heroic about it.'

'Oh dear.'

'I don't mean your father. Of course not. Your father was a hero. Certainly. And there were plenty of brave men. I mean – I mean to say that bravery doesn't seem to matter. Most of the time it's all so cold-blooded. So workaday. You're in the war like it's a job. It's like a big dirty factory where you have to keep the machinery working and the machinery is trying to kill you.'

'Oh dear.'

'You can do the job well – like your father – or you can do it badly, but the war's still there, just grinding along.'

'Poor Daniel.'

'And I don't think I was much good at it either. I mean I did what I was told and everything, but I have to confess I was pretty useless. Your father kept me out of it at the end. I wasn't there when he was hit. He'd sent me to the rear. He knew I wasn't much good.'

'Poor Daniel.'

'So, I really can't see why he wants me back. And as an officer? I mean it's very kind of him, but...' He trailed off, tried to say something else and gave up again. Molly took his hand.

'You shouldn't be ashamed of yourself. Daddy said you did splendidly, and if he thinks you're a good sort then you can't be nearly as bad as you think. 'Anyway,' she patted his hand briskly to show that the time for indulgence was now done, 'I don't believe there's any question of Daddy being sent back to France, and that means that you shan't be going either.'

Wyndham looked at her for the first time. 'Are you sure?'

'Well, he might be frightfully brave and everything, but he's also dreadfully old – he's past fifty, you know. Mummy says that this is a young man's war. She says too that the job they're giving him is something of a consolation prize, poor soul. It's only a training command, after all. After blotting his copybook, she says it's almost more than he'd a right to expect.'

He looked at her more sharply, wordlessly enquiring where the catch might be. She smiled reassuringly and playfully butted him with her shoulder. 'So, if you stick with the most exalted Lieutenant-Colonel Hugh Fitzmullen-Brophy, then it's pretty certain that you won't go next nigh or near the front ever again if you don't want to.'

'I don't want you thinking I'm a coward.'

'After you followed Daddy to France? I shouldn't dream of it. If the war's really like some sort of factory then you've put in your shift and now they're moving you off the factory floor. You'll still be doing your bit, only now your bit is looking after Daddy – just like you have been. No medals, but no white feathers either. *Now* what do you say?'

He held her hand again while he wrestled with his thoughts. He tried to conceal that those thoughts were largely concerned with taking her hand. Thinking she had driven a wedge into his resistance, she gamely hammered on.

'It's some dreadful camp out at Kilworth or somewhere. It'll probably be awfully boring, but you might like it. It's the Irish countryside, after all. It's what you came for. You can read your books and keep Daddy out of mischief, and by the time the battalion's half trained the war will be over. You've been a hero – whatever you say – and now you can do a necessary and dull job and not feel in the least bit bad about it. Besides, how can you not be in uniform at a time like this? I know you're not a British subject, but every man should be playing his part, whether he's a natural soldier or not. Why, even Sidney will be in uniform, and that man hasn't a soldiering bone in his body.'

She laughed. Wyndham looked hard at her. There had been vague mention of this Sidney character before, but that had been a long time ago. He'd gathered that the man had some sort of connection with Molly, but she hadn't advertised it and her father had been briefly dismissive of the man. That had been that. Wyndham was here in Kerry, a cherished guest and companion, and Sidney Bryant was far away, who knew where. But now, evidently, he was back, and Wyndham found he didn't care for the man at all. He cared for him less when Molly elaborated.

'It might be the very thing if he were still in uniform when we get married. It might make Daddy think better of him. I know it's only a temporary commission and it's only the Army Service Corps. Purely administrative, but still.'

She didn't notice Wyndham's jaw tightening.

The Army Service Corps. Aunt Sally's Cavalry. The military equivalent of the grocer's boy.

'So,' he said. 'Not the infantry then.' Not a fighting arm.

Whatever they said after that was of no matter. Molly was pleased that she seemed to have talked Daniel out of himself. Presently they went inside for tea. Whatever tension had troubled the house that day vanished when it became clear that Wyndham would be most happy to don uniform again.

13

Regulation uniform must not be worn at fancy dress balls, but there is no objection to military uniform of obsolete pattern being worn on such occasions.

—*Dress Regulations for the Army*, 1911

The uniform was a problem. An officer commissioned from the ranks was eligible for a uniform grant, so that was alright, but finding a decent military tailor who wasn't inundated with custom was too tall an order. It would all take too long to sort out, and Fitzmullen-Brophy wanted to be off to his new command as soon as possible. That was how Wyndham ended up wearing Fitzmullen-Brophy's hand-me-downs. He wasn't keen on the idea, but the alternative was to arrive at the battalion wearing his unloved hospital suit, so he reluctantly accepted the parcel of khaki that was unearthed from a tin trunk in the attic.

It was not the khaki that Wyndham was used to, being rather the pale Indian uniform Fitzmullen-Brophy had last worn on the Mohmand Expedition some six or seven years earlier. Wyndham tried it on, because there was nothing else for him to do, and was surprised to find that it fitted quite well. A little too long, no doubt, but that was really only noticeable in the cuffs, and was certainly an improvement on what he'd been used to. The first uniform he'd put on last summer had really been no more than labourer's clothes in a military cut. What he had now was an adventurer's costume – the uniform of an empire-builder. Even standing in his socks in a bedroom in Kerry he could feel the pull of the far horizons.

Unlike the newer style of tunic, this one had a closed collar, which Wyndham thought more fitting. He'd always thought how unsuitable it looked for a British officer to go into battle wearing a necktie. He was relieved to find that the tunic was matched with a pair of breeches, and that he wouldn't be obliged to wear the shorts that he'd uncovered first. Fitzmullen-Brophy's devotion to the cult of bare knees could be taken too far.

The sun helmet that would normally complete the outfit was to be left in the attic, which slightly disappointed him. His other ranks' cap would have to do instead, as would his civilian boots. Of such equipment as belt, field glasses, or holster, there was none, but Fitzmullen-Brophy had been kind enough to include with his gift a couple of books he thought might be useful in the making of a young officer. Wyndham saw that they were *Scouting for Boys* by Robert Baden-Powell and *With Kitchener to Khartum* by G.W. Steevens, of which half the pages were as yet uncut.

14

To-day I am in my age, and I know but a few men; I used to shake my spear bravely in the ice-cold morning.

—Lady Augusta Gregory, *Gods and Fighting Men*

Fitzmullen-Brophy was rightly proud of his ability to get around now, but walking all the way to barracks was clearly beyond him. A neighbour with a horse-drawn car was imposed upon to carry him, and while Fitzmullen-Brophy was politely grateful, he hated being still dependent on people, and especially on a neighbour who spoke incessantly of politics and horses all the way in to Tralee. Fitzmullen-Brophy, feeling unaccustomedly fragile, clung precariously to his seat while his driver held forth on the worthlessness of the government and how it was linked to the rising cost of horseflesh.

'Not that I'd part with this little lady for the world,' he said, indicating the neat five-year old pulling the car. Fitzmullen-Brophy knew the mare was five years old because his good neighbour had not been reticent in telling him, along with all her other points.

The man might not have been selling that particular beast, but was Fitzmullen-Brophy interested in a certain gelding, just perfect for a colonel with a bad hip, that had been especially kept back from the remounts officers, who'd have offered ninety or a hundred pounds like a shot, but could be had by Fitzmullen-Brophy for eighty and a handshake?

'Most kind, most kind. I will most certainly give it some thought. Ah! Here we are.'

Getting down from the car was a tricky business, but he

managed it by himself, and wouldn't hear of any further offers of help. He didn't want to be any more beholden to the good neighbour, and he wanted to be away from the man before he started up again on the Home Rule question.

'Jolly decent of you. Don't let me keep you a moment longer. I'll be perfectly alright from here. Thanks again.'

But he'd have to face it all again on the journey back, when both men had completed their day's business. He thought it might be a good idea to learn to ride Susan's bicycle. If it meant that he wouldn't be at the mercy of garrulous horsey types, it was even tempting to consider a motor car.

With the barrack gate in front of him he attempted a soldierly stride, but it came off as a lurch. The sentry who saluted him was clearly new to the job, but then so was most of the army nowadays. The old hands and wise heads had been scattered among the new formations. Either that, or they'd been bowled out by the Hun. There were bound to be a few left, however. The eager new colonels might have swept up all the talent they could on their way to their new commands, but the depot in Tralee was the address to which all fusiliers returned at some point There were always chaps passing through, between one posting and the next. It was just a matter of getting hold of the right man. Fitzmullen-Brophy had no qualms about filching good men from other units. A mere month ago he might have been ashamed to commit any act reminiscent of his dangerous escapade of last summer, but that had been before his promotion. He didn't think now about the merciless dressing-down and dismissal he'd received at the hand of higher authority when he'd been apprehended in unauthorised command of troops he'd unlawfully spirited away from Ireland. He thought only of his new command, and how this time he was going to do everything better. Just give him the men.

The omens were good, in that practically the first face he saw on the barrack square was both familiar and welcoming. It was the dog Bobs, who didn't appear as delighted as Fitzmullen-Brophy was at the reunion but deigned to trot over all the same and allow his ears to be ruffled.

'There's a good fella! Splendid! Jolly good! Now, how about you take me to whoever's in charge, eh? No? Never mind, I know the way. Good boy, Bobs.' And, his spirits bounding, Fitzmullen-Brophy limped off to see the adjutant.

The adjutant, alas, was a stranger to him. The young man was perfectly polite, and no doubt sincere in his offer to be of some assistance, but what help could a lad like that possibly be when he was so ignorant of the ins and outs of army ways? Where were the boys of the old brigade, what? The commanding officer of the depot was at least known to Fitzmullen-Brophy, but he had much to be getting on with, and none of it included the unofficial smoothing of paths and bending of rules for his honoured visitor. Fitzmullen-Brophy might have been a lieutenant-colonel now, but he was one of several to have lately been appointed thus, and that brought the total up to eleven, and that was just in this regiment. Lieutenant-colonels were going cheap these days.

So, after a friendly but fruitless interview, Fitzmullen-Brophy sought out the quartermaster, O'Connor, who was something of a constant fixture in the depot.

Over a drink in the mess O'Connor was able to impart all manner of information on affairs in Tralee, but he could be of no more help than anyone. Fitzmullen-Brophy was beginning to think that he might have been better off just sticking with the dog.

The talk turned idly to Fitzmullen-Brophy's wound and to the desperate doings at the front near Armentières last autumn, but O'Connor was merely making conversation. Plenty of wounded officers had come limping through Tralee these past months, and all war stories tended to be much the same. He listened with half an ear as Fitzmullen-Brophy tried to recreate the battle using two whiskey glasses, a small water jug and an ashtray. A box of matches was about to be emptied on to the table to represent German troop dispositions when O'Connor put a stop to it.

'Yes. Yes. Very good. Read about it in the papers of course. Capital show.'

'But the papers could hardly have given a proper picture. Just let me…'

'And I was talking to old Whatshisname about it, too, I recall. First-hand account. Enthralling stuff.'

Fitzmullen-Brophy left the matches alone.

'Who exactly are we speaking of?'

'Oh, you know. Fella who was there. Tip of my tongue.'

'Not young Fleming?' Fitzmullen-Brophy asked earnestly. Lieutenant Fleming had been the only other officer of his command to survive the fight. He'd been carted off with a bullet through his chest and not been seen since. If he could be got hold of then they'd be off to a good start.

O'Connor fiddled with his pipe. 'Mmm. Might have been Fleming. Fellows come and go. Especially these days. Hard to keep track.'

'Any of them still here, do you think?'

'Might be. One or two of the men, perhaps. You'd have to ask the sarn't-major.'

And that was how he found Moriarty.

'Begging your pardon, sir, but you don't want Moriarty.'

'Really, Sarn't-Major? Why ever not?' Fitzmullen-Brophy was sceptical of any man who thought to cast aspersions on those who'd held the line in Flanders, but only a fool ignores the advice of a sergeant-major.

'The man's useless, I'm afraid, sir.'

'Oh now surely it's not that bad. He did his duty at the front like all the rest.'

'That's as may be, sir. But maybe it proved too hard for him.

He washed up here last month out of the hospital and he's no bloody good. The MO put him on light duties, but he wasn't even fit for that. I don't have the heart to punish a man who's done his bit at the front, but it does no one any good to have the likes of him mumping around the place. Sets a bad example, sir.'

'So, what have you done with him?'

'Between you, me and the four walls, sir, no one cares where he is so long as he's out of sight and not disgracing us. We send him into the town on some errand that doesn't matter, and he usually settles himself into a pub for the day, and if he behaves himself then we let him alone. I know what you're thinking, sir, but honest to God, he's like a lamb. All we have to do is feed him when he comes back.'

'Sarn't-Major, that is no proper way for a Munster Fusilier to behave. I am frankly rather disappointed.'

'Sir, we both know the army's not what it was, but if you think of it like an extension of Moriarty's convalescent leave then it's not so bad. He'll get better. Peace and quiet and a few pints of porter can only do him good. We'll make a good soldier of him again yet.'

'I expect you're right. However, I think it's best that we go about it sooner rather than later. A firm taking in hand is likely all he needs. I'll see to it.'

'If you can make use of him, sir, then you may take him away with you, and the blessings of God on you, Colonel.'

15

'And I have nowhere to go from this danger,' he said, 'for I have no friend or comrade under whose protection I could go in any far part of the great world...'

—Lady Augusta Gregory, *Gods And Fighting Men*

Fitzmullen-Brophy was not going to approach Moriarty himself. An officer talking with a private soldier in a public house, no matter how good the cause, just wasn't done. So he sent Wyndham. Wyndham and Moriarty had been comrades after all.

Wyndham was not unwilling to meet his old comrade again, but the circumstances made him uneasy. It had been in a pub in Tralee that he had first encountered Moriarty. Certainly, that meeting had led to Fitzmullen-Brophy and the Royal Munster Fusiliers and the whole mad adventure on the Continent, and all of that was too vast a thing to be considered by anything so small as regret. But all Wyndham was reminded of now was how that first drink with Moriarty had led, by rapid stages, to a brawl in the street, and how his introduction to the regiment that night had been by way of a grim cell in the barracks guardhouse. It was Fitzmullen-Brophy who'd rescued him, and set him on the right path, and now it was Fitzmullen-Brophy who was sending him back to the place of his near ruin.

Wyndham stood a moment outside the door, calming his misgivings. He couldn't tell if this was the same establishment. All the pubs looked alike. He had marched to France. He had fought the Germans. He had bought dirty postcards in Paris. He could face down the disapproval of an Irish saloon keeper if it came down to it. He went in.

Moriarty was sitting by the fire. He didn't look up from his paper when the door opened. His expression suggested that he was making a point of it. Wyndham hesitated a moment and walked up to him.

'Hello, Moriarty,' he said, unsure.

Moriarty looked so much more presentable than when last they'd been together. Seeing as that had been in a forward sap, nearly knee-deep in water, in the southern part of the Ypres Salient, this was hardly surprising. But if this wasn't the muddy Old Contemptible of last November, it wasn't the bold fusilier of last summer either – the swaggering man in the scarlet tunic who held forth in pubs, talking big and daring the local toughs. This man, with his pint and his newspaper and his coat buttoned up, looked middle-aged. He raised his eyes, reluctant to see what the outside world was bringing him.

'Wyndham,' he said in his middle-aged voice. 'Mr. Wyndham. Merciful Jesus.' he stared for a while, and then he sniffed, and put aside his paper, and waited to see what Wyndham was here for. It didn't look as if he was expecting good news. Wyndham grinned – and that made one of them – and sat down, and put his hands on the table for want of anything else to do with them.

'I'm very glad to have found you,' he said, and was answered only with a slow nod.

Wyndham kept smiling. For all the awkwardness of the moment, he realised that he was filled with joy to see Moriarty again. They had never really been friends, but the only thing they had in common just happened to be the biggest thing that had ever happened to either of them, and they had lived through it, and now here they were, home and dry.

Moriarty sniffed again, and pulled his greatcoat more closely around him, and didn't take his eyes off Wyndham.

'Will you have a drink, Moriarty?' asked Wyndham. 'May I get you another drink?'

'Go on so.'

Drinking whiskey in the early afternoon was new to him, but Wyndham felt that Fitzmullen-Brophy's new scheme required a little lubrication for both the man selling and the man buying. When the whiskey for himself and the pint for Moriarty were bought and Wyndham was settled again, Moriarty surprised him by talking unprompted.

'You're looking well,' he said. He indicated the civilian clothes. 'So, are you out of the army or what?'

'I was. I think. I'm not sure. But I'm back in it now. As an officer. I'm to be a lieutenant.' Wyndham emphasised the *eff* in 'leff-tenant'. He had no idea why it was there, but it was his now and he aimed to be careful with it.

'An officer,' nodded Moriarty. 'That makes sense.'

'It was Major Fitzmullen-Brophy's doing, of course, only he's a colonel now – a lieutenant-colonel at least.'

'Right.'

Wyndham took the plunge. 'And he wants you to come back. They've given him a new battalion to train and he's looking for soldiers of experience. He's—'

Moriarty, so slow up till now, snapped. 'I'm not going back.'

Wyndham had his mouth open, but Moriarty didn't give him a chance, the words spilling out of him in a rush.

'I'm not going back. I'm not going back to the fucking front. They can throw me in the fucking glasshouse for the rest of the war but I'm not going back.' He swiped the cream of his pint from off his moustache and drank Wyndham's whiskey in one swallow. They faced each other for a tense moment. Then: 'Was that your drink? Sorry. I'll get you another.'

'Really—'

'No. I'll get you another. Sorry.'

Wyndham wasn't sure what had surprised him more: Moriarty's sudden show of spirit or his willingness to put his hand in his pocket.

Settled again, Wyndham tried a new tack. 'I don't think anyone's saying anything about going back to France. It's a training
command. I don't believe they'll let Fitzmullen-Brophy back in
the field again. Not at his age. Not after he was wounded.'

'And he wants me as a drill sergeant, does he?'

'I believe so. "A trained soldier". That was the term he used.'

'Ah Jesus. A trained soldier isn't even a corporal. He's just an
old bollocks who teaches square-bashing and is good for nothing
else. Old FitzEm can get stuffed.'

Wyndham surprised himself by persevering, by attempting
to work the magic that Fitzmullen-Brophy had used on him last
summer. He conjured up an enticing vision of a new Moriarty,
enjoying the station he'd always deserved: an authority, a master
of recruits. He could tell his old soldier's tales to a captive
audience and be spared the drudgeries of normal army life.

'Think about it.'

'I don't know. I don't know if I'd be good for that sort of thing
at all.'

'What are you talking about? Remember how we first met,
and you were holding everyone spellbound with your stories?'
That was something of a fiction, but if Wyndham was going to
face the memory of that first night in Tralee, then he was going to
do it through rose-coloured spectacles. Perhaps the whiskey was
doing its work.

'Think about it. You wouldn't want to be a sergeant. You'd
only have other sergeants to talk to, and you never got along
with sergeants. Instead, you could be a father or a big brother
or something to the new men. Tell them what you told me about
soldiering – about Alexandria and Calcutta.'

'I was never in Alexandria.'

Wyndham was nonplussed. 'But you told me all about it.'

'I was never there. I was in Port Said, only they hardly let us
off the boat.' He took a swallow of his drink. 'Not much to see,

mind, and the heat was only brutal.'

'Oh,' said Wyndham, and took a drink himself. 'Well, you could have had me fooled.'

Moriarty merely sniffed. Wyndham had noticed that the sniffing was some sort of involuntary punctuation with Moriarty now. He thought again of Fitzmullen-Brophy, that touchstone of regimental pride, and had another stab at it.

'Alright, Moriarty. So you were never in Alexandria, but you were out east. You were years out there – with the regiment. You were out east and then in France because you're a soldier. It's all you know. It's in your blood. You're a Dirty Shirt. You're not going to spend the war sitting in a pub.'

'I don't know.'

'You'll want more stories to tell.'

'I don't know.'

'Think about it. I'll get you another drink.'

Wyndham had been trying to acquire a taste for whiskey since he'd left home the previous summer. The pre-dinner drink he'd accustomed himself to taking when crossing the Atlantic had returned as the after-dinner drink in the Fitzmullen-Brophy house, where he joined the major in a glass by the fire. The manliness of the custom was attractive, but he'd never had more than one glass since that disastrous night he'd first encountered Moriarty and Moriarty's mate Private Lynch.

Now here he was ordering a second drink for himself in a pub that he didn't think was the exact place of his fall from sobriety and decency, but was close enough. He wondered if this was the price of virility: to ruin oneself in the pursuit of duty? He thought about the afflictions he'd suffered since he'd followed the major to war, and thought he might be right. To persuade Moriarty back to the colours he might be expected to drink himself to sottish decay.

He remembered Lynch, a fusilier of the old breed, with his repulsive mouth sucking in booze and his malevolent eyes sizing up the room. Had the army made him that way? Would it do the same in time to anyone who took the shilling? Would that nice young Daniel Wyndham, for instance, turn into a drunken hooligan who spat Hindustani obscenities through bad teeth?

He was musing thus when he returned to Moriarty and, wanting to get away from the 'I don't knows' for a while, tried to engage the man in reminiscence. He didn't want to talk about their one-time drinking companion, but that was at the front of Wyndham's mind.

'What became of Lynch?' he asked. 'He was killed at Étreux, wasn't he?'

'He was killed right enough. Half his head blown off, and him right beside me at the time. God rest the dirty bowsie.' He took a sup of his pint and stared hard at Wyndham. 'What makes you ask about Lynch? He was no friend to you.'

'I was just thinking.' Wyndham made a vague ineffectual gesture at their surroundings. 'That night.'

Moriarty grinned sardonically. 'God bless us. I thought Lynch would have us all killed.'

Wyndham's memory was shamefully hazy concerning that night. He tentatively asked, 'How so?'

'Christ, but that man was a troublemaker. A few drinks too many and a bit of a brawl is one thing. And sneaking late into barracks isn't the end of the world. But assaulting a civilian – Jesus.'

Wyndham thought of the two fusiliers in their best Saturday-night scarlet putting the boot in to some local hard lads, but a generous interpretation could have it that the hard lads started it. 'Assault' seemed too strong a charge to lay on Lynch, and Wyndham said as much.

Moriarty looked at him disbelievingly. 'Do you not remember?

Do you not remember at all?' And he cackled a little as he told how Private Lynch, desperate for more drink at the end of the night had manhandled the American gentleman to the extent that the gentleman had fallen and hit his head.

'Matter of fact,' continued Moriarty, 'I don't remember whether he knocked you down and you knocked yourself out or whether he clouted you one in the first place. He was a rotten fella altogether and you wouldn't put it past him. Anyway, I forget. I had a bit of drink taken myself as I recall.'

'But,' said Wyndham. 'But.' He gathered his thoughts and tried again. 'But weren't we all drunk? I mean to say, wasn't I drunk?'

'Yourself? Not a bit of it. Sober as a judge. Sober enough anyway. Sure, you'd only had a couple.' Unaware of the impact of this revelation, Moriarty went on. 'Lynch was an awful fella, but d'you know he spoke well of you. He was a desperate fucker for holding grudges, but when word got around you'd kept your mouth shut and named no names he was almost sorry for beating you up and robbing you. Christ, but I think the Germans did us all a favour in shooting him.'

Wyndham said nothing to this, too astonished at having his past so suddenly rewritten. The disgraceful episode that had delivered him into the hands of Major Fitzmullen-Brophy and thence into the army had not been very disgraceful at all. What he'd always believed to have been a death-dealing hangover brought on by swinish overindulgence had in fact been concussion, and not his fault at all. There had been no sin to expiate, no need to find redemption. He stared in long silence at his glass and saw that he must have emptied it in his distraction. Then he started to laugh, and kept on laughing in what looked to Moriarty like an attack of almost silent hysterics. After an uncomfortably long time, Wyndham wiped his face, blew his nose, and with a final hiccupping giggle said:

'I need a drink.'

After that strange exorcism Wyndham returned to his mission with a stronger heart and wheedled and jollied and persuaded Moriarty for all he was worth.

In the course of the afternoon the 'I don't knows' evolved into 'I'll think about its' until finally becoming a triumphant 'Alright so'. When Wyndham emerged into the daylight it was with elation. He had done what Fitzmullen-Brophy had asked him, and that was the least of it. He felt liberated of a burden he didn't know he'd been carrying. He was worthy of the colonel's trust, of his own rank, and of his own manhood. The euphoria wore off on the long walk home, to be replaced by an uncomfortable fuzziness, but when he told Fitzmullen-Brophy the good news, generous drinks were poured and the dryness in Wyndham's throat and the tightness in his head were dispelled.

The celebratory mood continued through dinner. Wyndham was a fount of witty observation and amusing anecdote. After dinner he went down to crushing defeat at whist, but that was a source of merriment for him and his partner, who was Molly. He took that partnering, and her laughter, as a good omen.

16

They gave him a drink of remembrance, and after that drink there would be no place he ever saw, or no battle or fight he ever was in, but it would stay in his memory.

—Lady Augusta Gregory, *Gods and Fighting Men*

St. Yvon.

Wyndham had had the man in the spiked helmet clear in his sights and then the rifle had bucked into his shoulder and he hadn't been able to hear what Moriarty had said first, and he couldn't quite remember what Moriarty had said later, but he remembered, as clear as anything, the scream of the incoming shell a little after that, and Moriarty had said, 'Five-nine,' because Moriarty had been an unconscionable know-all, even in the face of imminent death.

Wyndham woke up from his doze then, as he always woke up when that scene played out in his head. He was in the sitting room, and there was the sound of dogs and women outside. Molly found him.

'There you are, Daniel. Stand over in the light and take off your coat.'

He shook his still-fuddled head. 'I'm sorry. What?'

'Stand over by the window. I'm going to make a start on Daddy's old tunic.'

He remembered. The tunic was too long in the sleeves and Molly had promised to do something about it. So he did as she told him and stood there, still not quite awake, while she knelt on the floor, her mouth full of pins, and busied herself with his cuffs.

He had grown up with women fussing at him, but this was the

first time he was properly at peace with it. Back at home he had been subject to endless well-meaning criticism about the way his hair was parted, or if his tie were suitable for church, or whether he had grown too tall, or not tall enough. Now the feminine attitude was the same – he was a man and thus needed endless work done on him – but the purpose was, for once, important. He was being fitted for an army uniform. He was being readied for battle.

'Five-nine,' he said to himself.

Molly looked up. 'Mmmf?'

'Nothing. Sorry.'

He would be going back to the war in an old soldier's coat, sewn by the old soldier's daughter. It was right that Molly should be kneeling, attending to him. He had earned it, just as he had earned the lieutenant's single pip. And he would earn it all again, twice and three times over if the war should still be waiting for him.

He saw that Molly's hair was beginning to come adrift, the way it always did around this time in the afternoon. He let himself forget that she was promised to another.

He would come back from the war – if he came back from the war – and domestic intimacy like this would be his due. He would have it all and he would treasure it. He would have the draughty house and the noisy dogs, the endlessly fussy Fitzmullen-Brophys and the piano that was forever out of tune because of the damp. He would be at peace. He would sleep sound at nights, with Molly warm and soft beside him.

He jerked back to reality, and a pin grazed against his wrist.

'Oh Daniel, do be careful! Look what you nearly made me do! I have enough to be getting on with without having to get blood-stains out of the cloth!'

He mumbled profound apology, hoping that she couldn't see him blushing.

17

Life and death come much closer in the night than they do in the day time, and the whole almost intolerable mystery of war is intensified a thousandfold.

—Mrs. Victor Rickard, *The Story of the Munsters*

The Fitzmullen-Brophy house had been a haven for Wyndham, even if it could have been warmer. However, being allowed to sleep alone and unsupervised – for the first time since last summer – had not been the perfect blessing he'd hoped for. There were too many nights when he found sleeping difficult.

What he wanted on nights like these was to go outside and walk around for a spell, but going downstairs would wake the dogs and the dogs would wake the house.

So, he sat on the edge of the bed, the night sweat cooling on him, and he thought about madness. He had read of the battle frenzy of the heroes and, in a way, he had even seen it. He had seen Sergeant Duffy, mild and amiable, fight like a bull in a narrow place. He had seen Robinson, the easy old soldier, go charging to his death, driven by grief and rum.

But it wasn't that sort of madness that had him thinking now, here in the dark bedroom. He was remembering how the army had carried on out there in Flanders. The army, that embodiment of order, had just carried on in the face of war, under the rule of unreason. The rage that unseated men in the fire of battle was perfectly understandable. What had him flummoxed was the routine obedience, the calm acceptance.

Not long after he had seen Duffy almost twist the head off a German soldier, and seen Robinson go roaring into an unequal bayonet fight, Wyndham had been sent to the rear in charge of some prisoners. Wyndham, who had so narrowly escaped being run through in the frantic melée, was told to take three Germans – one of whom perhaps being the very man who'd just tried to stab him – and escort them alone through the wilderness, and Wyndham had just nodded and yessir'd like he always did, because that's what you did in the army, whether they were telling you to climb up over the parapet or paint white stones white.

That sort of madness.

He could see it still. The holes and ruts had been filled with water, mirroring the wet grey sky, and the duckboard track laid over the soggy ground showed the way back from the kingdom of madness. He had seen Germans before this: as grey shapes across the waste, or in the blurring fight in the farmyard. Here, though, he could study them for the first time. Here he could see his enemy.

They were all wrong. He had lived only a few months in his khaki world, but it had become his whole world, so that now he could only see perversity in their odd-coloured uniforms, their peakless caps, their tall boots. A kindly sergeant had advised him on how best to murder those men, but even as he'd nodded he'd known that he'd never do any such thing.

Last November, alone, he'd silently shepherded those beaten men along that duckboard track – their three to his one, and he not even sure if he knew how to use his rifle, and certain that he would not use a bayonet.

Now, in this chill room in Ireland, the scene replayed differently. He saw his charges getting away from him. He saw the one in the lead, ever lengthening his stride until he was bounding like some Spring-heeled Jack across the littered fields, and Wyndham calling ineffectually after, knowing that the bolt would stick on his rifle, that the trigger would jiggle uselessly under his finger, that the bayonet would come loose from its lug and point harmlessly askew. And that's when, in Wyndham's dream, the Germans turned and smiled, showing small wet teeth through their bearded faces.

And that's why Wyndham had woken up at three o'clock, and was sitting here, beginning to shiver, his feet going numb, thinking about madness.

His dreams weren't usually so specific, nor did he usually remember them on waking, but wake he invariably did. He would come out of a dream, as now, or he would just find himself wide awake, staring into nothing, seeing what he'd seen in Flanders. Out there he could put up with it because everybody did, but here, alone in a civilised bedroom, free from the shared delusion of the war, he saw it all as a sane man might, and he flinched.

Had he really lived in a world where men laboriously excreted into empty food tins and casually threw them over the parapet? Where men ate their cold preserved meat alongside their half-buried dead? Where crouching in thigh-deep water all the live-long day was safe and normal, and standing upright and stretching deserved a bullet to the head?

And he thought then – as he so often found himself thinking in these cold hours – about the man he'd shot at near St. Yvon, just because the man had been standing above ground, dry-footed and insolent. He never knew if he'd hit the man. In the light of day, when his mind was level, he believed himself justified in firing that shot. The German was his enemy, and Wyndham's cause was righteous.

But in the dark he wasn't so sure. In the dark he knew that *Thou shalt not kill* was the immutable law.

And in his sleep, sometimes, the German he'd shot at was a devil like the Spring-heeled Jack of the nightmare just past. Maybe he hadn't killed him. Maybe you couldn't kill such a thing. Maybe Wyndham had just angered it.

Maybe it was waiting for him back in the place of madness.

II

TEMPORARY, ACTING, UNPAID

*You will yet have hard work before you
can call yourselves efficient soldiers...*

—John Redmond, Woodenbridge, 20th September 1914

18

Sons of small farmers in County Clare, shoeless vagabonds of County Kerry, herders of Ballyvegan, much wanted 'moonlighters' from the bare rainy headlands of the south coast... And these were, one and all, of that quaint, crooked, sweet, profoundly irresponsible and profoundly lovable race that fight like fiends, argue like children, reason like women, obey like men, and jest like their own goblins of the rath through rebellion, loyalty, want, woe or war.

—Rudyard Kipling, 'The Mutiny of the Mavericks'

The 11th Battalion should never really have existed. The fault lay in the over-hasty expansion of the army for which no one was prepared. Kitchener had asked for a million men. A million and a half came forward, with more following every month. The army that had never had to absorb more than a few thousand a year – and had to work hard at getting them – was now practically turning men away at the door. This embarrassment of riches would have overwhelmed the army in the best of times. In wartime, with the organisation supposed to handle this sort of problem otherwise occupied with urgent wartime concerns, the raising of the new armies was necessarily haphazard.

Before the war a young man would have submitted himself to the recruiting office, or simply walked up to the barrack gate, and been weighed, measured and sworn in before being posted off to the regimental depot for recruit training. After that, when it was reckoned that he wouldn't disgrace the regiment too badly, he'd have been absorbed into the home service battalion where they'd make a proper soldier of him. Without any great flood of volunteers, time could be taken over the lad.

When the flood did come, it was beyond the army's capacity. Indeed, it appeared to be outside the army's control. What had once been the relatively undemanding preserve of the recruiting sergeants was now in the hands of the patriotic worthies, the civic demagogues and the brass bands. Sometimes, the army's only contribution to the hoopla was a wounded veteran hauled up onto the bunting-festooned stage to make a few suitable remarks. The rest of it was all impassioned speeches, appeals to manhood and lurid reminders of the plight of gallant little Belgium.

The patriots were not ashamed to enhance the showmanship of their appeals with a little creative chicanery. For want of hard evidence of German atrocities, a couple of actresses might be willing to dress up as nuns and wear pillows stuffed down the front of their habits. It was hoped that there were more than a few young Irishmen out there who would be more outraged at offences to religion and womanhood than they were knowledgeable about the facts of life. By the time they'd have questioned how heavily pregnant Belgian nuns could possibly have found their way to, say, Galway, within a couple of months of the German invasion, the army would already have them securely in its martial embrace.

The army didn't care about the methods used. Gullible boys, heedless adventurers and broken-down veterans; the under-age, the over-age and all those wrongly passed fit by doctors who were paid by volume rather than medical scrupulousness: the army would sort them out by and by. For the time being all were welcome. The army was dizzy with recruits – drunk with recruits. And such recruits! The inevitable king's bad bargains aside, Kitchener's men were a superior breed by far to what the army was used to. Better fed, better educated, and hardly a one of them had been up before the beak or had got a girl into trouble. The spirit of come-one-come-all prevailed, even as the organisation creaked at the seams. No one thought of rejecting men lest they never come forward again. If some bigwig was itching to raise yet another new battalion, then let him at it. Any organisational difficulties could be sorted out later.

And that was why they let Colonel Lord Roscrea take his show on the road. He was paying for it out of his own pocket, after all. Roscrea had soldiered gallantly in his youth and he was still a fine figure of a man, with his hawklike face adorned with an iron-grey moustache and his frock coat adorned with the medals of Afghanistan and Zululand. He spoke in market towns about Ireland's fighting men – the men from days of yore and the men now fighting the Germans in Flanders. He spoke about Brian Boru and Patrick Sarsfield, the Duke of Wellington and Lord Roberts. He conjured up a dream of a new Irish Brigade, happily glossing over the fact that the original Irish Brigade had been an implacable enemy of England. It mattered not a whit to Roscrea. Patriotism requires fervour and not clarity.

And the men came forward to take their place in Ireland's army, even though it was an army that had been no more than sketched out in Roscrea's mind. As was so often the case right across the kingdom, the new recruits, upon taking the shilling and swearing fealty to the crown, were anticlimactically sent home again and told to wait for a bit. Their call to arms would not be sounded by the bugle but would be delivered by the postman. There just wasn't any way to accommodate all the recruits yet. Until the army could clothe and feed and house them, the new breed of heroes would have to stay at home.

And then one Saturday morning Lord Roscrea fell off his horse and broke his leg, and his personal recruiting drive was ended. Without his vision and energy to complete the creation of a new army formation, the few hundred men he'd signed up were all there were. In time the army took charge of the matter.

By then the new battalions of the Irish regiments had taken shape, and had taken their places in the army's grand scheme of things. Thus, it came about that Roscrea's recruits, when the postman finally brought them the notification, were instructed to report to Knocknahanna in the northern part of County Cork, and the 11th (Service) Battalion of the Royal Munster Fusiliers.

The Royal Munster Fusiliers didn't need an eleventh battalion, and didn't quite know what it was going to do with one, but it was damned if it was going to let recruits go to waste.

In daylight, and on their way to their new home, Wyndham felt the spring chill through the lightweight material of his new uniform and wrapped himself tighter in the ill-fitting greatcoat they'd given him on his discharge from hospital. He worried about regulations. He worried more about looking out of place.

His worries were unfounded. When Kitchener's volunteers arrived in their hundreds of thousands, they quickly cleaned out every quartermaster's store in the kingdom and kept the clothing factories vainly scrabbling to keep up with demand. In Ireland, where the army had a considerable presence and where the rush of men had not been so dramatic, the situation was not quite so severe. Nevertheless, it had been a case of first come, first serve, and the 11th Munster Fusiliers were late to the feast. Companies paraded in a mixture of khaki and scarlet, and even Post Office blue, with civilian clothing – much abused by camp life – a constant undertone.

Thus, the man who saluted at the gate was in proper uniform, albeit with an incomplete set of accoutrements, but the first man to be seen after that was in pinstripe trousers gone at the knee, a working jacket of dirty white canvas, and a splendidly coloured forage cap of the sort that a fashionable cavalry regiment had been wearing when Queen Victoria was still on the throne.

It was only when he entered the officers' mess that Wyndham

had cause for self-consciousness. Fitzmullen-Brophy had given him urgent instruction on regimental etiquette. Evidently, being introduced to the mess had been something of an ordeal back in the 1880s, and Wyndham guessed that gaffes had been committed that still shadowed Fitzmullen-Brophy's memories.

It helped a little that the officers of the 11th Battalion convened in surroundings less intimidating than was usual. There were no portraits glaring down from the walls, joining everyone from the senior officers to the mess waiters in merciless judgement on the new arrival. Instead, there was the bar of a commandeered hotel, with nothing to advertise its relationship with the army except for two men in uniform.

Their names were McCarthy-Moore and Curran, and they too belonged to a breed that the Munster Fusiliers of olden times would not have readily recognised.

They were correctly dressed, even if it had taken frantic effort and outrageous expense, and their bearing was likewise proper because they were so very determined to show that they could adapt to their new element. In civil life they had been men to be reckoned with. They were going to show the army that they were more than fit for military life, too.

And now here was this new man in a lived-in uniform that betokened foreign service; a man with a broken nose and a scar under his eye; a man who wore a hat and coat straight off the quartermaster's shelf.

'Good afternoon, gentlemen,' he said. 'My name is Wyndham.'

'McCarthy-Moore,' said McCarthy-Moore, gruffly.

'Curran,' said Curran, with rather more self-assurance.

19

The Army can no longer be left as a refuge for ignorant, stupid, and vicious young men.

—*The Naval & Military Gazette,* 1857

Bartholomew Curran cut an impressive figure, no matter what the situation. He was tall, and his studied posture made him look taller still. He knew how to stand so that his broadening middle appeared more as a swelling chest, giving him stature rather than girth. In civilian life, when not in the wig and gown of his profession, he had been dressed by one of the best tailors in Dublin. Now the same tailor had applied his demonstrable taste and skill to khaki barathea and whipcord. Curran had declined to match the uniform with a hairstyle cut *en militaire*, because the curls framing his high brow enforced his patrician good looks.

He was known in all the better drawing rooms and was married to a well-connected lady whom he never saw anymore.

A career at the bar had not served to calm his restlessness, nor had several love affairs been enough for his romantic nature. Thus, he had sought an outlet for his passions in nationalist politics. He contested a Unionist safe seat in the name of Home Rule and was, as expected, convincingly defeated, but the gallant gesture was what appealed to him and it whetted his appetite for further heroic stands. The frock coat of parliamentary politics suited his figure, but he was seduced by the uniform of the Irish Volunteer movement. Where the Home Rulers offered words, the Volunteers promised action.

When he'd first put on his new green coat, with the shamrock rank badges on his cuff, he'd murmured to the mirror the catechism of the patriots of 1798:

'What do you hold in your hand?'
'A green bough.'
'Where did it first grow?'
'In America.'
'Where did it bud?'
'In France.'
'Where will you plant it?'
'In the crown of Great Britain.'

What was better than politics?
This.

As his party leaders negotiated in London through the summer of 1914, Curran was making speeches, recruiting, drilling and trying to organise illegal arms shipments. He imagined that by the end of the year he'd be dead or in prison. The prospect simultaneously sobered and exalted him.

'Whether on the gallows high or the battlefield we die, what's it matter if for Ireland dear we fall?'

But the European war came and deferred his patriotic martyrdom. For a few weeks the thunder of 1798 and 1848 was stolen from his ears. Ireland would not be gaining independence for the time being, neither by her own efforts nor the gift of the Westminster government. The burning business of the spring and summer was sensibly disposed of as if it had been no great matter. The factions that had been preparing for sectarian civil war calmly accepted that the Irish Question would be resolved as and when, and, meanwhile, they would serve within a still United Kingdom to aid in the war against Germany.

Curran, if momentarily nonplussed by how quickly the national crisis had been defused, was able to change mental tack readily enough. Whatever perfidies the English had in store for Ireland would be revealed in time and addressed in time, but the German outrages in Belgium were an offence to God and civilisation that must be met forthwith. When his party endorsed the British war effort, Curran, like many another, saw no betrayal in changing his uniform.

The Volunteers' cause had been right, but so was the cause of the grand alliance against Germany and, although he did not care to admit it, an actual war in France was so much more exciting than the amateur sabre-rattling that had occupied him in Ireland. He had hoped to be off to the front earlier (and ideally, home in time for Christmas), but neither the army nor the war worked that way. He might have found a place in one of the earlier Irish units to be sent overseas, but that would have meant enlisting in the ranks in that first enthusiastic rush, whereas a gentleman of Curran's calibre was naturally holding out for a commission. After all, he'd already been fitted for a uniform, and only needed to know what regimental insignia was needed. Despite his many and sound connections, the commission was longer in coming than he'd hoped, and he'd been obliged to settle for the 11th Munsters – the fag-end of the army's expansion in Ireland. Still, unlike the enthusiasts who'd thronged to the colours in August and spent the winter under wet canvas, he'd been able to spend the winter in Dublin, well fed and much caressed by that part of society which appreciated the sacrifices a man made in fighting for king and country.

Whether in court, the hustings, or the army, Curran was playing a role, and he was honest enough to admit it. His convictions were real, even if the outward show was sometimes a necessary imposture. But he was worried about being revealed in the company of real soldiers. So far, he had been relieved to encounter only novices like himself. There had been the brief interview with the colonel, of course, but Fitzmullen-Brophy was a forthright gentleman of the sort that Curran was long used to. And then this Wyndham had shown up: this American adventurer who'd been fighting beside the colonel while Curran had still been admiring his new uniform in the mirror; this soft-spoken man with his rumpled tunic and battered face. Curran must have been more than a dozen years older than this Wyndham, but he had no scars on his face.

Like Curran, Laurence McCarthy-Moore had also heard from the colonel about Wyndham's arrival, and while he hadn't quite been expecting a desperado with a dagger between his teeth, he was certainly not overawed by meeting Fitzmullen-Brophy's American soldier in the flesh. He wasn't about to cast aspersions on Wyndham's courage or manliness, but McCarthy-Moore was a man who tended to judge other men by the strength of their handshake and their fearlessness in social situations. The colonel's comrade-in-arms scored poorly on both counts. Nor did Wyndham's broken nose impress him. McCarthy-Moore had played rugby for his school and his university, and was happy to play it still when opportunity allowed. He knew all about broken noses.

Like Curran, he was a barrister, although younger and not yet as successful, and, again like Curran, he was a Home Ruler, even if his political life had never extended beyond attending the odd meeting and casting his ballot for John Redmond's party on election day. He hadn't a radical thought in his head. He voted Home Rule because his family always had, and because it was right. Irish independence was just another aspect of standing on your own two feet. Work hard. Study for your exams. Play the game. If it all goes wrong, you have no one to blame but yourself.

Lead by example: that was another principle that had been drilled into him. The war was right, and McCarthy-Moore was not going to let other men fight it for him. He was as yet unmarried, but if sometime in the not-too distant future his little daughter might sit on his knee and lisp, 'Daddy, what did *you* do in the Great War?', he wouldn't have to look like that fellow on the poster. He'd have stood up for gallant little Belgium.

If it had been down to Wyndham and McCarthy-Moore alone, the battalion would have died that very afternoon. One read books while the other played rugby, and neither was comfortable at small talk. Curran was their saviour, easily demonstrating how he'd made such a success of himself in the salons of Dublin. He made the ordering of a round of drinks seem like a great conspiratorial escapade and then he skilfully guided the conversation clear of everything that might prove controversial or tedious. Having been given nothing else to do, they stayed talking through the afternoon, and when a more senior, more regular officer looked in at them, and frowned in disapproval, they knew they were united in subaltern brotherhood.

20

The character and credit of the British Army must chiefly depend upon the zeal and ardour by which all who enter into its service are animated, and consequently it is of the highest importance that any measure calculated to excite the spirit of emulation, by which alone great and gallant actions are achieved, should be adopted.

—Historical Record of the 88ᵗʰ Foot, or Connaught Rangers

The officer who had cast a censorious eye on the convivial meeting in the mess was Major de Roche. He had been with the battalion a few days longer than the rest and felt most proprietorial about the whole business. And well he should: he was second in command, after all. As Fitzmullen-Brophy and everyone engaged in the building of the new armies were daily reminded, there was a besetting dearth of trained officers. Untrained officers, alas, were two-a-penny, as the three idle characters drinking whiskey in the mess in the afternoon amply demonstrated. Officers like de Roche had their work cut out for them if that sort of thing was the regular state of affairs nowadays.

In de Roche's world, a second-lieutenant was a creature to be seen and not heard. Subalterns were like puppies, either timorous or boisterous, and to be disciplined either way until they knew enough to be useful and not so much of a nuisance. He most certainly didn't hold with new-made subalterns being much above the age of twenty-one. In the old army – the proper army – it had certainly been the case that an occasional man, through diligence and sobriety, might gain a commission from the ranks, and be perhaps in his late twenties when he first set foot in the officers' mess. But such birds were few, and of a different breed. They certainly didn't set a tone of amateurism and dissipation such as was being unfortunately shown in the 11th Battalion. De Roche rather hoped that the colonel would do something about it. As for himself, he had no taste for tussling with over-age subalterns, and besides, there was work to be done.

So much work. De Roche suspected that it was his thorough training – so rare in today's army – that would be his downfall. He should be in France now, gaining recognition and advancement with his regiment, instead of stuck here with this dribbling infant of a battalion. De Roche wasn't even a Munster Fusilier, or a Munster man for that matter. Mayo was his county and the Connaught Rangers his regiment.

The Connaught Rangers were the regiment that had once upon a time established the fearsome reputation revelled in by all Irish soldiery. A hundred years before, they had been the Devil's Own Regiment of Foot: bewhiskered young ruffians from the mountains and bogs who had formed the backbone of Wellington's army when he'd driven Bonaparte from Spain. They had become more civilised since then, being largely accustomed to speaking English and wearing shoes, for example, and as far as de Roche was concerned, that made them all the better. Esmonde de Roche was a man of education and refinement, but he knew that in his veins ran the blood of the men who had stormed Badajoz in 1812. He was quite sure it would show itself, given a chance.

But the great chance was being held from him. He'd been home from India on leave when the war broke out. The home service battalion of his regiment, bound for France in a hurry, had no place for him. There is no point in returning to India when his own battalion was likely to be summoned from there any day. And the army, of course, was not slow in finding him a job that had nothing to do with the workings of the Connaught Rangers. Of course not. De Roche was one of those precious officers who had *passed Staff College* and had ever since had the letters *p.s.c.* attached to his name. An officer like Captain de Roche *p.s.c.* could not be allowed to go to waste – not with the army in such ferment.

In France, the 2nd Connaught Rangers had met with rough handling similar to that which had wiped out the 2nd Munster Fusiliers. The 1st Battalion came home from India to be committed to the Western Front, and there it had stayed, bleeding steadily. Meanwhile, de Roche remained in Ireland. He steadfastly resisted the temptation through all this to just hang it all and head off to rejoin his regiment. Fitzmullen-Brophy had done something like that and it had caused no end of trouble. An understandable impulse, certainly, but you couldn't run an army if fellows were apt to act off their own bat in such a manner.

So, de Roche stayed and did whatever administrative jobs they gave him, and now they'd given him this. Lieutenant-Colonel Fitzmullen-Brophy was the right sort, up to a point, but he had simply no notion of building a battalion. And, alas, he was only a Munster Fusilier. De Roche had nothing against the Munsters, but they just weren't the Connaught Rangers. Also, there was something in the nickname 'Dirty Shirts' that offended his fastidious nature.

To show his allegiance to the Rangers, and his detachment from this slapdash creation of Kitchener's, he continued to wear the crowned harp badge of his old regiment. He was particular, however, to have his uniforms altered to display on his cuffs the major's crowns that came with his new appointment. It was an acting rank only, but that was no reason to be improperly dressed.

At present, the only other regular officer in the battalion was Doyle, who wasn't a Munster Fusilier either. He was an Irishman but had been commissioned into the Duke of Cornwall's Light Infantry two years earlier. His quiet regimental existence at the Curragh had ended suddenly in August and the war had accelerated his young life beyond imagining. Since last August he'd been shot twice, promoted twice and, if such a thing were technically possible, he'd have lost his virginity twice too.

Now he found himself here, proud of the captain's pips that came with his acting rank, still somewhat troubled by the wound that had invalided him home in December, and aching for a third sexual encounter with a delightful friend of the family who, in a transport of enthusiastic compassion, had taken advantage of him during his convalescent leave.

He'd been in Cork, appearing before a medical board, when he'd been nabbed by Fitzmullen-Brophy, who'd just been provisionally passed fit by the same board and had high hopes for future employment. In the short time that they'd shared in a waiting room, the friendly old major had positively grilled Doyle, as was his way, and in no time had learned all about his antecedents, education, and military service. A week or so later, with Doyle reeling from the discovery of sex, he received a letter from Fitzmullen-Brophy offering him a job. Doyle's regard for his own regiment – his father's and his grandfather's old regiment – was overridden by his new-found and urgent desire to tarry in Ireland a while longer.

Since he'd arrived here there'd been nothing to do except bag the best quarters, wander around looking vaguely busy, and write letters filled with clumsy yearning. As far as duties were concerned, he supposed the new CO would put him in the picture soon enough. Until then, the sergeant-major could run the show.

Up until now, the battalion had been run by a reserve officer who'd been put out by Fitzmullen-Brophy's appointment and had reassigned himself elsewhere in silent protest. Two opportunistic officers who'd been helping him took advantage of the brief interregnum to hasten back to their units in France, leaving the senior NCO unhappily in charge.

This was Sergeant-Major O'Meara, who had been merely Sergeant O'Meara last month. Rheumatism had sent him home from France, and he worried that he just wasn't up to the job of soldiering anymore. He also worried that he didn't know the first thing about commanding a battalion – even one understrength, and of willing recruits. He'd been in the battalion transport in France. That's how he'd survived Étreux: by getting the wagons out as ordered, well ahead of the German encirclement. He knew wagons and he knew horses, and he knew the army's way of handling both. He didn't trust himself to be responsible for anything more: certainly not the duties of a regimental sergeant-major.

And he didn't trust Lieutenant-Colonel Fitzmullen-Brophy. The man was a fire-eater. Everyone in the regiment knew that. This was the man who'd gone haring off to war on his own account with a company of untrained men last year. What was to stop him from doing the same thing again? How many men had made it home from that adventure? O'Meara had met a cook-sergeant named Duffy when they'd both been passing through Tralee. Duffy had been one of the men who'd gone off with Fitzmullen-Brophy and here he was back in Tralee with a hole in his face and a few fingers missing from his hand. And the man had only been a cook.

And now they'd only gone and promoted the mad Major FitzEm, who could hardly be expected to have mercy on a transport sergeant with the rheumatics. God help us all, thought O'Meara. If he were a drinking man he'd be drinking.

21

Only the Table Round, that is indeed, as it seems, a rivulet from the same river, is bound in a like fellowship.

—Lady Augusta Gregory, *Gods and Fighting Men*

The colonel had been quick to adopt a dog. His own dogs had been left behind in Tralee (so Susan would have something to scold, he liked to joke), but it was absurd that he should be stationed in rural Ireland and not have a dog. As colonel, he would find the loneliness of command eased. The men, sleeping under canvas, wearing ragamuffin clothes with their civilian boots giving in, would be immensely bucked by the cheerful addition of a battalion mascot.

The dog may have been cheerful. It was certainly exuberant.

He had named the last regimental dog Bobs, after Lord Roberts. This one he christened K, after Kitchener of Khartoum, who always signed himself with that single initial. Field-Marshal Lord Kitchener didn't have the same connection to the Munster Fusiliers that Roberts had, but he'd been born in Kerry, and that would do. The dog, his namesake, lacked the great man's maturity and forceful direction but had an abundance of energy and was a more direct presence in the life of this New Army formation at least.

K was half-grown and undisciplined when he'd been palmed off on Fitzmullen-Brophy, and the indulgent colonel was not a man to treat a dog harshly, even when it was as full of sin and selfishness as this one.

K grew proud on army beef and marked the battalion and

everything in it as its own. Its name never quite caught on in the ranks. There they knew the colonel's dog as 'that little black fecker'. After it unwisely picked a fight with a swan it was briefly humbled, but it never learned to respect human authority.

In the end a deputation submitted itself to the colonel. Some officers, whose expensive new boots had been worried by the dog, were inclined to call for shooting the beast, but they had to content themselves with a compromise that barred K from the mess.

The officers' mess was already too small. The hotel it had been prior to the war had been uncomfortably small too, and out of the way, and generally so unsuccessful that the owner had been pleased to let it to the army for the duration, even though he'd been sure to gouge every penny he could out of them, insisting that it was some sort of rural Irish Savoy and the beating heart of the local economy. Pleading also that it was his home, he'd even arranged to stay on the premises as a sort of caretaker, which meant extra money from the army. The arrangement was a persistent irritation to Fitzmullen-Brophy who held that an officers' mess was a sanctuary, to be forever free of the interference of women and civilians. He had enough to be getting on with in organising the new battalion without having to argue with this wretched hotelier about who was really in charge here. Also, with this man still occupying space, there was less room for his officers. He had few enough, to be sure, but the juniors were already obliged to double up, and if any more were assigned they'd have to be billeted in nearby houses.

In Flanders Wyndham had enjoyed a favoured position at battalion headquarters, which had allowed him to sleep on a shelf in the cupboard of a wrecked farmhouse. He had shared it with one other man, who'd had the floor space beneath the shelf, and they'd both appreciated their privilege. Before that, there had been the barracks in Tralee, with its enforced intimacy and permanent damp. Accordingly, sharing a modest hotel room with an agreeable comrade was no great hardship. McCarthy-Moore happened to be that comrade, and as he was neat in his person and Spartan in his habits, the two men found harmony. Curran, on the other hand, although he'd steeled his spirit to the rigours of a soldier's life, hadn't quite considered that those would include communal living. He'd grown too used to his comforts and his independence, and had no appetite to a return to a life he'd happily turned his back on when he'd left school. Also, he had too much in the way of possessions, and he and his luxuries had a habit of spreading out to fill all available space in a most unmilitary way.

They had servants, drawn from the ranks, but while they could carry coal buckets and fetch hot water, they made poor valets. The sort of men who knew the ins and outs of gentlemen's attire had not joined the army to skivvy for the epaulette gentry, so the job fell to simpler souls who'd always had their own clothes looked after by their mothers and hadn't learned the first thing yet about military kit. Wyndham, as the one-time ranker, was obliged to look after his own uniform as best he could, while simultaneously acting as instructor to his servant and McCarthy-Moore too. Curran was unlikely ever to learn. After a crisis of laundry, he came to an arrangement with a local woman who kept his uniforms spruce. Fitzmullen-Brophy disapproved, but he could hardly have his officers looking scruffy either.

He, naturally, had a room to himself, and the most promising of the soldier-servants, whom he drove mad. Downstairs he maintained an office, where he was obliged to spend far more time than he cared to, wrestling with the army's red tape. He tried to push as much of it as possible onto Major de Roche so that he could be out and about, keeping his eye in and his hands on, knocking the battalion into shape with the force of his personality. Alas, when it came to enforcing *esprit de corps* the best he could hope for some days was dinner with his officers. Here he could at least impress upon them the etiquette and traditions of the service and, in convivial atmosphere, infuse them with regimental spirit.

He did rather wish, though, that he had somewhat grander surroundings in which to work. In his time, he'd dined off the regimental silver in Aldershot, sipped iced champagne under flyblown canvas in South Africa and toasted the queen in fine old port in Rangoon, with the mercury at a hundred and five and everyone's collars grey and wilted with sweat. A small country hotel in County Cork, with the manager hovering nearby to see that the crockery didn't get broken, just wasn't quite the thing. In an effort to militarise the mess, and introduce comforts more fitting to gentlemen, he appointed Curran as mess president and gave him firm guidelines as to what was expected.

Curran might have been new to the army, but he was clearly a fellow with standards. His first decisive act was to write away to a decent wine merchant he knew. Then he gave a stern talking to the cook and the servants. After that, he addressed himself to the decor. The parlour (henceforth *never* to be referred to as the parlour, but always as the anteroom) was lacking in promise. There were a couple of inoffensive and barely noticeable pictures on the wall that could be readily done away with, but it wasn't as if the room had been overflowing with civilian knick-knacks and fripperies. There had already been a row over the Sacred Heart of Jesus being banished from the front hall. Fitzmullen-Brophy had insisted on that, but had tactfully stopped short of replacing it with a coloured picture of King George V, cut from an illustrated newspaper. That instead now hung in its cheap frame in the dining room.

'I'm afraid it all makes a rather poor showing,' sighed Curran. 'I'm thinking of some sporting prints. Maybe some Indian scenes. I've got on to a bookseller in Dublin who deals in such things. It's not as if we can have the colonel's portrait in oils though, is it?

Not exactly falling over ibex heads and tiger skins either. I don't suppose you brought back any trophies from France?'

'Afraid not,' admitted Wyndham, but he thought about it for a moment and added: 'But trophies wouldn't be right. I mean we haven't been in action yet. I mean, when we were in France we were part of the 2nd Battalion. Even if we had a German helmet to hang on the wall it wouldn't really be ours.'

'Suppose not.'

'And we don't hunt and we've never been to India.'

'You're not being much help, Wyndham.'

'Sorry.'

They stood silently a little while longer before Curran spoke again. 'But I do take your point. Regimental tradition's all very well, but it's not *our* tradition, is it? We're not here to fight for the empire. Tiger on our badges or not, we've nothing to do with India. We're Irish. Even you, my American friend – for the duration of the war, at least. And I'm damned if we can't have Irish traditions we can't celebrate. Let me think about it.'

The result, unveiled before Friday night's dinner, was not a stuffed animal or a stand of captured arms, but a large decorative sign, skilfully run up by an artistic young sign painter in the battalion. Before uncovering it, Curran, glass in hand, gave a dedicatory speech.

'Colonel. Gentlemen. I am new to this proud old regiment, and I have been avid to learn as much as I can of its traditions. I was not, to give you an example, familiar with the regiment's motto, and indeed was obliged to ask the colonel. And you, sir, were so kind as to tell me that the Royal Munster Fusiliers have as our motto, "Heaven's Light Our Guide", which is certainly a pious sentiment but, as you yourself pointed out, a trifle uninspiring for a man of action, who would undoubtedly find a prismatic compass a more practical guide.'

Fitzmullen-Brophy joined in the laughter, not caring in the least that he'd said no such thing.

'The 11th Battalion,' Curran resumed, 'is honoured to partake of all that the regiment has been and done down the ages. The regiment's countless gallant fights across India, Burma, and South Africa are an example to us and an inspiration. But, gentlemen, they are not our fights. We have our own battle to fight, and our own traditions to make, and I think I can say that it becomes us to have our own motto, too.'

He said all of this with a smile on his lips, because men who must have dealings with death are light-hearted even in their reverence.

'I have taken these words not from the Latin that we most of us have forgotten, nor from any high-minded evangelical tract of the last century (with sincere apologies to whomever granted the regiment our motto).'

More laughter.

'No. Instead I have looked among the deeds of Irishmen – of the heroes of yore – which is to say that I've been rooting in the library of our own Lieutenant Wyndham.'

Good-natured shouts.

'And so, ere our soup get cold, I give you the words of Cuchulain – an Ulsterman who knew not the narrow sectarianisms that bedevil the Ulster of today, but a true Irish warrior. Indeed, dare I say, that with a little of the colonel's discipline behind him, perhaps he'd even have made a true Irish *soldier*.'

And with that, caring not at all that some of his audience might have had no notion of who or what Cuchulain might have been, Curran deftly uncovered the sign. It was framed with Celtic scrolls, and tigers and harps, and bore the words:

I will make my doings be spoken of among the great doings of heroes in their strength.

He proclaimed the words aloud lest his audience had trouble with the ornate Irish script or the heroic syntax.

'I do not propose, gentleman, that this is something we should be shouting as we close with the Germans on the battlefield, but rather let it stand as an aspiration and a reminder. We are the 11th Munsters. We'll show them what we can do!'

The applause was the sort of appreciative bellowing made by men who can't clap because they are all holding drinks. Then Fitzmullen-Brophy, beaming, stepped up, said, 'Jolly good. *Jolly* good. Quite splendid,' and they all cheered again and went in to dinner.

The evening went swimmingly after that. Wyndham was particularly pleased. He was filled with good wine and good fellowship, but most of all he was delighted that he had finally – *finally* – come across someone who shared, or at the very least acknowledged, an interest in Ireland's legendary past.

He looked at the faces round the table, of men who were willingly shedding a measure of their individuality in order to fit in. All of them with shining red faces above khaki collars, khaki ties, khaki tunics, and Wyndham was just the same. He'd joined the army so he could be a man, and a man among men, and here he was, with the wine red in the cup and the warriors of Ireland around him at the table.

Hugh Fitzmullen-Brophy was a far cry from Finn, son of Cumhal, and the officers of the 11th Munsters were no Fianna, but, thought Wyndham in his contentment, they were making a rather good start.

So contented was he, in fact, that he was not quite shocked into speechlessness by the colonel addressing him by his Christian name. Never – not even in the months he had lived under the man's roof, almost as one of his family – had he been addressed as anything other than Wyndham. This in no way belied a genuine affection, but Fitzmullen-Brophy had always been Sir and Wyndham had always been Wyndham. Only to the women had he been Daniel, as he had always been to his own family. And now, suddenly, he was Dan, because the mess was home: a place of ease and relaxation where familiarity and jocularity reigned, and where, while the senior officers naturally retained the respect due to their age and rank, the junior men were known by Christian names and nicknames.

But there were no other nicknames as yet. The officers had mostly come to the regiment not from school but from sedate civil life, where even close friends might be addressed by surname only. And these were serious men, dedicated for the duration. So, until the rest of them could get a little more raffish and unbuttoned, Fitzmullen-Brophy would have to settle with calling Lieutenant Wyndham 'Dan', and hope that the trend caught on.

22

I hope the officers of Her Majesty's Army may never degenerate into bookworms. There is happily at present no tendency in that direction, for I am glad to say that this generation is as fond of danger, adventure and all manly out-of-door sports as its forefathers were.

—Lord Wolseley, 1897

The new officers were diligent in learning their trade. The stack of War Office publications that appeared in the mess disappeared rapidly as the students of the military arts set themselves to their studies. Wyndham had opened *Infantry Training (4-Company Organisation) 1914* just after dinner, but Curran borrowed it from him 'just to look something up', and that was the last Wyndham saw of it that evening. For want of anything else, he resorted to *Scouting for Boys* to see if that might help him in taking charge of a platoon of fighting men.

Wyndham instantly knew that he might as well have been looking into the soul of his commanding officer and mentor. Clearly, both General Sir Robert Baden-Powell and Lieutenant-Colonel Hugh Fitzmullen-Brophy were men whose mission it was to create young patriots who were sound of wind and clean of limb. The health of the bowels and the wellbeing of the Empire were evidently the concern of all right-thinking men, and Wyndham well remembered how he'd marched from Tralee to Maubeuge with the motto 'Be Prepared' ringing in his ears.

The book's uplifting stories and sound advice were all very well, but he found that the moral rather outweighed the practical.

The practical skills, evidently, were largely something in which a leader should already be versed. Wyndham thought this rather a shame, seeing as he'd been hoping for something concrete along the lines of how to read a map without making a fool of himself in front of his men, or how to outflank a German position and play a notable part in winning the war.

He could, if he chose, practise making a button out of string, but instead he studied the Scout Law (written all in capitals as the Law of Moses had no doubt been), wondering if it could be applied to his own situation. He wondered if the rules held true with the word 'fusilier' substituted for 'scout'.

A Scout's honour is to be trusted, was the first commandment and, applied to a soldier, was a sound ideal, if not quite a universal law in the army as Wyndham knew it.

A Fusilier is loyal to the King, and to his officers, and to his country. Well, that translated easily. Indeed, it went without saying. These were the *Royal* Munster Fusiliers, who solemnly toasted the king after dinner every evening. He read on, taking heart.

A Fusilier's duty is to be useful and to help others. Fair enough.

A Fusilier is a friend to all, and a brother to every other Fusilier, no matter to what social class the other belongs. That might be pushing things when it came to life in barracks and in camp, but he remembered how it had been at the front, with officers and men sharing both the danger and the squalor. The colonel was right: this Baden-Powell fellow was worthy of respect.

A Fusilier is courteous. And so he should be.

A Fusilier is a friend to animals. And why not?

A Fusilier obeys orders. Why, naturally. Unthinkable otherwise.

A Fusilier smiles and whistles. He does *what*?

Wyndham's faith in the scouting movement received a bad shake. *Scouts never grouse at hardships, nor whine at each other, nor swear when put out*. No. Sorry. That just didn't apply to fusiliers. Grousing, whining and especially swearing were what soldiers did along with breathing. Nor, he considered when he read the last law, were fusiliers thrifty in any degree. This book, while admirable in many respects, would not be his salvation. He kept it by him, though, because its uncompromising optimism cheered him. The War Office manuals, whatever their worth, had no power to inspire.

23

The Irish soldier is not difficult to lead: he will follow any man who is just and fearless…

—Major Bryan Cooper, *The Tenth (Irish) Division in Gallipoli*

Sergeant Rafferty was the reddest man Wyndham had ever seen. From looking at his sandy hair it was possible to guess that he'd once had one of those fair Irish complexions, but years exposed to the sun of Africa and India had put paid to that. A lifetime of heavy drinking couldn't have helped either. The redness radiated out from every part of him. His nose was a dark and angry red. His eyes were glassy beads of grey-blue set in red. Even his yellow-brown teeth seemed to reflect the red that surrounded them.

He was a sergeant because he'd asked to be a sergeant.

The recruiting party had brought a holiday atmosphere to town that hot August afternoon. On that day patriotism meant the United Kingdom and the red, white and blue was all in fashion. It was the sort of mood that would make people stand an old soldier a drink, so Rafferty had gone home and got his medals out of a drawer. He hadn't intended to re-enlist, but with a couple of jars inside him adding to the warmth that came from being a minor celebrity of sorts, the idea had grown on him. Having presented himself as an old imperial hand, and being of mature years, it would have been beneath him to go back in as a private. A private was all he'd ever been in all his years of service, but by rights, in fairness, in all fairness, he should have been a sergeant. The rank of sergeant was befitting his experience and dignity. And a sergeant got two and fourpence a day. The landlady was after him for the rent and his India General Service Medal was all that was holding the front of his coat together so, when it appeared that no one else was likely to buy him a drink, he'd shouldered his way through the good-natured crowd and stood to attention in front of none other than Lord Roscrea himself. They'd eyed each other's medals, and Rafferty, with a horse-coper's wink, had asked if Roscrea would be needing any sergeants. That was all it took.

When the battalion formed, he'd been disappointed to find that the rudimentary sergeant's mess was under-supplied with the comforts of life, and that the nearest public house wasn't very near at all. But all this would be remedied in time, and until then there were the recruits to lord over.

Given the camp's primitive state, Rafferty was limited in the ways he could exercise his authority. Kit inspections were impossible without kit, and so that meant drill and nothing besides drill. He kept them at it until he got bored, and then he'd assign some pointless cleaning tasks, delegate the unnecessary supervision of it all and go off in search of rest and refreshment.

When the inevitable officer arrived to take charge, Rafferty wasn't too bothered. He could produce any number of excuses for his negligence, and you could double that number if the officer was a new-made subaltern. Still and all, he wasn't pleased with the appearance of this Lieutenant Wyndham. He was an odd one, and Rafferty found it hard to get the measure of him.

The platoon was engaged in the usual morning's desultory square-bashing in a meadow when the new platoon commander walked up in his rumpled pale khaki. Rafferty roared at the men to come to attention and snapped off a quivering, glaring salute that was designed to intimidate anyone who might be new to this sort of thing. Lieutenant Wyndham returned the salute correctly, but showed neither the earnestness of the novice nor the offhand style of the experienced officer.

'Number six platoon, sergeant?' he asked, with no more

military ceremony than if he'd been asking if this bus went all the way to the station.

'Number six platoon, yes *sir*! Sergeant Rafferty, *sir*! Platoon all present and ready for inspection, *sir*!' Rafferty, in contrast to Wyndham's attitude, was announcing to anyone within earshot that he and the platoon weren't leaving until they'd got the fight they'd come for.

'Very good, Sergeant. Very good,' said Wyndham, and Rafferty wondered at the accent. Combined with the uniform it made him suspect that he might be dealing with some sort of colonial type. He'd seen them in South Africa – men casual in their military punctilio, but natural horsemen and deadly shots. This Wyndham was too young to have been in South Africa, but that proved nothing. The empire was wide, and there was always some fighting going on somewhere.

Wyndham inspected the men because the sergeant had said they were ready for inspection and it would have been impolite to ignore them, but as he looked along the ranks, with every man avoiding his eye, his qualms fell away. These weren't like the old soldiers of last year, wily and cocky. These men, just like him, were new to the job. The proof was there in the hard-worn civilian clothing mixed with ill-suited military uniform. And these men were so obviously of a different species to the recruits with whom Wyndham had bunked down in Tralee last summer. The men in front of him were no ignorant wretches, enlisted for the pound of bread and shilling a day. That man on the front rank, with his bow tie and weathered homburg, might look shabby and comical to the military eye, but Wyndham recognised him as an adventurer and a patriot. The only real differences were that Wyndham had received his call personally from Fitzmullen-Brophy. That, and of course, that Wyndham had already been through the disorienting rigours of recruit training, and taken his place in the trench, and earned the tiger badge on his cap.

When Wyndham turned back to Rafferty he was smiling broadly. This was rather outside Rafferty's experience. New officers tended to hide their ignorance by looking too closely at details they couldn't see or by feigning indifference to the whole show. Both approaches tended to end with a brief, 'Carry on, Sergeant,' which was an acknowledgement of who really was in charge.

Instead of such an abdication, Wyndham looked brightly at Rafferty and asked, 'What shall we do now, Sergeant?'

'Sir?'

'Well, you seem to have drill well in hand, and I don't imagine there's much more that can be done until arms are issued. How about games?'

'Games, sir? Like football, do you mean?'

Wyndham thought of the wealth of educational exercises outlined in the handbook from the night before. 'Games in stalking!' he said. There was a delay while he realised that the first book he'd pulled from his tunic pocket was a O'Growney's *Simple Lessons in Irish*, but the required text was found in due course.

> *Stalking and Reporting: The umpire places himself out in the open and sends each scout or pair of scouts away in different directions about half a mile off. When he waves a flag, which is the signal to begin, they all hide and then proceed to stalk him, creeping up and watching all he does. When he waves the flag again—*

'Really, sir – half a mile? We can't have the men scattered all over the parish!'

Wyndham held up a finger.

> *When he waves the flag again they rise, come in, and report each in turn all that he did, either by handing in a written*

*report or verbally as may be ordered. The umpire meantime
has kept a look-out in each direction, and, every time he sees
a scout, he takes two points off that scout's score. He, on his
part, performs small actions, such as sitting down, kneeling
up; and looking through glasses, using handkerchief, taking
hat off for a bit, walking round in a circle a few times, to give
scouts something to note and report about him. Scouts are
given three points for each act reported correctly.*

'Ah now, sir! In all fairness! You can't be teaching men out of a child's book like that, sir.'

'Sergeant, this "child's book" was strongly recommended by Colonel Fitzmullen-Brophy.'

'Be that as it may, sir—'

'And was written by *General* Sir Robert Baden-Powell.'

'Ah, but sir!'

'But it will be *fun*, Sergeant. Now, we will need a signal flag.' And it was clear that young Mr. Wyndham had the bit between his teeth and was not paying heed to his wise old sergeant. The men, also, were easily infected with enthusiasm for the game. They were sick of drill, and even if not all of them saw the point of the exercise, it was a grand day to be allowed to range freely about the countryside. That class of thing wasn't something that Rafferty held with at all. Fun? The new lieutenant wasn't just peculiar: he was wandered.

24

I never knew a man that was in a battle that liked to speak of it after. They'd sooner be throwing hay down from a hayrick.

—W.B. Yeats, *The Celtic Twilight*

Moriarty was off by himself, taking it easy in the lee of a wall. Skiving had always been his nature, but these days he liked a quiet place out of the wind for its own sake. He just wasn't comfortable in the open spaces. He had finished his cigarette so had no excuse at all to be here when Sergeant Rafferty found him. In the old days, Moriarty would have had some excuse at the ready, but nowadays he couldn't be bothered, especially with someone like Rafferty.

But Rafferty wasn't here to push his weight around. After a companionable remark about the weather and the offer of a cigarette, he got down to business.

'Your man Lieutenant Wyndham,' he said.

'I know him,' answered Moriarty guardedly.

'Sure I know you know him. I just wanted to ask.'

'Go on so.'

Rafferty was pointedly ignoring their disparity in rank, remaining friendly, even conspiratorial, despite Moriarty's neglecting to address him as sergeant.

'You were out in France with him, isn't that right?'

Rafferty hadn't been to France, and no matter how many stripes Rafferty sewed on his sleeve, Moriarty would always have that advantage over him. And Rafferty wouldn't be here like this unless he wanted something.

'That's right,' admitted Moriarty, seeming to grudge the information, beginning to play Rafferty like a fish on the end of a line. 'Me and Wyndham, we were out together. The Aisne, Wipers, the lot. Of course, he was only in the ranks then, so we got to know each other well. I could tell you stories.'

'I'd heard he was in the ranks alright, but tell me – he's a quare one, isn't he? What's his story at all? He's an American, isn't he?'

Rafferty had dropped the pretence at casualness, and the rush of questions was making this too easy for Moriarty.

'Ah, he's a quare one alright. Did you notice the tunic he has on him? He'll tell you he joined up only last year, but that tunic's seen some service. You don't need me to tell you that. And if you look close you'll see that it has the marks of different rank badges on it.'

'And what would that be about, do you know?'

'Mister Wyndham doesn't like to talk about his past. I asked him about it once, when we were sharing a trench, but you could see the questions were making him angry, and you'd know better than to make a man like Dan Wyndham angry.'

'Is that so? He seems quiet enough.'

'He seems quiet enough, alright, but sure it's the quiet ones you have to watch. Isn't that always the way? Did you see the broken nose on him?'

'I did. What's the story with that?'

'Well do you remember Sergeant Duffy? Ah sure you wouldn't. You weren't there. Well anyway, Duffy was a huge man. Ask any of the old sweats and they'll tell you about his boxing.'

'And he broke Wyndham's nose?'

'He did, but it wasn't in the ring. It was up the line, and Wyndham went mad with him – with a man practically twice his size – and Duffy had to put Wyndham down, and I'll tell you that it was no easy thing.'

'Mother of God! What was it about? And what's he doing as an officer now if he's offering violence to sergeants?'

'I'll tell you. First, you don't want to set too great a store by King's Regulations at the front. You don't want to stand on your rank out there. Things get too serious for that. I'll tell you how it was. We'd been fighting for days. No rest at all. We were outflanked and outnumbered and practically surrounded. This was at Wipers – Eepray – you'd heard of that? Well, we'd run out of ammunition and the Huns were coming at us in crowds and it was all bayonet work. I'll tell you that my uniform was so stiff with German blood I couldn't have sat down even if I'd had the chance.'

'Jesus. They tell me it was bad alright.'

'It was bad enough. Would you ever have another fag on you? Good man.' He tucked it behind his ear and took another drag on the cigarette he already had on the go. 'So anyway, we hold on and the Huns break off the attack – sure you knew that or otherwise I wouldn't be here talking to you – and we'd taken a few prisoners. Now most of us just wanted to sit down and have a smoke and some tay, but Wyndham was still fired up.'

He paused to examine his cigarette with apparent distaste. 'Are these Woodbines? I thought that you'd be able to afford something better with sergeant's pay.'

'Never mind that, man. What did Wyndham do?'

'He tried to kill the prisoners. Went after them with his bayonet. Just him, and twenty-odd prisoners, and they're scattering like rabbits, and that's when Sergeant Duffy waded in and tried to calm him down.'

'And Wyndham hit him?'

'They were belting each other like heavyweights. D'you know, I don't think Wyndham knew what he was doing. Himself and Duffy used always get along grand. Duffy was a fair man and Wyndham liked him. Jesus – I'd hate to see him with a sergeant he didn't like.'

'Jesus.'

'It's a frightening thing to see him lose his temper – but do you know?'

'What?'

'I think he's even more dangerous when he's calm.'

'What do you mean?'

'Remember I fought alongside him for months, so I know what I'm on about.'

'Go on.'

'Well, there was this one time when we were going to raid the German trenches. The general needed to know about the German dispositions and that, so me and Wyndham volunteered to sneak over there in the night time and see what we could see. Two men would have a chance where a whole battalion might get cut to bits. So anyway, we're about to set out when I see that Wyndham has this big knife on him – huge big knife – and you could see straight off it didn't come from Birmingham or Sheffield, or some government stores.'

'What was it so?'

'Shut up and I'll tell you. So, I didn't ask because we were just about to go over the top – we were to split up so that if one of us was caught the other might get through – and I didn't see him until we made it back. So, we're back and having our tot when I ask him about the knife, and he gives me a wink and takes it out to give me a look, and he takes out these two big hanks of hair as well.'

'*Hair*?'

'Scalps, boy. German scalps, all dripping with blood.'

'Jesus!'

'That's what I said. He told me then that the knife was a gift from a Red Indian chief called Chief Bloody Hand. I knew better than to ask any more. I told you he doesn't like to talk about his past.'

'Chief Bloody Hand?'

'That's what he told me.'

'And where was this, do you suppose?'

'Out near Wipers, I told you.'

'No – the Red Indian Chief.'

Moriarty remembered the adventure stories Wyndham had been obliged to invent for the amusement of bored comrades who wanted the Wild West in preference to the Irish heroic legends that fascinated the American. 'Oh – that was out in Abilene.'

'Abilene? Where's that?'

'Abilene, Texas,' said Moriarty. 'Out in the Dakota Territory. I'm surprised you didn't know that now, Sergeant. A man of your calibre.'

'I was talking to your man Moriarty,' said Rafferty to Wyndham the next day.

'Oh?' Wyndham had been long enough among the Irish to learn that the phrase 'your man' did not necessarily denote possession, but was a mere familiarity. He did not care to be familiar with Rafferty.

'He's a bit of a character, isn't he, sir?'

'Indeed?' said Wyndham. He was far from knowing all the army dodges, and didn't quite have Rafferty bracketed as a fraud yet, but he'd seen that the man was a tyrant when he needed to look busy and an idler the rest of the time. Wyndham did not like Rafferty. He did not like Rafferty's joviality, and, standing this close, he did not like the smell of Rafferty's breakfast.

'You were together in France last year, weren't ye, sir? He was telling me about it. I believe he was pulling my leg a bit.'

Wyndham, who'd been cultivating his aloofness when it came to Rafferty, deigned to look him in the face. The sergeant's grin remained in place.

'Private Moriarty and I,' he said, 'did indeed serve together.

Under Colonel Fitzmullen-Brophy's command. In Flanders. How precisely, Sergeant, would you consider him "a character"?'

'Ah you know, sir. I wasn't saying anything against the man at all. I just got the feeling that he was a bit of a one for the tall tales. The old soldier's stories and that.'

Wyndham knew little enough about Rafferty's record. He knew, though, that the man's service had not been in the Munsters but in some other regiment – some lesser regiment. He was no true Dirty Shirt and he had never known the tortured line that ran between Armentières and Ypres.

'I wonder what stories Moriarty told you, Sergeant. I wonder what stories he left out.'

'Sir?'

Wyndham spoke with barely disguised impatience, like a man explaining something he really shouldn't have to. 'You've heard of Étreux, I imagine? Moriarty was at Étreux. Do you know how many men got out alive, Sergeant? Precious few. Moriarty was one of them. He was carrying another. A wounded officer. Carried him a night and a day. Twenty miles through German lines. He'd have been recommended for a decoration only the officer had died during that first night.'

'Mother of God. I never knew that, sir. You weren't at Étreux yourself, were you, sir? Were you still off in America then?'

Wyndham was tired of Rafferty, and his imagination had failed him for the time being.

'I prefer not to talk about my past, Sergeant,' he said coldly.

25

Each fight was a game, each one was a sport.

—Lady Augusta Gregory, *Cuchulain of Muirthemne*

Besides drill without arms and route marching, the only activity open to the battalion was games. Fitzmullen-Brophy was all for games. He was not alone. Whoever had acquired the land for the camp had been sure to adhere to the standard army practice of choosing enough flat space for a parade ground and a football pitch. Details like shelter and drainage could be sorted out later.

Wyndham was an utter stranger to organised sport, but if an exemplary old soldier like Fitzmullen-Brophy was insisting on it, and a serious young lawyer like McCarthy-Moore took it so seriously, then who was Wyndham to disagree?

Rugby football and Association football – or rugger and soccer as they were apparently known – were to be the chief activities. Games were to be played by all ranks at platoon and company level. The phrase 'weather permitting' was never used. The last time Wyndham had stood with bare knees on a rainswept field had been at the Battle of the Aisne, but McCarthy-Moore assured him that rugger was not as dangerous, and that he could have a hot bath afterwards. The way he told it, however, suggested that just because C Company's first game would not determine the fate of France, that was no reason at all to treat it lightly.

'Shoulders well down in the scrum,' he would earnestly lecture, and Wyndham would repeat, 'The scrum,' and nod gravely, sure that he'd know a scrum when he saw one.

Or: 'Mark your man.'

'Of course.'

Or: 'Don't take your eye off the ball.'

'The ball. No, certainly not.'

Unsurprisingly, Wyndham proved useless on the pitch. His experiences in Tralee and France had inured him to the rough and tumble, but he was just too polite for this sort of thing. He persisted though, because the colonel expected it, and McCarthy-Moore's patient instruction deserved it. In his own strange way, he came to enjoy the whole business, even though for an annoyingly long while he kept forgetting not just the rules of the game but which game he happened to be playing. Were you allowed to catch the round ball or was it just the pointed ball? Think quick – here it comes.

His teammates learned soon enough never to pass to Lieutenant Wyndham, who was clearly away with the fairies, and that at least saved him from the personal and professional discomfort of being tackled by the lower ranks. McCarthy-Moore knew no such discomfort. Minor disciplinary problems in his command were often dealt with on the playing field by the troublemaker being pounded face-down into the turf. King's Regulations might not have strictly approved, but the Irish Rugby Football Union could take no issue.

Curran deemed himself too old for such pursuits. In deference to the colonel's views on outdoor exercise, he did go so far as to acquire tennis equipment, but even after they'd laid out a court of sorts, the ball refused to bounce on the damp ground, so he gave up.

26

We gave ourselves up in old times to mythology, and saw the Gods everywhere. We talked to them face to face, and the stories of that communion are so many that I think they outnumber all the like stories of all the rest of Europe. Even today our country people speak with the dead and with some who perhaps have never died as we understand death...

—W.B. Yeats, *The Celtic Twilight*

Manly sporting activity having limited allure, Wyndham still kept his books and indulged in his unmilitary fancies. It did no harm, and was just another eccentricity in an officer corps that was filled with odd types these days. Every so often, his fancies even revealed some relevance, like when a motto had been found for the battalion, or that time when Wyndham happened to find something that sharpened his interest in fieldcraft.

'Curran!' he said. 'Curran, come and have a look at this.'

This was more animation than the self-contained Wyndham was wont to display in the pursuit of his duties, and Curran was particularly bemused that Wyndham's excitement should be prompted by an Ordnance Survey map of all things. He bent over the map, following Wyndham's finger.

'What, precisely, am I to be looking at, my dear fellow?

'There! Look. See?' Wyndham sounded almost like a child in front of a toyshop window.

'A cromlech?' said Curran.

'A cromlech! A rath!' said Wyndham delightedly. 'Right here.

Practically right in back of the hotel. I've never seen one before.'

'Well then, Lieutenant Wyndham, my young bucko, you shall see one now. Let's go and have a look.' He was astonished at Wyndham's enthusiasm and, as they got their coats and set out, it occurred to him that it would be best to offset the younger man's potential disappointment.

'There might not be anything at all to see, you know,' he said. 'Not so much as a standing stone even. Certainly not dolmens or stone circles or whatever it is you're imagining.'

'I want to see it anyway. They're always mentioned in the sort of stories I've been reading, and I've been in Ireland months without ever seeing one. I dearly want to see one, Curran.'

'Very well then. If it turns out to be less than advertised, we can look on our little jaunt as a map-reading exercise. You think that might be it up there, beyond that little stand of trees? I seem to have left my compass behind.'

They stared again at the map in the fading light and checked their bearings as best they could before striding decisively up the slight slope. Their puttees were wet from the long grass by the time Wyndham eagerly pushed through some brushwood at the neglected upper edge of the undistinguished field.

Curran looked about in vain for some identifiable relic of ancient Ireland. 'Do you think this might be it?' he asked, sorry that they had come even this short distance for so little reward.

'This is it,' said Wyndham, evidently quite pleased with their find.

'It seems to be no more than some sort of mound,' said Curran, experimentally stamping on the ground.

'What are you doing?' asked Wyndham.

'Oh, just seeing if there are old stones hidden in the undergrowth or – you never know – the hollow echoes from fairy caves beneath. No luck, I'm afraid.'

'It doesn't matter,' said Wyndham. 'This is the place.'

'Well, I must say I'm pleased that you're so satisfied with it, Dan, old man.'

'Look at it,' said Wyndham. 'Never been ploughed. Never been grazed. Generations of farmers leaving it alone because they knew what it was. You may laugh at fairies, Curran, but this is a fairy fort.'

'You seem uncommonly easy to please, Dan. You must have made for an exceptionally gratified tourist. One wonders what an impression a genuine megalithic monument might make on you.'

'This will do me quite well for the moment. Those trees there: those are rowans if I'm not mistaken.'

'I don't believe you are. Rowans indeed. Shall we be getting back? Who knows what further wonders a six-inch-to-one-mile map may reveal.'

'You go. I believe I'll stay awhile.'

Curran was reluctant to leave when his brother officer was acting so oddly, but Wyndham appeared to be at peace. He certainly didn't have the appearance of a man contemplating hanging himself from a rowan tree.

Wyndham heard him going, and felt the silence reclaiming this neglected spot. It had been Moyle who'd first told him about fairy forts and rowan trees. Wyndham had come to Ireland searching for the Celtic heroes, for the gods and fighting men, and the closest thing he'd found was Lance-Corporal Joseph Moyle, marksman first class, who had commanded a section dug in near a stand of rowan trees in disputed fields north-west of Armentières. Wyndham had never forsaken his interests, but while he'd told the old Irish stories to the men in the trenches to stave off his own and their boredom, he'd given up early on trying to learn folklore from them. They didn't have any. Their world was the army, and their legends were the regimental deeds on long-ago Indian battlefields. Only Moyle had seemed to have an inkling of what fired Wyndham. Only Moyle seemed to have retained some thread of a link to Ireland's mystic past, and one night, almost within earshot of the German line, Moyle had pointed out the rowan trees and told what he knew about ancient magical places – the places that he knew as raths and fairy forts and the Ordnance Survey noted as mounds or cromlechs.

Moyle was dead now and the trees were shattered. This place, whatever it was, remained. That was good enough for Wyndham. It would have to do for Moyle.

27

And what he saw this time, was a young strong man, with high looks, and with two red stripes on his body.

—Lady Augusta Gregory, *Cuchulain of Muirthemne*

It was another cold morning on the parade ground. The sun was shining and the rain was holding off, but there was a cold breeze and the ground was soggy under the men's feet. They had mastered the rudiments for the most part, so there was no real need for a trained soldier to be at them every minute, bawling at them to learn the difference between their left and their right. Moriarty had nothing much to do, but he was keeping his eye on them. As was so common now, he was looking faintly aggrieved, and, despite his soldierly bearing, he was somehow giving the impression of being hunched. But that was not what drew Wyndham to him.

'Moriarty, there is something different about you today.'

'Sir,' said Moriarty, and no more. Wyndham's tone was light, but Moriarty's demeanour suggested that he was feeling beset, and openness should not be expected of him.

Wyndham chose not to indulge in guessing games with a sulky former comrade, and cut straight to the heart of the matter.

'Are those corporal's stripes on your sleeve?'

Wyndham did not ask in any authoritative way. He was pretty sure about what he was looking at, but he still felt new at all of this and wasn't taking chances. Furthermore, he had no intention of giving offence. Nevertheless, Moriarty's lack of response suggested a hint of indignation. Either that or guilt. Wyndham was in no mood for it.

'Moriarty, you are wearing corporal's stripes.'

Silence. Moriarty didn't look Wyndham in the eye, but that was nothing new. This time, though, his gaze was fixed on a squad of men drilling. Wyndham, rather than try and stare a reply out of him, followed his look and pushed on.

'I didn't hear anything about your being promoted.'

No response.

'Somebody would have told me, I'm sure.'

Moriarty glowered and exhaled loudly through his nose, but still said nothing.

'Moriarty,' asked Wyndham sternly, 'it pains me to ask, but have you promoted yourself?'

The squad of recruits was putting on quite a competent display, but Moriarty glared at them as if watching for some hint of mutiny.

'Moriarty?'

'If I might speak freely, *sir*.'

'Oh, go on then.'

'Do you see those gossoons over there?'

Hoping the answer wouldn't prove to be too obscene, Wyndham asked what a gossoon was.

'A kid. You know – some young fella who knows nothing. A wet-behind-the-ears kid.'

Wyndham experienced a moment of happy enlightenment. 'I think it's pronounced *garçon*,' he said.

Moriarty turned his face to Wyndham for the first time. 'It is *not*,' he said, exasperated that such a well-travelled intellectual could be so ignorant about so much.

'All right then,' said Wyndham, with more patience than he felt was warranted.

Moriarty returned his attention to the men. 'Do you see him?' he said with vehemence. 'Do you see him there? Do you? *Do you?*'

Wyndham looked at the squad, which was now standing

easy, except for one man who had stepped forward to talk to the instructor.

'Do you mean Dineen?'

'Look at him, look at him, *look at him!*'

'At Dineen? The man who's talking to the sergeant?'

'*He's talking to the sergeant!*'

'Moriarty, calm down.'

'The lick! The dirty little teacher's pet.'

'Moriarty, please calm down.'

Moriarty looked Wyndham in the face again and his frustration almost seemed close to tears.

'Tell me what's wrong, Moriarty.'

Moriarty sniffed deeply and gathered himself.

'That little gobshite,' he said.

'Dineen? He seems perfectly alright. Seems to have the makings of a good soldier.'

'*Seems to have the makings of a good soldier*,' sneered Moriarty, in mocking imitation.

'Moriarty, please.'

'Sorry. But you know.'

'Tell me.'

Moriarty spat out the verdict. 'That fella's no soldier – not a real soldier anyway. You and me, we've been in the trenches. I was at Mons. I was out in Rangoon. Where's that little prick been? I'll tell you. That little prick's been in school, getting his first-class school certificates, and he's been going to mass and saying the rosary. Little gobshite. Little Legion of Mary gobshite, with his first-class school certificates.'

Wyndham didn't like where this was going at all. He hardly knew Dineen, but he painfully remembered the last time one of Moriarty's one-sided hatreds had been allowed to run on. Shots had been fired that time.

'Moriarty, please.'

Moriarty's litany of condemnation tailed off for a moment. He looked at Wyndham, appealing for understanding.

'Do you not see what I'm saying at all?'

'I don't think I do.'

'That fella's no fucking soldier at all.'

'So you said.'

'But they're going to make him a lance-corporal.'

'They are?'

'Of course they are! They have to make someone a lance-corporal and it's going to be him because he's a good little Christian Brothers boy and he's learned all his drill and he sucks up to the sergeants and the officers and all.'

It was true. Every squad that graduated from uselessness needed one man to take responsibility. In such circumstances lance-corporal was merely a temporary appointment which allowed the more senior NCOs to delegate the menial and elementary tasks, and it meant that they only had to shout at one man when everything went wrong. A man like Dineen was an obvious candidate for such a position. The light dawned on Wyndham.

'So you made yourself a corporal,' he said.

And now Moriarty was hunched again, and looking straight ahead.

'You made yourself a corporal so you wouldn't have to take orders from men like Dineen.'

Because it was now the time for all good men to stand up, Moriarty gritted his teeth and said, 'I did.'

'I'm pretty sure that's not allowed, you know.'

'You can take the stripes off me if you want.'

Wyndham knew a challenge when he heard it, and did not excite his old comrade's truculence any further.

'I'm not going to do anything,' he said reasonably. 'But someone's bound to notice, you know.'

Moriarty looked at him again, his jaw set. 'I'm willing to take my chance. The army doesn't know what it's doing these days. If you can be an officer, I can be a corporal.'

'Moriarty!' Wyndham was genuinely affronted that his imposture had been so easily seen through.

'Ah sure, but you know what I mean. And the colonel isn't really a colonel either, is he? Anyway, if a kid like that is a soldier then I'm a corporal. I'm more of a corporal than the likes of him will ever be.'

Wyndham had no reply. He walked off briskly, hoping to get away before retribution came down on Moriarty – either that, or before Moriarty thought to elevate himself any higher.

28

One diary remarks that the writer of it can never forget 'the dark, damp, dismal mornings with the bugle of a light infantry battalion playing reveillé round the barrack square. No wonder the people in Ireland drink.'

—Lt-Col Frederick Whitton,
The History of the Prince of Wales's Leinster Regiment

The camp at Knocknahanna had been chosen because the ground was fairly level and the land was available cheap. The location wasn't convenient to anywhere at all, but the army reckoned that such isolation guarded the recruits from distractions and temptations. Far from the bright lights and the fleshpots of, say, Kilworth, a battalion of young men could be whipped into shape with greater efficiency. If it all proved too Spartan for some, well, the middle-of-nowhere quality might make desertion all the harder.

Huts had been erected to serve as offices and storerooms, but accommodation was lagging behind. Half the battalion was still sleeping in tents.

In fine weather the men would have been happy enough to live so close to nature, but fine weather was not to be expected – not in Ireland. Not in spring.

All instruction and training happened out of doors. That meant stamping up and down on the space designated a drill square until it got too muddy and another space had to be so designated. The men were putting up with it well enough, but their willingness had its limits. Five days of blustery rain brought them dangerously close to that limit.

Moriarty wasn't used to cheerful recruits. In his army, recruits were small parties of fearful men who knew their place from being roared at day and night by the instructors and either bullied or ignored by the rest of the men in barracks. This mob was different. Practically every man-jack in camp was new to this life, and so wasn't ashamed of his ignorance. The tone of this new army was good-natured amateurism. Men went about their duties readily, and laughed when they got it all wrong, and laughed as they worked to set it right again. Moriarty didn't trust recruits who weren't harried and oppressed. He didn't like their good nature. He suspected that their laughter might be directed at him.

Then came that wet week, when the tents leaked and sometimes blew down in the wind, and the men weren't smiling any more. Moriarty found he didn't care for that either. A sullen recruit had to be watched. And the weather too made him uneasy. It wasn't as bad as Festubert, but as he watched his step crossing the mud, and felt the rain whipping at his face, he couldn't help but think of the machine-gun bullets smacking out of the wet unknown at kneecap height.

The men were assembled waiting for him. Few of them had greatcoats. Every day since Sunday: wet clothes by day and wet blankets at night, and devil a hope of getting anything dry. They were hoping to be spared further exposure. A few hours of dull lectures, with everyone crammed together standing in a leaky hut, would be heaven compared to this.

'Right!' began Moriarty, after bawling them to attention. 'We're drawing shovels from stores. I want you all to get digging.'

The disappointment was written plain on their suffering faces.

Digging practice trenches according to the book was never a popular exercise, even though they understood that it was necessary. They were soldiers now, and they knew that earthworks were what characterised the modern battlefield. Indeed, those old terms – the battlefield, the front, even the war itself – were all expressed now in that single phrase, 'the trenches'. So, if they were to be fighting from trenches, it made sense that they should be proficient at digging trenches, even though few of them had been labouring men before they enlisted, and none wanted to be out here in the rain, shifting wet earth and getting blisters, while Corporal Moriarty shouted at them to dig faster and deeper, ever deeper.

Every so often someone would stop, and straighten his back and survey the work, perhaps hoping that Moriarty would be satisfied, but to no avail. All instructors cultivated an angry and hectoring style, and all lost patience from time to time, but Moriarty appeared to be in the grip of genuine emotion as he strode from one hole to another, urging ever greater effort.

'Hurry up, ye gobshites! Do you think the Hun will leave you have a rest? Do you think he'll not shoot you because you're having a fag? Get your heads down! Get your fucking heads down!' And as the men worked he took to pelting them with clods of earth. 'Those are bullets!' he shrieked at them. 'You're dead! You're dead! You're dead!'

The weather was as bad the next day. Cigarettes wouldn't light. The food was waterlogged and cold. The men's clothes were still muddy from the day before and their hands were clawed from digging. They stopped their griping as Moriarty approached, but they didn't stop until they were sure he'd heard them.

The rain was blowing directly into Moriarty's face, so he did an about-face and ordered the men to line up on the lee side of him. He cast his eye on the line of pale faces, squinting and grimacing in the rain. There were faces missing – a fair few faces.

'Where's Finnerty?' he asked. He noticed the absence because Finnerty was the tallest man in the unit.

'Finnerty is sick, Corporal.'

'*Sick?*'

'The doctor marked him down sick, Corporal. Him and Higgins and O'Loughlin, Corporal.'

'Cronin too, Corporal.'

'It's the rain, Corporal. The cold and wet got at them.'

'I'm not feeling very well myself, Corporal.' There followed a burst of coughing, which was echoed down the ranks.

Moriarty never knew if this was just a pathetic appeal to his better nature or a mutiny in the making, because just then Wyndham sloshed up with the colonel's order that all outdoor training was cancelled for the day.

As the men trooped off to what would probably be a lecture on hygiene or somesuch, their innate optimism began to resurface and Moriarty heard some relieved laughter and forced jokes.

Suddenly, he yelled at them to halt, and rapidly strode to where they could all hear him. They saw he was quivering with anger.

'Ah Jesus, would you listen to yourselves? There's nothing at all wrong with ye! Call this a bit of water? I was five years out in Burma and it rains non-bleeding-stop for three months of the year. Three months! Every blessed day! There's water up beyond your shins and it's full of snakes. *Snakes!* The water's as warm as tea and the same colour, and the snakes swim around in it and they'd ate you if they had half the chance!'

His voice was almost breaking with passion.

'I don't want to hear another word out of any of ye about the rain. Call this rain? Go out to Burma in the monsoon. Go on! I'm sick of looking at the lot of ye!'

After another wet day, and a lengthening sick list, a generous programme of leave was instituted. Moriarty's squad was sent off *en bloc* for a week, while he retired to the local pub until they came back. There, as had been his habit in Tralee, he kept to himself. The only trouble he gave the landlord was a constant complaint about the poor choice of newspapers available.

At the end of the week the weather was much improved and so were the men. Moriarty could hear them as he came back from the pub. He'd had company he didn't want in the form of another couple of old sweats like him who were back from their own leave and weren't in the mood to sober up yet. So, Moriarty, even though he wasn't in the humour for it, had drunk more and stayed out later than was his habit. When he cut himself loose it was dark. Following the road was no bother, but when he turned off onto the unmetalled path leading to camp he realised he was in danger of becoming lost. He had never been afraid of the dark before, but then a lot of things had been different before – before the maze of little trenches near Armentières and Germans infiltrating through the dripping trees, where you couldn't see your hand in front of your face and you couldn't hear anything until it was too late. The warmth of the beer fled out of him, and he stumbled along, close to panic. Then he saw dim lights just ahead and knew he was home.

He slowed down, and let his hammering heart settle. His men were back, and new huts had been completed for them while they'd been away. He could hear their happiness. Christ, but it didn't take much. Not a bother in the world on them now. Poor ignorant bastards had no clue at all. No clue about the Huns in France. No clue about everything that would crawl up and kill you in Burma, even. What you'd hear at night in the Burmese jungle would put the heart across you – noises that would turn your hair white.

All was indeed well with the recruits. They were telling stories and sharing out treats brought from home, all having a laugh before bed, when in burst Corporal Moriarty, wild-eyed and evidently with drink taken.

'*Spiders!*' he shouted to the room at large. 'Spiders as big as your hand! As big as your two hands! And they'd bite you and you'd swell up and turn black and die roaring. *Roaring!*'

And then he was gone again, back to his own hut. Back to his troubled recollections.

29

Our fathers they left us their blessing –
They taught us, and groomed us, and crammed;
But we've shaken the Clubs and the Messes
To go and find out and be damned
...
So some of us chivvy the slaver,
And some of us cherish the black,
And some of us hunt on the Oil Coast,
And some on the Wallaby track:
And some of us drift to Sarawak,
And some of us drift up The Fly,
And some share our tucker with tigers,
And some with the gentle Masai.

—Rudyard Kipling, 'The Lost Legion'

Despite its isolation, all sorts of characters blew into the battalion from time to time. Military officials inspecting this and that, rapacious civilians seeking to profit from several hundred clueless soldiers stuck out in a field, and even a few recruits to be welcomed and kept a close eye on before they changed their minds.

But the most colourful arrival yet seen was a small man who strode into camp one wet spring day and, spying Wyndham, asked directly to see the colonel. He was dressed, just like Wyndham, in hot-weather khaki of old-fashioned cut and, unlike Wyndham, his complexion matched his outfit, being so sun-baked and weather-beaten that he was without doubt the darkest white man that could be imagined. His hair though – what could be seen of it under a broad-brimmed hat – and his moustache were pure white. Despite this, Wyndham could see that the wizened little man might not be all that old. He had an energy in his manner and a glittering in his eye that marked him as one not to be easily written off. When he asked to see the colonel, he asked in such a way as to suggest that seeing colonels was how he usually began his business. He wore no rank badges, but he was of the type that Wyndham would automatically address as 'sir'.

'The colonel, sir?'

'Fitzmullen-Brophy, isn't it? Most grateful if he could see me. If you'd be so kind as to tell him, Lieutenant. Devereaux's the name.'

Wyndham could have given him directions to the office, but he was curious as to who this Devereaux might be, so he escorted the visitor himself.

Fitzmullen-Brophy, as was usual this time of day, was behind his desk, worrying at the battalion's worth of paperwork before him and making life wretched for his clerk and the adjutant. When Wyndham announced the new arrival, he frowned in curiosity and came out to have a look.

'Foxy Devereaux, by heaven!'

'FitzEm, by God!'

'Well I never! How long has it been?'

'Fourteen years or thereabouts, I expect.'

'South Africa.'

'South Africa.'

The two old warriors beamed at each other and Wyndham noticed the pronounced resemblance between them. Devereaux was a head shorter and had been left out in the sun for longer, but they'd evidently come out of the same stable.

'Gentlemen,' said Fitzmullen-Brophy, addressing Wyndham

and de Roche (who'd deigned to come and see what the new at-traction was), 'this is Major Devereaux, late of the regiment.'

'Late of the Cape Mounted Rifles, too, as a matter of fact, by way of the Somaliland Camel Corps.'

'Well come and have a drink and you can tell me all about it.'

The war in South Africa had played merry hell with the old regimental structure of the army, what with men being turned into mounted infantry and odd new units being created to deal with the far-flung scrappy nature of the war. For an officer seeking advancement and not fussy about where he got it, it was a land of opportunity. Devereaux had stuck with the Munsters for as long as things were interesting, and then sought a secondment to something more colourful and improvised. After the war, he'd stayed in Africa.

'Bechuanaland, Matabeleland. Superb country. Ruined now of course. All settled. Ended up in the Sudan. Magnificent country. There when I heard about the war. Eight weeks' trekking to get to Somaliland. Found a billet with the Camel Corps. Nothing doing. Poor show. Thought I'd come home and have a crack at the Hun.'

'Stout fellow. How can I help?'

'Rather looking for a job, old man. Nobody was interested in Dublin so had a nose around Tralee. Said you were out here. Said you might need another pair of hands.'

'Why that would be perfectly splendid, Foxy. Can't quite think at the moment what there is for you to do, but a chap of your experience is always welcome.'

'I'll take command of a company, FitzEm. Take a step down in rank. I don't mind. I believe my regimental rank is still only captain.'

'We'll see, Foxy. We'll see. In the meantime, let's have another drink before lunch. Then you can meet my officers. Damned fine bunch, if I say so myself.'

Fitzmullen-Brophy presented his old comrade as a feather to the battalion's cap, and urged the gentlemen around the table to learn all they could. For his part, Devereaux told tales that conjured visions of the vast burning wilderness where men were truly tested.

Initially, he insisted that boiled rice was all he could eat and heavily watered whisky all he could drink, but the cooks were not men to take orders on short notice, so Devereaux found that he could stomach roast mutton (and in surprising quantity, too) and wash it down with the quite-decent wine with which Curran had supplied the mess.

His Africa habits reasserted themselves that night when he insisted that a tent had always been good enough for him. This was an immense relief to the officers who were already living on top of each other.

In the course of a few days, Devereaux was accepted as a fixture in the regiment. He greeted the dawn swathed in as many layers of woollens as a man might need for a night in the howling wastes of the Sahara Desert, as much as for a night under canvas in north County Cork. He spent his days imparting outdated military wisdom to the officers as a sort of emeritus company commander. He never did take that step down in rank. His assurance and leadership, it was felt, made up for his unfamiliarity with all that the War Office publications were describing as modern warfare. In the evenings he contributed to the happy life of the mess with his fund of comic songs from a bygone era.

For sentimental airs and suchlike Irish favourites, there was no one to match McCarthy-Moore's rich tenor, but while Devereaux didn't have much of a singing voice, he had an inexhaustible memory for rollicking, risqué crowd-pleasers. He also had a treasury of African tales involving wild beasts, pitiless men and a killing climate – often all three in the same story. Seeing as the senior officers set the tone in after-dinner entertainment, he was a welcome counterbalance to Fitzmullen-Brophy and de Roche. The colonel, while he was eager in his efforts to jolly his officers along, had an awful singing voice and an inadvertent but wearisome tendency to repeat his anecdotes. De Roche, for his part, did not sing at all, and his conversation consisted of sedate sporting reminiscence and toothless social gossip.

Devereaux was, in short, a success. It was considered a great pity then, that he should have come down with a severe chill after only a week. A civilian doctor recommended indoor nursing, and Devereaux was duly conveyed to hospital. A fortnight later word came directing that his gear be packed up and sent to an address in Dublin. The 11th Munsters would be hearing no more advice on how to track a wounded lion, nor would they delight in joining in a naughty version of 'The Broken-Hearted Milkman'.

And yet, such was the youthful forgetfulness of the battalion that it took no time for the old soldier to vanish from memory. Devereaux had come from the past and returned back to it. Only a few weeks later Wyndham found himself humming, 'She was only a corporal's daughter, but now she's an officer's mess,' and it took him some little time to remember how he might first have heard it.

30

Tut-tut-tut-tut went the Maxims.

—G.W. Steevens, *With Kitchener to Khartum*

It was hugely liberating to discover that inexperience was pretty much universal in the battalion and nothing to be ashamed of. Thus, with casual optimism, Wyndham volunteered to take charge of the machine-gun section. The battalion didn't have a machine-gun, but then the battalion didn't have much of anything, and they weren't letting that stop them. Wyndham reckoned himself qualified for the job because he had picked up the instruction booklet and skimmed the contents pages. None of it made much sense to him, but he felt up to the challenge. Besides, he was the only one of the new officers who had seen a machine-gun. The gun had been out of action at the time, but Wyndham had been right there next to the man who was bringing it to the rear, and had even helped carry the tripod.

Flowing underneath this feeling of capability was the current of uneasy memories that had been troubling him for some months now. He remembered that other machine-gun – the German gun dug in dangerously close but still out of reach – that had chopped at the sandbags above his head when he'd shivered in an entrenched position known as the Piggery, and still managed to trouble his sleep with its vicious bark.

If he had to be doing with machine-guns in future, then he'd much rather be behind one than in front. He would read the manual and learn how to draw the teeth of the beast.

Wyndham had become bored with commanding his platoon, where there was not enough to keep him busy and what there was

was often a source of frustration. He could do without the endless drill and the exercises in which most of the military necessaries were present only in make-believe. The new job would take him away from Sergeant Rafferty, too.

There was no shortage of volunteers who were doubtless feeling the same way about drill and Rafferty. Wyndham had his pick of the handier and more intelligent men, and set a couple of them to study the machine-gun manual and copy out the relevant bits in their best handwriting. The rest he took with him into the village. They couldn't free themselves from make-believe, but Wyndham was determined that their military fantasy would have more substance.

A broom handle might stand in for a rifle as far as drill with arms was concerned, but it lacked weight, and Wyndham's military experience had deeply impressed him with how bloody heavy everything was. If his men could not learn the mechanics of their weapon for the time being, at least they should become familiar with its mass and sheer physicality.

The local blacksmith looked at the sketch that Private Foley, apprentice draughtsman, had done up, and supposed that he might be able to do it by Tuesday next. He asked a few technical questions, but Wyndham couldn't answer on the grounds that he had no idea and it was probably all a military secret anyway. The blacksmith was unimpressed by military secrets and said that it would be Tuesday and would cost two pounds ten.

'He's robbing you, sir,' said Foley. 'Two pound ten for a load of scrap? He's robbing you.'

'You shut up, you little scut,' was the blacksmith's answer to this, but Foley stood his ground, which Wyndham thought was pretty good, seeing as Foley was a slight fellow and the blacksmith was built like, well, a blacksmith. Foley made a convincing case for military economy, and the soldiers departed with the smith's wrath upon their heads. A dummy machine-gun was subsequently rigged up out of an old mangle and a broken bicycle salvaged from the yard behind the officers' mess. In recognition of his courage and initiative Wyndham promoted Foley to lance-corporal. On second thoughts, he made him up to full corporal. It seemed to be the way promotion worked these days, and what sort of an officer would he be if he couldn't do the best for his men?

Fitzmullen-Brophy was simply delighted with the gun, which gave Wyndham the excuse to promote O'Flynn (bicycle repairs, Mitchelstown) and Donovan (general handyman, Listowel) who'd helped Foley build the thing.

Flushed with the colonels' approval, Wyndham boasted of the excellence of his men after lunch, which caused his brother officers to come to the defence of their own platoons, whose qualities, they suddenly felt, had gone too long unrecognised. That afternoon brought a rash of promotions which spread in subsequent days as the subalterns competed in advertising how well they were getting on. Seeing as all these new ranks were unofficial and unpaid appointments, higher authority took little notice. It was only when the army started to make some headway with the clothing shortages and the battalion paraded in something that approached complete uniform, with new NCOs' chevrons proud on far too many new sleeves, that the colonel put a halt to the wholesale elevation of raw recruits.

There was still a woeful lack of weapons, but with the battalion finally clothed as soldiers, Fitzmullen-Brophy was proud to send his men out on exercises. The war had been fought from trenches when he'd left it, and evidently was still being fought from trenches as it was, but that couldn't last. Once the French pulled themselves together and the British built up sufficient strength, then a war of movement would be restored – a proper war, like South Africa. The men must be prepared for it.

Ordnance Survey maps were duly issued and schemes by which platoons and companies would manoeuvre across country, learning their fieldcraft as they went, were outlined. With the weather improving it was a popular prospect for all. As so often, the battalion muddled through on the strength of team spirit and a willingness to give their best effort to any task. Men got lost – whole platoons got lost – but they found themselves again, and trailed home as best they could, determined to give it another go and do it better next time.

To hone his men ever sharper, Fitzmullen-Brophy took to pitting units against each other, with infiltrations and mock battles that kept everyone amused as long as the rain held off.

On one of these exercises Wyndham's machine-gun section, accompanied by Curran's platoon, was to secure a given position some miles distant and hold it against D Company, or the whole German army, as the case may be.

They made a good show as they marched along – or at least a better show than hitherto. Every man had a suit of khaki, whether it fitted him or not. Rather too much equipment was held together with string, but the men marched with self-assurance.

Curran cast a critical eye, and considered that the wooden battens carried instead of rifles marred an otherwise pleasing martial spectacle. He spoke aloud, because speaking aloud was his great talent. As it happened, Moriarty was his only audience. It turned out that Moriarty had nothing to say about martial spectacle, but merely nodded and sniffed to show he was paying some sort of attention.

Curran saw no use in treating the other ranks merely as retainers to be ordered about, seen but not heard. He had a strong democratic instinct and saw every man, if not necessarily as an equal, then certainly as a potential vote.

'No doubt, Moriarty, a seasoned soldier such as yourself must think we amateurs are making a poor show of things, eh?'

Moriarty nodded solemnly. Condescension and jocularity from officers, indeed.

'You'll have noticed, I suppose, sir, that Mr. Wyndham doesn't carry a gun,' was what he said by way of reply. As it happened, the eccentricities of Wyndham's uniform had caused some quiet comment among his brother officers, but deficiencies in equipment were so widespread that any officer who'd managed to procure a revolver was secretly very proud of the fact, and Wyndham's lack was of no note.

Curran cast a proprietary glance down at the russet leather holster on his own belt, getting shinier and more officer-like every day. 'Is there a reason for that, Moriarty?'

'I won't say anything against him, sir. Himself and myself soldiered together, you know. Wouldn't say a word against him, but Dan Wyndham has a temper on him.'

'Really, Moriarty?' Curran didn't like to be talking about a man behind his back, but he couldn't resist finding out about people either.

'He'd never carry a gun because he'd be afraid he'd use it on one of his own men. He said as much to me, sir, when they made him an officer.'

'Moriarty, you are pulling my leg,' said Curran, stern and jovial all at once. But he had his doubts nonetheless. Moriarty was not a man who ever seemed to be joking, who never even seemed to be quite in the world the rest of them inhabited. The man's gaze was always fixed on some distant point, as was the case now. Moriarty was looking off across the fields, but Curran suspected that what Moriarty was seeing was a different country – a country where the truth was hard and laughter was unknown.

Curran watched the mock machine-gun being manhandled across a ditch. He looked at Wyndham supervising them, and he thought how Wyndham had seen that dark country, too.

Indeed, perhaps a part of Wyndham had never left.

'Oh, good heavens, but he's doing it again,' said Curran.

'Sir?'

'The colonel will have our heads,' said Curran, and hurried up to intercept Wyndham. 'That's the wrong way, Dan! We need to be over there! To the right, damn it!'

They were growing steadily more proficient at map reading. In truth, it was no great feat to navigate across two miles of countryside in daylight, but the officers were proud nonetheless. They had been in the army long enough to understand how every simple thing could often be so damned difficult. But Wyndham would become wayward on occasion, such as now. Having found their way to their objective, he would wilfully disregard orders and military good sense when it came to the deployment of forces. So far, his failure had been met with no more than exasperation from Fitzmullen-Brophy, but such indulgence couldn't last, and Curran, for one, was just too old to receive a dressing down as if he were some schoolboy.

'Over there!' said Curran. 'On that rise! Where you are is no good, damn it!'

But Curran had learned that, at times like these, Wyndham could be positively mulish. Curran should have known. He should have paid more attention to the map. Then he'd have seen what that rise was marked as. Lieutenant Wyndham never sited a gun or countenanced the digging of a trench on a fairy fort.

31

The Heroes' Hall in Valhalla is the richer at the Munsters' expense.

—Lt-Col H.S. Jervis, *The 2ⁿᵈ Munsters in France*

The 2ⁿᵈ Battalion of the Royal Munster Fusiliers had been the battalion on home service when the war broke out. That meant they were understrength, and most of the men in the ranks were being trained up for their posting overseas and some real soldiering. In August these youngsters had been joined by older men recalled from the reserve and the hastily mobilised battalion was sent to the Continent as part of the British Expeditionary Force.

They formed part of the rearguard on the retreat from Mons, until they were cut off and surrounded near the village of Étreux. They made their last stand in a walled orchard near the village, and that is where many of them remained for ever after. There were a hew handfuls of survivors who managed to make their way out, but the 2ⁿᵈ Munsters were finished for the time being.

They had been three weeks on active service and one day in action.

While the 2ⁿᵈ Battalion was being slowly and painfully rebuilt, the 1ˢᵗ Battalion, straining at the leash since August, was finally let loose. These were the imperial veterans, tempered by their years policing Burma. As soon as the empire could spare them, they were sent off to fight the Great War. By the time they arrived, however, the war had grown even greater. It was not the Germans they would be sent to fight but the Turks, who had come into the war on the German side in December. The navy having proved unequal to the task of knocking them back out of the war, the army hastily cobbled together a force to secure the Dardanelles Straits and open the way to Constantinople.

In April of 1915 the Munster Fusiliers, along with the Dublin Fusiliers and the Hampshire Regiment, led the assault on the Turkish beach. The navy had smashed down the fortress there, but a small Turkish force clung to the ruins. They possessed the resolve of men fighting for their faith and fatherland, and four machine-guns also. After the Irish and English troops had made their gallant attempts to storm ashore, aerial reconnaissance reported that for fifty yards offshore the sea was red with blood.

After their first day in action the 1st Munsters, like their sister battalion at Étreux the previous summer, ceased to exist as an independent and effective fighting force. What was left of them had to be temporarily amalgamated with what was left of the Dublins in a single, understrength scratch battalion.

Moriarty had survived Étreux by the skin of his teeth. He had been with the 2nd Battalion because there'd been nowhere else to put him. He was really a Depot Company man, mooching around Tralee waiting for his discharge when the war came. By rights he shouldn't even have been in the depot. By rights he should have been out east still, with the 1st Battalion where he belonged. And now he was reading in the paper about all the mates he'd left in Burma and how, like the lads who'd tried to hold off the Germans around the orchard at Étreux, they wouldn't be coming home again. The long road back from Rangoon had ended at a place with the undistinguished name of V Beach.

'Where's that at all?' asked Sergeant-Major O'Meara.

'Gallipoli,' said Moriarty, putting the emphasis of the third syllable. Gally-*Pole*-ee. 'It's in Turkey.' He had learned as much only this minute from the newspaper which included a map that might have been of Donegal for all Moriarty knew, but he'd never shown ignorance yet of world events and, even in his bereavement, wasn't going to start now.

And it certainly was the shock of loss he was feeling. This mob he was with now, and all those other showers in the training camps around the country – they were just some wartime expedient dreamed up by Kitchener. The two regular battalions had been the real regiment, and that meant that the regiment had been killed. It wasn't that he thought of the regiment with great affection, but it had been his home since he was nineteen, and while he'd done his damnedest to get out of it from time to time, it still held the only real loyalty of his heart. And the regiment was dead, twice over now. And how close had he come to dying with it?

He remembered Christmas in Festubert with a shiver.

Fitzmullen-Brophy made a short speech to the battalion about the regiment's heroic traditions, how the men at Gallipoli had added to them, and how every Munster Fusilier must carry on those traditions. The men listened, clear-eyed and resolute. They would follow the men of the regulars. The fight under the apple trees in France, the Aegean sun shining on bright bayonets and reddened surf – these were what they'd signed up for.

Moriarty was not so sanguine. Old FitzEm could spout off at the young eejits all he liked: there was no fooling a man who'd been there.

A few weeks later the colonel chose to keep silent on the theme of noble sacrifice. He still believed in everything he'd said to the men, but the news from France that May came too close on the heels of the news from Gallipoli, and lacked the epic quality of that sun-drenched, blood-soaked shore.

In May of 1915, almost within sight of the ground where their December attack had gone down into the cold mud at Festubert, the reconstituted 2nd Battalion was sent into a similar attack with similar results, only on a larger scale. The 2nd Munster Fusiliers, twice destroyed and twice rebuilt since the previous August, saw its fighting strength reduced by two thirds in a bloody day at Rue de Bois.

The men of the 11th Battalion, learning their trade here in Ireland, were sobered by the seriousness of war, but they strove all the harder to hasten the day when they could join in, and show that they were the equals of the men who'd gone before.

Moriarty, who'd personally known so many of the men who'd gone before, thought about how a single bad day was all it took to destroy a battalion. He thought how luck and judgement had no part in this war. Neither the 1st nor 2nd Munsters had put a foot wrong. They'd just gone where they were told and a day later their number was scratched off the order of battle.

The destruction was never total. That was probably what kept everyone going. There were always survivors. But this survivor thought about a freezing hole near Festubert, and how just going where you were told would never be enough for him again.

32

Irishmen

Avenge the Lusitania

Join an Irish regiment today.

—Recruiting poster, 1915

In May the Cunard *Lusitania* was torpedoed and sunk within sight of the Irish coast. Nearly twelve-hundred people lost their lives. It did Wyndham nothing but good.

He was as appalled and disgusted as anybody by the event. It was a barbarity on a par with the Rape of Belgium, and a reminder, should one be needed, that he was enlisted in a just war. But a letter from his sister indicated how his stock had risen considerably at home. In the space of a few months he had gone, in the eyes of the staid community in which he'd grown up, from a somewhat dreamy boy to a feckless wanderer to a wild adventurer. But now, thanks to the *Lusitania*, he was a crusader in a noble cause, a warrior for civilisation and decency.

That letter was followed a few days later by one from a certain Penelope van Wyngarden, who was not considered by the good people of Lowell to be in the least bit fast. An unsolicited letter from her, warm with approval, was thus a prize indeed. Too bad that Wyndham was several thousand miles away, with little hope of timely return, or he could have capitalised on his newly bestowed nobility in rake-hell fashion – or so he liked to dream.

The regiment was looking at him in a new light, too. He had gone from being the colonel's tame Yank – an amiable eccentric – to being the vanguard to America's vengeance against Germany.

Dan Wyndham had seen at the very beginning that the Hun had to be given what for, and had answered the call without hesitation.

His star waned, however, as the year lengthened and the armies of the United States failed to follow Wyndham in their multitudes.

'I see your President Wilson has sent another angry note to Berlin, Wyndham. What earthly use is that?'

'To be fair, I believe he was forced by the German navy to play by the rules.'

'Harrumph. The only way to make Fritz play the game is to give him a sound thrashing. And where are your Yankee troops, eh? Where are your ships, man?'

Wyndham got sick of making excuses for everything the US State Department chose to do without consulting him. He got tired of taking the blame for America's failure to declare war. After a while he found it easier not to advertise that he even came from Massachusetts. As far as anyone was concerned, he was a Munster Fusilier, and that should be enough. He hadn't yet got around to claiming that he was Irish, but once, in a railway compartment with two gentleman loudly damning the international situation, he had found it easier to own to being Canadian.

Penelope van Wyngarden never did write a second letter to him.

33

As I was going down the road, feeling fine and larky-o,

A recruiting sergeant says to me, 'Now you'd look fine in khaki-o.

'The king he is in need of men, come read his proclamation-o.

'A life in Flanders for you then would be a fine vacation-o.'

—Seamus O'Farrell, 'The Recruiting Sergeant', 1915

Early summer found the little battalion healthy and proficient in drill, if still only partially uniformed and depressingly under-equipped. Fitzmullen-Brophy was proud of them, but ever aware of how their small numbers had failed to grow since he'd taken charge. A few men trickled in, but only enough to offset those weeded out for uselessness, those older men discharged for medical unfitness, and a few youngsters reclaimed by angry parents.

The 11th Battalion was isolated, but not so much so that Fitzmullen-Brophy hadn't heard of other battalions readying for posting overseas, making up their numbers by poaching from other units. His command was small enough as it was, and there was no reason why it couldn't disappear entirely at the whim of some rapacious seniors. Aggressive recruiting, he decided, was the solution.

The band, like everyone else, was wanting in everything but spirit. Nevertheless, properly rehearsed in a few rousing tunes and kitted out in the best that battalion possessed, the colonel reckoned they were capable of putting on a creditable show. He chose a fair day in Mitchelstown for that show, and he envisaged himself on a flag-bedecked platform rallying masses of Ireland's young manhood to the colours with his words while the sun flashed off polished bugles and bayonets. Alas, while the weather promised to be favourable on the appointed day, Fitzmullen-Brophy came down with a disgraceful head cold he felt would rob his oratory of some of its power. Still, as he told his officers, a well-run battalion should be prepared to overcome the loss of anyone, no matter how important. Curran, as an accomplished public speaker, would take charge of the operation, assisted, if necessary, by McCarthy-Moore, who likewise had no fear of crowds and moreover looked the most impressive of any of them in uniform. Wyndham volunteered to come along as stage manager, or whatever was needed, because he fancied a day out.

They set off in Curran's motor car. He had appeared with it on return from his last leave in Dublin, and Fitzmullen-Brophy had no reservations about appropriating it as a battalion asset. Curran was an awful driver, but he was the only one who could drive, and at least he got them where they intended to go without injury. Wyndham and McCarthy-Moore were crammed into the back along with the recruiting paraphernalia while Moriarty sat up front next to the driver. Moriarty was coming because Moriarty was a law unto himself and, besides, he might be useful when it came to performing menial tasks beneath the dignity of commissioned officers.

'If I could have ten shillings, sir, I'll be off to the pub,' he said, after they'd arrived. He said it so unassumingly – as if NCOs were supposed to be scrounging money from their superiors so they could spend the day getting wearily plastered – that Curran's hand was half-way to his pocket before Wyndham interjected.

'Moriarty! What on earth are you talking about? You are most certainly not going to the pub. You're here to help us recruit.'

Moriarty turned on Wyndham that look that was so familiar

– that look that asked how on earth a fellow such as Wyndham could reach manhood and still remain so profoundly ignorant. 'Recruiting's done in pubs, sir. Everyone knows that. You pour drink into a fella, tell him stories and convince him that soldiering is the life. When he sobers up, he's already taken the shilling and it's too late. It's traditional.'

Wyndham was about to formulate an argument in defiance of tradition when Curran said, 'Five shillings. After the meeting. And after you've helped putting the stage up. And I'll want change. And there'd better be some recruits to show for it.'

'Of course, sir.' said Moriarty, with a suggestion that he didn't care to have his honesty and sobriety impugned.

The stage was a couple of planks on top of a couple of crates. In front of it was a sign saying, *Vacancies still exist in the 11th Battalion Royal Munster Fusiliers. Enlist today*. Flanking this were two other notices commanding the reader to *Remember Belgium* and *Remember the Lusitania* in emphatic businesslike black on white (Private O'Regan, sign painter, Youghal). Behind the stage, crossed, were a Union Jack (government issue) and a green flag with gold harp (provided by 2/Lt. B.P. Curran 11/ RMF). Surmounting them, and unfortunately rather smaller and less colourful, was the unofficial battalion flag – a Bengal tiger (Miss M. Fitzmullen-Brophy, Tralee), stitched with more competence than artistic flair or zoological accuracy.

All was in order by the time the band arrived, sweating like bejesus after an eight-mile march in the fine sunshine, and they in the best uniforms as could be gathered from the whole battalion. It was a small band, with no professional musicians in its ranks, but there had been plenty of time for practice through the spring. After all, it had either been that or peel more spuds.

They announced themselves with 'The British Grenadier', which was the standard march for all fusilier regiments and was nice and jaunty. Then, having marched through the fair-day crowds, and luckily not being impeded by any livestock, they formed up on one side of the stage and launched into a tune that Wyndham had come to recognise as 'A Nation Once Again'. Curran had organised the musical programme, and had assured Wyndham that this nationalist anthem was not in the least subversive and was perfect for their purposes.

Wyndham could see now that Curran was in his element, surveying the gathering crowd with a gleaming eye from on top of a box and breathing deeply in preparation for the coming address. The crowd gathered because there's only so much looking at cattle you'd want to be doing; because a bit of music was always welcome; and because a public meeting might promise all manner of entertainment if the hecklers were up to the mark.

They hushed as the band came to a finish and waited for Curran, his chest swelling and nostrils flaring, to cut loose. He did not disappoint.

'Fight for Ireland!' he declaimed.

'Fight for Ireland! That is the appeal I make to you today, my countrymen!

'My name is Bartholomew Curran, and, while I stand before you in the king's uniform, I am an Irishman, first, foremost, and forever. When last I appealed to the people of Ireland I spoke as the Irish Parliamentary Party's candidate for Carlow South. I spoke then about the necessity – the vital necessity – for Home Rule. That struggle for Home Rule has now been won. John Redmond has seen to that. Moreover, your efforts and your votes have seen to that. But there is more that is asked of you yet.

'Today I speak as a soldier of the Royal Munster Fusiliers, and I speak of the necessity – of the vital, the moral, the historical necessity – of joining in the greater struggle.'

On rolled Curran in similar vein, the rhetorical cadences issuing forth in endless stream. It was good stuff. It was a sermon and a history lesson rolled into one. It was a concert with Curran's voice the orchestra. It took the audience from Dunkirk to Belgrade, riding with Clare's Dragoons, flying with the Wild Geese, marching as a nation.

'And an independent Ireland will be counted among the nations by proving herself on the battlefield!

'My friends! My countrymen! *Has there ever been a just war from which Irishmen have shrunk?*'

Wyndham felt that he'd have joined up that very minute if he hadn't already been in uniform. He felt that at least they could sell tickets to Curran's next performance.

The audience, however, did not flock forthwith to the colours. They didn't even applaud. Was it possible, thought Wyndham, that they could be unmoved by such oratory? Could it be that they heard the like every fair day?

But not only was the favourable reception limited to one or two approving nods here and there in the crowd, and a lone 'hear, hear' from a well-dressed old gentleman at the back, there was actually some dissent to mar the sacramental silence deserved by the close of Curran's appeal.

The dissenter didn't have Curran's ringing voice, but he had rehearsed his line nicely.

'You can take the king's shilling, but that doesn't mean we have to! The red coat is an Irishman's shame!'

Wyndham was dumbfounded. He considered calling out for the heckler to be arrested, but wasn't sure of his legal authority in the matter. But as he stood flustered, with McCarthy-Moore outraged beside him, and Curran drawing breath for what would surely be a devastating riposte, the defence of the regiment's and Ireland's honour was voiced from an unexpected quarter.

'Shut up you, you fool!'

Moriarty wasn't comfortable much in open spaces these days, but years of standing sentry and the last months of being in charge of a squad made him used to being looked at. He stepped up from his place beside the stage to get a better look at the heckler. He identified a likely suspect.

'Who said that? Was it *you*?'

His target was a young man, evidently of the farming class, looking righteous and truculent in the presence of two men much like himself in appearance and most probably father and brother. He had said his piece to Curran and wasn't going to back down before Moriarty. As far as he was concerned, any rejoinder to his just accusation would be a lie.

'You know nothing, you,' Moriarty said to the young man, and then: 'How tall are you?'

The young patriot looked confused for a moment, but it was clear Moriarty had already dismissed him and was looking at the young man next to him.

'You. The brother. How tall? Five foot nine? Am I right?'

The patriot's younger brother had his mouth open to answer, but Moriarty was in full flight.

'Five foot nine inches and twenty years of age, am I right? Twenty years of age and you've never had a pair of trousers that weren't handed down to you! Is that your brother, is it? You're wearing his trousers! Aren't you? And that's your father? And you're breaking your arse for him seven days a week?'

'Keep it clean, Moriarty,' hissed Curran, in vain.

'How much pocket money did he give you? I'll bet he'd never give you more than two tanners to bless yourself with, and you have to go around looking like that and you've never been to bed with a girl!'

'*Moriarty!* For heaven's sake, man.' But it was no use. This was Moriarty's moment. The spittle was flying.

'The army will take you if you're over five foot three and nineteen years of age, and they'll give you two suits of clothes as soon as you're in the door and seven bob a week and you can do what you want with it and you won't have to work your arse off for your oul fella or listen to your brother talk political shite.'

His verdict on Ireland's emotive political issues as 'shite' drew a growl from one section of the audience. It was enough to make Moriarty take notice, and shift his attention to a party of hard-handed rural manhood that was quite happy to prove just how independent Ireland could be.

'What are *ye* looking at? What are ye even *doing*? Standing around scratching your bollocks waiting for a fight to start? You want a fight? Go on away and fight the Germans! Show them what hard men ye are!'

And then one of them made the classic move of squaring his shoulders and taking a step forward, while two of his fellows made the equally classic move of laying restraining hands upon him while the crowd, evidently knowing the challenger's capabilities, made some room. Moriarty didn't falter. He roared above the heads of the crowd.

'You think I'm afraid of you, boy? I'm not afraid of any of you! You're nothing! I'm a Munster Fusilier! There's eleven battalions of me!'

And then Curran gave an order and the band struck up with, 'God Save Ireland Say the Heroes'. One of the trumpets was off key, but volume was what counted, and it was delivered. Curran, marking time with his fist, sang the words with gusto enough to bring Moriarty to a standstill and, remarkably, to get enough of the audience to join in. Wyndham was hugely impressed.

In a show of solidarity McCarthy-Moore somehow made space for himself on the platform, which wondrously bore all their weight, and when the music finished he announced in his best referee's voice that enlistments would be accepted directly, but if any potential recruit would care to hear more, his questions would be entertained in the saloon bar of Ahern's Hotel.

And as the little stage ceased to be the big draw in the square,

Curran ostentatiously handed ten shillings to Moriarty and told him to be about his duty.

When the band marched home that evening they were accompanied by a round dozen of high-spirited young men. The officers, equally merry, drove home singing rebel songs. Only Moriarty, sunk in the front seat, declined to join the general jollity.

III

SHORT, MAGAZINE, LEE-ENFIELD

Fusil *(fiū·zil)*

1. A fire steel or tinder-box.

2. A light musket or firelock.

Fusilier *(fiūzilīᵊ·ɹ)*

Originally a soldier armed with a fusil.

—*Oxford English Dictionary*, 1ˢᵗ Edition, 1901

34

Now-a-days things are different; the men are better educated and have finer feelings, and esprit de corps, carefully fostered and maintained in every good regiment, is an immense factor in the prevention of crime among soldiers.

—Augustus Mockler-Ferryman, *Annals of Sandhurst:
A Chronicle of the Royal Military College*

Lieutenant-Colonel Fitzmullen-Brophy stamped his foot to test the firmness of the ground and the soundness of his leg. Both seemed to be answering nicely. Summer had come, he was feeling fitter by the day, and the battalion was shaping up well. *His* battalion was shaping up well.

They could drill and they could march, and with every man with one almost-complete suit of khaki to his name, they were exhibiting a soldier's pride that warmed their colonel's heart. Not good enough for mounting guard at Dublin Castle yet, of course, but keen. Keenness made up for so many shortcomings, and without it all the spit and polish in the world wasn't enough.

And his officers were keen, too. Fearfully keen. Jolly keen. Not a man-jack of them had been through Sandhurst, and here they were bringing themselves and their platoons up to a very creditable mark. Which only went to show, as far as Fitzmullen-Brophy was concerned, that Sandhurst wasn't everything, you know. Fitzmullen-Brophy himself had never been there, after all, and look at him: commanding a battalion.

There were a thousand and one things still to do, of course, but he was confident that they'd all be made right in time. What worried him, however, was how long the higher-ups would leave him and his battalion alone. How long would it be before someone with red tabs on his collar bowled up out of the blue and judged a company or two's worth of men to be fit for overseas, and there they'd be – gone – and the battalion down by half its strength or more. The fact was, although he preferred not to acknowledge it, there was no good reason for the 11th Battalion to exist except to train up replacements for the units already at the front. Fitzmullen-Brophy's command was really little more than a sort of a shop where the greater regiment could pick up replacement parts. But isolated out here through the spring, he had been entertaining dreams of leading his battalion, under its own flag as it were, into battle. He had raised it from its infancy. Surely it was only proper that he should lead it into the world?

It was all in the lap of the gods, but he reckoned that the better he was able to present a fully trained and integrated body of fighting men, the better his chances of keeping the battalion together.

A platoon came by, marching to attention. He returned their officer's salute with a hearty encouragement.

'That's the ticket, McCarthy-Moore! First rate! Best bally marching in the battalion!'

It was certainly a smart display, and Fitzmullen-Brophy knew that the grimly competitive McCarthy-Moore would thrive on the extra approbation. The man would hardly let standards slip now after being so publicly complimented. That was the ticket indeed. Man-management. Find an officer better at it than Hugh Fitzmullen-Brophy.

But the precision on show also advertised a great shortcoming in the battalion. McCarthy-Moore's men were still drilling with those awful dummy rifles, just as the other platoons were, just as Wyndham's section were still wheeling around that odd contraption and calling it a machine-gun.

A battalion without rifles was not a fighting force, and a battalion that couldn't fight was no battalion at all. It was just a collection of men, who could be posted elsewhere at the army's whim, leaving nothing but the empty title of 11th Munsters.

Fitzmullen-Brophy had written sheaves of letters to higher authority, badgering them for equipment. Taking one last deep breath of the clean outdoors he headed back towards his office. Time to get another damned letter on its way.

Every man gave himself wholeheartedly to the regiment. More correctly, they gave themselves to the battalion. The regiment was too great, too nebulous a concept, but the battalion was here – among these rows of tents, here in these fields. Fitzmullen-Brophy showed them that. His dream of the 11th Munsters became their dream, and every man did his best to realise it, to please the colonel, to make themselves worthy of his vision.

Even before there were uniforms or weapons, or even proper accommodation, they all were doing their best to conduct themselves as Munster Fusiliers. To do less would not just betray their colonel but would make mock of the sacrifice they'd made in enlisting. With the colonel holding his light aloft for them they were soldiers. Without it then they'd just be a muddy field full of big eejits.

They had few of the trappings of their new calling, but they had faith. McCarthy-Moore grew a moustache because regulations demanded it. Wyndham did the same to advertise his allegiance to the old army. Of the new officers, only Curran declined to efface his old identity. He had spent enough years cultivating a particular appearance, and felt himself too old to change things now.

It was a season of improvisation. Fitzmullen-Brophy's

overwhelming optimism in his new command admitted no obstacles that could not be overcome by every man trying his very hardest. Material wants should mean nothing in the face of several hundred willing men and their pooled skills and experiences. These skills were applied even where they were somewhat tangential. Thus, just as Wyndham was made machine-gun officer on the strength of having once seen a machine-gun, so McCarthy-Moore, on the grounds of being a keen rugby player, was made acting medical officer. Why not? As Fitzmullen-Brophy contended, the man was the very picture of physical fitness and would be well used to the sort of injuries suffered by healthy young men living an outdoor life. (They'd originally had a civilian doctor on call, but he'd pushed off when he found the military life unappealing. A poor sort.)

Like all the officers, McCarthy-Moore took his new duty most seriously, but most complaints were treated with the advice to 'walk it off'. Lesions of various sorts were treated by the instruction to 'run it under a cold tap'. The few, more serious and puzzling cases received a rigorous examination consisting of a frown and the question, 'Are you feeling alright?' Only when walking it off and running it under a cold tap proved ineffective was the patient excused duties and advised to take to his bed.

Fitzmullen-Brophy heartily approved of this approach. 'That's the stuff, McCarthy-Moore. No sense in mollycoddling them. Weakens them in the long run, you know. Saw it in India. Treat a man like an invalid or – God forbid – tell a man his life's in danger, and he'll believe you. Waste away in no time. Ridiculous. A fit man with a stout heart should be able to soldier on through just about everything except sunstroke and cholera. Carry on.'

The army's disciplinary and legal system was another thing with which the new officers had to acquaint themselves. McCarthy-Moore, a barrister at law, had a head start on Doyle, his company commander. Doyle had been a heedless subaltern in times of peace, and happily ignorant of all manner of military administration. Now, as an acting captain, he had to be judge and jury in the hearing of his men's transgressions. When presented with a thorny case he would have been a fool if he hadn't called on McCarthy-Moore's experience. The conscientious McCarthy-Moore was not willing to trust the matter to himself alone. He had, after all, been very junior in his profession. Thus, he requested the advice of Curran, who obliged him with his counsel, and the two men spent a hasty half hour – all the time allowed – with the *Manual of Military Law*. Wyndham, out of curiosity, asked to be included in the party. After all, no opportunity for an officer's further education should be missed, and besides, the concentration that C Company's legal department was putting into the case promised something sensational.

It was a little disconcerting to learn that the case involved nothing worse than the theft from the stores of some boot polish. Why, wondered Wyndham, would anyone want to steal boot polish, to the quantity of a single tin? It was true that there was a shortage of everything, and that the issue of boot polish had been temporarily suspended, but Wyndham remembered from his recruit days the stupefying commitment to boots – boots that had spent almost as much time on his hands as on his feet, being nurtured with blacking and soothed with the endless rubbing of a rag. Why would any soldier, excused from such an obligation, risk his liberty in the illicit quest for boot polish? And how was it that the culprit in such an unfathomable act should be Private Maguire?

Maguire was one of the men that Fitzmullen-Brophy referred to as 'steady', which was to say that he was older than the common run and not likely to prejudice good order with youthful hijinks. Sensible, sober, obedient: that was Maguire. He was also a labouring man in civil life, and thus no sort of dandy.

Marched into company orders, with his ill-fitting suit of khaki as presentable as he could make it, he was no one's idea of a really smart soldier. And now, in the custody of the company sergeant-major (acting), and arraigned before his company commander, even his reputation for steadiness was rendered meaningless.

There were four officers present, and as the Manual of Military Law had informed McCarthy-Moore, this was one more than was needed for a Field General Court Martial. It was a lot for a single tin of boot polish, but theft was theft, and justice was not something that the 11th Royal Munster Fusiliers intended to treat lightly.

Although largely ignorant of procedure himself, Sergeant Rafferty was the only proper soldier in the room, at least as he saw it. This shouldn't have been his job at all, but Sergeant-Major O'Meara was off sick, pleading the rheumatics again, and Rafferty, rather than do any actual work, had been happy to step forward in the interim. Pushing his weight about a bit more than was usual? He could do that. So he had small enough claim to the crimson sash of his new office, but he still thought himself more than a cut above everyone else assembled. Useless shower.

In truth, Doyle looked like what he was – the somewhat ineffectual scion of minor gentry, as yet under the age of twenty-one – while the new-made lieutenants were looking quite unmilitary. Curran was grasping his lapels in an unconscious courtroom pose, while McCarthy-Moore was leaning forward attentively, his knuckles on the table, as if he expected this case to take some shrewd turns. Wyndham, as always, had assumed the air of a bystander. He might as well have been waiting for a train.

Rafferty had them all bracketed. Doyle would do what he was told, and so would those other two, even if they didn't know it yet. Company orders in a tin hut and they were acting like it was the Old Bailey. Lieutenant Wyndham was the odd fella – the peculiar Yank with his funny tunic. He'd been out in France, and God alone knew where else, but he didn't know everything. These offhand officers knew damn all about King's Regulations and the smart running of a company.

'Prisoner 42398 Maguire apprehended in the stores without permission, in unauthorised possession of boot polish, tin of, one, *sir*,' Rafferty spoke unnecessarily loudly.

'Anything to say, Maguire?' said Doyle

Maguire, the steady man, standing to attention, admitted the offence.

'But why, man? What on earth possessed you?'

All four officers were looking at Maguire's boots which, like every other man's boots in the battalion, were greased against the wet but otherwise dull. Maguire stared steadily at the wall above Doyle's head and said nothing.

'You have a good record, Maguire. If you have nothing to say for yourself, I have no choice but to punish you according to the book.'

Still Maguire said nothing.

'Very well,' Doyle began, but Rafferty forestalled him, with a suggestion of smirk on his face.

'Sir. If I may, sir. The prisoner has been using boot polish to dye his hair and moustache.'

'He's been *what*?'

'Haven't you, Maguire? Haven't you been trying to make yourself look younger? Sure, we can see the grey coming out. Who do you think you're codding?'

Maguire declined to answer, but he quivered. Rafferty saw he'd touched a nerve. Anywhere else, and he'd have let the officers take things from there, but here? With these officers? He was happy to overstep the mark.

'What class of an old fool are you at all? Why didn't you go the whole hog and put on short pants when you enlisted? You could have told them you were only fourteen, but you had a letter from your parents. They might have believed you down at the recruiting office, but you're not going to fool me. How old are you really, Maguire? Sixty? Seventy? Go on – tell us.'

And that was when Private Maguire, the steady man, punched Sergeant Rafferty in the jaw with his hard labourer's fist so as to send him thudding against the wall.

Assault on a non-commissioned officer was a matter above company orders. Maguire submitted with dignity to being marched off under armed escort to close confinement while Fitzmullen-Brophy was informed of the dramatic developments in the case.

Fitzmullen-Brophy dispensed with the matter in short order and with a heavy heart. This sort of thing was no good for the battalion.

'Do you have anything to say for yourself, Maguire?'

'I mean no offence to you, Colonel, sir, but that man Rafferty's a gobshite.'

Wyndham, who along with the other officers was present at this new hearing, wanted to step forward in the accused's defence and confirm that the injured party was, upon my oath, sir, indeed a gobshite, but he kept still.

Maguire, with the dye out of his hair, could never have passed for forty now. For all his age and modest stature though, he stood proudly. Fitzmullen-Brophy let the bad language go. His need to understand this man was genuine.

'How old are you really, Maguire?'

'I'm fifty-four, sir.'

Not far off Fitzmullen-Brophy's own age and too old to soldier. A depressing business indeed.

'If it were just a matter of few years, I believe I could overlook it. But fifty-four? I'm afraid it just won't do, Maguire.'

'I have two sons in the army, sir, and a third who went down with the *Aboukir*. I couldn't but do something, sir.'

'Your motives are commendable, Maguire, and I am of course sorry to hear of the loss of your boy, but I greatly fear that none of this excuses your conduct. Your offences warrant severe punishment but none, I think, could be as severe as what I am obliged to do now. I'm afraid that you are to be discharged from the army forthwith. Dismiss.'

Maguire saluted for what was to be the last time and, not waiting for anyone to give the order, did a most creditable right-about-face and marched out. No one looked him in the eye, fearing they might see tears there.

When Maguire left the camp in a shabby suit of civilian clothes, Sergeant Rafferty called out a jibe about the Kilmainham pensioners maybe accepting recruits. The men accompanying Maguire moved to restrain him, but there was no need. He didn't even turn his head. Some men watching thought it a pity. That Rafferty could do with another thump.

35

The common people of this Country are naturally fond of times of Confusion because they have an Opportunity of indulging some favourite appetites such as Thieving and Cruelty.

—Lt.-Col. Samuel Bagshawe, Cork, 1753

Recruits kept coming, albeit in disappointingly small numbers. Fitzmullen-Brophy sent his officers out to beat the drum from time to time, but they never came close to matching that first haul of a dozen men. Every so often a party of men would be sent from the regimental depot at Tralee, bewildered, raring to go, or just dumbly accepting that the army was their lot now.

On one occasion a couple of men showed up at the gate, having specifically sought out the remote 11th Battalion. They gave their names as Linehan and Clark, and they'd walked the eight miles from the station, and before that, they said, they'd come all the way from Dublin.

'What do they want coming all the way down from Dublin?' asked Moriarty, with his bred-in-the-bone suspicion of Dubliners and all things Dublin. 'Is there no army above in Dublin for them?' He said this within earshot of the two men, having been summoned to take charge of them by McCarthy-Moore. Such a hostile welcome for the new arrivals pained McCarthy-Moore, but it didn't do to chide a corporal in front of the men, and any attempt at shushing Moriarty was a losing proposition.

'Just take them to the cookhouse for a cup of tea, Moriarty,' he said gently as he left them to it. 'Then see if the stores can kit them out with anything.' But Moriarty didn't appear to be listening. He had turned on Linehan and Clark.

'What are you doing coming all the way down from Dublin? Isn't there a Dublin Fusiliers for you to join? Isn't there any Leinster Regiment? Isn't there a Boys' Brigade or something?'

Linehan opened his mouth, but that was as far as he got. Moriarty was in no mood to finish up yet.

'Did you think we're just some gobshites you could just walk up to and join? Are you cute fuckers or something? Thinking you could just walk up and join? We're the Munster Fusiliers, boy. Do you think we just take anyone who toddles up to the gate?

'The lieutenant there already signed us up, Corporal,' said Linehan, as if that settled that.

'You! What's your name?'

'Linehan, Corporal.'

Moriarty leaned his face close to Linehan's and stared, daring a reaction, for as long as it would take to count to five slowly.

'Linehan,' he said finally, as if he had just discovered what was for dinner, and wasn't too delighted about it but was going to eat it anyway. He didn't like the way Linehan just stood there, not cocky, but not cowed either.

Clark respectfully butted in. 'Me Da came from Kerry, Corporal, and I'd an uncle in the Munsters. Linehan's got family in Kerry, too.'

Moriarty declined to look away from Linehan, and merely acknowledged the interruption with a: 'Shut up, you. I'll get to you in a minute.' Continuing to address Linehan he asked, 'Is that the case, is it?'

Linehan, calmly refusing to meet Moriarty's eye, affirmed that this was indeed the case, and added: 'Didn't care to enlist in a recruiting office, Corporal. Sure, it's only money to the recruiting sergeant and the doctor. Cut out the middle man, Corporal.'

Moriarty blinked for the first time and sniffed. 'What have you got against the middle man? You wouldn't, by any chance, be one of those socialist feckers, would you? One of those red Larkinites?'

'Irish Citizen Army, Corporal,' admitted Linehan, naming the Dublin workers' militia that had fought against strike breakers and police the winter before last.

'And that's where you learned to stand to attention, was it? And did you learn to drill there?'

'A bit, Corporal.'

'A bit. And that's what made ye marked men in Dublin, am I right?'

Linehan and Clark both remained silent, and that was all Moriarty wanted out of them for now. He'd got their measure.

'Cookhouse is closed,' he announced in satisfaction. 'Follow me, the pair of you, and I'll show you where you're to be bedded down.'

Before the war the Munster Fusiliers had been home to men from all over the United Kingdom – even from Dublin – but that had changed. With the great flood of recruits last autumn, the regiments hadn't had to look outside their recruiting areas anymore and the men, joining in droves, saw no reason to serve alongside anyone other than their own kind. So, it was odd, Moriarty's Corkonian prejudice aside, for two Dublin men to stray so far from home when the regiments of their own county and their own province would have been happy to enlist them. Even the blacklisted men who'd fought for the trade union leader Jim Larkin the year before the war had found a home in the Royal Dublin Fusiliers. But then, despite their admission, Linehan and Clark had never been Larkinites. Linehan and Clark weren't even their real names.

They had in fact learned their drill in the Irish Volunteers but, unlike Mr. John Redmond MP, they didn't agree that Ireland's cause and the United Kingdom's cause were one and the same.

Let the Germans overrun Europe. It was no business of the men who called themselves Linehan and Clark. They would do their fighting for Ireland at home.

After consultation with certain clandestine superiors however, it was decided that they should indeed answer Redmond's call and join the army, although they should stop short of going to fight the Germans. How short? It was reckoned that they need stay no longer than it took to be issued with rifles. And so they perfected their drill in the Dublin Fusiliers until each of them was deemed responsible enough to have signed over to him a factory-new Lee-Enfield .303, still coated in its protective chemical grease. They took their new rifles back to their quarters, assiduously cleaned them and then, at a prearranged time, threw them over the barrack wall to prearranged persons of certain political convictions. Then they smartly walked out of barracks, never to return.

It went so smoothly that it was decided to give it another go, and so the names of Linehan and Clark were adopted, and directions were given to Clonmel, and the home of the Royal Irish Regiment. On their own initiative the two men diverted to the Royal Munster Fusiliers, on the grounds that they were hopelessly remote, and even less likely to be on the lookout for two deserters from the Dublins.

They were disappointed to see that the man at the gate was armed with an elderly rifle of foreign manufacture, but by then it was too late. They'd been walking for hours and besides, Lieutenant McCarthy-Moore had spotted them. Seeing two able-bodied men who were obviously neither too young nor too old, he hadn't fussed over their lack of identification, and had briskly set about the technicalities of enlistment before handing them over to Moriarty.

Moriarty, in his turn, after trying very hard to find fault with their standard of drill, grudgingly admitted that they weren't completely useless and might as well be lumped in with a platoon.

There still weren't any rifles to be had, but Linehan and Clark bided their time. The 11th Munsters, gallantly muddling through, always tried to make the best of a man's civilian employment, and the two Dubliners, in keeping with their cover story of being staunch trade union men, had listed themselves as carters. This was another lie, but they did apparently know their way around horses and harnesses, so when a wagon was finally acquired they became part of the battalion transport. It wasn't exactly the keys to the armoury, but it would put them in temporary charge of all manner of government stores – perhaps even weapons – that might find better use in an Irish revolution than in a European war.

36

ENROL UNDER THE GREEN FLAG.
Safeguard your rights and liberties.
Help your country to a place among the nations.
Give her a National Army to keep her there.
Get a gun and do your part.

—Irish Volunteers poster, 1913

One Saturday afternoon Wyndham and Curran went motoring through the countryside. Their duties in camp, such as they were, promised nothing but tedium that day and could, they both felt, be put off for a while. The weather was fine, and they needed variety.

After an hour or so of Curran's truly dangerous driving, Wyndham suggested they stop for refreshment and a stretch of the legs. He desired a last moment of calm in case the return journey might kill him. The town where they stopped was indistinguishable from the other towns Wyndham had thus far seen: a grey main street with two churches and a small hotel, set down amid the green patchwork of dairy farms that spread all across the county.

The two officers took tea at the hotel, strolled the length of the main street, and were about to return to Curran's car when their attention was caught by the sound of words of command. They investigated down a lane and there, in a little grassy space beyond a low stone wall, they found a squad of men drilling. The man in charge wore a green tunic of military cut and a matching slouch hat, but otherwise everyone was in civilian clothing.

'Volunteers,' said Curran.

Wyndham by now knew enough not to ask, 'Volunteers for what?' He'd heard plenty about the nationalist militia, but had never yet seen them. He went closer. The Volunteer officer, seeing two officers of the crown forces rather than a pair of idle sightseers, turned to look at them with a suspicion verging on hostility, but Wyndham was so steeped these last months in military etiquette that he snapped off a very civil salute, and Curran was only a beat behind in following his lead. There was the slightest moment of surprise before the polite gesture was formally returned. Better yet, the Volunteer officer called his men to attention and had them present arms in recognition of the two visitors in khaki.

Curran held his salute impassively, but Wyndham beamed. He appreciated these little reminders that he was part of an international brotherhood of soldiery, and that the sometimes ridiculous rituals and evolutions in camp weren't just some dotty pantomime invented by Fitzmullen-Brophy. He and Curran retired to a less intrusive distance while the Volunteers continued self-consciously with their drill.

'Look at their rifles,' said Wyndham.

'They're not rifles.'

'I know. But they look very well all the same, don't they?'

'Those are hurleys, I believe.'

'Hurleys?'

'Hurling sticks. For hurling. It's a game – a little like hockey.'

Wyndham lit up with delight. 'Hurling sticks? Like Cuchulain used? Why that's wonderful!' In this modern world of motor cars and politics, shops and farmers, he had at last found a survival of ancient heroic Ireland. The young men in their cloth caps and country clothes were revealed to his eyes as the heirs to the Red Branch. He said as much to Curran, in laughing wonderment.

'Well, I suppose that's one way of putting it,' Curran smiled, gratified that thirty years of national resurgence and Gaelic revival should have such a successful impact on one romantic American at least.

'And they hurl those sticks somehow?' Wyndham asked, unable to drag his attention away from something so mundane as a length of curved ash wood. 'At each other?'

'No. I'm afraid you've been misled, dear fellow. Nothing to do with the verb "to hurl". No throwing of anything except the ball, as far as I'm aware. As I say – it's something like hockey.'

Wyndham had never seen a game of hockey, but admitted that this new knowledge did make better sense of some of the stories. They stood in silence a while longer, Curran wishing to be off, but Wyndham hanging on, wondering if there were more to see, looking at the sticks in the Volunteers' hands and thinking of Setanta striking down the hound of Culain.

'"I swear by the gods my people swear by, I myself will be your watch-dog, to guard your goods and your cattle and your house." That's it, isn't it, Curran? It's all most fitting. Didn't the Volunteers promise that they would guard Ireland while the army went off to France? Magnificent.'

'Some of the Volunteers at any rate. I must say I admire your perspective on Irish affairs. Come along now. We'd best be getting on.'

'I suppose so. Hurling sticks. Fancy that.' Wyndham shook his head, mildly astonished that an afternoon's idle diversion should have brought such reward. 'And they're using them as rifles. Perfect.'

He turned and gave the Volunteers one last look. All cultural symbolism aside, the hurleys did look properly martial, with the curved end closely emulating the stock of a rifle, and even the little lip at the other end giving quite a good approximation of the foresight assembly on a Lee-Enfield.

On the way back to camp, to distract him from the perils of Curran's driving, Wyndham clung grimly to his seat and shouted above the noise of the motor.

'What did you mean when you said "some of the Volunteers"?'

'What's that?'

'You said some of the Volunteers are contributing to the war effort. I thought Mr. Redmond had assured the government of their cooperation.'

'Ah. Yes. But Redmond doesn't quite command the Volunteers, you see. Some of them were more than willing to take up the army's duties. They marched the Royal Irish Regiment out of barracks in Clonmel last August, I heard. Proud to show that they were all serving the same cause. Then there are all those who answered Redmond's call to join the army. You know all about them, I'm sure. But there are quite a number, I fear, who still see Britain as the enemy and who see themselves as the only surety against a feared English betrayal. After all, they were formed expressly to hold the government from reneging on Home Rule.'

'Ah, I see,' shouted Wyndham, grateful in the engine noise and rushing air for Curran's training in public speaking. 'So what…,' he said, leaning in to Curran and praying the man didn't take his eyes off the road, 'What side do you think those men we saw today have taken?'

'Hard to say. There's a strong suspicion that those who don't follow Redmond have been infected by Fenianism. God alone knows how that will shape up. We can only hope that they see us as Munster men and not British soldiers.'

Wyndham thought about it as they careered onwards at twenty-five miles an hour. He'd been hearing about the looming threat of civil strife in Ireland even before he'd left America, but like so many others had thought that the greater war had nullified that threat. Now he tried to imagine how it would be if the 11th Munsters were called upon to fight their countrymen in the Irish Volunteers. The men they'd seen that afternoon had put on a good show. They'd been few, but then that was just one squad in one

184

little town. The Volunteers were a country-wide organisation, and there were a lot of little towns in Ireland.

On the other hand, he knew exactly the capabilities of his own men, who had energy and spirit, and whose drilling had come on well, but who were understrength and deficient in all the necessaries of war. And he thought about Ireland, and the men who'd fought for her down the ages, with musket and with pike, with sword and spear, and even, in the legends of Ulster as in the farmland of North Cork, with hurling sticks.

I will make my doings be spoken of among the great doings of heroes in their strength.

Wyndham knew that his war was just, and his loyalty to the regiment was staunch, but he unhappily suspected that the men with the hurleys had history on their side.

'And even their dummy rifles are better than our dummy rifles,' he said aloud.

37

'We put our religion into our knapsacks, sir, whenever our colours are unfurled, or where duty calls.'

—Unnamed subedar, 40th Madras Native Infantry, c.1835

Because it was a Saturday afternoon, Lieutenant-Colonel Fitzmullen-Brophy was taking tea with Father Bewley. The Army Chaplain's Department had not seen fit to assign anyone to the 11th Munsters, but the battalion had not been long wanting in spiritual guidance. Father Bewley was just one of two local priests from different parishes who had sought out the camp almost as soon as it had been established. They had been quick to settle between them their claims to the few hundred souls, with one hearing confessions on Saturdays and the other saying Mass on Sundays. Besides that division of sacred spoils, there was little enough to tell them apart in Fitzmullen-Brophy's eyes, except that Father Bewley, the Saturday priest, came by bicycle, while Father Davis, the Sunday priest, came in a pony and trap.

Fitzmullen-Brophy was particular in showing hospitality to the visiting clergymen, and not just because one did well to keep in with the local witch doctors. Roman Catholicism was a dangerous thing, after all, and while Irishmen made the best soldiers in the army, whatever their faith, their native flightiness had to be kept on a tight rein. That was what army chaplains were for. A civilian padre on the other hand, a Catholic padre, an Irish Catholic padre, might not only fail to understand the army's moral jurisdiction over its men, but had been known in the past to attempt to subvert it.

That was why Fitzmullen-Brophy was taking tea with Father Bewley. If the priest had just been spending the last two hours hearing the darkest secrets of young fusiliers' souls, then it was incumbent on the commanding officer to keep a close eye on the father confessor. Not, of course, that the secrets of the confessional were under discussion. Indeed, Father Bewley was such a lively talker that he could carry on for hours with nothing but a single reminiscence or an observation on the weather to start him off. Perhaps this was helped by the tea in this case being whiskey,

Fitzmullen-Brophy didn't care for whiskey in the afternoon, as it gave him a bad head and spoiled his appetite for dinner, but that was part of the price one paid for command, and a necessary precaution against runaway religiosity in his battalion.

It had never been a real problem in the old days. The old army had been full of unrepentant sinners, and new recruits learned quickly to discard the niceties of Christianity, such as saying their prayers before bed, or refraining from theft, adultery, coveting that which was their neighbour's and occasionally killing. This new breed, however, showed an uncommon piety. Private Dineen, for instance, although a most promising recruit, had been found saying the rosary in the evenings. Indeed, he had been leading almost his entire platoon in the rosary, as if he were some sort of spiritual authority. Also, he was apparently organising a sodality. Fitzmullen-Brophy didn't quite know what a sodality was, but it sounded frightfully RC. More worryingly, it was not covered by King's Regulations. It just wouldn't do. A man cannot serve two masters. Private Dineen could serve as an altar boy on Sundays, but, as Moriarty would have been delighted to hear, he would not be promoted until he recognised that his sole master was the regiment. Naturally the regiment answered to God, but it followed the correct chain of command.

And so Fitzmullen-Brophy spent an hour or more every Saturday trying to incorporate Father Bewley into the regiment's world, while the priest, for his part, happily sipped whisky and talked the colonel's ear off.

This Saturday, the colonel was relieved by the interruption of Major de Roche, who smiled a tight smile at Father Bewley and handed an official-looking piece of paper to Fitzmullen-Brophy.

'So sorry to interrupt, Father. Thought you should see this right away, Colonel.'

It was, as it happened, the best news Fitzmullen-Brophy could have hoped for, and a strong case for the efficacy of fervent prayer. He was herewith directed to make provision for the receipt of a shipment of rifles and ammunition due by rail on Monday. The God of Battles, or perhaps the God of Birmingham Small Arms, had heard His humble servant.

Even though he had two whole days to wait, the news galvanised him. Father Bewley was cheerily handed his hat and hustled from the room, with hearty apologies concerning pressing military business – 'But do be sure to call again, Father.' – and hasty instructions were issued concerning confirmation of orders and inspections of the battalion transport.

Rifles! Hundreds of them!

For Hugh Fitzmullen-Brophy and the 11th Royal Munster Fusiliers, although it was only September, Christmas had come at last.

38

We must accustom ourselves to the thought of arms, to the sight of arms, to the use of arms.

—P.H. Pearse, 'The Coming Revolution'

The delivery of the rifles was no small thing. It wasn't like rolling up to the post office and signing for a crate of chickens. The army could be quite punctilious when it came to the transfer of weapons, so there was security to be considered alongside the military formalities. More than that, there was a ceremonial element to the proceedings that needed to be honoured. Taking receipt of government weapons was a rite of passage. The battalion had been running around with toy guns long enough. Today they would be putting on long trousers. This was why the trip to the station had turned into something of a procession.

A wagon was obviously needed to carry the cargo, and an officer of sufficient responsibility should be at hand to make sure that all was correct. In this case that meant Major de Roche, and no one would suggest that Major de Roche should ride in the seat of a common wagon. So, Curran's motor car was once again pressed into battalion service. Wyndham was still apprehensive about Curran's driving, but he fancied an excursion to town to get a haircut, and de Roche had no objection. An extra officer in his entourage was in keeping with de Roche's dignity.

Then there was the escort. A dozen smart men would accompany the wagon there and back. Their smartness was all-important. Fitzmullen-Brophy would boast the quality of any of his men against any other regiment in the kingdom, but it was a regretful truth that their appearance was not precisely the thing.

When there was nothing to hold personal equipment together except string, Fitzmullen-Brophy made sure that it was quite the best string, worn in a neat and soldierly manner. But it was still only string. Twelve full sets of webbing gear could, however, be assembled for Monday's ceremony of the rifles, and the men to whom this gear was assigned had spent all of Sunday night busy with Blanco and Brasso. The canvas weave was made glassy-smooth and the brass fittings might almost have been gilded. Wadded cardboard squared off the otherwise shapeless pouches. Men sat up through the late-summer evening putting a high gloss on their boots, while their good trousers lay sandwiched between boards, the creases soaped to keep them sharp.

It was an eight-mile march to the station at Mitchelstown, but with little to keep them occupied these last months except route marching and cross-country runs, eight miles wasn't a bother to them. The only load they'd be shouldering would be the battalion's few precious Lee-Metfords. These prized possessions were obsolete and had no available ammunition, but they were government issue and uniform in appearance. The men carrying them would do the battalion proud.

'Rifles, short, magazine, Lee-Enfield, point three-oh-three inches, Huns for the shooting of, two hundred and fifty. Ammunition, ball, ten thousand rounds. Sign here, sir.'

De Roche didn't care for the flippancy of this young officer with the clipboard, but he did seem to have managed to get his work done without losing anything or keeping them all waiting. The escort had arrived on time and in good order. Neither Wyndham nor Curran had shown themselves up with unmilitary behaviour. Linehan and Clark, the two transport men, seemed competent to handle the loading of the wagon by themselves. All in all, things were proceeding without a hitch. Just get this little lot home and unpacked and the battalion could perhaps get down to some proper training. At least they'd look more the part, and no longer be burdened with that ridiculous miscellany of shotguns, rook rifles and relics of the Zulu War, not to mention all those shameful wooden props.

He checked his watch against the station clock, annoyed at the four-minute discrepancy. He'd set his watch by the clock in the mess, which was set from the hotel manager's watch, which was roughly synchronised with the angelus bells. And now he had no guarantee that the railways of rural Ireland were scrupulous in their timekeeping. That was the trouble with Ireland. No proper appreciation of punctuality.

'Gentlemen,' he said to Wyndham and Curran. 'We shall see the wagon and escort on their way. Then I hope you will do me the honour of joining me for lunch.'

Lunch with Major de Roche was naturally not a boozy, matey celebration, but there was something to celebrate nonetheless. Wyndham in particular was well pleased. A duty had been performed efficiently, the battalion was elevated in status, and he himself was looking very fine. It wasn't just the haircut. He'd been given leave some while back to go and be fitted for a new uniform, which had recently arrived. He'd thought to keep it aside for military high days and holy days, but de Roche had insisted that he be properly dressed for this public appearance. So here he was, a vision in tailored khaki and russet leather, perfectly happy to be bored by de Roche's conversation. Who knows, he thought. With his horizons broadening all the time, perhaps he too might someday move in the polite society of County Mayo or the Punjab, and so should know what's what.

Curran seemed less at ease, and de Roche noticed.

'I say, Curran – do please attend.'

Curran, who'd been looking at a pair of men outside in the street, and turning his head ever more to follow them, whipped his attention back to de Roche. 'I do beg your pardon, Major.

You were saying what a pity it is that we're unlikely to get any polo in at camp. I agree entirely, of course. Such a pity, yes. Forgive me – I was distracted by someone I recognised.'

His lips pursed, de Roche looked out the window. 'That fellow in the brown suit?' he asked, clearly disapproving of the man's attire.

'The man next to him, as a matter of fact. I was at one time briefly acquainted with him in my professional capacity.'

De Roche did not care for officers having had any professional capacity outside the army. Curran was a gentleman, and had practised a gentlemanly profession, but still. He was an army officer now, and one should put lesser things behind one, particularly when one has been obliged in the past to associate with characters such as those who'd just passed their window. Fellow looked like a commercial traveller of some sort or, given Curran's profession, might even have been a member of the criminal classes. Clearly the wrong sort, either way. He consulted his watch.

'I think perhaps it is time we were getting on, gentlemen.'

The wagon and escort should by now have been halfway home, and it was intended that the officers should overtake them and then lead the way back to camp – low-key, but triumphant all the same.

After their march to town the escort had been rested and fed, and treated to absolutely no more than one pint of beer apiece, and they were still going strong and keeping their heads up when the officers caught up to them. The new-made corporal who'd been put in charge of them was looking anxious though. As well he might. The wagon, driven by Linehan and Clark and carrying the pride and hope of the regiment, was nowhere to be seen.

'Whatever do you mean, "gone"?' snapped de Roche.

'They just speeded up, like, sir. I thought they might be having a joke on us or something, but they just speeded up and wouldn't slow down.'

'And where did this happen, Corporal?'

'About two mile back, sir. We picked up the pace and that, thinking that maybe we'd catch them up, or maybe they'd stop and wait for us or something.'

And that was the truth. Hoping to find the wagon around every turn of the road, he'd had the men doubling along, with them getting shagged out and him getting frantic. His first independent command and he'd gone and lost a whole general service wagon and a load of rifles. Jesus, Mary and Joseph.

The officers were soon feeling the very same as they sped the rest of the way back to camp. Every bend in the road revealed nothing but hedgerows and an increasing sensation of nightmare. Was this even the right road? Was there a turn-off they'd missed? Was the wagon even now rolling into camp, with Linehan and Clark up in the seat wondering what had happened to everyone else?

But they were speeding past familiar landmarks now, and this had always been the only road, and the wagon was lost, and two hundred and fifty rifles and ten thousand rounds of ammunition had disappeared. Under their charge. Dear God.

When he heard the motor, Fitzmullen-Brophy hastened to the scene, eager to receive the War Office's bounty, and was taken aback to see de Roche, half rising from the front seat, looking rather pale and opening and closing his mouth like a landed fish. He never found out what de Roche had been trying to get out, because Curran was in there first, speaking at dealing-with-hecklers volume.

'Bit of trouble, I'm afraid, Colonel!' he shouted, manfully forcing the car into a three-point turn. 'Wagon's broken down!

Nothing to worry about! Rifles are safely locked up in town! Left the escort there guarding them! Just stopping by to let you know! Nothing to worry about!'

And drowning out Fitzmullen-Brophy's protests with a horrible grinding of gears, he was heading fast back the way they'd come.

De Roche, clinging to his seat and looking sick, stared disbelievingly at Curran.

'You lied to the colonel,' he said.

Either Curran didn't hear him or didn't care. As they sped back, de Roche reflected that Curran's lie was nothing he could do anything about just now and had at least bought them time. When they found the escort again, he had regained a measure of his self-possession and he took charge. The men were to pair off and beat the countryside, exploring every laneway and byroad, heading back in the general direction of the town where they were to rendezvous when it got dark. They were not – absolutely not – to speak to anyone of this matter.

Having set the search in motion, de Roche now faced the daunting business of informing higher authority, which meant the colonel, and probably higher than that, which meant disgrace. Curran, however, had other ideas.

He explained: 'I don't imagine the men will find anything. Linehan and Clark didn't get lost. They stole those rifles, and I'll wager they didn't do it without a careful plan and a few necessary accomplices.'

'What do you mean?' asked Wyndham. 'What's it all about? Do they think they can just sell a wagonload of army rifles like that?'

'Oh no. Not selling at all. I imagine they're planning on using them. Don't worry, old fellow. Not on us. At least not any time soon. But time, nevertheless, is of the essence.'

'Indeed, Curran,' interjected de Roche. 'But unless you have better ideas, I rather fear we must alert the colonel and also the police forthwith. A watch must be put on all roads and railway stations.'

'Not yet, sir. If I may hazard, those rifles won't be moved very far very soon. Too risky. No doubt we'll find parts of the wagon holding up the roof of some shed in due course, and those two horses will turn up for sale somewhere down the line, but those rifles will still be in their crates, cached somewhere no one is likely to find them.'

'What makes you think all that?'

'I rather hate to tell you this, Major, but I've done this sort of thing before.'

'You mean track down thieves, Curran?'

'I mean steal government arms, Major.'

39

We want recruits because we are able to arm them. In a rough way of speaking, we have succeeded already in placing a gun and ammunition therefore in the hands of every Irish Volunteer that has undertaken to endeavour to pay for them. We are in a position to do as much for every man that joins us.

—P.H. Pearse, 'Why We Want Recruits'

They left de Roche in town to coordinate the search and maintain the fiction told to Fitzmullen-Brophy. The time that Curran had said was of the essence had little to do with the pursuit of Linehan and Clark and much to do with how long the CO could plausibly be kept in the dark. De Roche appreciated this. The reputation of the 11th Munsters was of considerably more importance than the havoc that could be wreaked by modern firearms in the hands of revolutionaries. They left him with his conscience and his worries while Curran fired off a couple of urgent telegrams, before leaping into his car again and speeding himself and Wyndham away, back down the road they'd taken so much more peacefully on that Saturday drive all those weeks ago. It was late afternoon before they came to a stop in what Wyndham thought might have been Doneraile, but all these little towns blended into each other. He was pretty certain, though, that this was where they'd stopped for tea that time.

He sat in the car while Curran spoke, evidently at random, to a few people in the street. His demeanour suggested a tourist asking directions more than an officer of the crown investigating treasonous larceny. When Curran returned, he just said:

'Shouldn't take long.' And then, because silence wasn't his habit: 'The good thing about Ireland, you'll find, is that everybody knows everybody else. That's why those rifles are going to stay buried under stacks of turf for the time being. You can't move that amount of illicit goods without someone taking notice and word getting around. Do you know what happened in Dublin, July before last? About a week before the war broke out?'

Wyndham had been undergoing the purgative transformation of recruit training in Tralee at that time, and hadn't been keeping up with the newspapers. 'Remind me,' he said.

'We – the Irish Volunteers, that is – brought a cargo of rifles into Dublin. Landed them from a private yacht at Howth, just north of the city. Broad daylight. Everyone knew about it. The police were called out, the army was called out, the press was there. No secrecy at all. We only carried it off because half of Dublin was crowded all around us. Strap a rifle to the crossbar of your bicycle, throw your coat over it, and away you go. The authorities could hardly stop everyone in Dublin with a bicycle – especially not with the crowds taking the part of the Volunteers.'

'I remember hearing something about it now,' said Wyndham. 'There was shooting, wasn't there?'

'That's right. The Scots fired into the crowd on Bachelors Walk. Dreadful business. And they never did manage to get any of our rifles, although we did get some of theirs. Only a few mind, and it was entirely by the way. I fear I was rather exaggerating when I told de Roche about stealing government arms. I am, however, versed in transporting and concealing unlawfully obtained weapons. Out here in the country a damn great army wagon is too slow and too conspicuous. So is a fleet of shady individuals from out of town pushing bicycles with their coats wrapped around the crossbar. Ah! Here we are. The very man.' And Curran was off again to intercept a man walking by.

The polite tourist manner was absent this time. Now Curran

was a figure of brisk authority, not bullying, but not to be gainsaid either. The man he'd waylaid didn't seem anything but ordinary, although looking at him, Wyndham realised that he'd seen him before, and then the man had been wearing a green slouch hat. Wyndham couldn't hear what was being said, but it seemed to be a pattern of demand and refusal that ended at last with a curt nod of the head from the man who'd been resolutely shaking it up until now. That appeared to be enough for Curran, who returned to the car, looking satisfied that he'd got this far at least.

'That was that Volunteer officer, wasn't it?' said Wyndham. 'Does he know where the rifles are?'

'I very much doubt it, but as I say, everyone knows everyone else around here. He may not be bosom pals with renegades like Linehan and Clark, but he'll know all the Volunteers in the area. He's agreed to send word up the chain of command.'

'Good heavens! That's admirably public-spirited of him.'

'I did, I must confess, intimate that I might have the garrisons of Fermoy, Buttevant, and Kilworth tearing the neighbourhood apart if he proved less than cooperative. All he has to do is send a message to someone who'll send a message to someone else who will, I fervently hope, get in touch with someone we might speak with. We're to go back to Mitchelstown and wait.'

Waiting was something de Roche had been doing already, and it had been telling on his nerves. When he found out that Curran had been unable to conjure up the missing rifles by his little jaunt out the country, he was set on returning to camp and laying everything before Fitzmullen-Brophy. Accepting responsibility and displaying initiative were all very well in theory, but deceiving one's commanding officer to such an extent just wasn't on. Furthermore, he was dashed if he was going to keep on carrying the can for this ghastly affair. Before he left, he told Curran to continue with his harebrained intriguing among his nefarious political connections, and told them both to ensure that the escort, now assembled forlornly at the station, did not run amuck.

Just before the post office closed, Curran sent off another couple of telegrams. He also, by the force of his personality, the king's commission and a pound note, persuaded a clerk to stay unofficially on duty, with orders to keep the lines of secret communication open through the night.

After that they waited in the hotel bar until it closed, and after that they sat in the car as the town slept around them.

'It's at times like this that I wished I smoked,' said Curran. 'At times like these one sees the virtue in cigarettes. A cigar after dinner is fine, but it's part of dinner, and I always felt that the excessive smoking of cigars would have a detrimental effect on my voice, which for a man in my profession might prove disastrous. A cigarette on the other hand is a simpler thing, an unfussy thing. Have you ever noticed, Wyndham, that a man who is smoking a cigarette doesn't fidget? He merely sits or stands, inhaling and exhaling. His breathing is regulated, and his hands are occupied. He is at peace, yet all the while receiving the stimulating benefits of tobacco.'

'I think I know exactly what you mean, Curran. I was always intending to take up the habit for that very reason. Pretty much all the men smoke cigarettes. I remember when I first joined, Moriarty told me I'd start in no time, but I never quite managed it. The problem is that when you're really in need of something to perk you up and keep you calm at the same time, there just isn't the opportunity. Sentry duty at night, for instance. Smoking's forbidden. Obviously. Then there's the nuisance of keeping everything dry. That was what kept everyone complaining when we were at the front. Also, of course, like you and your voice, there was Major Fitzmullen-Brophy and his insistence that cigarettes were bad for a fellow's wind. Perhaps I'll follow his example and take up a pipe.' Then, after a short silence, he added: 'What do you think the colonel will do when he's been told about the rifles? Dear Lord. There's set to be the most unholy rumpus. He'll have the whole battalion out combing the countryside.'

'Yes. That's what I told them.'

'Told who?'

'The people I need to get in touch with. I said plainly that the whole province is likely to be under martial law by dawn if we don't get those rifles back. I say "plainly", but the truth is I had to be pretty circumspect, which even at a ha'penny a word still managed to come dear.'

'But just to be clear: do you really mean to tell me that you know who the culprits are – I mean beyond Linehan and Clark?'

'Oh no. But I'll warrant that I know people who do know, or at least I know people who can certainly find out, and they're the people who should be out beating the bushes and shaking the trees for us.'

'And these are the Volunteers, and not this Citizen Army that Linehan and Clark said they were in.'

'Almost certainly.'

'I'm afraid I'm being rather slow on the uptake, Curran, but aren't the Volunteers on our side? Or rather, if they're not quite on our side, haven't they agreed to, um, suspend hostilities for the duration of the war?'

'Well yes and no, old man.'

'But can't it just be a case of finding out who Linehan and Clark answer to and telling them to give us our rifles back?'

'Not as such, I fear. The Volunteer chain of command has become rather tangled by differing loyalties. It all depends on how the individual might interpret what defending Ireland really means. Even if I still had rank in the Volunteers – even if I had high rank – there'd be no certainty I could exercise complete control over every unit.'

'So?'

'So, I plan to make a great deal of noise and threaten to make much more noise in the hope that someone with useful authority sees reason. Reasonable or not, secret cabals don't care for noise. So here we sit, waiting for them to open negotiations.'

'I see. I think.'

Wyndham had an uncomfortable thought.

'So, these Volunteers – the ones who stole a load of army rifles.'

'Indeed?'

'And intend on using them in some sort of armed uprising?'

'Perhaps.'

'Well, it occurs to me that they're the sort of desperate fellows who might not care to listen to reason.'

'It's a possibility, alas.'

'But has it occurred to you that, seeing as they know you might cause trouble for them, and they know we're waiting out in the dark and everything...'

'Are you suggesting, dear fellow, that they might be about to have us assassinated?'

'No – no, of course not. It's just that... Well, yes, as a matter of fact. It's crossed my mind.'

'Nonsense, man. We're perfectly safe. That sort of thing doesn't go on – at least it doesn't go on anymore. I mean to say. Really.'

'I'm sure I'm getting alarmed over nothing, Curran. Pay no attention. I do apologise.'

'Quite alright.'

They sat in uneasy silence, one or other of them striking a match from time to time to take a look at his watch.

They had a momentary alarm a while after midnight when a figure did appear out of the darkness, but it turned out to be a policeman, wondering why two army officers were sitting in a motor car in town in the middle of the night. Curran was all effusive charm and broad hints that important military business was afoot, with assurances that the good constable should not be troubled. Wyndham might have been imagining it, but he thought he heard Curran's accent become more noticeably Irish. It was still rounded and plummy, but there was less of the barrister and more of the country squire to it. Whatever it was, it did the trick.

After the policeman had said goodnight they sat, speaking quietly of this and that – anything to pass the time. Despite the chill, Wyndham fell asleep, and dreamed disturbing dreams of other nights spent out in the perilous open.

When he awoke it was first light, and he was stiff and mortally cold. Curran was snoring beside him. A curious dog was inspecting them, and a cart could be heard coming up the street from behind. Wyndham got up, clumsily, deciding that he needed somewhere discreet to relieve himself before the town woke up. He stood beside the car, working his muscles, taking in the scene and waiting for the cart to go past. He nodded to the driver. Just two men getting a head start on the day. Nothing out of the ordinary going on at all. The driver, who might have been delivering milk, nodded back and said: 'Mister Curran?'

Wyndham nodded, then shook his head and then, trying to speak, found that his teeth were chattering. The man looked at him unsympathetically. 'I'm told to tell you to be on the first train to Fermoy,' he said and, flicking the reins, he resolutely said no more. By the time Wyndham had shaken Curran awake it was clear that the man would not be coming back to exchange civilities.

40

'Eternity is not long enough nor Hell hot enough to punish such miscreants.'

—The Right Reverend Dr. David Moriarty, Bishop of Kerry, 1867

De Roche had no end of trouble in finding a means of getting back to camp. One might think that a person willing to help one of His Majesty's officers in distress would be more forthcoming, but it was nearly two hours before a good gentleman of the neighbourhood was happened upon who declared himself only too delighted to furnish de Roche with the loan of a horse. Had de Roche been willing to accept a bicycle or to hire a pony and trap then doubtless he'd have been on his way much earlier, but such modes of transport were out of the question. Just because they were the Munster Fusiliers was no excuse not to consider the tone of the regiment. Besides, de Roche had never ridden a bicycle before. It was bad enough for a field officer in uniform to be seen riding such a conveyance, but quite another thing entirely for the same officer to be seen falling off one. The Munsters might not have had the same cachet as the Connaught Rangers, but there was no need to make things worse. Especially on a day as bad as this one.

When Fitzmullen-Brophy was informed of the calamity he initially felt faint.

It had been an unsatisfactory day, a day of triumph postponed, with the dissatisfaction turning to worry with every hour the rifles failed to arrive. It really was something he should have seen to himself. It might be said that a commanding officer had no business overseeing such mundane business as equipment deliveries, but to that Fitzmullen-Brophy might retort that everything was a commanding officer's business. From what he'd understood from Curran's hastily shouted explanation the day before, it seemed that nothing was too much out of order, but that didn't keep him from suspecting that things had gone awry. Someone, perhaps, had *not been prepared*. That someone could have been any one of the officers and men tasked with the morning's work, but the sad fact was that anything that went wrong was ultimately the CO's fault.

And now here was de Roche laying open the whole disastrous affair, and Fitzmullen-Brophy had to absorb the enormity of mislaying his command's fighting capability.

It shook him, but, where a lesser man might break down and weep at his disgrace, the commanding officer of the 11th Munsters did not even sit down. He did grip the back of his chair hard, but he mastered himself while, in a voice that sounded distant in his own ears, he demanded that de Roche go over it all again. As he listened, Fitzmullen-Brophy dug out a map of the neighbourhood, and in short order he was calculating times and distances.

'No point in raising the alarm,' he said with unerring decision. 'Take all bally day to get men here, and even then they'd only make things worse. I believe Curran has the right of it in thinking that the thieves have gone to ground. If they see half the 47th Brigade preparing to comb the county they'll have those rifles vanished who knows where before we even get started.'

He didn't need to add the obvious – that raising the alarm would lead by short and inevitable steps to the battalion becoming a laughing stock and all their careers deservedly in tatters.

'No, de Roche. We must act now. Where a whole brigade will muddle, a few men with initiative on their side might have a fighting chance. Curran's scheme, whatever it might be, might bear fruit, but we mustn't sit idle hoping that it does. We must act now.'

'Of course, sir. Tell me what to do.'

Fitzmullen-Brophy's instinct was to hand-pick a band of resourceful men who would sally forth in darkness and, with speed and guile, locate what had been stolen, get the better of the thieves, and return in victory in time for breakfast. He reckoned that, half trained or not, he could find plenty of stout-hearted lads who'd be eager for such an escapade. Even armed with sticks, these countrymen in their own country would be just the ticket, like the Pathan tribesmen recruited on the Northwest Frontier to fight other Pathan tribesmen. He had a moment's sad reflection that in the country up by the Afghan border the custom was for soldiers to sleep securely tied to their rifles. It was a custom he might seriously think of instituting if they ever got out of this pickle. Meanwhile, though, he had to admit that even the best men he had would only be blundering through the dark if he couldn't first locate the missing rifles. That meant scouting. He considered the officers under his command. Good men. Fine men all. But…

'I'll go myself. Nothing else for it. You are to remain here in readiness.'

'Very good, sir.' Although, of course, there was nothing very good about any of this – not least allowing an elderly colonel with a bad hip to go wandering alone at night in search of desperate and heavily armed thieves. 'But surely, sir, you won't be going alone?'

Fitzmullen-Brophy was thinking hard. 'No,' he said. 'Find Moriarty.'

41

I have often been asked why we exposed ourselves to such danger? My answer has always been that there was a charm in the open-air life of a scout from which one cannot free himself after he has once come under its spell. Give me the man who has been raised among the great things of Nature; he cultivates truth, independence, and self-reliance.

—Robert Baden-Powell, *Scouting for Boys*

Moriarty wasn't just a regular soldier. Moriarty was an Old Contemptible. He and Fitzmullen-Brophy had held the line together in Flanders. Since he'd been salvaged from that pub in Tralee he hadn't quite been restored to military vigour and rectitude, but he had been nowhere as bad as the sergeant-major in Ballymullen had warned either. Well, now was the time to put him to the test properly. Tonight, he could show whomever gave him those corporal's stripes that he was worthy of them.

And that was how, as midnight approached, Fitzmullen-Brophy on the horse that the government had bestowed on him to befit his rank, and Moriarty on a bicycle commandeered from the owner of the hotel, came to be riding down a country road to foil an Irish uprising and save the honour of the regiment. Some way behind them, marching under the command of the young Captain Doyle, came a dozen men, prepared to use their dummy rifles as cudgels, but having no idea what they were about or why.

Fitzmullen-Brophy had never been comfortable on horseback. He had never found a horse in all his life that matched his temper. They were always too obstinate or too skittish. This one he had once tried to swap with the 9th Leinsters for a dozen coke stoves, but he was grateful now that the deal had fallen through, even if this ride would give his hip the very devil. He couldn't have stayed in camp. People thought him fidgety, but they misjudged him. Inaction galled him, that was all. He absolutely could not sit still when there was work to be done. Now, for all that the theft of the rifles was a disaster that could destroy his command and ruin his career, it felt good to be doing something about it. He'd been too long behind a desk. Now he was back in action.

Speed and surprise were the order of the day. Ground was to be covered expeditiously. The enemy must be sought out and taken unawares. His wound might be giving him gyp, but he was still a man of action. The threatened infirmities of the body were as nothing to his years of experience and his hunter's instinct. As much could be said about Moriarty, devil a doubt.

'You were in Burma, Moriarty?'

Moriarty wasn't used to cycling, and was annoyed with having to keep pace with the colonel's horse.

'I was, sir. Nearly five years. Up Shwebo way.'

'So was I. So was I. Thirty years ago, mind, but I imagine the country's pretty much the same. Wild country. Wild people, too.'

'I suppose so, sir.' Moriarty wobbled the handlebars from side to side to keep his balance. He was in no humour for old soldiers' reminiscences. He was in no humour for any of this. The colonel had put him in the picture regarding what tonight was all about, and it was no good reason at all to be keeping a man from his bed. The last time he'd followed old FitzEm, nearly all of them had been killed, and there'd been almost a whole company of them. Now they were off hunting Fenians in the dark and there was just the two of them. Madness.

The Huns were an enemy you could get the measure of. They were the ones over in the opposite trenches who wore grey uniforms. And you had a rifle and all your mates had rifles, and there was artillery somewhere to the rear of you. None of that had seemed comforting at the time, but Moriarty was beginning to see it differently now, out here in the dark, with no one but this old man who was too clueless to be scared, and somewhere a gang of bastards who thought nothing of waltzing off with a wagonload of army property. And just because the old fool had been sniped at by dacoits back in Burma, back when God was in short pants, didn't mean that they were safe from getting murdered on this dark road.

Madness altogether.

What were they expecting to find anyway? Would Linehan have thrown away his cap so that it hung on a bush to mark where they'd turned off the road? Would Clark have left a handy trail of cartridges for them to follow?

Fitzmullen-Brophy had gazed hard at the map before they'd set out. There were several ways the fugitives could have gone, but his instinct favoured one little road that branched off to the south. They came to it now. It was nothing more than a boreen with grass growing up the middle, and no indication one way or another that it had seen any traffic that day, but indecisiveness would not serve their cause this night. Down this lane they turned, the ageing officer with the bad hip and the self-appointed corporal who was afraid of the dark.

The bicycle, of course, had not come with a lamp. Scant moonlight shone down from a sky that was clearer than they'd any right to expect. They could make out where they were going, but the shadows were blacker than the inside of your hat. A slight turn nearly put Moriarty into the ditch, and when he righted himself he wasn't sure of his direction at all. There were trees overhanging this bit of road and only the sound of the colonel's horse put him right.

'Blacker than the Devil's back passage,' he muttered.

'Hush, man!'

'Beg your pardon, sir.'

'Be quiet, Moriarty. Do you hear that?'

There was nothing except the wind in the trees, but when Moriarty started moving again there came a drier, crisper rustling.

'There! Do you hear that?'

'Sorry, sir, but that's me. There's a bit of paper caught on my leg. I must have picked up off the hedge.'

There was a moment of thoughtful silence. Then: 'Show me.'

That was senior officers all over, getting distracted by something of no consequence at all and not believing your explanation until they'd wasted time by having a look at it themselves. Fools altogether.

Moriarty pulled away the paper that had tangled around his shin and brought it to where he could just about make out the colonel. It seemed about the size of a sheet of newspaper but was the wrong type of paper – stiffer and somewhat waxy.

'It's plain old brown paper, sir.'

Fitzmullen-Brophy ignored Moriarty's rather surly tone and felt the paper between finger and thumb. He sniffed at it, then sat up straighter in the saddle, casting his eyes about the landscape. Moriarty couldn't tell, but the colonel had set his teeth in a humourless grin. The game, evidently, was afoot.

'Rifle oil, Moriarty. Rifle oil, if I'm any judge.'

Moriarty had a sniff himself. Maybe it was, he thought, but you might use that class of oil for all sorts of things. Did rifles come from the factory wrapped up in brown paper? He realised he had no idea. He did know, though, that just about every sort of parcel came in brown paper. Meat from the butcher's came in brown paper. Cake from your granny came in brown paper. The stuff wasn't exactly scarce. He peered at this scrap and didn't see the War Office's broad arrow on it. The colonel was grasping at straws.

'Go back to the main road. Find Captain Doyle. Make sure to

set him on the right road. Then get back here as fast as you can. I shall go on a bit and investigate further. Hurry, man! And for heaven's sake don't make any noise!'

'The colonel's found some brown paper, sir.'

'What on earth do you mean, Moriarty?'

'Paper, sir. Brown paper. He thinks it might be something to do with the missing wagon. *I* don't know. He wants you to hurry along.'

Moriarty's scepticism did not deter Captain Doyle. Marching down country roads in the middle of the night on the orders of one's commanding officer was just something one should be expected to do in the army. Having only the faintest idea why was just another part of the picture. All he'd been told for certain was that a GS wagon had gone missing and that potentially dangerous elements had been involved in its disappearance. Now, evidently, the colonel had a notion that it might have been found. Corporal Moriarty being less than enthusiastic about the scheme was neither here nor there. Moriarty was an odd one, but Doyle had been two years in the army and had known odder. He set his men in motion in the wake of the corporal who had been instantly lost to the night.

The ride back was bad on Moriarty's nerves, and things only got worse when he found he was lost. The stupid thing was that it was impossible to get lost. He'd been up this road once, back down it once, and here he was going up it again. There was no turning off anywhere. It wasn't a road you should be able to get lost on. But nothing was familiar about it. Every bush was the same as the next, every shadow as dark as the last. And then, when he was sure he'd come to the place where he'd left the colonel, the colonel wasn't there. He cycled on, becoming more uncertain with every turn of the wheels. His back was hunched and his shoulders began to ache with the tension. When he craned his neck to see what might be seen his neck felt naked. The reasonable part of him was saying that the colonel had just pushed on ahead, pretty much like he'd said, and the colonel being the colonel, and unable to leave anything alone, had most likely lost the run of himself and was either poking around where he shouldn't or following bits of windblown litter all the way to Tipperary. But the reasonable voice was being drowned out by the whimpering of a frantic animal – an animal that had crouched in trenches and huddled in holes while bullets cracked just overhead.

He nearly came off the bike when Fitzmullen-Brophy hissed at him from out of the dark.

'Moriarty! Do be quiet, man! Whatever kept you?'

Moriarty cursed quietly to himself as he fumbled his way towards the colonel. 'I've told Mister Doyle, sir. He'll be along in a bit.'

'Very well, but we can't wait for him. If it took you this long by bicycle, heaven knows how long it will take him by foot. And he'll be making an appalling racket. No. At the very least we must carry out a reconnaissance by ourselves before they're alerted to our presence.'

'Who'll be alerted, sir?'

'It might be nothing, but I'm dashed if we're taking any chances. Farmhouse. Just off to the left there. I'll cover the front. You have a nose round the back.'

'Me, sir?'

'Don't be a fool, Moriarty. Of course you. Here, take this.' And Moriarty felt a pistol thrust into his hand. 'Be careful with it. There's a gap in the hedge you should be able to get through. Go on, now. And be careful.'

Be careful. What Fitzmullen-Brophy called a hedge was what people in this part of the world tended to call a ditch, which meant a steep bank overgrown with whatever vegetation wasn't getting in the farmer's way. As a field boundary it was emphatic. To make a proper gap in it would take several strong men all day. The gap the colonel had spoken of was no more than a space between the hawthorn that grew thickly all over. As Moriarty scrambled up it on the third attempt, he found that a single strand of barbed wire had been laid across the top. He was lucky not to tear his hand on it, but the combination of earth and wire on this black night did nothing for his humour. As soon as he was across on the other side he pulled the colonel's pistol from his pocket and pointed it resolutely into the darkness. Any fucker who might come at him would find out how they'd held the line in Flanders.

It was the manic barking that alerted Fitzmullen-Brophy. He didn't care in the least to be stuck out here, but even if his hip weren't still troublesome, a commander's job was to command, which in this case meant establishing himself where he was. If he were to go creeping about on his own, then there'd be no one to tell Moriarty or Doyle what to do and the whole business would become a muddle in no time. So, he stayed in the shadows by the farm gate, his horse tethered some distance back, and watched and waited.

He was thinking how everyone was being so exasperatingly *slow* tonight, and wondering if Moriarty wasn't stopping for a smoke, or Doyle dawdling on the road, when the noise started.

The barking was followed in short order by a light appearing at a window and the sound of someone coming out the back door. Fitzmullen-Brophy came out from hiding. If an innocent farmer had been disturbed then he'd be needed to calm everything down. If, on the other hand, a nest of Fenian cut-throats had been surprised, then Moriarty had provided an excellent distraction and given Fitzmullen-Brophy the element of surprise.

He moved swiftly around the side of the farmhouse, aiming to approach the scene of the action from behind. The action, when it came into view, was lit by a paraffin lamp in the hand of a man whose other hand was wielding a stout stick while at the same time endeavouring to keep his trousers up.

'Come out!' he was shouting. 'Come out where I can see you, you dirty hoor you!'

Moriarty shouted back from the darkness, 'Get that fucking dog away from me! I'll kill it! I swear!'

'You touch that dog and I'll have the head off you! Come out!'

Fitzmullen-Brophy, not seeing anyone likely to rush to the farmer's aid with a Lee-Enfield .303, thought it time to step in.

'It's all right, Moriarty,' he called out and, to the farmer, 'It's all right.'

The man whipped around. 'Who's that?'

'The Army. Now please calm down. Everything's quite all right, I assure you.'

Clearly not reassured, the farmer brought up his stick, and voices were now adding to the clamour.

'Michael, what is it?'

'Da, what is it?

'*Do* put down that stick, my good man, and please keep your hands where I can see them.'

'Sir, if he doesn't get this dog off me I swear to Christ I'm going to shoot!'

It was a near thing, but matters settled down without violence being done. The vehicle on top of which Moriarty had taken refuge was a farm cart and not an army wagon. The weapon which the son of the house brought belatedly to his father's aid was no more than a kitchen knife. There wasn't so much as a shotgun in the place. By the time Doyle's men came up the farmer had left off his threats of legal action and the kettle was on the boil. Moriarty hadn't quite calmed down, but Fitzmullen-Brophy was at his beaming best, broadcasting geniality, along with a shilling for the boy with the kitchen knife, and a winking suggestion that he should come and look up the battalion when he was a few years older, what?

A few fields away, at another lonely house, the commotion hadn't been enough to wake anybody, and the men calling themselves Linehan and Clark slept easily through it, content at their good day's work.

42

Ireland armed will, at any rate, make a better bargain with the empire than Ireland unarmed.

—P.H. Pearse, 1913

There had been no time to wash or eat before catching the Fermoy train. Maybe that was deliberate, thought Wyndham. They'd been given no chance to do anything except follow the sole instruction they'd received. No time to communicate with the authorities. No time to plan.

And now Wyndham felt grimy, and he couldn't tell if the discomfort of his stomach was down to nervousness or to missing breakfast this morning after missing dinner last night. He and Curran had been each other's sole company for long enough that they had nothing left to say. Curran spent the journey with his hands steepled in front of his face, thinking. Wyndham looked out the window, although the Ireland on show was not the Ireland he'd come so far to see. Pleasant in its way, but too dull. Too cultivated.

A man stuck his head into their compartment. 'Excuse me, gentlemen. Do you see that little bit of a wood over yonder? Just beyond that there's a lane. Wait there. Oh yes, and would you ever mind explaining things to the engine driver? Thanks.'

And then he pulled the communication cord and was gone. The two officers were still sitting open-mouthed as the brakes screeched.

'Were you expecting something like this?' asked Wyndham, bracing himself as they came to a halt.

'Not as such. Come on, though. I'll take the conductor and you can deal with the driver.'

Wyndham alighted and made his way forward, trying quickly to assume the mantle of authority. By the time he reached the engine he was striding along exactly like one of His Majesty's officers about His Majesty's business. He returned the driver's glare of consternation with a peremptory wave.

'Carry on. Military business. No need to concern yourself, thank you. On you go!' and, unsure how long he could keep up the act, and perhaps a little alarmed at how exhilarating the abuse of power could be, he checked to see that Curran was following before striking off across the fields.

He pretended he couldn't hear the driver's questions and execrations as they went. He felt giddy. *I stopped a railroad train. And got away with it. Just like that. The only way to travel!* Their purposeful military stride wasn't enough. He wanted to skip. As they heard the train puffing away he tried to express his delight to Curran, but the older man was having none of it, and was vexed that this usually bookish and self-contained fellow could find fun in such unsuitable circumstances. Wyndham was chastened, and Curran's displeasure, after the uncomfortable night and the anxious hours, caused his joy to dissipate. They were hungry and over-tired, and were walking into God alone knew what, and there was nothing funny about it at all.

They found the lane where they'd been told it would be, and they waited like the man on the train had told them. They waited in silence. Enough time went by for them to doubt they were in the right place, and each walked a hundred yards or so along to see if there was anything to be seen, before returning to his companion with nothing more than a shake of the head. At last a man came along: a perfectly ordinary man that Wyndham would have had trouble picking out from a crowd.

'You're late,' he said to them.

Curran wasn't having this. 'We have followed your people's instructions to the letter, and without the least delay.'

'Well, you should have been here half an hour ago and half a mile farther along. Come on. You're to follow me.'

They followed him, and despite their cold welcome, they found him quite communicative – for an agent of a secret revolutionary organisation.

'They were wondering where to have the meeting,' he said. 'The Volunteer headquarters in the town would have been the most convenient for everybody, of course, but sure the captain wouldn't be holding with this class of activity at all. Himself and a fair few of the others are dead set against this sort of thing.'

'You mean stealing army rifles?'

'That kind of thing. Fecking cowards. They're quick to put on uniform and spout off about Ireland, but they're just as quick to start going on about the government keeping faith and Redmond's promises and all that crack.'

Curran nodded sagely. Wyndham gathered that the split in the Volunteer movement was being discussed.

'Anyway, even if those fellas were on our side we could hardly meet in the Volunteer Hall, could we? Sure, half the world would know about it before dinner time. There'd be some fellas who'd be wanting to take minutes of the meeting. Ah sure Christ.'

'So where are you taking us?' asked Curran.

'You'll see when we get there – or at least we will if you'll hurry along. Anyway, like I was saying, we were wondering. Like how were we supposed to get you out here without the whole world knowing about it? Someone suggested putting you in the back of the bread van, but there was no way of getting hold of the bread van, and besides, what would they be doing delivering bread out here at this hour of the day? It would cause talk, even more than having a pair of British officers coming along on a pony and trap.

'So anyway, we had the bright idea of just stopping the train. I say we had the idea, but actually 'twas the fella you're here to meet. That's the higher ranks for you. Making the bold decisions. Would you ever hurry along?'

Wyndham knew that he should be paying close attention to their route so that he could guide men back here when the time came, but there was nothing in the least remarkable about the surroundings. The lane was more hemmed in and overgrown than some, but it was just another country lane, and there were no landmarks visible. They made their way at last to a house that was equally undistinguished – tumbledown, isolated, perhaps not even inhabited in the usual run of things. There was another man waiting for them. He had a pistol in his hand.

'Did you search them?'

The first man, realising that something perhaps important had slipped his mind, quickly turned to survey Wyndham and Curran. Their belts, not as shiny as they should be this day, were devoid of weapons. 'I did. They're unarmed.'

'Grand so. Go out and keep watch.'

'Could I not have a cup of tea first?'

'Alright. Put the tea on and then you can keep watch. Gentlemen,' he turned to the officers, 'will you sit down?'

It was with such an air, thought Wyndham, that Napoleon might have greeted his vanquished foes in his tent.

There was no refreshment save tea, and nothing to do except wait as morning turned into afternoon. The man with the pistol was not talkative, and Wyndham and Curran were disinclined to talk to each other in his presence.

The silence was broken eventually by the return of the sentry. 'They're on their way,' he announced, and shortly after there was the sound of horse-drawn conveyance pulling up outside.

There was nothing about the three men who entered to mark them as members of any sort of armed force. True, the man who'd been in charge at the house did address one of the new arrivals as 'sir', but that was about it. There were no uniforms, no weapons, nothing to suggest that these three men were doing anything other than taking a drive to look at a piece of land that might be for sale.

'Curran,' said one of them.

'O'Keeffe,' nodded Curran, not deigning to rise from his kitchen chair, his arms folded. 'I saw you yesterday in town.'

'This is Martin,' said O'Keeffe, indicating the man who'd already been acknowledged as an officer by their keeper. 'There's no harm in you knowing who he is, just like there's no need to be telling you what might happen if you decide to get loose-lipped.'

Curran merely nodded, and looked at the third man. 'And I know you, too, I think. I saw you at Bodenstown last year. Your name…'

'Never mind my name.' That was all the third man had to say. He whipped the dust off one of the chairs and took a seat, seeming more of a spectator than a participant. All three men were of an age and all were dressed alike, but this man, Wyndham instinctively knew, was the one who mattered. Maybe more than that. Wyndham imagined, but imagined with a clear certainty, that this man in his nondescript suit, with his deep-shadowed eyes set in a still-young face, could watch the blood pool beneath the guillotine and think that it was not yet enough.

They got down to business around the kitchen table, Martin standing for want of enough chairs and the man with the pistol, who'd possessed so much authority such a short time before, sent outside.

'So,' began O'Keeffe. '*Lieutenant* Curran.'

Curran gave a dignified shrug.

'A British officer,' said O'Keeffe.

'An officer of the Munster Fusiliers. Of the Irish Division.'

'Indeed. But does that make you an Irishman still, Lieutenant? You know about the monument to the Dublin Fusiliers at St.

Stephen's Green, don't you? You know what they call it.'

'Traitor's Gate.'

O'Keeffe smiled. Curran didn't.

'You're on the wrong side, Curran. Just as Redmond's on the wrong side.'

'It's a just war, O'Keeffe. It's a necessary war. Ireland must play her part. It is how our independence can be assured – can be justified.'

'So you said at Mitchelstown a few months ago, I gather, but I don't care to argue politics with you, and I don't imagine that's why you're here either.'

'No. We both know that you have to give us back those rifles.'

'Is that indeed the case?'

'Would you have come out here if it were not? You know that the Volunteers will be hounded to the point where they'll turn you in themselves. You know that the country will be turned upside down in the search for those rifles, and not only will they be found, but so will every one of your secrets be uncovered.'

'Do you know, since yesterday your gallant colonel has been trying to turn the country – or at least the parish – upside down. So far he's uncovered nothing at all and done no more than sour the plain people against the British army even more.'

'Nevertheless, you have overreached. You must return those rifles.'

And then the third man, apart from the group with his back to the wall, spoke up. 'You've made your threats, Mr. Curran. Now what can you offer us?'

Curran looked at the three revolutionaries in silence for a moment, and then asked Wyndham if he would mind waiting outside.

There was no one to talk to except the man with the pistol and Wyndham knew it would be improper to engage him in polite chit-chat. Also, the arrival of the three men now inside with Curran had stripped this man of his authority, so what might earlier have passed for a disdainful reserve now looked more of a sulk.

Wyndham stood looking at nothing, reflecting with satisfaction that the army had instilled in him the most useful ability to stand still and keep his mouth shut for prolonged periods. He was curious to know the time, but he decided that to show any curiosity or concern was a sign of weakness. Let the other man look at his watch first. That would be a point to Wyndham. Better yet, let the man ask Wyndham the time. Two points. Or perhaps three. If the man fidgeted at all that would obviously be one point. Wyndham only had to hold his own and the game was his.

Time went by, with only the suggestion of murmured voices from inside. Wyndham was feeling a slight itch in his nose and wondering if he'd be sacrificing a point by addressing it with his handkerchief, when Martin stuck his head round the door.

'Where's Fahy?'

'He's up the road a bit. Keeping watch.'

'Tell him he's wanted. I'll stay here.'

Wyndham smiled at Martin, forgetting for a moment the conspiracy behind closed doors and pleased only that he'd won his little game. Martin didn't care to be smiled at.

'Would you be one of those who thinks we're all only play-acting, then?'

'Oh no – no, of course not.'

'You're not an Irishman, are you?'

'Ah – no.'

Martin snorted dismissively. 'You'll be taking us seriously soon enough.'

Fahy, the talkative fellow who'd escorted them here in the morning, reappeared, was sent inside, and came out again shortly, pushing a piece of paper into his coat pocket and seeking out his bicycle from somewhere round back. As he was departing, the other men came out. Curran nodded at Wyndham, but no one said anything.

A small two-wheeled carriage, which Wyndham had learned was known as an outside car, was brought for the three men, who mounted with barely a word and departed. The man with the pistol directed the two officers up the lane, with vague directions as to where they should go after that. Apparently, they could find their own way home.

'So, what happened?' asked Wyndham, when they found themselves alone. 'Do we get what we came for?'

'I believe so. I hope so, at any rate. I confess I feel it would amount to bad luck to say with confidence that it will all turn out well. I'll tell you as much as I may when we see how events transpire. Until then, I hope you'll forgive me for keeping you in the dark a little longer.'

'I see.'

'It's just that one never knows with men such as those.'

'Men such as those? But they're your men. You were a Volunteer officer, weren't you?'

'Indeed, but as I said, there are two kinds of Volunteer nowadays. That man O'Keeffe is very much one of the other kind. And his companion – well I'm afraid he's something of a different stripe altogether.'

'How do you mean?'

'Irish Republican Brotherhood, or I'll eat my hat. Dan, my old darling, you can now boast that you have met a real live Fenian.'

Fitzmullen-Brophy was still out questing, worrying himself into a state of distraction and running his men ragged. He had them paired off now, wandering far and wide, not quite knowing what they were looking for or why, sticking their noses into every likely corner. When asked, they might answer that they were hunting Fenians or fairies or German spies. At the start it had been a novelty, but they were all tired and hungry now, and were sick of the whole stupid business.

Back at the camp a boy on a bicycle rode up to the gate. He was perhaps twelve, and not quite big enough for the bike.

'Mister Fitzgibbon Murphy?' he asked the sentry, as if he didn't care one way or the other, but would like an answer soon because he had better things to be doing.

Although his army attestation form said he'd been born in 1895, the sentry was only seventeen and had spent the last few months being reminded of his utter lack of seniority. He knew he was better than the boy, but then he was obliged to stand here like a big eejit while the boy was free to cycle wherever the wind might take him. He asserted himself.

'Who?'

'Mister Fitzgibbon Murphy,' said the boy. 'I'm to give him something.'

'That's Fitzmullen-Brophy. And he's a lieutenant-colonel.'

'Yeah. So. I've got a letter for him.'

'He's not here. He's away.'

'So you can take it, so.'

'Wait there. I'll get the sergeant.'

'I'm not the telegram boy that has to wait for a reply. Take the fucking letter, you.'

'Don't you be using that kind of language! Give me the letter here.' He snatched it out of the boy's casual hand. The boy stayed where he was, half astride his tilted bicycle.

'What are you waiting for?' said the sentry.

'Give us a shilling.'

'Go on away. You're not the telegram boy, so you can't expect a tip.'

'A tanner so. Go on.'

'Go on away with you.'

'A fag so. Go on, you stingy bastard.'

'Fuck off out of it before I shoot you.'

The envelope the boy had handed over contained a short note and a helpful sketch map. De Roche was in the process of saddling up to find the colonel when Fitzmullen-Brophy rode in, a tired man on a tired horse. The note galvanised him, and he was off on the road again in an instant, riding de Roche's horse and having a squad of fresh men doubling along in his wake.

They found the wagon where they'd been told. The horses were gone but there it was, with a scruffy looking individual in attendance, smoking a cheap cigarette.

'Right,' he said, when the military came up. 'There she is. All yours. I'm off.'

'Stay where you are!' said Fitzmullen-Brophy.

'I will on my arse.'

'You're under arrest!'

'I am on my arse.' And, throwing down his fag butt, the man was through the hedge and away. Fitzmullen-Brophy was in no condition to follow, and his men arrived too late to see hide or hair of the man. It rankled, but at least they had the wagon. The cargo had been shifted about, but there were the crates, marked with the broad arrow. Fitzmullen-Brophy could have wept.

43

It requires a man of good judgment to select those rules that can never be relaxed, and for negligence of which men should always be punished, from the others that should not be enforced.

—Field-Marshal Lord Wolseley,
The Soldiers Pocket-book for Field Service, 1869

There was no heroes' welcome for Wyndham and Curran when they returned. They had left the morning of the day before, spruce and confident, to fetch rifles for the battalion. When they came back, tired and grubby and late, they came without the rifles, which had already been recovered by then. No one knew the whole story, and few enough even knew the half of it. There had been no intimation of perilous covert meetings or bargains struck with sinister men. All that anyone knew was that these two had had something to do with a wagon going missing, with two horses being stolen, with two men deserting, with the battalion's rifles going astray for a day and a half. Moreover, they'd been absent when it mattered, when everyone had been haring around the countryside. All that most knew was that the colonel could have done with Lieutenant Curran's fancy motor car when he was riding round all night and half the day, getting all in a lather, and now his hip was at him, poor man, so that the oul' fella could hardly walk.

The colonel's old wound was indeed troubling him after his time in the saddle, and although the crisis was now over, his temper had not recovered. He subjected Curran to a long private interview, from which Wyndham was glad to be excluded.

'Well, there's one good thing came out of that, at least,' said Curran when it was all over. Wyndham had been hanging around out of loyalty, not knowing what else to do.

'Which is?' he asked.

'The colonel has put me in charge of the armoury for the time being. I have been given to understand that a very dim view will be taken of me if I choose first to repair to the mess for a much-needed drink, followed by a bath and a change of clothes. No – to the armoury I must hie me, there to account for every rifle and every cartridge, and Lord have mercy on my soul if anything be found amiss.'

'And why, then, is that a good thing?'

'Because, my dear fellow, it makes it easier for me to hide the depredations of our nationalist friends.'

'What do you mean?'

'I mean that some of those crates are going to be empty of rifles.'

'Oh Lord.'

'Quite. I fear it was part of the arrangement I made with those men.'

'Ah.'

'Indeed. Did you, by any chance, get something to eat while the colonel's inquisition was in session? No? Shame, because you're coming with me. I'll need you to help.'

'What? Me? Really?'

'Who else? Don't worry – I have a plan. Of sorts.'

'Oh Lord.'

'*Nil desperandum*, Dan, old man. I'm sure we can have sandwiches sent over from the mess.'

There were sandwiches. There was also whiskey. Wyndham thought that addition a bit much. A glass after dinner was just the thing, but there was a whole bottle of the stuff, and no dinner for it to follow. He worried that Curran had perhaps been pushed over the edge of recklessness, but was glad to see that the man was all business, and didn't even notice the whiskey, let alone partake.

The armoury, like everything else in the camp that wasn't a tent, was a tin hut. Sergeant Rafferty had made it his own, because it gave him importance and a cushy job out of the rain. Seeing as the battalion's weaponry hadn't amounted to much at all up until now, he was able to take his ease and exercise his tyranny in equal measure. When occasion demanded, he would rise from his ease and grudgingly issue an obsolete rifle without ammunition as if the fate of the kingdom hung on its safe return. The borrower – whether officer or man – was invariably treated like some heedless truant who couldn't be trusted with a sack of turnips and never mind His Majesty's property.

Now he sat himself in a corner while Wyndham and Curran took charge of the inventory. He didn't offer his help, and Curran was perfectly happy that it should be so.

They hefted each crate onto the table and levered off the lid before marking the contents off on a clipboard. Moriarty would have been interested to know that the rifles were indeed individually wrapped in waxed brown paper. One of the crates contained the paper even though there were no rifles. The paper made up a few unhandy parcels of sods and stones roughly approximating the weight of ten Lee-Enfields. Wyndham, even though he'd been warned, stood aghast for a moment, but without hesitation Curran counted off ten imaginary rifles and routinely wrote down the information. Rafferty, sitting in his corner, had noticed nothing. Wyndham tonelessly concurred the count of ten rifles, shocked that so gentlemanly a fellow as Curran – an officer of the crown and an officer of the court no less – could so blithely commit a falsehood. Wyndham's faith in the justice system of the United Kingdom was severely rattled.

There was one other crate also packed with rubbish, and that meant that twenty new rifles were now in the hands of some secret society sworn to overthrow the government. Wyndham thought about what those rifles could do. He'd seen them in the hands of experts. Fifteen aimed rounds in a minute. Fifteen rounds at a man-sized target at two hundred yards, and the men he'd known in Flanders would have scorned anyone who could do no better. Wyndham had heard of the German dead piled up at Mons. He'd seen them fall at Armentières, as fingers tightened on triggers and thumbs pushed fresh charger clips into the magazines.

Over and over again.

Ten rounds. Rapid, independent. *Fire*.

The Volunteers, or the Fenians, or whoever, would surely not have the same standards of training (but then he thought of Linehan and Clark, and however many other deserters from the army there might be out there). But training or no, a bullet fired by a novice could be every bit as deadly as one aimed by a marksman. He couldn't be sure, but Wyndham suspected that there was a German NCO at St. Yvon who could testify to as much.

It was getting late, and Rafferty was getting more and more sour. He had suggested that he might be let go about his business – as if he had any business – but Curran had insisted that he stay, even though he gave him nothing to do until the long pantomime with the crates was finished. Then, just as Rafferty was beginning to stir himself hopefully, Curran announced that inventory should be taken of everything else in the armoury.

'If the job is to be done, it must be done thoroughly, Sergeant.'

And so every Martini-Henry, Lee-Metford, rook rifle and sporting piece was roused out by a grudging Rafferty, who clearly felt that if the job was to be done, it could be done tomorrow. His uncooperative attitude evidently bore fruit for, after an hour of labour that served only to clutter up the front of the hut with miscellaneous firearms, Curran finally gave in to

Rafferty's protestation that everything had already been checked, and everything was in order, and that the accounts could be tallied in the morning.

'Very well, Sergeant,' said Curran, in the tone adopted by every junior officer as had ever been thwarted by an obdurate old sergeant. 'Tomorrow morning then. I can leave you to lock up, I trust?'

'Of course you can, sir. You know *I'm* not going to allow any rifles to be lost.'

Curran pretended not to hear that. He merely said, 'Just leave everything here as it is.' As if Rafferty would even dream of doing a hand's turn more at this hour of the night. As if there was some sort of system to the great jumble of old firearms stacked on and around the table.

Trying to look as if he was still in charge, Curran stood with his hands on his hips and surveyed the room. His eyes most certainly passed over the neglected bottle of whiskey but he said, 'Have we forgotten anything? No? Good. Be sure to lock up now, Sergeant. Come along, Wyndham.'

Outside, Wyndham said softly, 'You forgot the whiskey.'

'I did not.'

'Are you hoping that Rafferty might, perhaps, pilfer it?'

'That is indeed my hope.'

'I know he's an odious man, Curran, but entrapping him in a charge of drunkenness or theft – or whatever it is you're planning – is surely unbecoming of you.'

'It most assuredly would be if that were the case, but I fear we are playing for higher stakes. Something rather terrible is going to happen and someone will have to take the blame. Now would you rather it be Rafferty or Colonel Fitzmullen-Brophy?'

Wyndham had been following Curran almost blindly since this ghastly affair had begun. This was the first time he wanted to plead with the man. What had been comradeship was now looking like a devil's bargain. He was forestalled by the appearance of two sentries coming to guard the armoury.

'Good night to you, gentlemen,' said one of them, which was perfectly cordial, but not quite what the formality of standing guard demanded.

'For God's sake, be quiet!' said Curran. 'And stay out of sight! You're far too early! Give it another hour at least.'

'Another hour, Mr. Curran. Very good, sir,' came the easy reply.

'Why in the name of God did they send you?'

'Sure didn't we have the uniforms and don't we know our way round? Calm down. You're grand. No one'll know it's us. Good evening, Lieutenant Wyndham. A grand mild night.'

Wyndham peered at the man's shadowed face.

'Is it Linehan or Clark?' he said.

'You can call me Linehan, but it doesn't matter. We won't be seeing each other again, I imagine.'

And the two Dubliners, with shiny new rifles on their shoulders, disappeared into the dark, leaving Curran cursing under his breath and Wyndham feeling sick.

The armoury burned down later that night. It seemed that a paraffin lamp, left unattended, had overturned. The hut was utterly destroyed, but it wasn't a total disaster. Despite the long two days they'd endured, Lieutenants Wyndham and Curran were awake and quickly on the scene, and they made valiant efforts to save what they could. Although the older weapons that made up the armoury's original inventory were lost, only two crates of the new rifles were destroyed in the fire – all the rest being saved. For Colonel Fitzmullen-Brophy it was little enough to salve the bitter blow. Yes, more rifles could always be found in time. The factories were turning them out by the million. Less easy to replace was the lustre of the battalion's reputation. Rumours had already spread about the 11th Munsters creating disturbances by night in the neighbourhood. There was talk of illegal searches, of thefts, desertions, of a train being stopped, no less. Maybe all of that could have been smoothed over, but the fire in the armoury lit up too much that would be better hidden for Fitzmullen-Brophy's good.

When it was all over he found himself in his office, his hip smarting, staring at the paperwork that amounted to a confession.

Two draught horses missing; two transport men deserted; one drunken sergeant left in charge of the armoury; the armoury burned; twenty new rifles lost, along with however many older models. And who was in command of all this carelessness, for what else could it be called except carelessness?

As he wretchedly set about accounting to the army's higher authorities for his disgrace, he would have been appalled to know that the misfortunes of his command would shortly be matters for discussion in even higher circles than the offices of the quarter-master general.

44

In making these recommendations I am influenced by the conviction based upon my knowledge of Ireland and Irish ways, that you draw the teeth from elements of possible internal disturbances whenever you remove from Ireland all regular Irish regiments, all the Army Reserve, and all the Militia Regiments...

—Lord Wolseley, 1895

Curran had stood and watched the armoury being emptied. The weapons that he'd helpfully left piled on and around the table near the door were silently bundled up and passed in the darkness down a chain of men, through the perimeter hedge, and out of Curran's control. No doubt they'd been spirited away, strapped to bicycle crossbars with coats draped over them. Perhaps such subterfuge had hardly been necessary. Here, in the middle of the countryside in the middle of the night, a man might have cycled along the road weighed down with all the stolen weapons he could carry, and no one to see him.

Curran had stood and watched, an appalled Wyndham by his side, and he'd thought it a mercy that the men clearing out the armoury were taking their task seriously. If Linehan and Clark had been treating the matter lightly earlier, they'd been all business when needed. There'd been no jokes, no nervous laughter, not from anyone. It was a mercy.

And there'd been no shooting, thank God. Linehan and Clark had stood ready, but no one had intruded on them.

There'd been some muttering at the end about the new rifles

that had been stolen, recovered, and were now again, seemingly, going a-begging, but this was why Curran had been standing here all the while. The deal had been made, and if these men had thought to break it – well then perhaps there might have been shooting. Curran had brought his revolver.

The shadowy men had perhaps cast covetous glances at the new rifles, but perhaps it had been too big a load for them. They'd left the crates for Curran and Wyndham to rescue from the flames. They'd also left the flames as something that Curran could see to himself. They'd not wanted any alarm raised before they'd got well away.

So, Curran, angry and resolute, and Wyndham, dulled with disillusion, had dragged out the crated Lee-Enfields, and then Curran had scattered packing straw and paper about, and had deliberately knocked over the lamp, and when that had failed to ignite the kindling, he'd struck a match, and then a second one, and that one had done the trick.

And then they'd both stood outside and watched until the brightness was clearly visible through the seams in the corrugated iron shed, and only then had they raised the alarm.

Once the whole furor had calmed down Curran and Wyndham had at last returned to their quarters, where Curran had filled Wyndham with enough whiskey to put him to sleep. Then he'd sat down and, smoke-grimed and weary as he'd been, he'd written his letter.

My Dear Stephens,

No doubt it comes as a surprise that I, of all people, should be writing to you but, despite the strong words spoken during the election, I recognised you then for a forthright and honourable opponent. It is for that reason that I now write.
It has become evident that the battalion of the Royal

*Munster Fusiliers, in which I now hold a commission, is
being infiltrated by nationalist agitators. You might scoff at
my speaking against nationalism, but while you and I might
differ in our respective visions of Ireland, it is Ireland that we
both cherish and both serve. We opposed each other fairly
in the arena of parliamentary politics: we both know that
there is no place for the machinations of secret revolutionary
societies.*

*So, while I remain a staunch proponent of Irish Home
Rule, I am also an officer in His Majesty's Army, and in both
capacities it is my Duty to uphold the Rule of Law.*

*Thus far, two Fenian agents have been unmasked in the
battalion, and though they escaped before they could be
questioned, the apparent ease with which they were able to
desert suggests that they had worked their will upon their
more impressionable comrades.*

*Worse yet, a determined attempt was made on the battalion
armoury by these men and by what I must suppose were
members of the local Irish Volunteer unit. It was only through
the valiant efforts of Lieutenant Colonel Hugh Fitzmullen-
Brophy that a great quantity of weapons and ammunition was
kept from being taken. I would say more, but the situation is
still very much in flux.*

*I trust that you will not spread this tale among the press, but
as you have the ear of Sir James Craig and are now a man of
influence both in Dublin and Whitehall, I earnestly implore
you to aid me in putting a stop to this rot. The Irish regiments
are true, and will remain true so long as they are removed
from malign persuasion. What I propose, and that for which I
seek your help, is that the 11th Munster Fusiliers be removed
from Ireland forthwith. In England, they would be insulated
from subversion while their training is completed. In France,
in the fight for Britain, Ireland, and Empire, all seditious*

thoughts will have long been washed away.
In this matter the causes of Union and Home Rule are one.
I put my trust in you, and I remain,
Your humble and obedient servant,
Bartholomew Curran, 2nd Lieutenant, Royal Munster Fusiliers

Another letter, of similar content but different flavour, was to be written to a mischievous Home Rule MP, and still another to a tame Dublin journalist of Curran's acquaintance, but these would wait until tomorrow.

McCarthy-Moore, who liked to rise early for a run around the camp, was always the first to see the morning papers. He was also the first officer to look beyond the sporting results, and one of the few to concern himself with political matters. Indeed, most were content to let McCarthy-Moore do their reading for them and then relay to them the more important news of the day. They did not care to be overly taxed at breakfast.

'I say,' he said. 'I believe this is about us. "Incident in North Cork", it says.

'Coverage of C Company's last-minute victory over the cooks and signallers in the battalion league, I imagine?'

McCarthy-Moore would never allow himself to be derailed by impertinence. He frowned at the speaker and rustled the newspaper to show that he was about to take back the floor. 'No. It seems to be about that unpleasantness the other day. Listen.'

In capable voice he read the article to the assembled officers, who were intrigued that the great outside world should have taken notice of them. When he was finished, they were unsure what to make of it.

'That doesn't sound much like us.'

'Got the colonel's name wrong for a start.'

'Bloody typical journalism.'

'Language, please,' said de Roche.

'And there's a letter, headed "Fenianism in the Army". By that fellow Stephens, no less.'

'And who's this Stephens?'

'Unionist MP. Curran stood against him in the last general election. Didn't you, Curran?'

Curran leaned back from his breakfast and looked at the ceiling. 'That I did. I confess I hadn't much of a hope, but it was a spirited contest nonetheless. I called him a shoneen and a Tory lickspittle, and he suggested that I was evidence that Saint Patrick hadn't banished quite all the snakes from Ireland. Good clean fun had by all.'

'Well, he's quite worked up now, it seems. "Fenianism in the Army". It has come to his attention through certain confidential channels that troops stationed here are under threat from agents of violent nationalism, and that these threats have manifested themselves in attacks on army camps and thefts of army property. Oh dear.'

'Oh dear?'

'He suggests that we are harbouring revolutionary elements in our ranks.'

'He must have heard about Wyndham's taste in books. He just didn't know that Finn MacCool commanded different Fenians altogether.'

It was a joke that aroused no laughter. Most of the officers just didn't get it, and the rest didn't think it very funny at all. Major de Roche fell into both categories. He did not care at all for the battalion to be mentioned in the papers, unless an officer happened to be marrying a lady of good family or had just performed creditably in a point-to-point.

'Gentleman,' he said, 'I must warn you that your conversation is straying perilously close to politics, and I'm afraid I must put a stop to it.'

Feeling as though they'd been caught singing dirty words to hymn tunes in church, the officers hurried to finish their breakfasts in silence before finding duties to occupy them elsewhere.

The next morning would not allow them to forget the cloud that hung over Knocknahanna. A nationalist member of parliament, eager for column inches and Unionist blood, published his riposte to the previous day's letter, in which he denounced his right honourable friend for denigrating the motives of southern Irish soldiery. In a nice piece of sophistry, the Home Ruler managed to convey that recruiting for the British Army and mobilising a nationalist militia were both good things, and any man who thought to disparage either was woefully lacking in patriotism.

The worst thing about this confused but stirring debate was that it mentioned the 11th Battalion of the Royal Munster Fusiliers by name. De Roche was scandalised. Fitzmullen-Brophy was distraught. After all they'd had to go through with heart-stopping alarms and midnight rides, this was just too much.

But it was really just the start of things or, looking at it another way, the end.

45

I am perfectly ready to admit that in the present condition of Ireland it would be impossible to recruit purely Irish regiments and leave them in their native districts.

—Sir Charles Dilke, *The British Army*, 1888

When Dublin sent someone, they sent Devereaux. Devereaux, who'd departed Knocknahanna as a major, returned as a full colonel, of all things.

'Acting rank merely, old boy,' he assured Fitzmullen-Brophy. 'Just a temporary appointment to keep me from getting tripped up by all the red tape. No need for fanfares'

But the old adventurer was so trim in the trappings of his new rank, and so assured in his authority, that it was obvious that he was used now to loftier heights, and breathed air more rarefied than that which sustained lesser men. Naturally, Fitzmullen-Brophy wished his erstwhile comrade all the success in the world, but it was a bit galling all the same, and made one wonder what was happening to the army if high staff appointments could be had just for the asking.

Tall and short, the two imperial veterans surveyed the ruins of the armoury, Devereaux poking the evidence with his stick, and the dog K making a bloody nuisance of itself as usual.

'It won't do, FitzEm. Won't do at all. Getting in the papers, what? Talk of Fenianism? Dublin is not pleased, I'm afraid to say.'

'It's wholly exaggerated, Foxy. No question about that. And except for a hut burned down there's no real harm done.'

'No? Then what about all the missing rifles?'

'But we got them all back. I grant you, a few were lost in the fire, but they were nearly all the old types.'

'But where's the evidence, eh? A few dozen rifles don't just turn to ashes, you know. Where are the barrels and the bits and pieces and whatnot? Look here, FitzEm, I know you want to sweep everything under the carpet, but I'm afraid it's not on. Gang of Fenians infiltrate the unit, try to make off with your rifles, you foil 'em, they try again, and this time the armoury burns down. That's the bare bones of it. Don't try to deny it. We have the good word of one of your own officers – and no I don't know who it is, and I wouldn't tell you if I did. You needn't worry. You come out of it most creditably.'

Fitzmullen-Brophy sputtered in his consternation. Dublin making enquiries; Devereaux promoted over his head; and now some frightful conspiracy uncovered – and all inside a quarter of an hour?

'But damn it all, Foxy,' was all he managed at short notice.

'The fact remains, FitzEm, that your battalion has been targeted by rebels, and that your camp is virtually under siege by Fenians, who are now armed with whatever they managed to get away with that night. Dublin is most concerned. I imagine that so will Whitehall be when they hear about it.'

'But. But.'

But there was no getting away from it. Fitzmullen-Brophy could hear the inevitability in Devereaux's voice.

'They're shutting you down, FitzEm.'

'But—'

'Oh, it's not that bad. They're sending you to England. Much healthier for all concerned. Better training facilities and not so many Fenians.'

Fitzmullen-Brophy, who had heard the axe whistling down on him, realised he would live a while longer.

'All of us?' he asked, his voice sounding faint in his own ears.

'The whole shooting match,' said Devereaux, happy to be imparting better news. 'You included. Oh, I imagine the battalion will be broken up and properly absorbed into 16th Division in due course, but we always knew that was likely to happen. It was never going to be anything more than a training command. Just not enough recruits. But not to worry, old man: it's still yours for the time being. Least I could do. Not much use being a staff-wallah if you can't look after your fellow Dirty Shirt in time of need, what?'

It didn't take long. In early October the 11th Royal Munster Fusiliers packed up and left. They had no idea if the army would be making further use of the camp, but they left it as neat and correct as possible. The good name of the regiment demanded it. To Curran, all that mattered was that they left. Other troops might move in, but that was not his concern, and nothing to do with the bargain he had struck in that deserted house near Fermoy. He had promised to remove a battalion of British troops from Ireland, and he was glad to keep his promise. He could not be sure what was coming, but he was content that his comrades and the good Irishmen in his care should have no part in it.

IV

ENGLAND

Go on drilling and make yourself efficient for the Work,
and then account yourselves as men...

—John Redmond, Woodenbridge, 20th September 1914

46

Irishmen might have the fighting, but not the privileges. The rough work of the service might be their portion; faithful before the enemy, they were not to be trusted at home.

—Colonel Sir Percy Herbert MP, June 1867

Ireland had never been a happy member of the United Kingdom, and this was reflected in the number of military stations built across the country in the century gone by. Even before the war, the army could be found almost anywhere, and the county the Munsters had just left had been positively alive with soldiers. So, given the profusion of garrisons in Cork (which were themselves mere shadows of the vast Curragh Camp in Kildare) and given the abundance of officers (sportsmanlike, impecunious, old-fashioned) who claimed Ireland as their own, it was sometimes easy to forget that the army was in fact British, and not Irish. But then all you had to do was look at Aldershot, and its satellite garrison towns, and the camps spread across the broad Salisbury Plain, and see it all in wartime, and you were in no doubt that you had found the army's true gravitational centre. It was the army's cradle, its school, its home.

It was a barrack square, much like any other barrack square, and Wyndham, having bruised his feet through recruit training in Tralee, saw nothing to excite his interest here. For Fitzmullen-Brophy it was different. He stopped to take it all in.

'Well, damme,' he said. 'Bless my soul.'

'Sir?'

'Why it's the very same, Dan. Can't imagine why it should

243

have changed, mind. Well, well, well.'

'You've been here before then, sir?'

'It's where I first joined the regiment, don't you know – oh – ever so long ago now. Still the very same though.'

Wyndham was pleased that the grey surroundings could evoke such happy recollections, and murmured something to that effect while Fitzmullen-Brophy gazed fondly at the landscape of his youth.

'There – right there. That's where they had me stand on my first night. Middle of the parade ground, and me in just my night-shirt and my busby. Lord!'

'Your nightshirt, sir?'

'And my busby. It was all something of a jape, you see. Welcoming me to the regiment and that sort of thing. I must confess I didn't think much of it at the time, mind. Felt rather put upon, if I'm honest. Frightfully cold, too. But they did it to all the young chaps. Did it to old Tummy Belcher when he arrived a while later. I felt rather sorry for him, of course, but at the same time I was jolly glad that they hadn't just been singling me out.'

He stared into the past. 'Poor old Tummy.'

Wyndham remembered Major Belcher as a well-fed sort whose discourse could be summarised as: the dogs, and how everything has gone to them.

'A fine officer, sir. A sad loss.'

'Thank you, my boy.' Fitzmullen-Brophy pulled himself together and they resumed their progress across the barrack square. 'God be with the days, Dan.'

'Sir?'

'God be with the days. You've never heard that said? It's what we Irish tend to say when we're being sentimental.' And he smilingly repeated the phrase in a passable stage-Irish accent.

Wyndham thought about it, and nodded. 'God be with them indeed, sir.'

'Of course, you can't bring them back. It's not just me getting long in the tooth or poor old Tummy getting killed. The old army's gone. The war's changing everything. Still: there's still the regiment, what? And still fine young chaps like yourself coming up, what?'

'Yes, sir.'

'But old traditions will be forgotten, alas.'

'A great pity, sir.'

Fitzmullen-Brophy laughed. 'I don't suppose anyone will make you stand out here in the middle of the night, what?'

Wyndham was content to reflect that he had never been issued with a busby, and moreover that his chosen night attire was pyjamas.

'God be with the days, sir,' he said.

'This place again,' said Moriarty, dumping his kitbag. As a corporal – if he was a corporal – he was entitled to a room of his own at one end of the barrack, but it wasn't a room: just a paltry partitioned-off space. Hardly what you'd call swank.

'You've been here before, Corporal.'

'I have. Long time ago now. Before I was shipped out east. Before you were born, practically. When you were running around in short pants anyway. Here, give us a smoke.'

'Is there anything you could be telling us, like?'

'I could be telling you to keep your mouth shut and do as you're told, but there'll be plenty to tell you that. Or maybe not. The army's gone to the dogs lately, but I'm telling you that there were some right terrors here once upon a time.'

'Is that right?'

'Desperate men. Fierce men altogether. Have you on jankers as soon as look at you. Especially you, Cronin.'

'Why me, Corporal? What did I do?'

'Look at the state of you. You're like something left out for

245

the binmen. In my young day they'd take the head off you for not polishing the soles of your boots. The soles of your boots! You young gobshites know nothing. There was a colour-sergeant here long-go, name of Weston. If Weston took one look at any of ye you'd have been locked in the spud hole for fourteen days, no question. And there was no crying to your mammies or writing to your MP in those days. Weston was a right bloody terror.'

'Are you telling us you were afraid of him, Corporal?' That was Finnerty, the cheeky bastard. 'A man like yourself?'

Wearily Moriarty pinched out his cigarette and stuck it behind his ear. Finnerty might have been the tallest man in the unit, but that was all the more reason to cut him down to size. Moriarty stepped up to him until he had to look right up the man's nose to make eye contact.

'I used to be like you, Finnerty. I used to be a big young eejit who thought he could give lip to non-commissioned officers. I thought I could get smart with a man like Colour-Sergeant Weston. I thought I could appear on parade with the soles of my boots unpolished.'

Finnerty looked down on Moriarty. 'Ah now, Corporal.'

'Ah now, Finnerty,' and he jabbed his forefinger into the man's chest. 'Colour-Sergeant Weston pokes me with his pace-stick. Like this, see? And he says, "There's shite at the end of this stick", see? And I say, "There's shite at both ends", see?'

Finnerty laughed – nervously, because he wasn't sure if this was that sort of joke.

'Fourteen days in the spud hole, Finnerty. Fourteen days he gave me, and nothing but bread and water.' The finger was still jabbing at Finnerty's chest, and it was beginning to hurt. 'Count yourself lucky, boy, that the army's not what it was. Count yourself lucky that I'm a mild man.'

If he had to bunk down with these men under the one roof, there was no point in letting them take liberties.

'Somebody give us another fag there.'

As he lay back on his cot and blew smoke toward the ceiling, he thought of Sergeant Weston who really had been a terror, and had once put the young Private Moriarty on a charge for losing a brush. Maybe the story with the pace-stick had really happened. He'd known an old soldier who swore it had happened to him. Then again, he'd heard other old soldiers telling the very same thing about other colour sergeants. Oh well. He'd been fined over that brush and that had been a right bloody nuisance because it had kept him skint for yet another week. In the end though, that hadn't been so bad, because instead of going on the town on Saturday he'd mooched around barracks and ended up in the garrison library. He wondered if that was still there. Grand place. Lots of peace and quiet. Maybe they still had *Pears' Encyclopaedia*. Grand read. Probably not, though. Army had gone to the dogs.

Fitzmullen-Brophy's Munsters were no longer being left to their own devices in a field a long way from town. They were more evidently part of a greater organisation now, even if it was still ramshackle in places. One sign that the age of unfettered improvisation was over was the assignment of a medical officer. This was a properly qualified gentleman with a university degree and a commission in the Royal Army Medical Corps, and that was a great relief to McCarthy-Moore. A full-blown typhus epidemic could break out now, or the whole of B Company could fall victim to an attack of Housemaid's Knee, and he wouldn't be sent scurrying to the pages of the *Field Service Pocketbook* in desperate search of a remedy. That handy War Office publication was sound on the principles of first aid, and most illuminating when it came to the diseases that preyed on horses, but it was perforce limited. There were some promising elixirs advertised in the 1914 edition of *Old Moore's Almanac*, a steadily diminishing copy of which could be found in the outside lavatory at Knocknahanna, but battalion funds were already strained. An actual physician was more than welcome.

The new MO was an Irishman – as were so many military doctors – and that comforted the battalion, and in contrast to McCarthy-Moore's energetic pursuit of the men's health through fresh air and cold water, his approach was more relaxed. He would attend to the sick list after breakfast, but the rest of any given day would find him in the mess, where he proved most amiable company. 'Dose them with purgatives, old boy,' he explained to McCarthy-Moore. 'The Number Nine pill, bestowed generously, unstoppers the genuine cases and discourages the malingerers. That's four fifths of army medicine.'

The remaining fifth, evidently, was venereal disease, which the army took rather more seriously than constipation. Thus, the MO was mandated to deliver a most alarming lecture, complete with graphic visual aids.

There was the expected mixture of revulsion and ribaldry. Once the shock had worn off, many of the better-brought-up young soldiers were scandalized at the implication of immodesty on their part. They didn't need to be told that England was an immoral country, but this was taking things too far. Other innocents were not so much outraged as intrigued. It wasn't that they actually intended to be corrupted, but it was interesting to learn how it might come about.

It had been hoped that things would be more efficient in England, but that was not always the case. Kitchener's new divisions were scrabbling for the necessaries of military life just as they had been in Ireland, only here there were more of them. The Irish formations had been better off than most with regard to organisation, having had first pick at the wealth of Ireland's over-sized peacetime military establishment, but the 11th Munsters had proved to be something of a neglected child – late in coming and slow to catch up. By the time they came to England, their parent formation was stocking up on everything available, preparatory to going to France, leaving Fitzmullen-Brophy's command to make a living for itself on the scraps and leavings.

Wyndham, as machine-gun officer, thought it time to exercise some initiative. Thus, when he discovered an armoury, he marched in in an officer-like manner and requested one and, if at all possible, two Vickers machine-guns, .303 calibre, please.

The ironmongery that had been the focus of his and his men's training thus far had been left behind in Knocknahanna. Major de Roche had insisted on it. He would have been mortified for the regiment to display such silliness in Hampshire, where other regiments might see them. So here, at what he took to be the fountain-head of the army's bounty, Wyndham thought to remedy matters. The storeman to whom he addressed himself was unimpressed.

'I am sorry, sir, but I cannot accommodate you.'

'This is the armoury? You have such things as Vickers guns?'

'Correct on both counts, sir. It is the armoury, but I'm afraid you can't just walk in off the street and expect us to issue equipment to you, sir. This isn't Fortnum and Mason, you know.'

'I don't think I care for your tone, Corporal.'

'Indeed, sir. If you would care to speak to my sergeant, I can fetch him for you. Sarn't Watson!'

A sergeant, calm and professional, appeared at the counter. 'Sir?' he asked.

'I would like two Vickers machine-guns please, Sergeant.'

'And you are, sir?'

'Machine-gun officer, 11th Munster Fusiliers.'

'In that case, Lieutenant, I am afraid we cannot accommodate you.'

'And why not?'

'In the first place, sir, this is not Selfridges. In the second place, there are no battalion machine-gun officers anymore.'

And it seemed there weren't. Overcoming his indignation, Wyndham listened as the two smooth NCOs told him all about how the machine-guns and their crews had been taken away from the line battalions and into the newly formed Machine-Gun Corps. Wyndham, it seemed, was out of a job.

'There are still battalion trench mortar units, I believe, sir, if that's any help,' said the armoury sergeant, although Wyndham doubted the man's engagement in his problem.

'Trench mortars,' said Wyndham, hoping to provoke a more helpful reply.

'Yes, sir,' interjected the corporal. 'Only we don't issue those either.'

Wyndham was given command of a platoon again. He didn't mind. Sergeant Rafferty was gone, and the men had been trained up well enough to keep him from making too big a fool of himself. Also, he wangled things so that Moriarty was one of his corporals. The man's waywardness made it so that none of the other officers wanted him, even if he was wise in the ways of pre-war standards.

The 10th (Irish) Division had been there before them, and the 16th (Irish) Division was quartered all around the district, so that the people of Hampshire were growing well used to hearing Irish accents, and even to being outnumbered in their own streets and public houses by Irish soldiery. Curran thought it most interesting.

'Interesting?' said Wyndham. 'How?'

They were sitting in a teashop, watching a party of Munsters strolling outside.

'Well, I don't suppose you saw much of the English papers before the war, but the more rabid ones rather gave the impression that the Irish were akin to savages, and that to allow them a measure of independence was dangerously irresponsible. Look at the editorial cartoons and you'll see the Irish as brutal yokels led by black-hearted assassins. At his best, Paddy is a jovial rogue, always spoiling for a fight. And now here is Paddy in his multitudes, swarming across England's green and pleasant land, and behaving himself very nicely indeed. I've even heard some of the locals say they prefer the Irish to some of the English troops – to Londoners, anyway.'

He gestured to the men who were milling about outside the post office.

'Look at them. They write home to their mothers and they even say their prayers at night. A better argument for Irish self-government than the English could have imagined. Not a Fenian dynamiter to be seen.'

But that had been in November. Next April it all changed.

47

Mighty were the deeds that were done upon that day at the ford by those two heroes, the champions of the west of Europe; by those two hands which in the north-west of the world were those that best bestowed bounty, and pay, and reward.

—A.H. Leahy, *Heroic Romances of Ireland*

The 16th (Irish) Division was sent to France in December, but Fitzmullen-Brophy's command stayed behind. A few recruits drifted in over the winter, but the battalion never reached anywhere near full strength, and because of that it remained unfairly far down in the queue for resources. Fitzmullen-Brophy was convinced that active service would be all the finishing that his men needed – that a whiff of gunsmoke would accomplish more in an instant than all this tedious training – but the spring came and lengthened, and still they languished in Hampshire, sometimes shuttled from one camp to another. They had come nearly three hundred miles closer to the war, but they may as well have stayed in Ireland for all the good it did them.

Such were his thoughts as he opened his post one morning. The letter from Susan could wait until he needed cheering up. The official-looking envelope could certainly wait until breakfast had done its fortifying work. The third letter was a harmless-looking handwritten missive, but he instantly wished he'd never opened it. It was an accusation from an anonymous Irishwoman (who signed herself 'a Mother') accusing him of vainglory and shameful irresponsibility in stealing away poor boys from Ireland and leading them to their deaths in Flanders. He seemed to remember the tone and the signature from a year or more before – even the looping blue handwriting was depressingly familiar – but why was this wretched woman writing again now? Why was she harping on, after such a long interval, about something done with in the first months of the war? And what on earth was this beastly nonsense about his unearned reward, bought with the blood of innocent Irish youth, no less? Dreadful.

The letter could go straight into the wastepaper basket, but the words were a wound to his heart that he knew would trouble him all day.

But it turned out not to be so. The official correspondence drove away all pain and doubt, replacing them with an astonishment and delight that positively bowled him over. He had been expecting something wearisome requiring him, in imperious tone, to furnish details of this, or account for that, when both this and that were largely unknown to him. Instead, he found himself reading the bare bones of an adventure story in which he himself was the hero. In spare prose the story unfolded of how on a certain day in November of 1914 Major Hugh Fitzmullen-Brophy had performed an exemplary service deserving of nothing less than the Distinguished Service Order.

'For conspicuous gallantry and devotion to duty when in command of a company. He repelled the enemy's attack, organised a counter-attack, and drove the enemy completely out of the menaced area. It was largely due to his courage, initiative and leadership that this important success was obtained.'

He read it again. And again. He fanned himself with the paper. He summoned his clerk to read it for him. When de Roche arrived on the scene to confirm the matter, he found his colonel almost prostrate in his chair, a look of tearful ecstasy on his face.

Fitzmullen-Brophy did get around to reading his wife's letter in due course, and found that it explained everything. Some retired senior officer with a soap box had been making loud noises and writing letters. This might have gone on unnoticed had it not been for the intervention of a Nationalist MP who raised complaints about the unfair neglect of worthy Irish officers. Fitzmullen-Brophy certainly remembered a few fusty old imperialists who had lauded his escapade, even while so many others had questioned or condemned it. For the life of him, though, he couldn't guess why a Home Ruler should trumpet his cause. Deuced odd, but there it was. Susan included the relevant newspaper clippings.

She appeared in person, and in a new hat some weeks later, so as to accompany her hero to London for his investiture. She was treated by the happy battalion with all the ceremony due to the colonel's lady, and more. Molly was not with her. Wyndham didn't know if that were a good or a bad thing for him, but he was gloomy all the same.

As it happened, the king had a chill on the day of the ceremony, so the award was bestowed by his uncle the Duke of Connaught. What matter? It was a grand day out, and an absolute pinnacle to Fitzmullen-Brophy's career.

The descent came almost immediately.

48

*In this supreme hour the Irish nation must, by its valour and
discipline and by the readiness of its children to sacrifice themselves
for the common good, prove itself worthy of the august destiny to
which it is called.*

—Provisional Government of the Irish Republic, Easter 1916

Easter was celebrated with all the ostentation that the Church of
Rome likes to show in the face of massed Protestants. Wyndham,
Church of England for the duration, missed the great spectacle,
but he knew all about it from artistic squabbles in the ranks.
Private Dineen, who regularly served at mass, and who pushed
himself to the fore in all religious observance, was to be upstaged
on this occasion. The bell he rang at the consecration was to be
replaced this time by a bugle sounding the General Salute, which
everyone thought right and proper, except Dineen, who did not
play the bugle. Moreover, he had a low opinion of the bugler's
devotion. The bugler did not say the rosary, or go to confession,
and he was often heard to take the Lord's name in vain. Private
Dineen, who had donned his white surplice and knelt through
many a cold morning from the earliest days in Knocknahanna,
did what he could to banish the sin of envy from his heart. But
that didn't mean that he was just going to hand over his duties to
the profane bugler with a clap on the back and best wishes.

The bugler complained to Wyndham about how he was being
unmercifully pestered by Dineen – morning, noon and night – all
through Holy Week, about how he should be doing his devotions,
and if he had to hear one more word out of that fucking Holy Joe

255

– begging your pardon, sir – he wouldn't be answerable for it.

Wyndham made peace by detailing the bugler for further practice somewhere out of the way, and wrote him a note excusing him the Stations of the Cross. Dineen, who could be trusted with money, was meanwhile sent off on a bicycle to investigate rumours of ducks' eggs for sale somewhere in the locality. The mess was eager to acquire anything in the way of luxuries for their own Easter dinner. Also, the Fitzmullen-Brophys would be back from London after the weekend, and deserved to be fêted in the finest style.

Sunday, when it came, proved a pleasant day in all respects. Spiritually cleansed and well fed, Wyndham spent the afternoon walking in the countryside, with a book in his pocket that he felt no need to open.

On Monday the weather stayed fair. The Munsters got back to their training. There were some comments about having to go to work on a bank holiday, but it was light-hearted grousing. Here in England the training was better organised and had clearer purpose. They had got used to the army's hardships, and found much to interest them in every new day.

In Dublin, armed insurrectionaries seized key points around the city and declared an Irish republic.

C Company had found that 'A Nation Once Again' was a fine song for route marches. It was perhaps for the best that when the good people of Basingstoke were yet again treated to it that day, they did not know that the green flag of revolution had been raised over Dublin's General Post Office, and that horses, and perhaps even men, of the 5th Lancers already lay dead among the broken glass of Sackville Street.

Over lunch the officers agreed that they might as well have the rest of the ducks' eggs now, because there really weren't enough to make a properly enjoyable feast for when the colonel got back.

A rebel assault on Dublin Castle was repulsed, but it had been a near-run thing.

On Tuesday, as the depot companies of the Royal Irish Regiment, the Royal Irish Rifles and the Royal Dublin Fusiliers moved in to engage the positions held by their countrymen, Lieutenant Colonel and Mrs. Fitzmullen-Brophy returned from London. The ribbon of the DSO looked very well beside the older medals for South Africa and India. Compliments and congratulations were universally and sincerely offered, but minds were elsewhere.

In late afternoon, as Susan Fitzmullen-Brophy wrapped her new hat in tissue paper, the guns of the Royal Artillery opened fire on the second city of the British Empire.

The Munsters were confined to camp. They never learned if this was for their own good, nor did they know from how high up the order had originated.

The mood was unsettled. Wrong was being done, but it was hard to say who was doing it. Ireland was striking for her freedom, but the 11th Munsters were stuck in England. The army was engaged in a desperate fight just across the sea, and the 11th Munsters were kept out of it. It was a bad week to be an Irishman in khaki. For some there was a feeling that if they'd only waited: if they'd only listened to their friends who'd scorned Redmond's appeal, who'd refused the king's shilling, then they wouldn't have had to wait long too long before they got their fight. They'd have got their fight, and it would have been in a grand cause, and they wouldn't have had to go through a year and a half of Brasso and Blanco, and saluting the bloody Union Jack. It was a bad week to be an Irishman in khaki.

The rebels surrendered on Saturday, but the next week was little better.

'Dreadful business.'

'Dreadful. Thank God the Munsters had nothing to do with it.'

'One advantage to our depot being in Tralee, I suppose. All the same, a dreadful affair.'

'Quite.'

All the time there was a constant prowl for news. It was too infrequent, too contradictory, too vague, and none of it was good. Wyndham, who had thought he'd gained a firm grip on the Irish Question, found added complications and confusions with every newspaper he read.

Talking politics in the mess was out, of course, and would have been particularly bad form in these fraught times, but it was safe to seek the wisdom of a level-headed brother officer like McCarthy-Moore.

'Who or what is Sinn Fein?' asked Wyndham, studying the front page.

'That's pronounced *Sinn Féin*, as a matter of fact. Gaelic, you know.'

'Sinn Fein. I see. So, what is it?'

'A political party dedicated to republicanism.'

'Fenians, you mean?'

'A semi-respectable mouthpiece for Fenianism, yes.'

'That makes things much clearer. Thank you.'

A week or so later, and dramatic news still coming from Dublin, Wyndham sought out Curran. Ever since Easter Week he'd been reluctant to talk to the man – particularly about this.

'You've seen the newspapers, I suppose?'

'Naturally. Dreadful business.'

Wyndham didn't want to ask what precisely it was that Curran found dreadful, afraid that it would differ too radically from the views prevalent among the other officers.

'So, you've seen this?' Wyndham held out one of the illustrated papers. It wasn't that he'd been concealing it, and he wouldn't have said he was being furtive, but in easier conscience he might have been put in mind of how he'd once passed on a packet of pornographic postcards to a comrade in France.

Curran didn't say anything about the fifteen grainy portraits reproduced on the page, but gave a tight-lipped nod. Wyndham didn't want it thought that he was making accusations, but he held the paper in front of Curran until Curran was more forthcoming.

'I knew Pearse,' he admitted at last, putting his finger on the blurred photograph. 'Not intimately, but I knew him. A remarkable man. One really couldn't be surprised at how he met his end. He, most of all. He always gave one the impression that he would embrace martyrdom.

'I met several of the others, too, of course. Briefly. From time to time. We all moved in the same circles. One saw the same faces whether it was at Volunteer manoeuvres or a play at the Abbey.'

Wyndham singled out one picture. 'How about him?'

'I really can't be sure. The extremists had their own little circles for the most part. I tried to stay clear.'

It wasn't an answer that satisfied Wyndham, but then he wasn't sure what he'd wanted from Curran. In private he stared at the little oval picture, hardly bigger than a thumbprint. A single photograph taken who knew how long ago, under who knew what circumstances, copied and miniaturised by whatever mechanical process and run off the printing press in the thousands – the subject might not have recognised himself in the end. But Wyndham looked at the deep-shadowed eyes of one of the fifteen executed men, and thought of the house near Fermoy and the man with whom Curran had haggled for stolen arms.

49

Then nodded, and kindly, as friend nods to friend,
'Old man, you fought well, but you lost in the end.'

—Rudyard Kipling, 'The Ballad of Boh Da Thone'

'That's it, FitzEm. It's all up.'

Fitzmullen-Brophy was glad – if glad was the word – that it was Devereaux who brought the news. Devereaux had come all the way from Dublin especially, which was pretty big of him seeing as he was a brigadier-general now.

'Your lot's off to France forthwith, or at least as close to forthwith as can be managed. The farther from Ireland the Irish troops are, the happier everyone will be. That doesn't include you, I'm afraid, but I'm sure you guessed as much. There isn't any bally battalion anymore. You never even had two full-strength companies to your name, and I don't imagine there'll be too many young Irishmen flocking to the colours for the time being. It's as I warned you: your men will be sent where they're needed. De Roche can take charge until a proper billet is found for them.'

He saw Fitzmullen-Brophy's mouth open in question.

'You're for home. I'll do what I can for you – don't fret. Least I can do for an old Dirty Shirt, what? Especially one who took me in when I was just a poor orphan myself. Another training command probably – if there are to be any more jolly old training commands. Don't fret. Damn fine business with your DSO. My congratulations. Stand you in good stead, that will.'

Fitzmullen-Brophy tried to get a word out, but couldn't get beyond, 'I say.'

'Have a drink, old boy. Make you feel better. Shan't join you, I'm afraid. Train due shortly. Must get up to London. Cheerio, old man, and good luck.'

Fitzmullen-Brophy did not have a drink. He wasn't the sort. Drink was for good fellowship or for dealing with sudden shock, and he refused to consider this a sudden shock. It was just the sort of misfortune that a soldier must accept. Nothing more. No good crawling into a bottle every time there's bad news. He was still in command, and for as long as he was in command there was work to do.

Except at just this moment there was nothing. No men to inspect. No papers to sign. Nothing to do but think.

He thought about his prospects, which were admittedly pretty dim. Of course, he could go home to Susan, but much as he adored the dear old thing, he'd been hoping for a few more years in harness. And it wasn't every day that a great war such as this came around.

He thought about some gossip doing the rounds a while back. About how a colonel had disgraced himself during the retreat from Mons and been cashiered. Instead of locking himself in a room with a bottle of whiskey and a revolver, the fellow had chosen the only other honourable route open to an officer and a gentleman. Word was that he'd enlisted in the French Foreign Legion, where he'd performed acts of gallantry until he'd redeemed himself. Hadn't let his age get in the way at any rate.

Fitzmullen-Brophy sat immobile behind his desk, his eyes unseeing, and thought about it. Giving it all up and starting again, under a different flag. He even imagined how he might dye his moustache with boot polish like poor old Maguire had tried. But he barely spoke a word of bally French, and the blasted dog had just that morning got at the boot polish and made the most fearful mess.

That brought him back to reality. He pulled himself together, and sent for de Roche so as to begin the formal sad business of abdication.

50

Not long before their departure for France Wyndham received a letter from Molly. There were some general remarks about domestic life in Kerry, but the gist of the letter was that she was doing her damnedest to resume her life in Dublin as soon as possible. It didn't seem to matter to her that not much of Dublin might be still standing, but if her father had lost his job she most certainly did not want to be in Tralee should he be coming home again. Anyway, she was *so* grateful for everything that Dear Daniel had done for Poor Daddy and did *so* hope that he would remain safe and well, and that everyone was positively certain that the war would be over this year, and she signed it with, 'All my love, Molly'.

All my love.

He had seen her at Christmas when he'd returned to Tralee on leave. There hadn't really been anywhere else to go. She had kissed him on the cheek when they'd met and again when they'd parted, and both times it had made him unutterably sad. He'd gone back to England early just to avoid meeting her fiancé, and had spent the rest of his leave as a tourist, moping about some of southern England's more eminent churches.

And now he was being sent back to the Great War. Now, when they might never meet again, she was breezily sending him all her love.

He smiled as he read it. A month ago – a week ago, even – he might have brooded over her letter, but now, seeing as he had a few minutes in hand, he was able to dash off a cheerful and off-handedly affectionate reply with hardly a qualm. Molly was a dear girl – a dear friend. He had been foolish to think anything more. He was wiser now. He had been warned for overseas, and that had stripped away all the fictions and illusions. Across the Channel the war was waiting for him, and the war cared nothing for callow infatuations. If he had to die, he was damned if he was going to get himself killed because of a supposed broken heart, and he was sure that his last thoughts would not be of Molly Fitzmullen-Brophy. She could send him all her love, but it meant little enough. The warning for overseas had confirmed him as a soldier, and as a soldier he would live and, if need be, die. Dear Molly. He didn't need her.

Oh – and he had fallen in love with someone else.

It had been wholly unexpected. Amidst all the hullabaloo of imminent embarkation there was the need for everyone to be inoculated against typhoid and whatever other fads were exercising the medical mind. No one was happy about it. Bullets were one thing, but needles were quite another. The officers had to stand by and make sure that everyone filed into the hospital tent, every man with his sleeve rolled up and grumbling fit to beat the band. It was really the job of the NCOs to act as overseers, but there was every chance that they'd have taken the opportunity to escape the injections themselves.

Wyndham had cajoled and shepherded his men through the ordeal, telling them that there was nothing at all to worry about. They came out, rubbing sore arms and giving him resentful looks, and then, with those sullen eyes upon him, he himself was obliged to pass through the canvas flap and submit to what would now doubtlessly be a rather blunt needle.

He remembered his time in hospital during the war's first winter. He was expecting some bored orderly in a stained apron, some veterinary's apprentice in khaki. Perhaps there were such characters in evidence. He didn't see them. What he saw was a frighteningly tall young woman whose frown turned to a scowl when she saw him.

'The last man told me he was the last,' she accused him. 'I was already clearing everything away.'

She had a marked Irish accent, and everything about her suggested that she was sick of it being mentioned by every soldier – English, Irish, Scots, or God knew what – who came shambling in the door. And if it wasn't her brogue it was her being tall. And what was a fine tall Irish lass doing here? Or what was a sweet young colleen doing amid all these rough men? And the officers were the worst for taking liberties. And if it wasn't palaver they were giving her, they were tongue-tied. This one was saying 'um' and goggling at her. He had to be told to sit down and take off his tunic.

Wyndham bared his arm and looked into her hard grey eyes. They were too much for him. He looked down instead, and had a moment to contemplate her feet, incongruous in tennis shoes, before something that felt like a cross between a knitting needle and a branding iron was rammed into his upper arm.

He nearly swooned.

'Well at least you didn't bawl out like some of them do,' she said, plying an alcohol swab. 'Go on now. Are you sure there's no more?'

He croaked something to satisfy her, and made his wobbly-legged way out.

She had springy red hair. You could tell that even though it was hidden under a headscarf.

He straightened himself and turned to have a last look at her. He felt immensely brave doing it.

Inevitable freckles spattered across broad cheekbones. Flaws on flawless skin.

She looked up from her work and her frown sharpened again.

'Did you forget something, Lieutenant?'

He shook his head a little, and smiled a little, and blushed deeply, and was gone.

'Jesus, Mr. Wyndham, are you all right? That ogre in there didn't spare you I see. Jesus, but she'd put the heart across you, sir!'

And the men laughed and swore, and said that they hoped the Germans might take more pity. Wyndham smiled along with them, but he wasn't really there. His arm hurt like fire, but that was nothing.

He'd had the heart put across him.

Committing himself to an approach on a hostile redhead took courage, and Wyndham had enough for that. But he needed a plan. It was Doyle who came, unintentionally, to his aid.

Captain Doyle's youthful carnality was well known in the mess, and he was forever skirting the prohibition on talk of ladies. At lunch, though, the talk was of inoculation, and of men using sore arms for an excuse to get out of duty, and Doyle used that to work in a reference to the latest object of his impure affections. It wasn't that he boasted of conquests or wanted to present himself as a man of the world; he just had something of a one-tracked mind. Also, he probably hoped that free and widespread discussion of all matters sexual might broaden his knowledge and thus his chances.

'I say, did you chaps notice that astonishing piece in the hospital tent?'

'The tall girl? You thought she was something?

'Oh, rather!'

'Hmm. Quite bad-tempered, I thought.'

'But didn't you think she looked a smasher?'

'I'm a happily married man, young fellow-me-lad, so she's all yours.'

Not, thought Wyndham darkly, *if I can help it*.

He spent a disturbed night, between erotic dreams of warrior maidens on the one hand and detailed plots to foil, and, if necessary, murder his company commander on the other. But Doyle's inability to keep his lusts to himself gave Wyndham the opening he needed.

In the anteroom before lunch Doyle was talking about her again – just happened to be talking about how he just happened to come across her.

Now, back in Cork Doyle had fixed upon a handsome woman who'd set his pulses racing by bicycling past the camp twice in the same week. Assiduous and indiscreet enquiry had eventually revealed her to be the wife of a neighbouring Church of Ireland clergyman, and thus out of bounds, and Doyle's single-minded attention to the affair had provoked a mixture of amusement and exasperation in the mess. So now, if Doyle said he just happened to run into a certain young female, it was odds-on that he'd spent all his time prowling about the hospital and its environs, likely badgering all and sundry for details of his prey. Wyndham didn't even have to guess. He'd straight-up asked the company sergeant-major where Doyle might have been found, and he hadn't asked just once either. Those games of stalking he'd learned from Baden-Powell's book were paying their dividends.

Doyle had rank and his family had land in County Meath, but Wyndham was older, more widely travelled, had a better moustache to his credit and had (possibly) shot a man in cold blood in the Ypres Salient. He saw no reason to back down.

On hearing his beloved spoken of lightly, a younger man might have been driven by instinct to strike the loose-lipped speaker, or turn on his heel in rage and shame. But Wyndham was made of cooler stuff, and so bided his time and listened. What Doyle had learned in a morning of ham-fisted investigation, Wyndham might find out with a few subtle questions over a drink in the mess.

'Is this that tall nurse you're talking about, Doyle?'

'That's the one. Something of a honey-pie, wouldn't you think?'

'Hmm. Not sure if we're thinking of the same girl. A Miss Murphy, I believe?'

'No, no. Her name's Maxfield. Didn't learn her Christian name yet, mind.'

Maxfield? Maxfield? *Not Maggie Mavourneen or Bridget Macushla-Macree then? Well, well.*

The day after that Doyle was still talking about her, but he was much put out.

'I ran into that nurse again – quite by chance actually – and do you know? She was smoking a cigarette!'

'Really?' said Wyndham, scrutinising his rival for the smallest weakness.

'A cigarette! Can you credit it?'

'Perhaps she was merely holding it for one of her patients?'

'No, no. This was outside.'

'Where outside?'

'Behind that big marquee tent. Down by the side of the hospital proper. Out-of-the-way place. I happened to be passing.'

'And this was in broad daylight?'

'Broad daylight. About eleven.'

'Remarkable,' said Wyndham, knowing exactly where he'd be at eleven the next day. 'Look here, I know we're busy right now, but might I have a few hours this afternoon to run some errands?'

The pleasant towns of Hampshire could not boast the luxuries of London, but it wasn't hard to find a jeweller at short notice. Where time was short, money would have to suffice. Napoleon had probably said something to that effect.

'Good afternoon. I'm looking for a cigarette case. A particularly fine one.'

The jeweller was happy to provide such for six guineas, which the lieutenant paid in cash, although he did seem unsure as to what a guinea was. That didn't surprise the jeweller nearly as much as a young officer's – and an Irish officer at that – ability to produce such a sum without apparent reluctance. The gentleman declined to have the case engraved. No time.

That suggested to the jeweller that the lieutenant was for France, and that made him doubly happy that he hadn't paid by cheque. It would be too painful to ask a bereaved family to honour a cheque.

Wyndham walked quickly. It made it easier to forget that he'd just parted with more than a fortnight's pay. His next stop was a genteel tobacconist.

'Good afternoon,' he said without preamble, 'but do you happen to know what brand of cigarette the Prince of Wales favours?'

'I beg your pardon, Lieutenant, but I'm afraid that I'm not acquainted with His Royal Highness's tastes.'

'A pity. We are expecting a visit, and it wouldn't do much for the tone of the regiment if I were to offer him an inferior cigarette – should he ask, of course.'

'Indeed not, sir. But if I may make so bold, I do have something in a most superior blend that he might like. Despite wartime shortages I am pleased to say that we have these. They're Russian, as a matter of fact.'

Wyndham desperately hoped that it would take Doyle a day

at least to overcome his reservations concerning the Modern Woman and her flagrant habits. He reckoned that this morning was his best and probably his only chance. Seeing as money was no object, he shamelessly bribed an orderly to confirm Nurse Maxfield's location and then, as the hour of eleven approached, he wandered around the back of the hospital, hoping that his timing wasn't off. After all, there are only so many times a fellow can wander casually around the back of a military hospital in the course of a morning.

He saw her coming. He nearly ruptured himself trying not to look furtive. A direct approach or nothing.

'Good morning, Nurse Maxfield,' he said, with an open smile and an unmilitary tip of his cap. She did not look pleased to be meeting him, or anyone, but she returned his good morning as she eyed his cap badge suspiciously.

'Munster Fusiliers,' he admitted. 'We met a few days ago. There's no reason you'd remember.'

Her eyes narrowed. 'Are you a friend of that Captain Doyle?'

'The Boy Doyle? He's my company commander.'

'Is that what you call him – the Boy?'

'We're very fond of him. May I offer you a cigarette?'

She looked at him, sensing a trap, and looked over her shoulder to see if they were observed. Then, because a cigarette was a cigarette, she deigned to take one from the most elegant case held open for her.

'Matron would only have me shot,' she admitted, as she accepted a light.

'I wouldn't dream of telling,' he said gallantly, squinting from the cigarette he lit for himself. 'They're Russian, as a matter of fact.'

The smoke made him dizzy, or was that victory? Whichever – he mustn't push too hard. Aim for and achieve a limited objective. Remember Patroclus at the walls of Troy. Remember that German machine-gun at Armentières. 'Please don't let me keep you, Nurse Maxfield. I really must be getting along.'

'Then good day to you, Lieutenant—?'

'Wyndham. Dan Wyndham.' And he waved a little salute as he went on his way, suave as you please.

He was unable to engineer another encounter. Only once more did he get a chance to be at the back of the hospital at eleven, but she wasn't there. After that his duties kept him busy.

All the while he watched Doyle like a hawk, in case the young captain had broadened his mind on the subject of women who smoked cigarettes in public. If such a change was so much hinted at, Wyndham was fully prepared to vow that Nurse Maxfield not only smoked, but picked her nose, mistreated dogs and voted Sinn Féin. Doyle stayed out of the picture, but the day of embarkation drew ever nearer, and Wyndham was no closer to learning even her first name.

It was an outbreak of measles that saved him. A division from the north of England brought it with them, and suddenly the barracks and tented camps were emptying as the hospital wards filled up. Wyndham had suffered the disease in childhood, so it was deemed safe to dispatch him to the hospital where nearly two dozen fusiliers needed to be accounted for.

He was standing in a corridor, lost, when there she was, right behind him.

'Lieutenant Wyndham, isn't it?' she hissed. 'I'm very sorry, but could I trouble you for a cigarette?'

He fumbled for his case, at a loss for words, as she explained that she was having the feet run off her, and – thank you very much – and she wouldn't know what she'd have done otherwise, and then she was gone, with the contraband hurriedly stuffed into an apron pocket.

After that he devoted his life to his men stricken with measles, and would have done as much had they been in a leper colony.

The next time he met her, the outbreak was threatening to explode into an epidemic, and although he had caught glimpses of her striding by, they'd had no chance to speak. He was on his way back to barracks and his regular duties when he stopped outside to light up. He was beginning to enjoy it. He was rounding the big marquee tent when he saw her bearing down on him. She stopped him with an urgent gesture, and quickly checked right and left before taking the cigarette from his unresisting lips and putting it between her own. She took a deep, blissful drag, and another, before returning it. Then she gave him a grateful smile and a guilty little wave and was gone.

She'd *smiled* at him. His lips and hers had drawn on the same cigarette. He wasn't much good for anything for the rest of that day.

He was far too smitten to be smooth now. The next day he sought her out with no pretence or subterfuge and asked her directly if he might take her to dinner. She turned him down without hesitation. He tried again the day after that, but scaled down his ambitions. Tea in a teashop? She said no to that one, too, but at least she didn't act like she was being insulted. On their last meeting he suggested that they have a convivial smoke somewhere out of the way.

'It's not allowed,' she said. 'Would half an hour suit? You might have to wait for me.'

It was more than half an hour, but he'd have waited until his waiting constituted absence without leave, if that's what it took.

'You're very nice,' she told him firmly. 'But I'm not walking out with soldiers. Not even officers.'

'But I'm off to France in a few days.'

'And sure everybody's off to France. And what were you hoping to achieve in a few days? No, don't tell me.'

He had nothing to say to that, but she conceded that he might write to her, if he liked. When they parted she wrote down her name and address for him and, after a moment's thought, followed it with an abrupt peck on the cheek. 'Maybe after the war,' she said, and then she was gone.

He went back to the jeweller when he had an hour to spare. He bought himself a more practical cigarette case and handed in the gold-plated tabernacle of his hopes to be engraved with the letters NM. He requested that it be wrapped nicely and sent on to a Miss Nora Maxfield at the garrison hospital.

After that, with a soaring heart and a dull ache in his testicles, Wyndham prepared to go back to the war.

51

*I had a dream in my sleep a while ago... of wounded men, of a
wind of terror, of keening that overcame laughter.*

—Lady Augusta Gregory, *Cuchulain of Muirthemne*

Warned for overseas. Originally Wyndham considered the
phrase to be just another instance of the menacing tone that the
army added to almost everything. If they could hardly give an
instruction without shouting, then naturally they were going to
make a notice sound like a threat.

But as the busy days slipped by the phrase sounded ever
more ominous. Wyndham had made peace with the war once
before, after he'd first come under fire on the Aisne, and had
known thereafter that he would not forsake his comrades or
his commander. The war had outworn his initial resolution, but
enough else had befallen him in the year and a half since that he
had gained a new acceptance: the war was still waiting for him
and he would go to it. Maybe he would finish the war or the war
would finish him. Time would tell.

But not so resigned to the warning for overseas was his fellow
veteran – that other survivor of the ragged band that had been
known, in the mind of its commander at least, as the Fitzmullen-Brophy Commando.

'Mr. Wyndham? I beg your pardon, sir, but I think you should
come and have a look at Corporal Moriarty.'

The warning for overseas meant kit inspections. Moriarty's section
had thought they'd got beyond this class of thing. Not only had
they months of soldiering to their credit, but here in England
the Irish country boys found that they compared very favourably

against soldiers from English industrial towns. There were dances. There were even invitations into people's homes. In short, there was extra incentive for making yourself smart.

But evidently it wasn't good enough for Moriarty. They were used to his moods, but the announcement of imminent foreign service had made him morose, and whereas, before this, his moods might often have manifested themselves in a lackadaisical approach to soldiering, now he was prone to bouts of tyranny. Today had been a particularly bad case.

'What's this? *What is it?*' The offending article was picked off the breast of O'Loughlin's tunic.

'It's a bit of thread, Corporal.'

'A bit of thread? *Only* a bit of thread? From sewing the frills on your knickers is it?'

'Ah now, Corporal.'

'Shut up! *Shut up!* You're a bloody disgrace! Your kit's a bloody disgrace! Sort it out!'

And it needed sorting out, because Moriarty was sweeping it all onto the floor and kicking it. That was the sort of thing you did to new recruits. They thought they'd got beyond it.

'*Jesus*, Mary and Joseph!' said Moriarty, having moved on to the next man. 'What do you call this?'

The true answer would have been, 'My mess tin cover, Corporal, only it got dropped on the floor when it was still wet and then there wasn't the time to get it squared away properly,' but Finnerty knew that this was one of the times when the true answer wouldn't be the right answer.

'No excuse, Corporal,' he said instead.

Moriarty held the imperfectly presented, mess-tin-shaped canvas pouch under the man's nose, momentarily speechless with frustration. Then he flung it out the window.

'What are you going to do without a mess tin cover, Finnerty?'

'Em – I'll get myself a new one, Corporal.'

'No, you *will not*! Because you'll be dead! Because if you go wandering around without a mess tin cover the light will catch off your mess tin and a sniper is going to see you and he's going to put a tiny little bullet into your big stupid head! Do you hear me?'

'Corporal.' Of course he could hear him. They could probably hear him over in France. Over the noise of the guns.

The next man, Higgins, had made the mistake of having notions. He'd thought he was a smart soldier.

'What in the name of the all-merciful Christ is *this*?' Moriarty roared.

'Bottle of hair oil, Corporal.'

'Bottle of fucking *hair oil*? And are you planning on humping this around with you? Entrenching tool, hundred and fifty rounds of ammunition, greatcoat, three days' rations, *and a bottle of fucking hair oil*? I'll show you! Pick up your kit! All of it! Not like that! Bundle it up in your blanket! Now hold it up! Do you feel the weight of that? That's nothing, boy! Finnerty! Get up on his back! Do as you're told! Do you feel that, Higgins? You'll be marching thirty miles a day over bad roads and that's the weight you'll be carrying! And Finnerty'll be bleeding all over you! A German sniper got him! Because he lost his fucking mess tin cover! There'll be bits of his brains going down the back of your collar and you'll carry him fucking miles to the aid post, only it'll do no fucking good at all because there's fuck all you can do with a head wound like that!'

And then Moriarty fell silent and blinked a couple of times at the grotesque piggy-back in front of him. Then he threw the bottle of hair oil out the window.

'Go on out and clean that up, Higgins,' he said, matter-of-factly. 'And get your hair cut while you're about it. Fucking hair oil.' Then, to the room at large: 'All of ye! Get your hair cut! If there's enough hair left for me to grab a hold of, then I will. Tell the barber that.'

He moved on down the line of cots, not really inspecting anymore, not really talking to his men anymore.

'There'd be lice in your hair. You'd be crawling with lice. And you'd get a head wound and the dirt would get into the wound. And the bits of hair. And the lice and all, I suppose. Damn all they can do for you then. You think you're a good soldier with your kit all squared away, but that's not going to help you. The Hun will see you and you'll die caught in a hedge with two little holes in your chest. Isn't that the way, Whelan?'

'I'm Daly, Corporal.'

'Daly. Bloody Daly. Where's Whelan so?'

'There's no Whelan, Corporal.'

'No. There's no bloody Whelan.'

'He went to have a bit of a lie-down after that, sir. Only he hasn't got up since. I wouldn't want to be the one to disturb him. Not when he's in bad form. We just thought an officer should be told. In case it's anything serious, like.'

Wyndham saw genuine concern on the face of the cropped-haired man, and when he went up to the barrack room there was the same delicacy shown by the rest of the men – all with brutally shorn hair – who slipped out and left Wyndham to it.

Moriarty was in his little cubicle, curled up with his face to the wall. Wyndham sat down and put his hand on Moriarty's shoulder, and kept it there while he softly repeated Moriarty's name. At last Moriarty turned and looked at him, his face wet.

'I was asleep,' he said. 'And then I heard you. Only it wasn't you I was hearing.'

He sat up a little. 'Do you remember Corporal Sheehan? He was the one who took you for drill back in Tralee, I think.'

'That's right.'

'I thought you were him. For a while there. When I first heard you. I thought it was him talking to me. He was talking to me on

277

the way up to Festubert. Christmas before last. "Come on out of that, Moriarty", he was saying to me.'

He pulled himself up properly and wiped his face.

'Sheehan. He was killed then. Not right then. Shortly after.' He sniffed deeply. 'Sheehan. He wasn't the worst.'

'I suppose not,' said Wyndham, remembering the screaming bully of his recruit training.

The two men sat side by side on Moriarty's cot, remembering and not speaking for a long while. Outside they could hear the rest of the world keeping a tactful distance. At last Moriarty sniffed again, slapped his hands on his knees and stood up.

'I'm not going back. I said that to you in Tralee. I'm bollocksed if I'm going back to the blessed trenches.'

'I really don't think they're giving us much choice.' Wyndham wasn't arguing. He wasn't trying to convince. His words were simple facts, gently spoken just as though he were still murmuring Moriarty's name over and over.

Moriarty shook himself, as if to banish all soothing. 'I'm not able for it,' he said.

'But we're winning the war now. It might not be all that bad.'

'Shite. We were winning the war two years ago, too, and that was two years ago.'

'It might be all over by the time we get there.'

'More shite. It was supposed to be over last year.'

'They'll probably find you a safe job in the rear. An experienced old soldier like yourself.'

'They'll put me in the line, an experienced old soldier like myself. They'll put me there to keep an eye on the young fools who haven't learned anything yet.'

'Have a cigarette.'

'I'm surprised you're so meek and mild about it all. There'll be no FitzEm looking after you now.'

'Why don't we have a drink?'

'Where? In a pub? What's wrong with you at all? We can't go drinking in a pub. They'll see us.'

'Somewhere quiet. I can get us something from the mess.'

'Do what you like. You're not talking me into anything.'

'Stay there. I'll be right back.'

Evening found them beyond the firing range, walking up and down among the gorse bushes, a bottle going from hand to hand and the lights of their cigarettes dancing in argument.

Wyndham returned to his quarters a little unsteadily, but in much better spirits. He was sounding forth with what he considered to be a particularly fine rendition of 'The Boys of Wexford' – at least until he caught the disapproving eye of the sentry.

'Dineen,' he said, with avuncular condescension, 'you have the makings of a perfectly good soldier, but I am afraid you are rather too prim. Goodnight.' And he went on his way, giggling.

McCarthy-Moore, still awake and reading something, was likewise disapproving when the door to their quarters was opened with theatrical suddenness.

'Was that you making that racket, Wyndham?'

'I believe it must have been. I do apologise, McCarthy-Moore.' And then, because he hadn't stumbled over the double-barrelled alliterative name, he repeated it. Nothing to it.

'Wyndham, are you drunk?'

Wyndham stood in a moment's solemn contemplation, swaying slightly.

'Yes. Afraid so. Decidedly so.' He leaned back against the wall, misjudging the distance but saving himself from a tumble.

'Decidedly so. *Heroically* so.' He gave a little laugh. '"God save Ireland", say the heroes.'

'What on earth possessed you, man?'

'Duty. The morale of an old comrade. Moriarty was feeling

blue. Much better now.'

'You've been drinking with an Other Rank? For heaven's sake, don't let anyone find out!'

'Drinking with an old comrade, my friend. Two Old Contemptibles. Two contemptible old Dirty Shirts. I believe I should sit down.'

'I believe you should go to bed.'

'You're a good friend, McCarthy-Moore.'

'A better one than you deserve in your state. Go to bed.'

'I will.' He sat down on his cot. 'But just in case we all get killed, I wanted to tell you that you're just fine, McCarthy-Moore. No end of a fine fellow.'

'Good of you to say so. Now shut up.'

'Goodnight, my dirty-shirted old comrade.'

'Goodnight, and shut up.'

'God save Ireland.'

And he lay back, with his boots still on, and let sleep and whiskey take him.

52

And then they were brought into the hall of heroes... and they were given every sort of food and of drink that is to be found on the whole ridge of the world.

—Lady Augusta Gregory, *Cuchulain of Muirthemne*

The last mess night of the 11th Royal Munster Fusiliers – the last night before they bade their dear old colonel farewell – was an uproarious and sentimental affair.

Fitzmullen-Brophy raised his glass amid the tumult and called for another toast. In a little while he would be so tight that he'd have to be helped to bed.

'Gentlemen! To wives and sweethearts!' he called, his face gleaming.

'And may they never meet!' roared back his officers, in the prescribed response.

'No, no! Listen to me! I really mean it. Where would we be without the womenfolk, what? What would we be without the dear dears, God bless 'em? I mean to say, here's to them, God bless 'em! Here's to womanhood!'

'Well said, sir! Hear, hear!'

Amid the toasting and the singing, Wyndham found himself in close conversation with Doyle.

'I say, Dan – did I hear it right when someone said you'd been to Paris?'

'That's right. Just after the Aisne. Why?'

'Well, I was just wondering, you know. I mean, is it true what they say?'

'About what, old man?'

'Well – you know – about the girls and that sort of thing.'

Doyle's time in France had been taken up with military matters. Survival had driven all other considerations aside. Also, back then he hadn't really thought much about girls 'that way'.

'So, is it true, Dan?'

Wyndham swirled his drink around, happy that this excellent whiskey could be followed by another one every bit as good.

'I'm afraid so, Boy. Every word. The French women are utterly without shame. Slaves to their appetites.'

'Really?'

'Your virtue will be assailed on every side. I myself barely escaped Paris without ravishment.'

'I say!'

'You'll need to conserve your strength.'

'I suppose I should.'

'No more chasing after pretty nurses.'

'No. No, I suppose not. Thanks. Thanks awfully.'

They had been given the sanitary lectures, but a good NCO took every opportunity to reinforce discipline and hygiene. In the wet canteen Corporal Moriarty swayed to his feet and shouted into the din.

'Remember what the MO said! If you stick your langer into the wrong girl it'll only fall off! But sure it doesn't hardly matter because the Germans will only shoot it off otherwise!'

And he sat down heavily and let the men revel.

V

FRANCE

War-battered dogs are we

Fighters in every clime,

Fillers of trench and grave,

Mockers, bemocked by time.

War-dogs, hungry and grey,

Gnawing a naked bone,

Fighters in every clime,

For every cause but our own.

—Emily Lawless, 'Clare Coast 1710'

53

*Or there is the Army ... in which you can wear the uniform of
your country and do good work in every climate under the sun...
In such a career you have plenty of adventure and you are among
good comrades and friends.*

—Robert Baden-Powell, *Scouting for Boys*

It was a different France and a different war.

When Wyndham had first arrived in France it had been by way
of a picturesque Breton fishing port, where Fitzmullen-Brophy's
rogue band of fusiliers were given the welcome they were due as
France's saviours. The squalid journey and the seasickness had
been quickly forgotten in the celebration.

This time there were no speeches, no open arms. The war had
become a machine, and the men fed along its conveyor were no
longer the heroes of 1914. As far as the army was concerned,
they were of no more note than the crates of stores and bales
of horse fodder that were stacked and loaded in Southampton
and unloaded and stacked in Le Havre. The French might still
think well of the British soldiers, but if so, it was hardly evident.
Prices were high. Service was brusque. Too many thousands,
and hundreds of thousands, had tramped down the gangplanks
and through the streets for allowances to be made for them. At
best, the barbarous English were tolerated as just another onerous
necessity of war. The war had to be fought, and the price of
victory included shortages and bereavements, and the British.

So, there was no band at the quayside and no free drinks in

the cafés for the Munsters. There was just the army, checking its papers and directing the stores and the men onward. It was all routine. Wyndham remembered the alarm that had spiced the French air when first he'd breathed it, but that crisis was long passed. The Germans had been driven back from Paris, but not back to Germany. 1914 had turned into 1915, 1915 to 1916, and the war was still there. Nothing to get excited about. Move along there. Your train's that way.

It was a different battalion, too. Indeed, as the powers had decreed, it wasn't a battalion at all anymore. After the over-age, the under-age, the short-sighted, the measly, the sergeant-major martyred with the rheumatics, and the otherwise useless had been weeded out, there were, as Devereaux had unkindly pointed out, not even two full-strength companies. Then, without a by-your-leave, another fifty men and three officers who'd been momentarily separated were shamelessly appropriated by the 8th Battalion, never to be seen again. Poaching had always been a considered threat, but Major de Roche had never imagined that it should be so sudden and so flagrant. If anything, though, it kept what was left together as never before. They were the chosen few, and they intended to stick together, defiantly calling themselves 11th Munsters a while longer.

In Cork they had been children, happy in their ignorance. In Hampshire they had been like the new boys in school, unsure and outnumbered. Here, in France, they had to stand up for themselves, and they found joy in it.

They celebrated Doyle's twenty-first birthday with more genuine warmth than they'd have felt back in Cork. The officers' mess was now wherever a table could be found and whenever time allowed. On that day it happened to be at a jolly estaminet outside Béthune where the wine was plentiful.

The Boy Doyle (never quite knowing who had first bestowed that nickname on him) still wore his captain's pips and would wear them until they took them away, and he drank that day like a captain of infantry should, until they made him lie down in the shade for the rest of the afternoon. Curran made a witty speech, Wyndham delivered quite a successful comic recitation, and they all sang lustily. To prove to the world that they were warriors, and not a gentlemen's drinking club, a bayonet was used as a cheese knife.

Major de Roche was not loved, but he was loyal to his men and they to him. He proved himself a capable administrator, worthy of the *p.s.c.* he appended to his name, even if his punctiliousness often proved wearing. He did not like France for its untidiness and inefficiency and its being full of the French. He took a dim view of the war for much the same reason.

The Munsters did not cherish de Roche they way they had Fitzmullen-Brophy, but it made a nice change to be free of the endless admonitions to *be prepared*, of the intrusive concern for their diet and the state of their bowels, of the sermons against cigarette-smoking, of the maddening insistence on fresh air, of the ceaseless mothering. They'd been sorry to see him go, but they didn't need a mother anymore.

They expected at any day the order that would assign them to a parent unit and then, perhaps, commit them to action. De Roche was only a caretaker until then, but he was enjoying his independence, and nurtured hopes that he might hold onto it. However, he accepted his fusiliers were too few to justify a separate existence for much longer.

'Not much more than three hundred men, I'm afraid.'

'Three hundred was enough at Thermopylae, sir.'

'That is not a helpful remark, Wyndham. I do wish you would take things seriously.'

54

The black troops have precisely those qualities that are demanded in the long struggles in modern war: rusticity, endurance, tenacity, the instinct for combat, the absence of nervousness, and an incomparable power of shock.

—Général Charles Mangin, *La Force Noire*

It was another of those little towns that had not been ravaged by war but had known the passage of tens of thousands who didn't mind where they put their feet, or care about the paintwork, or bother over who was going to pay for that broken window.

It was another of those towns where they just didn't know how to boil an egg properly.

Major de Roche looked with grave dissatisfaction at his breakfast. It was too, too tiresome.

As commanding officer, he thought it proper to breakfast alone, and the other officers agreed with him. He certainly did not care to be disturbed by such an apparition as now filled his door. It was an exceptionally tall black man in khaki uniform and a red fez that made him taller still. Seen at a distance, or when, say, one was properly prepared, the man would have been considered most picturesque. Looming over one's breakfast, he was positively alarming. He had something to say, but de Roche was having none of it.

He flapped his napkin at the man. '*Imshi! Jao!* Wyndham! Make this fellow go away!'

Wyndham, who'd been trying to slip unobtrusively through the room at that moment smiled politely at the exotic intruder and gestured outside, but the man persisted in his attempt to communicate.

De Roche, exasperated at how ineffectual junior officers could be, said, 'Explain to him that the *sahib* is having his breakfast and doesn't speak his dreadful Hottentot language, but *do* make him go away!'

'I believe he's speaking French, sir.'

'Then speak to him in French, man, but for heaven's sake do it outside.'

The exchange in the street outside was courteous but, of necessity, stilted. Wyndham's French was suitable for requesting a change of hotel room or praising his hostess's garden, while the Senegalese sergeant knew just enough of the language to supervise matters at platoon and company level. Translated, it ran thus:

'Pardon me, but the officer is taking breakfast.'

'Pardon me, but I wish to speak with the English officer.'

'I am an officer.'

'Please come with me. My officer is very sad.'

Intrigued, and not having it in him to say no, Wyndham complied, but when he saw Moriarty gawking from nearby, he summoned him to accompany them.

'Who's that fella at all?' asked Moriarty, who would most certainly have spoken with the same tone and volume if the fella had understood English. 'Would you look at the cut of him.'

'I'm not sure, but he speaks French and I think he's a sergeant.'

'Sure of course he's a sergeant. Look at the scars on his face.'

And it was hard to miss them. The man had arrangements of parallel scars cut onto each side of his lean face.

'Three on each side. That means he's a sergeant.' Moriarty trotted closer to the man to look properly at his uniform. 'He's got a fez on his head and anchors on his badges. Is he supposed to be the Turkish Navy or something?'

'I'm really not sure.'

'Have the Turks surrendered so? I'm not so up on the news lately. They don't get the *Cork Examiner* out here.'

'I think perhaps he's African. *Excusez-moi, monsieur le sergent, mais vous-êtes Africain?*'

The man nodded. What else would he have been?

'Sure, what else is he going to be but African? Look at the big black head on him.'

The African, the American and the Irishman strode quickly down the street until they came to an estaminet. The rest of the African squad was collected outside, with that disconsolate look common to soldiers who have been buggered about for too long. Inside was a white officer, also with anchors on his collar, collapsed in a chair, attended by another black man and glared at by the woman of the house.

The sergeant explained: 'Sir, here is my officer. He is very sad. The woman does not help.'

'Why is the officer sad?'

'Sir, the war makes him sad. He drinks wine. He sleeps. I do not know the orders.'

Wyndham was nonplussed. '*I* do not know the orders.'

'Ousama has the orders.' And he gestured to the man attending the officer, saying something in their own language. Where the sergeant was impressive on account of his height and bearing, the man Ousama was unnerving in his own way. You could perhaps get used to the tribal scars and the great squared-off blade at his belt, but his unfaltering merry grin did not match at all the dangerous look in his eyes.

He gently rummaged in the pockets of the officer's bemedaled tunic, all stiff with dirt, and pulled out a paper. Then he planted a tender kiss on the top of the officer's drunken head. The sergeant merely took the paper from him.

'Ousama is also very sad.'

'Such a shame.'

'The war makes him sad also. He is very brave, but he does not like the cannons.'

'I do not like the cannons.'

'The woman does not like the black soldiers. She does not give them wine.'

'Such a pity.'

'Ousama gives her a Boche head for wine but she does not like the Boche head. She wants us to go. But we cannot go without the orders. Sir, here are the orders. I do not know the words.'

Wyndham took the grubby paper and scanned the French army officialese.

'There is a train,' he said.

'There is always a train.'

'You must go quickly. You are late.'

'Sir, we are always late.'

'Can you wake your officer?'

'We do not like to wake him. We can carry him.'

Satisfied to have found such an easy solution to the problem, and happy to have played his part in the great alliance of nations, Wyndham made to leave, but saw that Moriarty had entered into a staring competition with the man Ousama.

'Tommy,' said Ousama, grinning. 'Tommee.' He had his great blade in his hand, running his fingers along its edge.

Moriarty just stood his ground, saying nothing.

The sergeant suggested – although Wyndham couldn't be sure – that the English soldier might like a severed head. All Wyndham could do was say that they were Irish soldiers and they really must be getting on. The train would not wait. The comrades-in-shellshock would have to cement their reconciliation some other time.

Outside, the soldiers picked up their gear and fell in, their stricken offer borne patiently from the estaminet. The fusiliers saw them to the station, and Wyndham sorted things out for them with a railway official. The railway officer frowned at the movement order and at the dozen or so men with their supine officer.

'Sergeant,' said Wyndham, 'he says there are wagons for 2nd Company. Four wagons. He says he cannot wait for the rest of you.'

'We are 2nd Company, sir.'

'Ah. Such a shame. Very sad.'

'Thank you, sir.'

As they loaded aboard, Ousama gave a little bow to Moriarty. '*Merci*, Tommy.'

Moriarty returned a curt nod. 'Mercy yourself, Sambo. Look after yourself, son.'

But Ousama wasn't finished. Bowing again, he handed Moriarty something large and round, wrapped in a sandbag. Moriarty accepted it stiffly, but deigned not to inspect it.

'Is that us so, Mr. Wyndham?'

'I believe so. Let's go back.'

As they walked away, Moriarty's curiosity got the better of him and he peeked inside the sandbag. Wyndham averted his eyes, but then had a look to confirm Moriarty's finding.

'It's a fucking cabbage,' said Moriarty. 'Your man gave me a fucking cabbage.'

Wyndham turned to give one last wave to the train, where the Africans were falling about in laughter.

'That was decent of them,' he said.

55

And thus let our name be magnified and enlarged from on high in glory, before we be divided and scattered through lands distant and strange.

—*Lebor Gabála Érenn:*
The Book of the Taking of Ireland

They scampered along after the coat tails of 16th Division, coming to rest in late June behind the Loos sector. The previous September Loos had been the scene of a battle so terrible that legend spoke of German machine-gunners, sickened by the slaughter, standing up and waving back the attacking British. It was quieter now, and reckoned a suitable place to condition Kitchener's Irish for the front. A spring spent in the trenches had seasoned them for more strenuous activities planned for the summer. This quiet seasoning had cost several hundred casualties, but that was the sort of thing that everyone else had long become used to, and so the Irish should get used to it, too.

De Roche's command was leery of the rapacious 8th Munsters, especially when it was learned that they had cannibalised the 9th Battalion. The 11th – a battalion in name only, and that name not even recognised anymore – knew that it was their fate also to be swallowed up, but they guarded their independence while they could. Perhaps that was their mistake. Perhaps de Roche should have just surrendered his men to 8th Battalion and have done with it, instead of sliding in late and unannounced, keeping up a pretence at detachment. Perhaps it was just the army's perversity, and nothing could have been done to prevent it, but as it fell out, the men who had first been mustered in County Cork were to be given into the charge of the Dublin Fusiliers.

'Dublin?'

'I'm afraid so.'

'But I mean to say, sir.'

'Nothing to be done. Probably temporary anyway. Make the best of it.'

'I don't like to think what the men will say.'

It was all very well for de Roche, the Connaught Ranger. He was already in exile. But what about the innocent country boys? What about Moriarty?

'*Dublin?*'

'I'm afraid so.'

'Fucking Dublin Fusiliers? Are they having us on?'

'We should make the best of it, Moriarty.'

'I bloody knew I should never have come.'

Moriarty, self-appointed regimental historian to the lower orders, didn't do much to reconcile the men to the new association. The Royal Dublin Fusiliers, it transpired, had the effrontery to wear on their cap badge the Bengal tiger, even though their forebears had come from Bombay and Madras and not from Bengal at all.

'And they've got an elephant up there below the tiger. They'd have monkeys as well but there was no room for them. It's nothing to do with their time in India. Dublin Zoo paid for the advertisement.'

Wyndham had been to Dublin briefly, and had thought it a perfectly pleasant place, but he had also spent too long in Moriarty's company, and thus couldn't shake the suspicion that malice and depravity lurked under that city's elegant exterior. The events of Easter had confused him further. Was Dublin the true seat of Irish national sentiment, being the only place where rebellion had flared up, or did it mean that it was only in malcontent Dublin that such perversity could manifest itself?

Wyndham's resentment at the new order was not as sharp as that felt by Moriarty, or by many of his fellows, but he had served as a Munster Fusilier for two years now and was not in the least bit happy at having his allegiance taken so lightly by the army. On almost his first night in Ireland he had been told of the glories of the Dirty Shirts, and only a day or so later he had been issued with one of those shirts – granted, new from stores, but still. He knew why the shirt was dirty. He knew why there was a tiger on his cap badge. He had been taught the histories, and knew that he was one with the men of Bhurtpore and Delhi. They had stripped off their red coats and fought under the burning Indian sun, just as he had wrapped himself in rags and taken his place in the flooded trenches near Armentières. He was a Munster. He had a right to be a Munster. Who were these Dublins? What had they ever done? What had been his sin that he was to be cast among them?

He felt an unreasonable bitterness towards de Roche. Fitz-mullen-Brophy had always provided for his children, but as soon as the old colonel was gone, here was de Roche letting them be dragged off to the orphanage.

So, no: he wasn't feeling quite as mutinous as Moriarty, but he was far from happy.

There was some surly muttering among the Munsters when they were told the news. To add to the insult, they were expected to pick up everything and march the eight or ten miles to where the Dublins were presently billeted, and all this with the sun splitting the stones.

Bloody cheek.

And when the post at last caught up with them, Wyndham received a small parcel containing a gold cigarette case.

Dear Dan,

*I am sorry for not writing to you earlier, but I have finally
decided that I cannot accept your very generous gift. It is
far too expensive, and it would only cause talk. It is a shame
about the engraving but I'm sure a good jeweller would be
able to change it without it costing too much.*

Your friend,

Nora Maxfield.

56

Do not scatter many feasts to strangers; do not visit mean people that cannot receive you as a king.

—Lady Augusta Gregory, *Cuchulain of Muirthemne*

The Munsters were standing about somewhat lost, while their officers tried to hunt down someone who might be able to offer them aid and comfort. They were discovered by a field officer named O'Donnell, who had been out in France too long and who didn't care about whose feelings he might hurt. The bright sunlight was doing his head no good at all and the appearance of the new drafts was an offence to his eye.

'What in hell's name are they sending us now? Bloody gormless schoolboys! Look at them – milling about like bloody poultry!'

'I'll sort them out, sir,' said the adjutant at his elbow.

'See that you bloody well do. Bloody disgrace. Their officers should be damn well horse-whipped.'

It was unfortunate that Curran should have made his appearance then, as if on cue.

'Look at that chap there. Bloody middle-aged fop. No wonder this war's taking so bloody long.'

It wasn't evident that Curran had heard these comments, but when one sees a senior officer bearing down like a shunting engine, all noise and purpose and bursts of steam, it is wise to come to attention.

'Who the devil are you supposed to be?'

'Eleventh Munster Fusiliers, sir,' said Curran.

'No you're bloody well not. No such bloody thing. From now

on you're whoever the army tells you to be. Got that?'

'Sir.'

'And what in the name of Christ is this?'

This was directed at Wyndham who had come outside because, no matter what the odds, a man must stand with his comrades in the hour of peril. Given the heat of the day, and remembering the free and easy fashions that the army had sported on its way up to Mons, he was back wearing Fitzmullen-Brophy's old tunic. It saved wear on his proper uniform. It was also now attracting the blistering attention of this bloody-visaged major of the Dublins.

Wyndham saluted, and held the salute as he was subjected to pop-eyed scrutiny.

'Why,' snarled O'Donnell, 'is this young wart in tropical kit?'

'The major wants to know why you're dressed like that,' said the accompanying officer.

'He can bloody well hear me,' rasped the major. 'And stop saluting, you fool. What are you? Some sort of refugee from Mesopotamia? Your tailor stopped your credit? What?'

'I beg your pardon, sir. I merely thought it more suitable for the French summer.'

'What the hell do you know about French summers? Gone paddling at Deauville, have you? Pinched girls' bottoms at Le Touquet?'

Wyndham did not care for vulgarity, and he had better things to be frightened of than this bully. He thought how in his young day Irish majors had been kindly old gentlemen. With unwonted temerity he looked his assailant square in the eye.

'Marched all the way to Maubeuge, as a matter of fact, sir. And all the way back.' That *As a matter of fact* was probably rank insubordination in violation of King's Regulations, but at just this moment Wyndham did not care. A gold cigarette case weighed heavy in his pocket.

The major stopped dead for a moment, and seemed to take in

the scar across Wyndham's crooked nose for the first time. Then he barked with laughter.

'Ha! Blasted cheek! What's your name?'

'Wyndham, sir.'

'Why is an Old Contemptible only a one-pipper, eh, Mr. Wyndham? What were you all the way back from Maubeuge?'

'Other rank, sir.'

'Of course you bloody well were! Bloody good show, Wyndham! You may not be a gentleman but at least you're a soldier. Now bloody well pull yourselves together. The captain here will show you what's what.'

And leaving his adjutant to take the Munsters in hand, he was off about his business, somewhat lighter in his heart. Some traditionalists couldn't abide commissioned rankers, but they were worth their weight in gold out here. Back at home, of course, a fellow like this Wyndham wouldn't be the thing at all. His inability to dress and his bloody awful accent betrayed his base origins far too obviously.

57

We cannot win this war unless we kill or incapacitate more of our enemies than they do of us, and if this can only be done by our copying the enemy in his choice of weapons, we must not refuse to do so.

—Lieutenant-General Sir Charles Ferguson, II Corps, 1915

At least with the Dublins they belonged somewhere in the army, and the days of official neglect had come to an end. Indeed, the army was making up for lost time when it came to inducting the Munsters into the age of modern war. New equipment was issued to them almost every day, sometimes familiar, sometimes new and strange. Initial instruction was provided by harried quartermasters and tended to be rudimentary.

'It's a shovel: what more do you want?'

'It's a Lewis Gun. Don't touch it.'

Experts did arrive with approved training programmes and helpful hints. They put on their little performances, left a pamphlet with whomever was in charge, and moved on to the next unit. The officers and NCOs made up the first class of students to be taught, and it was their job to pass on what they'd learned to the lower ranks.

Wyndham now stood in front of his men with a grey flannel bag in his hands and a stern school-masterish tone to his voice.

'Phenate hexamine gas helmet, one. Rubber band, one.'

'Beg your pardon, sir, but a *what*?'

'*Phenate hexamine*.'

'How would you spell that, sir?'

'You wouldn't. The War Office will spell it for you. It's a gas helmet. Call it a gas helmet.'

'Very good, sir.'

'Sir! I'm after losing my rubber band. It flew off somewhere that way, I think.'

'Do *not* go looking for that rubber band, Daly. Corporal, give Daly another rubber band.'

'That's government property, Daly. Lose it again and you'll be on a charge.'

'When you smell gas, or when the gas alarm sounds, you are to place the gas helmet over your head *like so*.'

Wyndham had practised this bit so he didn't look too foolish. The flannel hood, soaked in a chemical solution, was pulled down over the head and tucked in at the collar. Having done so neatly, Wyndham then embarked on his explanation of how to breathe in the approved manner. As if in a schoolroom, several hands shot up.

'I beg your pardon, sir, but could you say that last bit again?'

'We can't hear you down the back, sir. You're all muffled.'

Wyndham pulled the hood off, somewhat annoyed, and gave it to them again. 'Upon donning the mask, place the mouthpiece in your mouth. Inhale normally through your nose and exhale – that's breathe *out* – through the tube provided. Like *so*.' And, turning the mask halfway inside out, he demonstrated sticking the little metal tube between his lips and blowing.

As the instructional leaflet had emphasised, and Wyndham had memorised, the wearer had to remember to breathe in through the nose and out through the mouth. The chemically impregnated cloth filtered out the poison on the way in, and the exhalations were expelled by way of the tube. The army wasn't sure that ignorant soldiers could be trusted to breathe as ordered, but the alternative was to have them poisoned. It was an awkward system, but just about workable. What it was not, however, was dignified. Bad enough that an officer had to pull a bag over his head, but there was one feature of the mechanism that threatened to prejudice good order and discipline.

A one-way rubber valve at the end of the little metal tube made sure that a man could not inhale through it. When he exhaled, however, the rubber valve made a disconcertingly flatulent sound. Wyndham, whose mind tended to be above such base humour, hadn't made much notice of this when he'd tried it out by himself. His boyishly innocent men noticed straight away, and were delighted.

'Silence in the ranks! Shut up, the lot of ye!'

As Moriarty roared, Wyndham said something unconvincing about this being a serious matter, and then disproved himself by blowing through the valve again. When the tittering was again calmed they were put through the drill, until the parade was all correct, with bags over their heads, making farting noises in ragged unison.

'And breathe in. And breathe out,' intoned Wyndham with his eyepieces fogged up and his voice indistinct even in his own ears. He pulled his mask up and ordered everyone to do the same. Everyone's faces were red and their chins beslobbered. There was much rubbing and grimacing, because the chemicals in the fabric, reacting with the sweat, were proving a powerful irritant to the skin. Wyndham tried to ignore it.

'When worn at the ready,' he went on, resolutely, 'the mask is to be worn rolled up on the top of the head and secured there with the rubber band.' His forehead was prickling like mad and he did not relish looking even more ridiculous wearing his gas helmet on top of his head like an old woman's bonnet. To his increasing irritation, he saw that he was losing his audience.

'Daly, pay attention. What's the matter?'

'I think I've got something in my eyes, sir. I think I must have got gassed.'

'Don't be foolish, man.'

'He does have a bit of a rash on his face, sir.'

'He's not gassed. There's no gas. Pay attention now. *When worn at the ready the mask is to be worn rolled up on the top of the head and secured there...*'

Then the elastic band flew off his sweaty fingers and hit Moriarty on the ear.

'Ow! Jesus! Who did that?'

Wyndham raised his voice to parade-ground pitch. 'You are to practise in your own time. That concludes this exercise. Dismiss.'

The new steel helmet was a simpler piece of kit and instruction in its use should hardly have been necessary, but Wyndham had learned that a young soldier will find every undreamt-of misuse of anything at all issued to him.

'The helmet is *not* – and let me repeat myself – *not* proof against bullets.' This announcement was being made because he'd overheard two men talking of testing the helmet's efficacy out on the firing range. He didn't know if tests were to be conducted with the helmet being worn by either of these experimental souls, but he didn't wait to find out.

'Sir? What use is it at all if it's not bulletproof, sir?'

'It is designed to protect against shrapnel and other debris.' This was fair enough. For men who lived below ground level all lethal threats came from above, and Wyndham still shuddered to remember how vulnerable a man could feel, pulling himself into an ever-tighter ball, with nothing but his fragile interlaced fingers over his head, and the earth of France and iron of Germany raining out of the sky.

'When we go into the line,' he went on, 'you will find it a blessing.'

'It's fierce heavy, sir. Do we have to wear it all the time?'

'You will wear it when under fire or when ordered. Any further questions?'

'Sir, if I was to give O'Loughlin there a clout on the head with my entrenching tool, would he feel it, sir?'

'No one – *no one* – is to hit anyone with anything, whether or not he is wearing a steel helmet. Dismiss.'

But, of course, somebody did go and test the new helmet with a shovel, although that was in McCarthy-Moore's platoon and thus not Wyndham's problem. For now, fingers crossed, the worst thing about the helmet for Wyndham was that it was yet another item of equipment to keep track of. For the men it was something else to keep clean and lug around on top of all their other gear. For an old soldier like Moriarty, who could remember when the army had standards, it was something of an offence to his sense of style. Moriarty had worn the fusilier busby, an eight-inch-high cap of black fur with brass fittings and a parti-coloured plume affixed to one side. Now he looked at this tin soup plate and sighed with disapproval. 'Jesus. The shite they expect a man to put on his head. The Germans will only be laughing at us.'

An English officer arrived to initiate them into the secrets of the Mills bomb. He was wary of teaching Irishmen how to use hand-held explosive devices, but orders were orders. After the lectures came the live practice, for which a low wall of sandbags was constructed as a safety measure. The apprentice bombers stood behind the sandbags, lobbed their grenades in the approved manner, and then ducked down. They did as well as troops do, which is to say that some were perfectly competent and some frightened the life out of everyone in the vicinity with their handlessness. Finnerty – normally a fairly useful soldier – provided a classic example of the latter when it came to his turn.

'Not like that, man!' shouted the instructor. 'Like I showed you! Don't throw it – lob it! Like a cricket ball!'

Finnerty had grown up on a small farm somewhere in the mountains between Cork and Kerry. Wherever it was, it was not cricket country. He had never seen a game, let alone bowled at a wicket. He stood confused, his unaccustomed steel helmet in danger of slipping over his eyes and a live grenade in his sweating hand.

The instructor, who'd met Irishmen before in the shape of the Ulster Division, tried another tack.

'Throw it like you're throwing a brick at the police!'

Finnerty had been a law-abiding lad all his life. Moreover, his mind had been suddenly wiped clean of everything he'd just been taught, except that the grenade's fuse burned down in five seconds. From where he was standing now, that didn't seem like a very long time at all. The instructor shouted at him again and Finnerty, all limbs, fumbled his hold, his throw, his attempt to recover – everything. It looked like a comically inept juggling act, only nobody was laughing.

Finnerty stood there stupidly while everyone else scattered like a jar of marbles dropped on a stone floor. Finnerty would have died there – died like a fool, as Moriarty put it – if Lieutenant McCarthy-Moore hadn't chosen to run towards him instead of away. He tackled Finnerty around the middle, carrying him over the sandbags, and he pushed Finnerty's head into the earth while a bare five feet away, on the other side of the barricade, two pounds of amatol and segmented iron did what was expected of them.

Except for a severe ringing in their ears, both Finnerty and McCarthy-Moore were unhurt. To emphasise how dramatically close an escape it had been, the heel iron of Finnerty's right boot had been knocked clean away. He was made to pay for the repair. That was only right.

58

And the men of Ireland were afraid their army would be too much weakened by little fights of this sort before the great last battle that was foretold would come.

—Lady Augusta Gregory, *Cuchulain of Muirthemne*

South. Something big was going on down south. The army was full of it. Even in a camp behind the lines in a quiet sector they heard about it. Down south, where the British, grown to great strength, had taken over a long stretch of the French line, something big was going to happen. Endless battalions, heavy guns, masses of stores – everything that an army would need for a summer offensive – were being moved south. The Munsters watched with interest, wondering if there would be enough war left for them when their time came. Meanwhile, at the beginning of July, it was judged that they were fit to take their turn up the line here at Loos.

In steady summer rain, burdened with all their necessaries and sweating abominably under waterproof capes, they marched up the straight road to see at last this object of all their efforts. The journey that had begun perhaps with a brass band in the street; with a patriotic speech appealing to the manliness of the listener; with Lord Kitchener's stare and command that could not be denied, was finally nearing its end.

They were not going into battle yet, but they were going into the trenches, into the place of danger, where the enemy waited a mere rifle shot beyond.

'Youse have nothing to worry about,' assured their guide. 'This is a grand quiet spot.'

'Cushy enough, mate,' said a voice from a unit marching the other way into rest.

'Mind you,' said the guide, having elicited this response to his greeting, 'Everyone says that.'

'Cushy?' asked Wyndham.

'Cushy. You know. Grand and easy, like. It's an Indian word, I suppose. "What's it like, mate?" you'll say, and they'll always say, "Cushy, mate".'

'And is it?'

'Cushy? Ah, it is and it isn't. We did lose a few fellas here alright the last time. Sure, you'd know yourself, Lieutenant.'

Because Lieutenant Wyndham had been here before, of course – back in '14, when it was another war entirely.

It had been another army entirely, too. Back then he'd marched with the veterans of the Transvaal and the Northwest Frontier: men who didn't have to guess if a word were Indian or not. Men who could swear fluently in bad Urdu, mixed with bad Arabic, with a few words of bad Afrikaans thrown in for good measure. He'd marched in with that contemptible little army and been carried out again on a stretcher, which was better than what most of those stalwart men had got. And now here he was again, himself the supposed veteran, and all the eager novices looking to him.

Not the men of '14 at all.

The faces were fresher, the moustaches fewer and sparser. Their equipment created a silhouette unknown to the old army. The steel helmets shiny with rain, drops of water circling crazily round the rim; the rubberised capes that smelled so strongly; the gas helmets in satchels; the picks and shovels, pit props and wiring pickets with which the unlucky men were burdened, were a far cry from the brave fellows who'd stepped out towards Mons with their collars open not two years ago. They'd been on their way to put the kibosh on the Kaiser, to chase him out of Belgium with their bayonets up his backside. These lads, loaded like pack mules and trying to keep the wet out, were here just to maintain the line. No heroics were expected. They were just expected to learn the routine of moving up and moving out again; to learn the weary workaday business of filling sandbags and clearing drainage ditches, while somewhere far in the rear the brass hats contemplated the campaign for 1917.

Different war altogether.

Or maybe not.

They were halted by the roadside, but instead of being given permission to fall out they were addressed by de Roche, who had just received a communication from a despatch rider sent from Brigade. A bulletin, to be read to all ranks.

De Roche cleared his throat and waited for silence – a gesture that meant nothing to a caravan of motor lorries that took their time in passing. Wyndham, standing at the front, heard it all clearly enough, but the ranks behind were a soft-voiced rhubarb of de Roche's words being relayed and questioned and repeated.

The import of it all was that a major success had been scored down south. The communiqué detailed advances of thousands of yards, of objectives overrun, of prisoners taken and guns captured. The Irish – and these men would have expected no less – had done valiantly. They were perhaps the wrong sort of Irish, being the Orangemen of the 36th (Ulster) Division, but fair dues. When de Roche called for three cheers, the Munsters freely acclaimed their Ulster brethren. They'd be getting their own turn soon enough, devil a doubt, and then the Hun would really find out what the Irish could do.

This spell in the line was just to put the finishing touches on their training. Then maybe they'd be going south.

And Major de Roche's address had told them that the south had a name now. The men of Ulster were earning their glory on the banks of the River Somme.

59

It must, nevertheless, be clearly understood that trench fighting is only a phase of operations...

—*Notes for Infantry Officers on Trench Warfare*, War Office, 1916

The trenches were much more impressive than when Wyndham had last seen them. He could tell that by how quickly it took him to get lost. The first trenches he had known had been at the Aisne, where they were simple ditches dug to shelter troops while they were in contact with the enemy. In Flanders a few months later the trenches had become more complex. Not only did they form a network of mutually supporting fighting positions, but they also had to serve as accommodation for the fighting men, even if that accommodation was rudimentary in the extreme. Wyndham remembered how, even in so small a patch of ground as Fitzmullen-Brophy's men had held, one could get so easily disoriented by any new digging or construction.

A year and a half later, he might have thought that the line at Loos had been deliberately designed as a labyrinth rather than a defensive system. Even with a guide he quickly lost direction.

The path up the line sank underground quite early on, and even though there was only the one way to go, it switched and zig-zagged at irregular intervals. This was to obscure the trench from observation and to baffle blast, but its immediate function was to flummox new arrivals. Once the approach trench branched off into various communication trenches, support trenches, and fire trenches, you might as well give up.

As Wyndham remembered from his first spell at the front, all troop movements took place at night, so what with the dark, and his inability, being below ground level, to see any landmarks, he just had to trust that the guide knew his left from his right. It was practically the first thing the army taught a man, but given the confusing directions he was hearing, Wyndham was suspecting that the guide might have missed out on that particular period of instruction.

There were signposts, but snippets of information like 'B Coy HQ', 'Keep Left', and 'Unlabelled Lines Liable to be Removed' did not build for Wyndham a coherent picture of the lie of the land. And then, just in case he was concentrating hard on where he was going, or about to start cleverly laying a trail of bread-crumbs, he would walk into a strand of telephone wire, which always seemed to be strung at eye level.

'Mind the wire there, sir.'

'Thank you. Mind the wire there. Pass it on.'

'Mind the wire. Pass it on.'

'What wire? Ah Jesus!'

'Quiet, that man!'

And so it went on, for what felt like miles.

They settled in eventually to a stretch of reserve line. There was a handover in which the Dublins shuffled out and the Munsters squeezed in past them. The outgoing officer imparted some necessary local information to de Roche and various stores were signed for. They dumped their gear in a headquarters dugout that was alive with fleas. Wyndham was intrigued that Major de Roche, who was given to berating the servants over a spotted tablecloth, merely ordered some patent powder to be sprinkled over his designated sleeping space, before getting on with things.

Wyndham spent the next few hours blundering about in the dark, trying to make sense of it all and look competent while he was at it. He eventually saw his platoon fed on bread and jam, watered on tea, and disposed in what he hoped was an alert and tactically sound manner. After that he was reminded that there was no real rest in the trenches, and certainly not for junior officers. He and McCarthy-Moore managed their responsibilities by endless consultation, periodically meeting up on their rounds to share timely advice and moral support. McCarthy-Moore respected Wyndham's prior experience and Wyndham was endlessly reassured by McCarthy-Moore's steadiness and good sense.

In the small hours they shared tea laced with whiskey in the dugout. All was well. No one had pilfered the rations, or deserted, or let the Germans through. Keep this up and the war mightn't turn out so badly. Occasional distant shells weren't even making Wyndham flinch any more.

Dawn gave them all a sense of solidarity. As was the unwavering custom all along the line, the men stood to their arms at that hour. They lined the parapet, staring with steely gaze out into the grey light, watching for a German attack, but men couldn't help glancing at each other. They saw themselves, grimy and resolute, with bayonets fixed, looking like real soldiers.

They learned the routine of the trenches, which for the men meant trying to sleep between stretches of watching and bouts of digging. This maze of trenches wasn't going to maintain itself. For the officers, it was constant nagging and supervision, with a surprising amount of paperwork on top of it all. There were missteps but no disasters. The Munsters learned their trade and did not disgrace the regiment.

Wyndham, in paying his compliments at neighbouring platoons, was even learning his way around pretty well. The Dublin Fusiliers had been in residence for some months and had made their mark by naming their trenches after their home town. Thus, the Munsters occupied a stretch of fire bays known as Dame Street, broken by a communication trench called Georges

Street, and ending at a noisome sump called College Green.

After a few days, word came that they were to be moved up from the support line to the front line, and the officers were encouraged to go up in advance to see how things stood. It was a journey of no more than three hundred yards up Middle Abbey Street, but the Munsters were conscious that they were moving into a more unforgiving realm. The Dublins, certainly, were in stern mood that day. Officers scowled through periscopes and men muttered darkly among themselves. Fritz, it seemed, had been taking liberties in the night. Fritz was playing jokes that the Dublin Fusiliers were not finding in the least bit funny.

De Roche, having seniority, was the one who asked what was going on and, tight-lipped, a captain of the Dublins gave up his place on the trench periscope.

'At two o'clock. Gap in the wire. A whisker to the right. Do you see it?'

De Roche saw it, and silently indicated that each of his officers should take their turns and see it, too.

His thoughts filled with German frightfulness, Wyndham was half expecting something along the lines of a crucified nun, so it took him a moment to recognise what he was looking at. It was a simple signboard placed by some daring patrol within clear sight of the Dublin trenches.

Irishmen!
We will not fire on Sackville Street!
The Royal Artillery will do that for us!

'Blasted cheek!' said someone, but of course it was worse than blasted cheek. The Hun had been allowed close enough to learn the layout of the Dublin trenches, and that was disgraceful. Worse, the Hun was making jokes about the Easter Rebellion, and that was in very poor taste. What was so much more insupportable than that was that he was trying to create a rift in the British Army, suggesting that English and Irish troops were on different sides. It wouldn't do.

'It won't do at all, gentlemen. That sign must come down, but we daren't make a move until nightfall. He'll have a sniper with his sights on that sign, devil a doubt, just waiting for us. No doubt he'll have a machine-gun on fixed lines waiting in the dark, too, but that can't be helped. I'll not abide that damn sign.'

Wyndham grimly nodded along with everyone else at the Dublin colonel's words, but then his blood chilled when he heard de Roche.

'My men can do it, sir. Least we can do.'

Least we can do for what? *What have the Dublins ever done for us? This is Dublin business!* But Wyndham's alarm was quieted by the Dublin colonel.

'Good of you to offer, de Roche. Would have expected no less. But not on, I'm afraid. Your men don't know the ground.' Wyndham breathed again. 'But don't fret. We'll have plenty for your fellows to be doing soon enough.'

And Wyndham, who had begun to think of himself as brave, found his palms sweating all over again.

60

'Get a bit of your own back, boys!'

—Captain Hugh O'Brien, 2ⁿᵈ Royal Munster Fusiliers, killed at Festubert

Higher authority was all in favour of some stunt to discomfit the Hun. Indeed, large-scale raids had been underway all along this sector of the front for weeks now, on and off. Anything to keep German reserves tied down and away from what was going on down south. So, when the Dublins first sent out a patrol to retrieve the German sign, the higher-ups were all for it. Further, they approved a madcap scheme to send a patrol into the German trenches to cause a little mayhem. Honour of the regiment and dear old Ireland aside, it would be worth a few casualties if it made Fritz hopping mad to the extent that he sent his reinforcements here rather than to the Somme.

What mattered not at all to the figurings of the brass hats was that the men who were to risk all for Dublin's honour would be Munster men. De Roche's men just happened to be in the front line when the decision was made, so to de Roche's men the task would fall.

'You'll take plenty of hand grenades, of course. Bomb them to blazes. Ideally, of course, you should pick up any signage you happen to see handy. Something in Gothic script for preference. A sign saying Unter den Linden or what have you would look bloody well hanging in the mess. A real feather in our cap.'

Perhaps then, thought Wyndham, *it would be simpler if I just brought you back a feather.*

Because it was to be Wyndham's show.

It was the fierce Major O'Donnell outlining the scheme, but

de Roche – who really should have been standing up for his own – was nodding as though he saw no reason why Wyndham shouldn't lead his men into the dark. Lieutenant Wyndham was an Old Contemptible after all, and had done this kind of thing before. Of course, Captain Doyle was an Old Contemptible too, but de Roche reckoned that he needed his company commanders. Also, the Dublin major, forgetting young Mr. Wyndham's name but remembering the spirit he'd shown that first time they'd met, thought that this was just the thing for the cocky young man with his unorthodox tunic and bruiser's face.

As fingers pointed at a map in the candle-lit dugout, and voices of authority laid out lines of approach and passwords, Wyndham's mind raced. Wasn't Private O'Regan in Currran's platoon a sign painter? Could he run up a convincing Unter den Linden at short notice? Would Major O'Donnell notice that the paint was still wet? And then he heard himself speak.

'I beg your pardon, sir, but I don't think the men are up to it.'

The Dubliner looked surprised. De Roche looked outraged. 'The devil do you mean, Wyndham?'

'I mean that while no doubt they're in fine fettle, sir, they've never been out in no-man's-land before now.'

O'Donnell looked sharply at de Roche. 'This true?'

'I'm afraid it is. But I really don't see—'

'Should have damn well said so, man. Can't send a platoon out on a raid if they don't know where they're going.' Wyndham felt his knees weaken in gratitude. Too soon.

The pitiless major thought for a moment. 'No. Can't have a whole platoon stumbling about in no-man's-land in the dark. But you can keep a grip on a half-dozen good men, can't you, Lieutenant?'

In the dim light he couldn't see Wyndham pale. 'Sir?' he said.

'It's a fairly clear path there and back. Level ground. You've done it before, lad. Take a trusted NCO. Don't be too ambitious –

not with so few men. But get right up to his parapet at least. And bring bombs. You never know what opportunity you might meet. Right. Settled? Good. Choose your men, Lieutenant, and then get some rest.'

Wyndham walked out on wobbly legs, his heart beating too fast. It had begun to rain.

He sat in the dugout, not seeing the map provided to him, not hearing the earnest advice of the officer of the Dublins who'd had some experience in leading patrols. The officer saw that he'd have to go through his instructions all over again.

'Look. It's all pretty simple. We'll show you where to start off – it's a fairly straight line until you get to here. Then you angle left from the tree stump and you should be able to get through the German wire. If you miss the stump then you might as well come home. You can throw a few bombs about to keep Major O'Donnell happy, but I wouldn't bother. If it's a choice between a Jerry bullet in my backside and Major O'Donnell being happy, I know what I'd pick. Sure, if you're going back to the Munsters soon you won't have to put up with him much longer. Have you got that now?'

Wyndham nodded politely, but it didn't look as though he'd taken anything in.

'The password is "Bray" and the countersign is "Howth". Got that? Don't forget or a sentry might shoot you.

Wyndham nodded again, but the Dublin officer still wasn't convinced.

'Look, it'll be grand. You'll be grand once you're out there. Don't mind that your nerves are at you. It's only nerves. Have some of this.' And he held out his hip flask.

McCarthy-Moore dropped by later, to find Wyndham alone, staring blindly at the trench map, a mug in his hand. One of the servants came in from the back, his voice more suited to a hospital ward than a dugout.

'Major de Roche says he should be getting a bit of rest, sir, but it's no use. I gave him whiskey in his tea to make him sleep, but he doesn't want to lie down.'

McCarthy-Moore nodded in understanding, waved the man away, and pulled up a box to sit on.

'Look here, Wyndham. I've heard there's something on for tonight, and I was just wondering. Would you mind if I went instead?'

Wyndham jerked awake.

'McCarthy-Moore! I wouldn't dream of it! I wouldn't consider it an instant. No! Thank you. But no.'

'Really?'

'Really! This is my show. It's very good of you, but this is mine.'

'But look here. You've done this sort of thing before. Wouldn't you like to let another chap have his chance? Me, for instance? It's what I came here for, after all. To France, I mean.'

'You're a good friend, McCarthy-Moore, but I just can't.'

'I understand. You should get some rest.'

Wyndham fumbled at his watch. 'No,' he said. 'No. I really have to tell the men. I need to find volunteers. Oh Lord.' He drained his mug. 'Give me a minute.'

'Take your time, old man. I'll see you later.'

It took a while, but Wyndham found his resolve. *What have I come here for, after all?*

The rain had grown heavier through the afternoon. Wyndham had the platoon assembled and he sloshed purposefully up and down the trench, brushing close up against the men who lined it on one side.

'We're going out on a raid tonight,' he said. 'We're going to pay friend Fritz a visit.'

'I want volunteers,' he said. 'But this isn't a job for just any-body.'

'I want poachers,' he said.

He paused and looked slowly around at them, his face a savage grin.

'I want the burglars and the thieves and the dog-stealers.'

He sounded as though he'd been rehearsing this little speech for the past hour.

'You, Finnerty! You got the makings of a second-storey man – an area sneak? Because that's what I want. That's what it'll take.

'Out there beyond the wire you'll need to be silent as death. You'll need ice-cold nerve and a heart as black as Satan's hat. I want men who'd wring a neck or cut a throat easy as breaking wind but a damn sight quieter.'

He stopped in front of every second or third man, chest to chest with them, staring hard into their faces, sneering.

'They told me you were desperate men. You a desperado, O'Loughlin? You itching to bring back a couple of Boche scalps?'

'Yessir!'

'What are you doing with yourself tonight, Cronin?'

'Going on a raid, sir!'

'Damn right you are, man! You're going out through the wire with a blade in your hand and murder in your heart. Isn't that right, Moriarty?'

'Sir!'

'Because it's not no man's land – it's ours!'

Moriarty followed him back down the trench. When they were out of sight of the rest he took Wyndham by the elbow. 'That was really good,' he said. 'Have you been drinking at all?'

'Moriarty! That is an impertinent question!'

'Yeah, well never mind that. Do you have any for me?'

Wyndham didn't know how to answer for a while, but then stammered that he'd see what he could do if Moriarty would follow him back to the dugout.

'Jesus. You should really buy yourself a hip flask. You know that? Officers know nothing these days.'

McCarthy-Moore called back as darkness was falling. He offered again to take Wyndham's place, but it was obvious that the answer would be a more resolute no than before. Wyndham was smearing boot polish on his face. Maybe it was the candlelight, or maybe there was a glitter in his eyes.

'Just came to wish you luck, Wyndham. See if there's anything I can do.'

'Very kind, McCarthy-Moore. There's nothing, thank you.' And then the pose and the clipped tones vanished a moment. 'Actually, would you mind terribly checking my revolver?'

'Of course.'

Knowing that the servants were on the other side of the curtain, Wyndham leaned close and whispered. 'Do you know – I've never actually fired it.'

'Really?'

'Never even used one. Not sure if I've even loaded it correctly.'

McCarthy-Moore smiled. 'Not very American of you. So much for six-gun Dan Wyndham anyway.'

Wyndham laughed, too loudly and shrilly. A servant appeared with a mug. 'A drop of tea before you go, sir. There's a bit of whiskey in there to perk you up.'

McCarthy-Moore helped Wyndham with his kit, checking this and tightening that, murmuring little reassurances.

'Yes. You're better off without a tie.'

'Hmm. In the left pocket, I think.'

'Bray and Howth. Nothing to worry about.'

Amicably sharing the same quarters for more than a year, they were used to these small practical intimacies, even though they still weren't comfortable addressing each other by first name.

And when the time came, they went out into the trench together and found the men, silent and bright-eyed, likewise attended by their mates who were giving them last puffs of cigarettes and checking the panoply of knives and clubs that had been conjured up for this escapade.

De Roche was also on hand, and he'd been joined by Major O'Donnell.

'Wyndham!' said O'Donnell, as though that he'd just made the effort to learn the name. 'Bloody good. Know what to do, eh? Bloody good. Tot of rum for the men when they come back. Damn big tot if they deserve it. Here, have a drop of something yourself to keep the chill out.'

But Wyndham wasn't feeling the chill. He wasn't sure what he was feeling, but it wasn't the cold. Major O'Donnell went on.

'Give it a few minutes. Got the artillery to lay on a bit of a barrage on your right. Diversion. Keep Fritz's head down. Keep him guessing. Feeling fit?'

'Yes, sir. Thank you, sir.'

'Bloody good.'

And they stood there in silence as the last rain fell.

'Any minute now.'

The moon broke through the clouds, and Wyndham felt better. He knew that the light would make him more vulnerable, but it was better than darkness.

'Where the bloody hell is that artillery?' And O'Donnell said something shocking about the habits of artillerymen that, despite his preoccupations, made Wyndham think that he'd never be able to look at a horse the same way again.

De Roche, to dispel the scandalous image, and to keep the men from tittering, said, 'Surely, O'Donnell, we can go ahead without the artillery?'

'*We?*' thought Wyndham.

'Of course we can, de Roche, but that's not the bloody point. The damned gunners might be asleep on the job, or they might just have got the wrong end of the stick. What if they put down fire at the wrong time and place? Such as when your chaps need absolute silence? Or maybe right on top of your chaps? Think of that. It's no bloody good. I'm going to telephone them.'

The night was so quiet that they could all hear him shouting down the telephone even though he was fifty yards away and underground. Then there was silence. Then there was the sound of the telephone buzzer and more shouting.

A messenger came to summon de Roche to the dugout. Wyndham was told to stand by. It took another hour of waiting before the show was definitely cancelled.

De Roche's men, the Dublin battalion – the whole of 16th Division should pack up their gear. They were being pulled out of the Loos sector.

They were going south.

The move was conducted with surprising rapidity. Within forty-eight hours of that harried telephone message, de Roche was handing over his section of the front to a company of Kitchener's finest, fresh from England, and Wyndham was outlining the situation to a teenage officer who was raring to have a crack at the Hun.

'Angle left at the tree stump and you should be able to find a way through his wire. There's really nothing to it, but I should leave it a few days if I were you. We gave the Boche something of a hard time while we were here and he's going to be on his toes.'

As if to lend truth to this tale, the German guns started up an exploratory shelling of the Irish line. It was custom and practice to bombard trenches when reliefs were being undertaken. After all, the handover meant that the trenches would be crammed with twice as many targets as usual. It wasn't that German intelligence was particularly up to date: it was just that, given the routine of trench life, it was a fair bet that something would be afoot on any given evening.

'I say, is it always like this?' asked the wide-eyed youngster, as the first shells searched for positions within a few hundred yards of them.

'Oh no. Sometimes it gets quite bothersome,' said Wyndham. 'Well, so long. I'm sure you'll figure everything out for yourself in no time.'

His haste was not indecent. The shelling was not uncomfortably close or heavy. All the same, though, there was no reason to loiter.

Moving out of the line was the same vexatious stop-start as moving in, with contradictory directions being passed up and down in the crowded night, and frustrating halts being made to allow the way ahead to be cleared, or for men behind to catch up. God forbid that anyone should have left anything important behind, because moving back against this jostling throng would win a man few friends. Some cursing in front of him announced that someone was trying to push through, and Wyndham would have pulled rank and stood his ground if he hadn't at that moment heard the call for stretcher bearers being relayed down the line.

'Beg your pardon, sir. One side, sir.'

'Who is it, do you know?'

'Haven't a clue, sir. Sorry there.'

But in no time the answer came. It was Mr. McCarthy-Moore, poor fella, and there was no need to hurry.

'God be good to him, Mr. Wyndham. That was rotten luck.'

If there had been anywhere to sit, Wyndham would have sat down, but as it was, there was nothing for him to do but stumble on through the dark, blindly following the men in front.

61

We are told that if Irishmen go by the thousand to die, not for Ireland, but for Flanders, for Belgium, for a patch of sand on the deserts of Mesopotamia, or a rocky trench on the heights of Gallipoli, they are winning self-government for Ireland. But if they dare to lay down their lives on their native soil, if they dare to dream even that freedom can be won only at home by men resolved to fight for it there, then they are traitors to their country, and their dream and their deaths alike are phases of a dishonourable fantasy.

—Sir Roger Casement, speech from the dock, 29th June 1916

They carried McCarthy-Moore's body with them on the way out, and gave him a most decent burial in a cemetery behind the lines. That was something, at least.

Wyndham grieved, but that was his own business. He was angry that he'd let himself forget the randomness and unfairness of it all. You didn't need to be a hero or a sacrificial victim for the war to kill you. All you had to do was don khaki and place your foot upon the duckboard track that led inexorably to the land without second chances.

The day they buried McCarthy-Moore near Vermelles was, as it transpired, the day that Sir Roger Casement was hanged in Pentonville Prison for his part in the Easter Rebellion. Curran read about it in the papers, but unlike his brother officers, Curran read about it in the sort of papers that would never be taken by the regimental mess. No, these were of a more political flavour, sent to him privately by a friend, and he made sure that it was in private that he read them, especially given how things had been since Easter.

Officially, Casement had been *convicted and punished for treachery of the worst kind to the Empire he had served.* And it was a fact that he had been to Germany and had tried to suborn Irish prisoners to turn their coats and fight in German uniform against the British.

But there were other views.

One sentiment, which could never have been voiced in the regiment, was that Casement's hanging had been an act of murder: *another instance of the perfidy and hatred of the English Government towards Irishmen and Ireland.* That certainly could not have been said aloud in the company Curran was keeping now. If his companions had been thinking men they might have been in more agreement with an editorial piece that had it that *Roger Casement's death is a miserable end to a life which for the greater part of its course was honourable and distinguished.*

He hadn't known Casement. He'd heard of him, of course, and had been following the trial in the court papers as well as he'd been able, but they'd never met. Odd, in some respects, seeing the circles they'd both moved in, and the convictions they'd shared – up to a point.

Photographs showed a dapper man, dressed and groomed to the edge of flamboyance. Curran recognised the style. It was something like his own had been once upon a time.

Strange to think of him dying a felon's death.

Roger Casement. Sir Roger. Dying at the end of a rope.

And what about Bartholomew Curran? A public man, after a fashion. A fighter in the cause of Irish nationhood. A life honourable and distinguished – up to a point. And now an officer of the crown, a holder of the king's commission, but facing, he feared, a miserable end to his life.

Curran was unhappy. Part of it was McCarthy-Moore's death. Part of it was that he'd been too long a soldier.

It was easy to give it all up for death or glory when you're young and know no better, or even when you're middle-aged and blinded by something new. The cause for which he'd put on uniform had been like the first giddiness of a love affair. It had given him foolish joy and hope. It had made him forget how he was just too old. Nearly two years later and the illusions were dispelled. Ideally, Curran should have joined up and been killed the very next day, before army life became dreary, before his shortcomings became all too plain.

In the trenches he had seen the Boy Doyle unconsciously in his element: brave because he was young, alert because he was young, sure because he was young. And Curran had somehow endured the noise and dirt and lack of sleep, but his heart had quailed any time he considered that this was a quiet sector.

Curran could lead. He was a born leader. He could stand on the parapet, his words of command louder than the guns, fearlessly urging his men to follow him. He knew he could do that. But could he get up on the parapet in the first place? He was sagging in the middle. His manly girth would soon be a paunch. His noble forehead was in reality a receding hairline. The war belonged to young men like Doyle and Wyndham. It should have belonged to poor McCarthy-Moore. Curran would not die tragically or nobly. Men nearer forty than thirty, men with spreading middles, couldn't – not when younger men were doing it. The younger men were heroic because they had futures to hazard, and that was the difference. If Curran still had such a thing as a future he did not contemplate it with pleasure.

He should really write to his wife. It was only decent. And he should really write to his solicitor, instructing that a hundred pounds be left to a particular friend in Dublin. The younger men didn't have to trouble themselves with distant wives and one-time mistresses. For all the sins of their minds and bodies, they were pure. They hadn't burdened themselves with the baggage of status and the impediments of comfort.

And that was another thing that Curran felt was beyond him: the burden. The literal weight. The marching order that had to be strapped on and carried through the hot dusty days. Fitzmullen-Brophy had been kind and had not obliged a gentleman of Curran's maturity to over-exert himself. De Roche, likewise, had been understanding. But the war didn't care. The war ordered and did not wait. The war sent you on down the road – red-faced, dry-mouthed, sweat-soaked – and it didn't care if you looked foolish, or even if you died in your tracks, too out of condition even to march.

A miserable end to a life that, for the greater part of its course, was honourable and distinguished.

Roger Casement had been brave. He may have been a traitor, but he'd had the courage to be a traitor, and if the nationalist papers had the right of it then Casement was going to be remembered as a man who died for Ireland.

Curran had once thought himself a rebel, but in joining up he had only been doing what so many thousands of others were doing. In the end result there was nothing to distinguish him from the ardent imperialists and the rabid jingoists. They all wore the same uniform now. And Curran found himself wondering if he hadn't put on that uniform for any reason better than that he'd thought it flattered him.

Whether on the gallows high or the battlefield we die, what's it matter if for Ireland dear we fall?

Casement would be remembered. Casement had made a difference. Curran expected that he would be leaving the world without mention or note.

62

Honest and brave soldiers, the world must go on without you, and those who are left to mourn you must face what remains in life with a little of your own fine spirit.

—Mrs. Victor Rickard, *The Story of the Munsters*

The division proceeded south, and at some high level there was undoubtedly some plan at work and some sense to it all, but it was not particularly evident to the men who tramped the roads in sweating columns or were crammed into rickety railway wagons that moved barely faster than a walking pace.

Officers carried less gear on the march and had more civilised accommodation on trains, but Wyndham didn't care much. He had given up on books somewhere along the way and now, when left to his own devices, he preferred to doze. When they finally came to Amiens, which was as close to a metropolis as the British Expeditionary Force ever saw, Curran had to persuade him to go sightseeing.

'Dammit, man, there's a cathedral.'

'There's a café, and I can see a free table. Let's see the cathedral later.'

Curran grudgingly gave in, but even after he'd got his way Wyndham was a poor companion. He wasn't interested in architecture or literature. He had nothing to say about politics or the war. He didn't talk about McCarthy-Moore. Before the unsatisfactory lunch dragged on to a second bottle of wine, Curran hauled them off for a look at the cathedral which, even half-encased in sandbags, was magnificent. Wyndham seemed happy enough to be let wander around, to the extent that Curran had trouble getting him out again when the time came to go.

'Just another few minutes,' he said, not taking his eyes from the great rose window. 'You go ahead.'

Curran was about to say 'damn it' again but realised he was in a church. 'Come on. The war isn't going to wait.' But he let go his irritation when he saw the faraway look in Wyndham's eyes.

Poor young Daniel Wyndham. How old was he? Twenty-three? Twenty-four? And so very far from home. And the strangers who had taken him in were all being lost to him. McCarthy-Moore. Fitzmullen-Brophy. The men of the old battalion, lying in shallow graves in Artois and Flanders, or scattered throughout the vast uncaring army. What was there left to keep a man, with nothing staying long enough to hold onto?

He took Wyndham's arm. 'Come on, Dan. Come on, my poor old comrade.'

Wyndham let himself be pulled by the elbow, and even managed a brief smile.

'We can come back tomorrow if there's time,' said Curran, as they walked back towards the sunlight. 'If the good Major de Roche gives us another opportunity to look to the care and feeding of our souls, at any rate.'

'I don't mind.'

'Well, we can see something else then.'

'I don't mind.'

'Let me give you a treat, Dan. What do you wish for?'

'I don't know.'

'Anything,' said Curran, in an excess of joviality.

'How about a girl with the initials NM?'

'What?'

'Never mind.'

An argument had begun over the name of the town. Apparently, there was a street in Dublin with the same name, so the Dublins who knew that this town on the Somme was pronounced 'Amiens' – a bit like 'amiable' – were wondering what the connection might be. Not that they expected the Munsters to know. The Munsters were only culchies after all. This attitude caused some friction, seeing as 'culchie', as was explained to Wyndham, meant countryman, which is to say bumpkin, which was at least enlightening to Wyndham – who thought he'd heard the term once before – but not good for the harmony of the unit.

'Do what you can, gentlemen,' de Roche told them. 'I'm rather afraid that we must rely on the hospitality of the Dublins a while longer. I was hoping that we could be attached to one of our own battalions by now – it's not as though there aren't any vacancies – but the high command seems intent on pushing us into the line any old how. It is most vexing, but it can't be helped. We must make the best of things, gentlemen. See that the men behave. Show the Dublins that we can hold to a higher standard than they.'

Unusually, Moriarty was not part of the trouble. Indeed, the true son of Cork City had even gone so far as to break up a beery fight between a Dub and a culchie, calmly persuading a Kerry private that the satisfaction of smacking a jackeen wasn't worth a spell on jankers.

'And it wouldn't be jankers on active service, son. It's FP Number One, and who needs that?'

They had all seen Field Punishment No. 1, by which an offender – when he wasn't having the bollocks sweated off him with pack drill, that is – was tied to a fixed object for several hours every day so that everyone could have a look at him. Such a spectacle was on show in the artillery park, where two miscreants were exhibited, spread-eagled on gun wheels, and the flies from the nearby horse lines all over them. Curious fusiliers had gone and had a look. If the cathedral wasn't your class of thing and if it there was no cinema show on, it counted as one of the sights. Wyndham was surprised that Moriarty was actually doing his bit to limit the practice. The Moriarty that Wyndham knew was always content to stand on the sidelines of any bit of chaos or misfortune, and glean from it whatever entertainment he might. And it wasn't even as if the potential brawler was in his section.

Wyndham hadn't really been noticing, but this change in Moriarty dated to when they'd been pulled out of the line at Loos. Since they'd been told of their move to the Somme he'd become less cagey, less jittery. He wasn't yet the swaggerer that Wyndham had first met in Tralee, but a calm had come over him that had not been there in all their time in Ireland or in England. With Wyndham in low spirits, it was even Moriarty who came to offer words of comfort.

'You know I'm sorry about Mr. McCarthy-Moore.'

'Of course. Thank you.'

'He didn't suffer.'

'I know.'

'Bit of shrapnel to the back of the head, I gather.'

'So they said.'

'His helmet didn't stop it. I suppose it did keep his brains from slopping out all over the place.'

'Moriarty!'

'Sorry.'

'For heaven's sake!'

'Sorry. Anyway, he was a grand man. I know he was your friend, like.'

'Thank you.'

'It was just the luck of the draw, you know. There's no need to be fretting yourself.'

'I'm not fretting.'

'I'm just saying. It'll probably never happen to you.'

'No?'

'Course not. The war mightn't last much longer, you know.'

'I seem to remember saying something similar to you when

we were still in England. I don't remember you sharing my point of view then.'

'Ah, sure that was then. That was before this big push. I've been hearing things since then.'

He didn't want to mention that the things he was hearing were not hugely hopeful.

One was always hearing things. The army was rife with rumour. It would be sworn that the battalion was off to Russia, that someone had seen with his own eyes the fur coats already in the quartermaster's stores. Or that fearsome new war machines were being assembled that would roll over the German trenches and crush everything in their path. Or that the Kaiser had run away and joined the circus. Moriarty was always happy to trade in such rumours. You might as well. It wasn't as if the army bulletins were much better at keeping you in the know.

But, rumours aside, it didn't take a genius to look at even the most triumphant newspaper and see that, even after two months of supposed successes, the maps didn't show the front pushing any further east. Fresh units were being fed into the Somme all the time, with nothing to show for it except knackered units staggering out at less than half strength a few weeks later. And Moriarty didn't need to read the casualty reports when he could talk to men who'd been up the line at the beginning of July. If he could get on with Dubliners he could certainly get on with Ulstermen, and a Belfast sergeant, happy for another drink, had told all him about the glory of the 36th Division on the first day of the battle.

Over and through the German defences the Ulstermen had gone, just as it had said in the official communiqué. They had pushed farther forward than anyone else that day, and they'd paid for their gallantry. With battalions cut down to companies, and down to platoons, and those handfuls isolated, pounded by their own artillery, bearing the full brunt of enemy counterattack, they had fallen back at the end of the day. The sons of Ulster were strewn in their thousands across the Thiepval ridge to show what manner of men they were. No one could have done better. Thiepval – an objective of the first hours of the attack – was still in German hands nearly two months later, as if to prove that if the 36th Division couldn't take it, then it couldn't be taken.

'No surrender!' the Belfast sergeant had growled, and slammed his glass on the bar.

Ordinarily, Moriarty didn't care about other mobs getting the shite kicked out of them, and particularly if those mobs were all Orangemen. The thing was, though, it wasn't just the Ulster Division. Ask anyone. Look at the hospital trains forever pulling out of the station. No free berths to be had on any of them.

And now the Munsters were for it.

Étreux. Festubert. Rue de Bois. Even bloody V Beach.

After those, was there any doubt what would happen?

Of course, Moriarty was easy in his mind now, when the only thing left was certainty.

At least the weather was better than Festubert.

63

As to those who today enter your service to help in your criminal wars, I deny them! If they die, if they live, it matters not to me, they are no longer Irishmen.

—Maud Gonne, 'The Famine Queen'

Out of the line an honest attempt was made to make de Roche's men feel welcome. The Dublins and the Munsters were on the same side in this war, after all. A battalion mess was established, if only for the few days they might have before being sent back into the line. Whether in Kildare or Karachi, there was no reason why gentlemen couldn't make themselves comfortable, and you could say what you liked about France, but the place at least wasn't short of wine.

Wyndham was not naturally gregarious, and after the loss of McCarthy-Moore he felt even less inclined to put himself forward among strangers, but Curran was there, and keeping to himself was something of which Curran was quite incapable. Here was a man who had no qualms whatsoever about chatting with even quite senior officers in the most affable manner, which was a little unexpected to those used to traditional regimental life, but a great asset to the mess. He was only alone in a corner with Wyndham that afternoon because the few other officers present were sleeping off lunch. The only one not dozing was a pink-cheeked youth listlessly turning the pages of *La Vie Parisienne*, looking at the pictures. Curran had nothing against the lad, but he had privately admitted that the young officer was too stupid to converse with the grown-ups.

Wyndham's conversation wasn't up to much these days, so

Curran was glad when one of the new Dublin officers looked in, unsure. A draft had come from home the night before, and this was Curran's first opportunity to meet the lieutenant who'd been in charge of them. He knew no more than that the man's name was Philpott, and besides his being new here, the thing that attracted Curran's interest was the attitude the other Dublins seemed to have towards him. He'd sensed it briefly at breakfast. The other officers weren't giving this Philpott the cold shoulder, but a certain awkwardness was evident, as though they'd just found out that Philpott's parents weren't married, or that his brother had been involved in a sensational divorce. Hardly Philpott's fault, but it tended to put a chap at a loss on first acquaintance. That, at least, was how Curran had read it, and he hadn't had found a way to ask any of the Dublin officers to enlighten him.

But now: 'Philpott, old chap! I say, come over here and have a drink with us!'

Curran at his heartiest was more than sufficient for his brother officers to stir themselves and plaintively request him to shut up, but Curran could take far louder protest in his stride. He stood up in welcome and gestured Philpott to a chair in lordly manner.

Philpott looked relieved. His cuffs bore two pips to the one apiece that Wyndham and Curran had, but his demeanour advertised that he was newer to this than they were. No servant of Philpott's had ever had to clean mud from this man's tunic or boil the lice out of his underclothes.

'I'm Curran. This is Wyndham. We're a couple of the orphaned Munsters they've no doubt told you of. Poor little lambs seeking brief solace from the great cruel world. What can I get you?'

Curran was very good. He could make a merciless interrogation sound like polite chit-chat. Wyndham supposed that that if any of Curran's clients had ever been sentenced to death, they'd have been sure to thank Curran sincerely and settle their bill before they were hanged.

Philpott, it was readily revealed, was from Dalkey, although his people had come from Wexford as, coincidentally, did his wife. He worked for some large respectable firm that Wyndham had never heard of, doing something that Wyndham immediately forgot, but Philpott talked about it in the present tense, indicating that his civilian employment was his real life. The army was only temporary. He wasn't even one of Kitchener's men, it turned out. He was Special Reserve.

Wyndham knew all about the Special Reserve. It was the side door through which he himself had accidentally slipped into the army a few weeks before the war had begun. Fitzmullen-Brophy had painted a picture of a jolly military club which a young man would find most beneficial to his character. There'd also been something of a take-or-leave side to the affair, by which young Wyndham, had he found this club not to his tastes, might have left at no more cost than a small payment by way of a cancellation fee. Wyndham remembered Fitzmullen-Brophy's promise to stump up the requisite few pounds himself if the army somehow failed to match up to his promises. Wyndham occasionally wondered if the offer were still open.

Curran was holding forth on the delights of Wexford, the charms of Dalkey, the good name of Philpott's employers and the high purpose of his profession, but he easily worked his way back to Philpott's military service. Under the gentlest of pressure Philpott revealed that he'd spent the war so far doing what amounted to clerical work in the regiment's depot company.

Curran nodded along with the story. 'The depot company,' he said. 'Of course. In Naas, is it not? Indeed. And so you were called up to Dublin at Easter.'

So that was it. That was the secret that was no secret. That was the subject that everyone was reluctant to broach. The reserve battalions and depot companies of several of the Irish regiments were scattered in and around Dublin, so with the police too shy to engage with armed rebels, it was the Irish soldiers who were handed the task of suppressing an Irish rebellion.

Wyndham could understand why the old army abhorred politics, and why they cherished wilful ignorance in preference to considered debate.

Curran, soft-voiced, pressed on, and Philpott, never having expected a sympathetic hearing, unburdened himself. Even after all these months the sense of confusion and outrage could still be heard. More than anything the rebellion was an affront to Philpott as an Irishman and as a Dubliner. Who were these rebels to overturn everything and bring ruin to his city? The elegant streets; all the fine shops; all the money that had gone into refurbishing the General Post Office. All gone. All wasted. And for what? How could an Irish Republic be worth all that broken glass and scorched brick? Think of the loss to business. And the insurance premiums! And martial law (so necessary but so regrettable). Telling good and honest people where they could and could not go in their own city.

No, he'd seen no atrocities – at least not on the part of the troops at any rate.

And no, he'd had no part in rounding up rebels and suspected rebels. And the executions in Kilmainham Gaol? He was frankly puzzled by the attitude of the public. It was one thing for the Sinn Feiners to defend their own, but how could decent, sensible Irish people suddenly take the side of arsonists and murderers? How was it that the government were now themselves the murderers? And how was it that the army, who were only doing their duty (so regrettable but so necessary), had now become not only murderers but traitors?

'Honestly, I was glad to be sent out of Ireland in the end. Of course I'm sorry to leave my wife, but it's becoming insupportable. Mostly things are all right, of course. Most people are perfectly reasonable. But then you meet a friend – someone you always thought a friend – and they ask you how you dare to wear that uniform. Perfectly reasonable people, and now they're talking about a republic. Of course I was sorry to go, but I imagined things would be less complicated out here.'

'Forgive me,' said Curran, 'but am I right in thinking that you've found things somewhat complicated out here, too?'

'Oh, I wouldn't want to say anything. Might be all my imagination. Everyone's been perfectly nice to me.'

'But?'

Philpott looked around and then leaned in.

'But I confess I'm a little uneasy.'

'Speak up. You're among friends.'

'Of course. Of course.' He hesitated a moment before pushing on. 'There's an ugly mood. Or at least I think there is. I've heard talk. There are men – I've heard talk – who are secret Shinners. Not so secret, I suppose. There's talk of revenge for Easter Week. They'll do violence to any officer who helped put down the rebellion.'

'Really?'

'I've heard.'

'Nonsense!' laughed Curran. 'We're rotten with Redmondites in this division – I'm one myself, you know, and young Dan here has the soul of an Irish rebel – but that's no reason to imagine Fenians hiding round every corner.'

And he carried on in this vein a while longer, joking Philpott's fears away.

But Wyndham wasn't so sure. At Easter he'd seen the hurt in the men who'd chosen the wrong adventure and missed their chance to fight for Ireland. He'd also, in his time, seen murder done in the trenches.

He noticed that it was time to be about his duties, and he was glad to get up from his chair and make his excuses. Once, when he'd first left home, filled with visions, he'd have considered that Lieutenant Philpott was not the sort of Irishman that Ireland deserved. Now, with new standards pushing out the old, he felt that Philpott was not the sort of officer that a fusilier regiment would miss.

64

There are riches, there are treasures of every colour in the Gentle Land, the Bountiful Land. Sweet music to be listening to; the best of wine to drink.

—Lady Augusta Gregory, *Gods and Fighting Men*

Wyndham felt that the rear areas were not what they had once been. And he wasn't thinking about the first time he'd been up the line in the autumn of 1914 either. Back then it was still being improvised. Back then it had been some sort of khaki gypsy encampment with added artillery, but there had still been military method to it. What Wyndham was thinking about now, in one of his periodic flights of romanticism, was how little the rear of Fourth Army resembled a proper rag-tag and bobtail. With its pipelines and railway lines and telephone lines, its ration dumps and rest camps and hospitals, it was all as ordered as a city. A dull city, a city without architecture, but all the same a busy working society, with every man having a job and everything squared away. Where, along these roads with their traffic police, might one find the campaign wives and the hordes of fatherless children? Where were the herds of plundered cattle and the roistering cavaliers dicing for looted church silver?

The unruly children did indeed swarm about, begging cigarettes or selling homemade sweets, but one soon tired of their persistence, their occasional thieving, and the fluency with which they could swear in English.

Certainly also, somewhere back here, there were houses where bored and overworked women serviced the soldiery that queued outside, trousers already draped over the arm in readiness, and a brief medical inspection awaiting them at the end of it all. There were, too, the houses where older women poured out *vin blanc ordinaire*, served endless plates of *pommes frites*, and ignored the inevitable ribaldries and the complaints about the thin beer.

It was exotic if you'd never left the United Kingdom before, but there comes a point at which egg and chips no longer broadens the mind. The routine of army life in the dusty fields beyond Amiens did not thrill a young man who had been out in '14 and still nurtured occasional dreams of heroism.

That was what made it easy to ignore the pedlar of souvenirs who had spread his wares out back of an estaminet. He wore greasy khaki instead of a slashed doublet, and the goods on display were a far cry from looted church silver. In truth, his stuff was even a step below what could be had from so many other dealers, but the man was new to the business. Until last week he'd been running a crown and anchor game which was a little more crooked than was healthy for him. A good kicking from a couple of aggrieved Sikh cavalrymen first made him consider a new line of business, and the arrival of the Australians, with their no-nonsense approach to gambling and their forthright means of enforcing fair play, finally convinced him to move on.

He bought his stock from weary Tommies who'd thought it a fine thing to pick up German gear at the front, but were finding it less desirable after they'd lugged it on top of all their own kit bloody miles in the hot sun. If some bloke was willing to offer a couple of francs for a steel helmet, and if the same bloke was making the offer outside a place that sold beer, then why not? The kid brother back home probably wouldn't be all that interested in a Jerry helmet anyway.

The Munsters were not in the market for souvenirs. They were on their way to where they could win all the trophies they could carry. A few did deign to look out of curiosity, because here, after all, were things that had belonged to the enemy. This is what a

German wore on his head. The next time you saw a steel helmet like this there'd be a Hun underneath it. That was something to think about.

But Moriarty had seen Germans up close before, and he'd seen better souvenirs for sale than this old rubbish. He'd shooed his men away, telling them to mind what they were about and to get along after Mr. Wyndham. But a moment later, when Wyndham turned to look, Moriarty was still tarrying with the souvenir man.

'Corporal?'

'Just a minute there, sir.'

'Corporal Moriarty!'

'I'll be there in a minute. Hang on.'

Wyndham told the men to wait as he strode back. It was too hot and he was tired of Moriarty's independent attitude.

'What's the hold-up, Moriarty?'

'You'd never give us the lend of twenty francs there, sir?'

'The price is forty francs, Paddy,' said the souvenir man, 'And I'm not doing nothing with no officer looking.'

'I'll give you twenty right this minute, and don't mind the lieutenant. He's grand.'

'What on earth is all this about, Moriarty?'

'Forty francs,' insisted the souvenir man.

'Twenty-five, and I saw a redcap patrol on its way here.'

'Thirty.'

'Twenty-five. Go on.'

The souvenir man gave in with a scowl, and Moriarty turned to Wyndham in triumph. 'So, do you have twenty-five francs there so? I'm a bit short.'

'Moriarty!'

'Ah go on. It's only about twenty bob in real money.'

'I am not lending you twenty shillings – or twenty-five francs – or any damn money at all!'

'Jesus! What were you going to spend it on?'

'Moriarty! That's hardly the point!'

'Ah go on.'

The souvenir man butted in. 'Do you want the thing or not?'

'Of course I do. Go on, Show it to the lieutenant. He'll change his mind.'

The thing was produced, and Wyndham had to admit to himself that he was intrigued. It was a smoothly finished wooden case of some sort, rather oddly shaped, with leather fittings. Not quite something to entice a rapacious 17th-century mercenary captain, perhaps, but something so much finer than the modern militaria Wyndham was used to seeing. Despite himself, he looked closer as the souvenir man opened a sort of lid at the narrow end of the case and drew out a most impressive pistol.

'Mauser automatic,' he said, as if he'd made it himself. He turned it in his hand to show the customers, and demonstrated how the polished wooden case – actually a holster – could clip onto the pistol's handle to serve as a shoulder stock. Against his will, Wyndham found himself reaching for his wallet. Moriarty hastened him by justifying the purchase.

'A man needs a personal sidearm,' he said. 'An NCO does anyway. You can't look to your men and be squinting through the sights of a rifle at the same time. And it bates a bayonet when you're fighting in a trench, and damn all elbow room. And it's a beautiful looking thing, isn't it? And sure if I have to get rid of it I can sell it for forty francs easily. Come on, so. We'd better be getting along before the redcaps arrive.'

There were no military police that Wyndham had seen, but he understood the need to maintain the fiction and be gone. He also knew he was guilty of unofficerlike conduct. He was further embarrassed when he saw that some of his men had hung back, and had seen at least some of the grubby transaction.

Private Higgins watched Corporal Moriarty stuff his fancy new pistol into his haversack. 'Bottle of fucking hair oil,' he muttered.

VI

THE SOMME

We knew that this time a battle of unprecedented proportions awaited us.

No less enthusiastic than the troops who had crossed the borders two years earlier, we were perhaps more fearful for the greater experience. We felt in the best conditions of spirit and ready for anything; words like 'retire' were banned from our vocabulary. Looking at the diners at that cheerful table, one could have sworn that the positions entrusted to them would not have fallen until after the death of the last defender.

—Ernst Jünger, 73rd Hanoverians, Guillemont

65

There are rumours of peace amongst the politicians, so it will be as well to have a go before they can mature.

—General Sir Henry Rawlinson, Fourth Army

It had come to be known as the Big Push.

It had taken nearly two years, but the British army in France was finally ready to take the offensive. They had made attacks before, but these had been small affairs to make corrections to the line or to provide support to the larger French efforts. Small or not, every time men were sent over the top from the shelter of their trenches. they suffered for it, and to these surges in losses were added the steady wastage, month on month, of men kept continually in the presence of the enemy. The British Expeditionary Force was being steadily reinforced, but the ceaseless toll imposed by the trenches meant that the growth was never as great as was desired.

But as 1916 opened, Kitchener's new armies were at last appearing at the front – unblooded to be sure, and in many cases inadequately trained, but they arrived in multitudes and in high heart. Along with them came the guns that had been so wanting since the war began. All the armies of Europe had realised uncomfortably early how thirsty this war was for artillery ammunition. For the British, with their hopelessly small army, things had been particularly bad.

The Old Contemptibles could remember the dark days at Ypres when their artillery could oppose the German onslaught with no more than a handful of shells per day. In the year that followed things had been little better. Not only did the munitions industry have to replenish the magazines emptied in the autumn's fighting, but they had to vastly increase capacity to meet the vastly expanded needs of the war, and of an army that was growing all the time. It was no small task, but the generals were confident that now, at last, whatever setbacks might await them could not be blamed, as before, on insufficient artillery support.

The British front lengthened. So long confined to Flanders, it now reached south all the way to the river Somme. Kitchener's men took over trenches held up until now by the French, and prepared to join in the war as more equal partners with their allies.

They had the men, they had the guns, and they were ready to win the war.

The plan was for a combined allied offensive, which would naturally be launched where the two allied armies met, on the Somme. The Germans had been entrenched there for nigh on two years and, following French attacks in 1915, had dug in deeper yet. Theirs was a strong position, but the feeling was in the British and French high commands that if the Germans could be broken here they could be broken anywhere. The British, however, were not so hopeful as to believe that the Germans would indeed be broken that summer. It was all very well to have finally the men and the guns necessary for an offensive on this scale, but they'd been disappointed before, and their confidence in Kitchener's novices was limited.

Hence the plan was not for a breakthrough but a push. The Germans would be pushed backwards from their strong positions, onto a line that would be necessarily weaker, and the British, following up, and learning as they went, would find that they wouldn't have to push quite so hard the next time. The Battle of the Somme might not win the war this year, but it would surely open the way for victory.

And how was this first great push to be achieved? The guns would do the work. The guns would smash the German trenches, and the British infantry, who could not yet be relied upon for anything more complex, would move forward, like pieces on a board, to occupy positions that the artillery would have won for them.

The plan was concocted by General Sir Henry Rawlinson, commanding Fourth Army, and it was subject to the approval and amendments of General Sir Douglas Haig, who commanded the British Expeditionary Force, and to whom Rawlinson owed money, which unfortunately made him reluctant to argue with a chief whose optimism occasionally ran away with him.

It was a sound enough plan, even with Haig's interference, and, given the lessons of the war so far, there was no obvious reason that it should fail so spectacularly and kill nearly twenty thousand British troops on its opening day. Indeed, seeing as the army could now actually absorb such horrific casualties, it was judged to be worth giving it a second try a mere fortnight later. This time they were a little less ambitious and a little more successful. Given that success, and the not unreasonable belief that the Germans could hardly stand up much longer to such a concentration of force, Haig let go of the brake, and authorised a continuation of the offensive.

It was now September, and the objectives set out for the first day of July had yet to be achieved, but the Battle of the Somme rolled onward.

There were still enough fresh men of Kitchener's armies to throw into the fight, and those new to it were eager to prove themselves, even if doubts were steadily growing among those directing the battle.

'Rawlinson's a bloody half-wit.'

'Oh, come now, sir.'

'Haig's worse. Has he even seen this ground? Does he have the slightest damned idea what we're about?'

The general, accompanied by a deferential staff officer, was endeavouring to make a proper appraisal of the battlefield, and it wasn't doing his temper any good. The sun was blazing down on the ridiculous tin hat he was obliged to wear, and the air was alive with flies.

'Blasted Huns can see us.'

'I believe that we should be quite safe if we keep still, sir.'

'Not *us*, man. I mean they can see our trenches and they can see every damned square inch of ground we have to advance across. Not a bloody scrap of cover.'

'There are the woods, sir.'

'The *woods* somehow neglect to extend from our start line all the way to the objective. Bit inconsiderate of them, hmm? Rather inconvenient, wouldn't you say? Also, I suspect that the woods, once everyone's artillery has played over them, will amount to little more than a tangle of matchwood, which will not only provide us with little in the way of cover, but might even prove something of an obstacle to our free movement. The woods, in short, are not going to be our salvation.'

'We do have the manpower, sir. The numbers are very much on our side.'

The general lowered his glasses to look witheringly at his subordinate.

'No doubt you were only a heedless youth when this war first started, so you may not recall how the numbers stood then. At Mons we had four divisions.'

As a matter of fact, the man had been a staff captain at Mons but wasn't going to interrupt his general in full flow.

'Four divisions, and only two of them in the line, and we held a whole damn German army off all day. Two years down the road and for this little stunt all we have to do is capture one wretched little village, and they've assigned three whole divisions for the task. One village. Three divisions. And the village is worth precisely damn all. When we take it we will be approximately twelve hundred yards nearer Berlin. Do you think that's progress, hmm? Now would you be so kind as to explain to me how the numbers are on our side?'

The staff officer kept his peace. He had been warned, on taking up this appointment, about the general's sarcasm. The general spared him further venom, and returned to his survey.

'Rawlinson's a damned fool. God help me, but I don't think three divisions will even be enough.'

'The French will be pushing forward on our right, sir.'

'Blasted Frogs.'

'They have been doing rather well so far, sir.'

'Blasted Frogs.'

'And then there's 16th Division available as reinforcement as well, sir.'

'Sixteenth. Bloody Irish. Bloody Johnny Redmond's little pets. Green as their seditious little flag.'

'Who knows, sir? They might be up to the mark.'

'They'll damn well have to be. With any luck they'll be too damn stupid to realise what they're in for.'

66

We would not give up our own country—Ireland—if we were to get the whole world as an estate, and the Country of the Young along with it.

—Lady Augusta Gregory, *Gods and Fighting Men*

As they had feared, the Irish were committed piecemeal to the fight, directed by generals other than their own. Many suspected that politics lay behind it: that there abided in the high command a deep distrust of ten thousand Irishmen, under arms and united.

But as the battle gathered shape the 16t[h] Division began to coalesce. Dribs and drabs, companies and battalions, might be sent forward, attached to other formations, but in the rear there were assembling units from half the regiments of Ireland.

The army's wanton disregard for local loyalties – of which de Roche's men had first-hand evidence – meant that the division was not exclusively nationalist in its character. Two battalions from staunchly unionist Enniskillen were there, as if (suggested Moriarty) they'd taken the wrong bus on the way back from the recruiting office.

And the division wasn't even exclusively Irish. Besides the overspill from Ulster, a battalion from Hampshire had found a happy home among John Redmond's men. The Hampshires were another regiment that vaunted their Indian heritage with the Bengal tiger incorporated into their badge, and their tiger found its natural fellowship with the tigers of the Dublins and the Munsters, but also with the crowned harp of the Royal Irish and Connaught Rangers. And onto each sleeve, whatever the regimental badge, was sewn the shamrock of the Irish Division.

An Old Army man like Moriarty could hold forth to his heart's content on the histories and shortcomings of all of these mobs, and how not one of them could hold a candle to the Munster Fusiliers, but a more romantic soul, with a longer and broader view, could see beyond the regimental rivalries and the redcoated history.

The mustering of the 16th (Irish) Division was something, said Curran, not seen since the days of Patrick Sarsfield.

'An Irish army, Dan. Think of that. A dream from down the ages, realised at last. Don't tell me that these are King George's men. There may be a Union Jack fluttering somewhere behind, but look at the harps. Look at the shamrocks. Listen to the songs.'

Actually, it was the popular music hall hits that were most often heard, with occasional new ditties added by way of the army grapevine. Wyndham was thinking particularly about something recently picked up from a Scots unit about Hairy Mary from Inveraray, but he didn't want to upset Curran.

'This is Ireland on the march, Dan. We're not hirelings serving an English crown. This isn't an English war. We're soldiers in the Great War. This is where Ireland stands up among nations.'

Wyndham was impressed. He felt that Curran needed someone to follow him around, recording his grander sayings in a little notebook. All he could say, though, was, 'Remind me. Who was Patrick Sarsfield?'

Curran looked at him with perplexed disapproval.

'The Jacobite Wars. William of Orange. Late seventeenth century. You'd heard of them?'

'Oh yes.'

'Sarsfield fought for Catholic Ireland.'

'I believe I remember now.'

'Good.' Mollified, Curran got back on track, and resumed his oratorical tone. 'He led the army in Ireland, and after the Treaty of Limerick he led an army of Irish exiles in France. He died in

French service. And at least none of these men need say what he said in the end.'

'And what was that?'

'Oh, that this blood had been shed for Ireland!'

'Whatever blood we shed here, Dan, will not be wasted. Poor Lawrence McCarthy-Moore knew that. He wore the uniform of a British king, but he died fighting for France, and for Ireland, and for all that's worth saving of the old world and for the new world that we're bringing into being.'

For Wyndham, the ghosts of Ireland's heroes were growing ever ghostlier with every day that the army and the war reshaped him. He would never have thought himself cynical, but he was sadly coming to know the true meaning of the word 'disillusionment', and he had never appreciated how much his illusions had sustained him until they were blown away. He had always admired Curran, but now he was filled with gratitude towards the man who could invoke such a noble dedication seemingly off the cuff. He didn't want to die. He had not reconciled himself to the gallant sacrifice. After the spell in the line at Loos he wasn't even sure if he had any appetite at all left for any of this. But now Curran had found the words to revive within him, if only for a moment, something he thought had staled since Fitzmullen-Brophy's departure.

'I'm glad I came,' was all he could say, but he meant it. More or less.

The solemnity of the Irish Division's undertaking was accentuated by the religious services that marked their imminent departure for the front line. Wyndham had been brought up with a certain distaste for the Roman Church, but he could see no fault in the Catholic chaplains who practised their calling here.

Back in Ireland the priests had been quaint men like the Father Bewley who'd attended them in their camp in Cork – faintly comical, old-womanish figures in black skirts, who bicycled about the parish taking tea and trading gossip. The army's priests were a different breed.

They were still surprisingly recognisable. Booted and spurred they might be, but soft bespectacled faces still spoke of the seminary and the framed photograph on a proud mother's mantelpiece. There was little evidence of muscularity. The services conducted throughout the division had nothing of the revival tent about them. The ceremonies of the church were older than those of the army. They did not draw attention to themselves with stamping and shouting. The chaplains went from unit to unit, performing what was sacred by way of routine. The purple stole was unfolded, draped around the neck, and the Latin phrases were read from a book. No melodramatics. No mumbo-jumbo. No holy rolling. It wasn't needed. These men didn't have to pretend. The words they spoke were divine, and they carried salvation in their pockets.

They would be coming into the line with the battalions. Whether it was ordered or forbidden was all one to them. But here, while they could administer the sacraments to large numbers and in the open air, they were making the most of things.

Wyndham watched humbly as night fell on eight hundred soldiers, kneeling bareheaded on the trampled ground between a ration dump and a veterinary post, and a priest in candlelight absolved them of all their sins from an altar of sandbags.

67

'I am your comrade henceforth,' he said.

—'Death the Comrade,' (traditional),
from Douglas Hyde, *The Religious Songs of Connacht*

Moriarty, in nosing around the affairs of this Irish army, had been astounded to discover that not all of them were Kitchener's children. For so long now he had been used to being one of the few remnants of the pre-war professionals. The real army. The soldiers who actually knew what they were doing. Over the past year he had fallen into the role of the solitary elder – the only one who remembered and honoured the old ways. In effect, he did and said what he liked, and no one who had not been at First Ypres or crossed the Indian Ocean on a troopship would dare question him.

And now he was brought up short to hear that this division, barely out of short pants, had recently incorporated the 1st Battalion of the Royal Munster Fusiliers.

The First Battalion. His own battalion. The one that he thought had bled to death last year in the shallows off Cape Helles. It was here. At least some of it.

He wondered how many of the old faces might remain. Surely no more than a handful.

And would any of them remember Private Francie Moriarty, who had sweated with them out in Burma? Moriarty, who was always the butt of Sergeant O'Sullivan's devilment? Moriarty the skrimshanker, who'd hoodwinked a boy of an MO into invaliding him back to Rangoon? Moriarty who must have spread it on thick there, because didn't he get himself shipped home before his time was up? That Moriarty?

No. Too much had happened to them since. They'd have other things to occupy them now – if there were any of them left.

He wasn't going to pay them a visit to find out, anyway.

He'd left that battalion and that life behind in Shwebo. No point in seeking them out on the Somme just to say his goodbyes all over again.

De Roche's Munsters were still green. Their time at Loos had given them a taste of the war, but no more than that. Worse, being no longer a battalion, they were in no position to acquire all the appurtenances of a battalion. Many of Kitchener's formations had come to the Somme inadequately trained, but they had the wherewithal to make good their deficiencies. They had equipment. They had specialists. All they needed was more time. The Munsters had only themselves – a few hundred infantrymen.

Some of them had been trained as signallers and whatnot, but what they'd learned had come from a book. They'd never had a telephone to bless themselves with. The machine-gunners had never had a machine-gun. They'd left their medical officer in England, and relied on their Dublin parent to see to their hurts.

It was a good thing that the Dubliners had picked up a wealth of experience at Loos in the spring, because the Munsters were in need of stretcher bearers far too soon. A long-range shell caught them as they were moving up towards the line.

'Who is it?' asked Wyndham. 'How bad?'

'Mr. Bradley and Mr. Cunningham, sir. It's bad enough.'

In the hotel in Knocknahanna, Bradley and Cunningham had occupied the room next door to Wyndham and McCarthy-Moore. Everyone had been united in the brotherhood of the service, but you can't live with a fellow for eight months without finding things you just don't like about him. Tensions were always appearing, for instance, about hot water, and who was using too much of it. Bradley had used too much of it. He was a hearty outdoors type, and McCarthy-Moore's great team mate and rival on the sporting field, and Wyndham had spent too much of his life standing barefoot on the landing, towel over his arm, listening to Bradley washing off the mud of the pitch and inexpertly singing school songs.

Wyndham would never have wished death by shellfire on Bradley but now, hearing that his fellow fusilier was at that moment bleeding to death, all he could think about was being tackled by him in a game of rugger. Or was it soccer?

Bradley had cannoned into him and Wyndham had been left lying in the cold mud, soaking wet, with his shocked lungs vainly trying to draw breath. Bradley had stood there, bouncing on his toes to keep the circulation going, and he'd asked Wyndham if he was all right. Sincere concern had not been evident in his tone. Then, not hearing anything to the negative, he'd advised Wyndham to be more careful in future and had got back into the game. Wyndham hadn't needed stretcher bearers that day, but it had taken a while for him to confirm that.

And Cunningham? Cunningham hadn't been as tall or as hearty as Bradley, but he'd imitated Bradley's casual team spirit by largely ignoring the notion of personal property. Cunningham had been a borrower. A borrow-first-and-ask-permission-later type. A borrow-and-return-damaged type. A book of Wyndham's had had its spine broken by careless hand – the hand of someone who'd discovered that he didn't particularly care for reading after all, but was sure that such trifling damage wasn't worth telling the owner about. Wyndham suspected that when Cunningham's kit was packed up it would be found to contain a tie with Wyndham's initials on it.

Cunningham had also possessed a poor singing voice.

Wyndham was surprised by the meanness of his sentiments,

but he had spent all the grief he had to spare on his friends and on himself. He suspected that if he had any more it would be wise to keep it for what lay ahead.

So, de Roche's men marched into the great battle devoid of everything but cleansed souls, hopeful spirits and able bodies. They'd have to make do without everything they hadn't got, just as de Roche would have to make do with two fewer officers.

68

To stand before such a storm of fire, much less endeavour to overcome a barrier so impregnable, required men whose minds, as well as frames, were cast in a mould not human.

—William Grattan, *Adventures with the Connaught Rangers*

The approach trenches were, as always, winding. It wasn't just the zig-zag that was built in to prevent enfilading fire. It wasn't just the necessity to conform to the contours of the land. The irregularities had been dictated by the course of the battle, so that the path no longer matched the destination. So even with there being only one trench, and it only going one way, it was difficult to believe that it would take them where it was supposed to. There was no guide. It wasn't felt that one was needed. Wyndham wasn't so sure. He led his platoon along, knowing it would be stupid to ask directions, but feeling the need to seek reassurance from someone. Anyone.

He had thirty men with him, and there were other men occasionally passing the other way, and all in such a tight space that their equipment caught in his buttons, yet he felt alone.

He halted on the pretext of letting the men in the rear catch up, but really to steady his nerves, to remind himself that he was not adrift in a nightmare, and that this was just the war. He checked his watch. What it told him was meaningless. He looked at his compass. That was worse. It didn't really matter what direction the trench was taking, but he thought it a bit much that his dull and dependable army compass should choose this moment to start mocking him. It couldn't seem to decide where magnetic north was. He honestly didn't care himself, but he really wanted the little brass device that had guided his youthful steps around north County Cork to tell him that the foundations of the world were still where they ought to be – to tell him to stop being silly and get a grip on himself. That shouldn't have been too much to ask.

He was still staring at the dithering needle when a signals sergeant, pushing his way past, helpfully told him that there was too much metal in the earth to get a useful bearing.

'But not to worry, sir. Just keep going straight on.'

He lit a cigarette, even though his mouth was too dry for him to enjoy it. Too much metal in the earth. Just how intense did the barrage have to be to interfere with the earth's magnetic field? As if he needed to ask.

The sudden barks of the small-calibre stuff were becoming more common the nearer they came to the front lines, and to work more on the nerves there was the occasional howl of a heavier shell as the German long-range guns quested for the British lines of communication. The trench was shallower than was safe because of the ceaseless pattering of debris, and more than once they came to a place where the trench had been obliterated entirely. Wyndham's shoulder muscles had been permanently bunched since they'd arrived at the battlefield. His neck hurt from the unrelenting tension and the weight of the steel helmet he was afraid to take off.

One of the Munster officers was coming back down towards him.

'What's the matter, Dan? Major de Roche wants to know what the hold-up is.'

What was the matter? He could hardly say that they'd taken a wrong turning or that one of his men had thrown a shoe. No. It was just that Second Lieutenant Daniel P. Wyndham was having an attack of the jitters.

'Tell him it's nothing. Tell him we're right behind.'

He was going to push on, if only to avoid being branded with the nickname Windy Wyndham, which he always felt was right there, inviting anyone to pick it up and use it. But they weren't pushing on just yet. Without warning – as was always the case – a whizz-bang struck nearby, no doubt exacerbating the magnetic anomalies of the soil, and causing Wyndham to drop his cigarette down the front of his tunic.

Everyone crouched on the floor of the trench, thankful for once for all the gear they had piled onto their backs. Their instincts were sound, because several more of the angry little shells sought them soon after, smacking their eardrums. When it was over, Wyndham's fingertips were white from trying to pull the rim of his helmet down as far as it would go. His ears were ringing, but he was able to hear the call for stretcher bearers even before he had a chance to ask if anyone was hurt.

The unsteadiness of his legs was perfectly familiar to him by now. Weak knees, he'd learned, had nothing to do with coward-ice. They were just something you got when distant strangers tried to kill you with high explosive and jagged metal. Nothing to be ashamed of. Nothing to worry about. Meanwhile there was the business of the wounded. His wounded. He pushed his way back down the line.

'Who is it? Who's hit?'

'I don't know, sir. Back down there, sir. In the rear, I mean.'

He kept on asking as he shouldered his way closer to the rearmost men, and just before he turned a last corner he got an answer.

'Moriarty, sir. Corporal Moriarty's hit.'

It couldn't have been too bad, seeing as Moriarty had been well enough to call for aid by himself. He'd been the very last man in the platoon, and there was a sizeable gap between him and the tail of the little column. If he hadn't shouted it might even have been a while before anyone missed him.

He was sitting upright, tightly gripping his thigh, his face white and his teeth clenched.

'Sorry, Mr. Wyndham,' he said, with an attempt at levity. 'Bit of shrapnel must've caught me. I'll be grand.' But then his face contorted and he swore at the two men who were hovering over the wound, afraid to touch anything.

'Go on away, the pair of you,' Moriarty told them. 'You know nothing. Leave me to the stretcher bearers or you'll only make it worse.'

They looked at Wyndham and Wyndham gave them a nod of dismissal before crouching down and having a look for himself. The 'bit of shrapnel' appeared to have struck Moriarty in the thigh, gone all the way through, and ended up in his calf.

'Jesus, but that hurts! I didn't think it would hurt that bad!'

'It doesn't look too serious. Just stay still. The stretcher bearers will be here soon.'

'Are Finnerty and Cronin gone? Can anyone see us?' He grabbed Wyndham's shoulder and shifted himself painfully.

'Moriarty, what are you doing? Don't move!'

But Moriarty ignored him and pulled free something he'd been half sitting on. 'Take this. Quick. Before anyone else gets here.'

'What are you doing? What is it?' But Wyndham saw what it was. It was the German pistol that Moriarty had acquired at a knock-down price outside Albert.

Wyndham thought that he was growing hard in the service. He would never have thought that his disappointment could be so deep.

'Moriarty!'

Even with the life's blood oozing through his fingers and turning his trouser leg black, Moriarty was sorry to see the look on Wyndham's face.

'It just went off. I must have done something with the safety catch.'

'Moriarty!' And this time it was less of a rebuke and more of an appeal.

'Look, will you take the blessed thing? Go on. I'll be fine if they pull a German bullet out my leg, but it mightn't look so well if I'm carrying the pistol that fired it. Go on. Sure, you paid for it anyway.'

As the stretcher bearers bustled round the corner, Wyndham stuffed the pistol into his haversack, feeling betrayed. The man who had first inveigled him into the army was bowing out, leaving him right in it.

69

The Battle of the Somme has again shown the decisive value of machine guns in defence. If they can be kept in a serviceable condition until the enemy's infantry attacks and are then brought up into the firing position in time, every attack must fail.

—Headquarters, 6th Bavarian Infantry Division,
3rd September 1916

Before the war Guillemont had been a village of enough importance to boast a railway station. The land roundabout was, to eyes used to the Irish countryside, flat and open. To those who'd learned the subtler elements of geography on the Western Front these past two years, the gentle undulations were more obvious. To the men of the 16th (Irish) Division, who'd lain prone in shallow trenches under German observation all through a long summer's day, the slight rise leading to the village was a hill of murderous intent. A few days before, they had left those trenches and advanced up that hill, and their bodies, and scattered parts of their bodies, marked their ordeal still.

The corpse-littered ground had until recently been pleasant, if unremarkable, farmland. It was now a desert. All the vegetation had been seared away by both sides' artillery. Guillemont itself had been likewise flailed by shellfire until its main street was no more than a furrow between low heaps of rubble. Had the shattered paths not still been leading there, the village might easily have been passed unnoticed. But its continued existence was still advertised by the attention given it by the guns that had turned the houses to rubble and now the rubble to dust. Thousands of feet up, the artillery observation aircraft could still see Guillemont clearly. It was a stain on the landscape the colour of pulverised brick.

Only on maps did it retain its former state, with streets and houses indicated, but even those maps were scarred all over with wandering lines of red and blue, the trenches of enemy and friend, which, alas, had more relevance than streets and houses now.

And the village had lost even the dignity of its name. In the mouths of the khaki soldiers it was 'Gillymong' – which seemed too sad and silly a rechristening for a place of such massacre and martyrdom.

Guillemont still had its inhabitants. Long before the first bombardment had come crashing down, the Germans had tunnelled deep, and through the summer the reinforced cellars had been both refuge and stronghold against the French and British onslaughts. The guns that had levelled the village above had been unable to destroy deep dugouts beneath, and down in the lamplit dark the Germans had sheltered from the fury, organised their defence, and tended their wounded, right until the moment the hand grenades came rolling down the cellar steps and the men in khaki followed them down to round up dazed prisoners or to finish the bomb's work with the bayonet, as their tempers suited.

There was blood still splashed on the walls of the bunker in which the Munster officers now found themselves. Nobody was likely to clean it up. You might as well sweep the front step while you were at it, except that being above ground, especially in daylight, was something of a risk. The Germans had been driven out of Guillemont, but they were still nearby. Particularly, they were in Ginchy, the next village, which lay only two thirds of a mile to the north, and it was to Ginchy the 16th Division, along with a few extra Munster Fusiliers, would be going next.

Wyndham and his brother officers were crowded round a table lit by a candle stuck in a whiskey bottle, and they were doing their best to look grave, attentive and intelligent as they stared at a map and listened to a lieutenant of the Dublins explain the battle to them.

The lieutenant was perhaps twenty-one or twenty-two, and his dark curly hair fell boyishly over eyes that had lost all trace of youth. His uniform was practically white with dust and could have stood up by itself. Perhaps, thought Wyndham, it was the only thing that was keeping him upright. He had a cigarette stuck to his lower lip, lit off the cigarette that had been there just before. His voice was dry with weariness.

'Ginchy,' he said, pronouncing it Gintchy, and making sure everyone could see it on the map.

'Our line runs roughly – and I mean roughly – to the south, with the French on our right. they're the ones dressed in blue. Don't shoot at them for Christ's sake or they'll only shoot back and they've got better artillery support.

'This bit here is the Quadrilateral. After the village itself, that's the main German position. A square of trenches surrounded by all the barbed wire you've ever seen, except we didn't see it until we were right on top of it. It's in a bit of a hollow and the grass is tall. Didn't even know it was there. That was the end of that attack, let me tell you.' He ran a hand down his face, pulling his eyes grotesquely open, and then lit another cigarette.

'Over here,' he went on, indicating two adjoining rectangles of woodland marked Bois de Leuze and Bois de Bouleaux, 'are Lousy Wood and Bollocks Wood. The Skins fought their way into Lousy Wood and as far as I know they're still there. Much good may it do them. Wood's pretty much intact. A lot of the greenery is still there, and that means so are the Boche, and they've got cover.

'This bit here, this is where you'll be. We took that trench so you're not to give it up. Do you hear me?' He glared at the Munsters and they quickly nodded assent. He recollected himself and went on.

'Right. I'll tell you the truth that it's a rotten bit of trench. The Hun can see into most of it and you can't move unless it's dark. We've identified no less than three machine-guns they've got sighted just on that stretch of line. We've called them Johnston, Mooney and O'Brien – here, here, and here. Or we think O'Brien's here. Bastard moves a bit. Johnston is dug in tight under some rubble and the artillery hasn't been able to do much about it. Mooney is the worst of the lot. All we know is that he's got this bit here enfiladed. Stick up your head to get a bearing on him and you're dead.

'There's no water except what you carry in with you. Your wounded will just have to hang on until dark, or until the Hun gives up and goes away. Any questions? No? Right. All yours.' And he pulled on his steel helmet and climbed out of the cellar on stiff legs. They never saw him again.

70

They pushed up from Guillemont, destruction all around them and visions of worse destruction working on their imaginations. To disrupt the coming onslaught the German artillery had drenched part of the British line with poison gas, and the sight of the casualties coming back – vomiting, gasping, blue with asphyxiation – was a grim enough introduction to the next phase of this Battle of the Somme. The officers tacitly decided that what they had been told in the cellar about the profusion of German machine-guns they might as well keep to themselves.

Good thing too, because, in classic army fashion, they were redirected without warning, and found themselves manning a position not quite where they were told they'd be.

And it was a position that seemed just a little too big for them. It was absurd, but an infantry battalion, with the healthy addition of a few hundred Munsters, could find themselves isolated on a mere few dozen acres of ground that they shared with three whole divisions. Their loneliness was hardly unique. At ground level there was nothing to see except the waste. Except for the corpses, the battlefield appeared empty.

'Wyndham, I want you to establish touch with the Skins over on your left.'

'Very good, sir.'

'Not sure exactly where they are, mind, but it's your job to find out.'

'Yes, sir.'

'Somewhere on the edge of the wood. Casey can go with you. He has a good nose for this sort of thing.'

Private Casey was one of the men that Major O'Donnell used as a runner – a cheeky Dublin guttersnipe who did as he pleased. His job kept him out and about, free of menial tasks and army tyrannies. He answered only to O'Donnell, and he was indulged because there weren't many who would volunteer to take his place.

'It's out beyond here,' he told Wyndham. 'I was most of this way earlier. A bit hairy, like, and you'll see where you've got to keep your head down. Bits of fellas all piled up,' he added with a grin.

He chattered as they wound their way along the shallow trenches, Wyndham trying to keep his head low and keep an eye on his nimble guide at the same time.

'You're that American officer, aren't you? I might go to America after all this. You never know. One side there! Officer coming through! New York, like. I wouldn't mind a bit of that. I'm sorry, Sarge, but would you ever move out of the way there? You'd see it in the pictures like. Ferocious tall buildings. I reckon I could do well for myself there. Alright stop. I said stop!'

The air was full of flies. Two bodies, disarranged and torn, lay where the trench petered out.

'Right. Give us a sec. Now either Jerry's got this place bracketed or he doesn't.'

Wyndham was about to suggest raising a helmet on a stick by way of a decoy, because that was something you did in adventure stories, which was no doubt what he was in now, but Casey had his own ideas.

'I say we just go over and chance it. If we really leg it a sniper won't be able to get a bead on us. The trench is bound to start again beyond. Anyway, there's sure to be a shell hole or something. Ready? Go.'

Wyndham scrambled after. If he was shot at he never knew about it. He landed in some depression a dozen yards farther on, sick with fright. Casey was taking it in his stride.

'That was easy. We should be grand from here on. So, do you know New York, like? Is it really the same as in the pictures? Mind yourself here. This bit doesn't look very healthy. Would you know anyone that I could talk to? To set me up, like? Stop! Don't move. Wait. No. False alarm. We're grand. I think.'

Ahead of them Wyndham could see the shattered wood. It looked a desolate place, but it seemed to promise cover.

'So how did you end up in the culchies – in the Munsters, I mean? I'd have stayed at home in New York. Girls in short skirts and all that. I suppose they wouldn't find it so bad out here – the Munsters, I mean. It's only fields and that. They should be used to that.'

A challenge was heard from just ahead. The voice seemed to be speaking English.

'Take it easy!' shouted Casey, showing caution for what appeared to be the first time, and after a tense moment he and Wyndham crawled the last few yards to a new trench, where a man the same colour of the landscape was keeping watch. A junior officer, every bit as dirty, was coming up behind him.

Wyndham dropped breathlessly into the trench and, wiping the sweat from his helmet band, politely asked, 'The Skins?'

'The Royal Inniskilling Fusiliers,' the officer corrected him, with a touch of testiness. 'And you are?'

'Munster Fusiliers,' said Wyndham. And then, considering the recent confused arrangements, 'Dublin Fusiliers.'

Lest the Inniskilling officer wondered if he were dealing with a particularly ill-prepared German spy, Wyndham said, 'Munsters and Dublins,' daring to be contradicted.

The officer stood a moment, and them snapped an order to the sentry. 'Tell Captain Mulryan that we have visitors from the

Munsters and Dublins.'

'Very good, sir. Visitors from the Taigs and Fenians.'

Wyndham was just glad that he didn't have to go into any explanations. In truth, he wasn't even quite sure why he'd been sent here. Establish touch? Did that mean he was expected to coordinate a battle plan with the neighbouring battalion, or would it be sufficient just to leave his visiting card? Asking the splenetic Major O'Donnell to explain himself would have been ill-advised.

He was grateful that the Inniskilling captain appeared to know the protocols for this sort of thing, and Wyndham was duly ushered into a tiny dugout roofed with fallen timbers where a mug of whiskey-laced tea was thrust on him with perfunctory hospitality.

A map was unfolded. Wyndham, this Mulryan, and another officer who was probably a second-in-command or somesuch, sat so close together that the map – of no great size at all – was touching the knees of all three of them. Wyndham told what he knew, and that seemed satisfactory enough. He was thanked, and that seemed to be it. As he struggled to his feet, though, he was advised to wait.

'Fritz gave us a thorough pounding at just this time yesterday. He's a creature of habit. Best to wait.'

So they waited. Wyndham was almost glad to see that the tension he felt was mirrored in the faces of the other two. He had seen too much offhand stoicism and grace under fire. The terrors of war were bad enough without everyone pretending that they were nothing at all. He couldn't have stood it if this Mulryan were to talk about cricket as they awaited the bombardment, coolly drawing on a cigarette all the while.

But the Inniskilling officers were both silent, and Mulryan kept glancing at his watch, and the tip of his cigarette burned hot and angry.

As if to spare them the suspense, the German bombardment

landed right on time. The three officers hunkered down in their inadequate shelter as the air outside filled with dust and smoke and splinters.

When it was over Wyndham made his goodbyes and was gone before anything worse happened. He'd had a sudden vivid premonition. He'd seen his mother, straight-backed in mourning, receiving the condolences of neighbours.

'Yes. Poor Daniel,' she was saying with tragic dignity. 'Killed in Bollocks Wood. With strong drink on his breath.'

He was pretty sure that this was Lousy Wood, but it was an unlucky place nonetheless.

'Come on, Casey,' he said. 'We're leaving.'

71

Artillerymen of the higher ranks were to some extent carried away by the weight of metal for the first time at their disposal.

— Cyril Falls, *The History of the 36th (Ulster) Division*

You had to admit that the destruction was awesome.

Wyndham was peering over the low parapet, supposedly assessing the tactical situation, but he really couldn't make head or tail of it. The enemy was somewhere over there and his own side was in various places roundabout, but he couldn't see anyone and he couldn't make out any trenches even. He'd really have to stand up to get a proper look, and he was hardly going to do that. Indeed, if he were sensible, and didn't care about this officering business or what anyone might think of him, he'd be keeping his head well down, and never mind the state of the damn battle and the dispositions of the troops.

But he was finding the destruction fascinating.

On their way into the line they'd passed the guns, and they took a long time in passing. The little guns of 1914 – the thirteen- and eighteen-pounders – were still to be seen. It was hard to miss them, there were so many. If they'd had numbers like that at Ypres, it was averred, they really would have been having their Christmas duff in Berlin. There might have been heavier stuff in the Salient that winter, but Wyndham had never seen any of it. Now you'd be practically tripping over it. All the big guns you could want, parked wherever there was room for them, banging away day and night, with the supply lines trailing all the way back to the munitions factories in Britain, and the factories not stopping either.

The British guns had given this area a thorough plastering, and the French guns to the south had joined in. Now that the ground was being hotly contested, the German artillery was working every bit as hard, seeking to shred the men of the Irish Division as they clung to their trenches. It couldn't have been an easy task to hit a narrow trench from a distance of two or three miles, but the German gunners were undeterred. If they didn't succeed with their first shot they would try, try and try again.

The Munsters were learning all about the German artillery. They'd picked up a bit at Loos, but their education was greatly intensified on the Somme. Already they had learned to distinguish one calibre of shell from another by the sound it made in the air.

The little ones were the whizz-bangs of course. You tended not to hear them coming until it was too late to do anything about it, but on the other hand they were only little, and if you were under cover you should be all right. On the other hand again, Fritz had masses and masses of them, the same way the British had their eighteen-pounders and the French their famous seventy-fives.

The bigger shells came in higher, so even though they were more frightening, they did announce themselves in good time. That wasn't much help if they announced that they were coming straight at you and you had nowhere to go, but you can't have everything.

Crumps were common. These were the five-nines with which Wyndham briefly and intimately dallied the winter before last. A crump was a no-nonsense sort of shell. Experienced soldiers had respect enough to use the term *Mister* Crump. Wyndham was in no mood to make Mr. Crump's acquaintance again.

Bigger than the crumps were the Jack Johnsons, which, like the heavyweight boxing champion, were black and knocked you out. Unlike the boxer, they were considerate enough to dig an enormous hole for you to be buried in. No Great White Hope had come forward to answer Jack Johnson. All you could do was hunker down and hope he'd miss.

Veterans talked knowingly of Flying Pigs and Hissing Jennies, but they weren't in evidence in this part of the front. Wyndham reflected that Moriarty would be gleefully absorbing all of this knowledge if he were still here, because he was never the sort to let himself be out-veteraned by anyone. But Moriarty had swindled his way out of the war. He'd abandoned a comrade with whom he'd once been on the receiving end of a five-nine – back in the old days, long before anyone called them crumps.

Maybe the aggrieved feeling was what kept Wyndham peering above the parapet. They'd callously put Fitzmullen-Brophy out to pasture, killed McCarthy-Moore, and let Moriarty weasel his way out with a self-inflicted wound. In time, no doubt, they'd complete the job of taking everything away from him. So why wait? Here he was, and the Germans were right there. If they wanted to finish the job, he wasn't hiding from them.

And part of him was still capable of wonder, and the view from the parapet was something to see.

The occasional bursts and fountains of earth were jarring or thrilling depending on how close or distant they were, but what entranced Wyndham was what they wrought.

Back in the Ypres Salient the shelling had just disarranged things and created more mud. Here it was remaking the world. It was stripping and scouring the earth. The railway station at Guillemont wouldn't have been worth a second glance a year ago. Now it was crumpled and twisted and picked up and thrown down – a disquieting marvel. The woods were scorched and splintered. The lanes and fields and houses had all disappeared, merged into the all-encompassing devastation. And over it all the irregular drumbeat of the artillery continued to play.

Awesome.

These were the works of human hands, just like the cathedral in Amiens. The destructive efforts of industrialised war would not fairly be placed beside the craftsmanship and noble purpose of the medieval builders, but if it came down to a straight contest between Amiens Cathedral and the artillery of the Somme, Wyndham knew what his money would be riding on.

72

The attack on such a system of defences as has been described demands in all ranks dash and gallantry of a very high order.

—*Notes for Infantry Officers on Trench Warfare*, War Office, 1916

So, there they were: a curving line of Irish battalions and bits of battalions. The Skins, the Dirty Shirts and the Old Toughs, with the Devil's Own and Paddy's Blackguards extending over on the left, and all of them edging closer to the German positions around Ginchy, pushing in from west and south, aiming to surround the village on three sides before rushing in and finishing the job with the bayonet, just as they'd done at Guillemont.

Wyndham, when he thought about it, was fascinated by how slowly the battle crawled towards its climax. The fire and death were immediate, but the lines on the map went forward in stops and starts. It was only a few hundred yards to Ginchy, and while the pressure was unrelenting, it was taking all week to close that distance. An advance might be conducted as a crawl or a rush, but it never progressed very far.

Wyndham remembered an occasion in childhood when an elderly relative had come to visit – an esteemed man and a crashing bore. He had fought for the Union in the Civil War, and although the part the had played had been small and of doubtful significance, it had given him license to hold forth about it for forty years.

Wyndham imagined a distant future in which he himself might browbeat a younger generation about the Great War for Civilisation. At least, he hoped, he would embroider a bit of colour into his account.

'Forward we went, with our bayonets bright. The flag of Old Ireland fluttered overhead. The music of bugles and bagpipes thrilled our souls and steeled our resolve. Before us, the barbarous German waited.'

'And then, Uncle?' a young relative might ask, desperately blinking back a yawn.

'Why then we went to ground after fifty yards and made tea!'

Not that making tea was easy. Every man carried a ration of tea leaves, because His Majesty's Government knew that the Empire could not fight without the stuff. And this was just the reserve supply. Tea came up from the ration dumps in quantity. Like the equally indispensable tobacco, it was eminently portable, but all you needed for tobacco was a light: it was a right bugger to boil water on the battlefield.

So far the Munsters' advancing had been done by night, and it wasn't so much advancing as being shuffled forward in a general rearrangement of the battlefield. It couldn't continue like that much longer though. All the pieces were nearly in position now. For days Wyndham had been waiting for the order that would commit them to the attack. The guns worked upon the lines. Trenches needed to be held and other trenches dug. Nobody was getting any sleep.

Wyndham watched a dixie of water being heated over a fire made up of a broken ammunition box and a few dozen biscuits. Army biscuits, it transpired, burned surprisingly well. They didn't give off a great deal of heat, but then there wasn't a whole lot to be doing other than carefully feeding a fire with them. Not in daylight.

The position the Munsters occupied now wasn't quite as naked as the one farther forward: the one that had been outlined to them in that cellar in Guillemont. That would be the jumping-off line for when the attack finally went in. Another Dublin company was in possession of it now. Every night their casualties were carried back. It was only just over there, beyond a slight rise in the ground, but to Wyndham it was another world. The slight rise was the last barrier between him and the full intensity of the war.

'How's it coming along, Higgins?' he asked, just for something to say. His eyes felt gritty. He was desperate to rub some wakefulness into them, but his hands were too dirty.

Private Higgins was kneeling by the fire, trying to get the most out of the meagre fuel. 'Ah Jesus, sir. It'll be half an hour yet.' All the same, Wyndham saw that he had the tea, sugar, and condensed milk handy, just in case the water decided to boil suddenly. Higgins had been tea man since they'd moved into the line. He understood the gravity of the job. He wasn't taking chances. When he could, he posted his mates as sentries at either end of the traverse, so if some big eejit came around the corner in a hurry he wouldn't knock the tea over with his big feet. He had taken off his helmet to keep it from slipping over his eyes – or worse, slipping off completely and knocking the dixie into the fire. Wyndham saw that his roughly cropped hair had been moulded by sweat and dirt almost into a cap. He remembered remarks about Higgins and his hair oil but didn't know what all that had been about.

The tea still wasn't ready when word came up from Battalion that they'd be moving forward.

73

'I swear by the oath of my people,' said Cuchulain, 'I will make my doings be spoken of among the great doings of heroes in their strength.'

—Lady Augusta Gregory, *Cuchulain of Muirthemne*

'Now?'

'Afraid so.'

'In daylight.'

Doyle outranked Wyndham by some degree, and Wyndham was a great respecter of authority. Nevertheless, he wanted to make damn sure that he wasn't being sent forward into deadly peril solely on the word of a beardless youth.

'You're sure?'

'Damn it all, Dan. Do you want to go and ask de Roche? Or O'Donnell? Or General Haig? All I know is what I'm telling you. They want us to go forward.'

'To the jumping-off trench? Are we jumping off then?'

'No. I don't know. Oh, for heaven's sake! Don't be such a bloody nuisance! Just have your men ready.'

Further enlightenment did come eventually.

The forward trench had to be reinforced or there just wouldn't be enough men left to mount any sort of attack when the moment came. And if the Germans took it into their heads to counterattack, well that didn't bear thinking about.

So, if the Dublin company had been so much reduced then the Munsters were being sent to man a deathtrap. It was small consolation that they weren't expected to be there for long. The final attack on Ginchy would have to be soon.

At least there was a communication trench – of sorts – leading the way forward. Like all the trenches roundabout it was too shallow. It also gave out just at the low summit of the rising ground, where it came under the direct observation of the German defenders. The body of a man with a shovel marked the exact point where Irish efforts had been finally halted.

It had rained on them on and off these past few days, and maybe a little of that poor weather could have given them cover now, but the afternoon sun shone with cruel indifference on them as they moved out. They were burdened not just with their usual kit, but with rations and extra ammunition and cans of water. Their destination was a desert outpost.

Doyle led the way. It was his company, after all, even though 'company' was something of a title of convenience, what with its only having a hundred or so men to its name, and Curran and Wyndham being the only other officers.

He led them, bent double, until they ran out of trench, and then he led them on elbows and knees until they came to the dead man's rise.

'Right,' he said to Wyndham. Just sit tight here and I'll go and have a dekko. We'll have to hurry after this, and I'd rather like to know where we're hurrying to.'

Wyndham liked Doyle, but no more than that. Now, though, watching him creep forward towards the deadly unknown, he felt a concern for the young man he wouldn't have thought possible. He prayed that Doyle would hurry, that the Germans wouldn't see him, that he wouldn't be harmed. But Doyle went up the slight slope with no more show of apprehension than if, perhaps, there was nothing worse than loud noise waiting for him.

And then, agonising minutes later, he came back.

'Right,' he said. 'It's a little tricky beyond here. Not much cover, I'm afraid. There's part of an old Hun communication trench, but that's all. But just keep low and go quickly and we should be all right.'

Wyndham could never have decried the optimism of the younger generation more than at that moment. He could hear a frightened voice automatically repeating the Holy Name over and over, somewhere behind him.

Jesus. Jesus. Jesus.

Just what I was thinking, thought Wyndham, and straight away checked himself for the frivolous blasphemy. His clothes were sticking to him. He hadn't been able to wash in days. His equipment was slipping and twisting to hurt and hinder him. At least let his soul be pure.

And then the Boy Doyle said, 'Right,' and stood up, and showed again the astounding yet casual courage that made Wyndham ashamed to have ever thought slightingly of him.

Maybe, thought Wyndham, *it's not really so bad. Maybe that's what makes it easy for him to go back there again*. But no. 'Tricky' was what Doyle had said, and it didn't do for an officer of British infantry to overstate the case. A girl might be a smasher, a horse might be a marvel, and a badly played ball might be a thundering disgrace, but a bullet-swept killing ground should never be much more than tricky.

There was nothing to do but follow.

Beyond the stray whizz-bangs that were as much a part of the atmosphere as the flies, all was quiet. But the Germans had their eyes open, and a hundred heavily laden men can only be so surreptitious. The Munsters had found a morsel of cover in what might indeed have once been a trench when a distant machine-gun announced itself. There were cries of alarm and hurt as every man hugged the ground even closer. Doyle somehow managed to push the front of the column forward to a safer position a few-dozen yards farther on, but no one else was willing to risk such a dash in the open. It was just too far.

With the machine-gun bullets drumming on the ground again, an approach on belly and elbows was the only way to go.

Even that was proving too much for some. Some were paralysed with fear. Some saw staying put as the only reasonable option. Curran just found the going too hard.

He was blinded by sweat and bothered to distraction by the flies, and that was before he'd even started crawling. When they'd set out, he'd thought bitterly about how he must appear, red-faced to the point of foolishness, puffing and blowing when the others – even the heavily-laden men – were moving easily. At the top of the rise, Doyle had gone forward like a hunter. Such litheness was beyond Curran – or rather fifteen years in his past.

After the last fifty yards his heart was tripping. He feared that his face was no longer red but clammily pallid. He laboriously crawled up to where Wyndham was.

'No damn good, Dan,' he gasped, but it wasn't at first obvious if he was speaking about the unit's prospects or just his own.

'We have to go forward,' said Wyndham. 'If we stay put they can get us with their artillery. It's not far. There's just this piece of open ground. Then we should be safe.'

Curran nodded, because that was all he was capable of.

In between the bursts of fire they organised the men into small parties, and when the Germans paused to let their gun cool, or to reload, or just perhaps to lull their targets into an illusion of safety, a batch of men began a rapid crawl towards where Doyle was now waving to them. They made it half way before the gun opened up again. Two men were definitely hit. All of them were frozen and prone to the ground.

Doyle was shouting at them, but his voice barely carried above the racket.

'I think he's saying we should run,' said Wyndham. 'I think it's the only way.'

But the men were reluctant to stand up. They were finding

which hollows in the ground were safe from the bullets and their officers didn't seem to be making much of a case for abandoning this moderate safety. Out in the open, the unfortunate few waited for a cessation of fire and then started moving again. A few crawled, out of fear or injury. The rest ran, and most of them made it.

Curran elbowed Wyndham. 'Remember what that Dublin man was saying? Back at Guillemont? He said three machine-guns had the measure of this sector. We have to move before another gun finds us.'

'That's what I was saying,' Wyndham shouted back.

'We have to move *now*! We have to run.'

'I know, I know. How do you propose doing it?'

And straight away he found out, as a great weight pressed briefly on his shoulder and Curran hauled himself upright.

He stood up straight, and thrust out his chest, and inhaled deeply. The machine-gun died away again as he strode out into the open ground and waved his stick at the men still clutching the earth.

'Come on now! Let's be having you, men! Come on now!'

For all the breathlessness of the ordeal just endured, his voice was clear and ringing.

'First group! Corporal Quinn! Stand up now! That's it, my brave boys! Come on now!'

And the men were obeying.

The German machine-gunner seemed to hesitate, but in the end he went for the larger target – Quinn's section scrambling across the open ground. But he was too late, and the men made it to shelter. A burst was then aimed at Curran, but missed, and as the gunner corrected, another group of Munsters was sprinting to join their fellows.

And so it went on. A few men fell, but most made it. And in the midst of it all, waving his walking stick like a banner and bellowing the encouragement he'd heard McCarthy-Moore use on the playing field, was Curran, somehow still unscathed.

He nearly got away with it. Miraculously, he *did* get away with it as far as the machine-gun was concerned, but as Wyndham had feared, the German artillery finally arrived to the party. As the last few Munsters made their rush, a salvo of whizz-bangs burst overhead, and one of the men to fall was Curran.

He was still alive, and no small weight to be dragged off the field by men already carrying more than was comfortable. A shrapnel bullet had dented his helmet and dazed him, and maybe that was what was making him grin, but Wyndham doubted it. They roughly bandaged his various wounds and pulled him along the rest of the way to the trench they were to occupy. There was no medical officer, but the Dublin company had been at this long enough to be able to treat shrapnel wounds. Thankfully, there was morphine, and Curran was soon no more of a problem than could be tucked somewhere out of the way until nightfall.

The line was every bit as bad as they'd been told. Only one machine-gun had fired on them on their way in because only one had a clear line of sight on their approach, but this straggling ditch in which they now found themselves was subject to the attentions of all three of the guns the Dubliners had identified. Standing upright, even standing up at all, was an invitation – depending on where you were in the trench – to Johnston, Something, or O'Bannion. Wyndham couldn't quite remember the names.

He was shown around by a young lieutenant with a tremor in his hands and stinking breath. The man went through two of Wyndham's cigarettes in the time it took him to explain how things were. Despite the desperate situation he was grinning all the time, as though he feared the Munsters might go away again if their welcome weren't effusive enough.

'There's damn all in the way of dugouts. Company HQ is

wherever the officer commanding happens to be, but there's a place at the corner just down there that's kind of sheltered. Kind of. Come on and I'll show you. Keep low.'

Aid post, machine-gun post, sentry post and company stores were all similarly just random locations. Those who occupied them, just random huddled figures. No one seemed to be doing anything other than staying low. Even that usually constant labour of trench maintenance was suspended. Wyndham was going to ask why nothing was being done to deepen the trench when he felt a springiness under his hands and knees.

'Those are the Huns. The ones we took this trench from. They buried them under the floor. We were going to dig them out and sling them in front of the parapet.'

'But?' asked Wyndham, horrified.

'But there were more Huns underneath those ones. We just gave up after that. Too much trouble. And the smell is bad enough as it is.'

Wyndham thought about the old superstition about walking over someone's grave.

'Our lads are here. Fritz gets the floor, we get the walls.' And he patted the earth wall protectively. 'God rest them.'

Wyndham nodded in understanding. He didn't want to have to open his mouth and taste the tainted air.

'If it rains again, I'm afraid this might all come down. We packed in six men here, and that's only here.' There was a crack in his voice. 'Look, you can see Private Byrne's hand coming through already. Oh God love us! Byrne's family have a shop on the North Circular Road. My father gets the paper there'

And to Wyndham's horror the officer, still grinning but with tears running down his face, took tender hold of the corpse fingers protruding from the earth.

'Have another cigarette, please,' Wyndham said.

'Do you mind? Thanks.'

Curran was conscious by the time it got dark. The German snipers were still active, so it wasn't safe to evacuate him, but they were going to do it anyway.

Wyndham sat by his stretcher and told him that everything would be all right. Not that it would be. The shattered unit that had been holding on here was pulling out. Doyle, Wyndham, and eighty-odd Munsters were being left in sole possession. De Roche and all the others weren't far off, but even that short distance was well-nigh impassable, and their own situation was no better anyway.

Curran was hazy with morphine, but he made an effort at lucidity. If a man like Curran couldn't hold up his end of a conversation he might as well be dead anyway. He sounded like a drunken man trying hard to keep up appearances.

'Sorry to be leaving you in the lurch like this, old fellow,' he said.

'That's all right. It's my lurch after all.'

They settled into silence a while. Then Curran asked, 'What do you hold in your hand?'

'What?' Wyndham looked down at the cigarette between his grimy fingers, and then saw that Curran was drifting into reverie or rhetoric. His eyes were closed and there was a smile on his bloodied face.

'What do you hold in your hand?'

'A green bough.'

'Where did it first grow?'

'In America.'

'Where did it bud?'

'In France.'

He was asleep but still smiling when the stretcher bearers picked him up. Wyndham, the American in France, fighting –

apparently – for Ireland, tried to get to sleep for an hour, but it didn't work.

This is your lurch, Daniel. It wasn't Lieutenant-Colonel Fitz-mullen-Brophy, or Private Moriarty, or Mister William Butler Goddamn Yeats. You took that shilling because you were a simpleton. A grown-up simpleton, a well-read simpleton, but a bloody fool all the same. And then you did it all over again. That's right. You got out once, but you couldn't stay out. Why? Over a girl? Over someone who was marrying someone else anyway? You don't deserve a girl. If Nora Maxfield took off all her clothes in front of you and said she was bored, you wouldn't know what to do. You'd mumble something about having to ask Major de Roche first.

What was the matter with you? If you didn't like your job you could have done anything else. Anything. You wanted a manly life? You could have gone prospecting in Alaska. You wanted a thrill? You could have played piano in a New Orleans whore-house. You wanted Irish heroes? You could have just read another damn book.

And you wanted to commit suicide? You could have done that, too, only you could have had a bath and a hot meal first and then made it quick.

'Wyndham? Dan? You awake?' It was Doyle.

'I'm awake.'

'I'm just on my way to find de Roche. You're in charge while I'm gone.'

Wyndham did the rounds. He didn't want to, but if his men were out in the dark, crouching on a mattress of corpses, then he could not in all conscience leave them alone. He had maybe two hundred yards of winding trench to negotiate, but it took him an hour, and it was an unnerving and loathsome business.

He prayed for Doyle to come back – not because he was lonely, but so that someone else could do the crawling across a charnel pit next time.

He did manage to doze off for a little while in the small hours, warning the sentries to wake him in good time for the dawn stand-to. His eyes were shut for no more than half an hour, and he felt no benefit from it. He was assessing his dwindling stock of cigarettes with some alarm when Casey the runner found him. As usual there was no salute and no respectful address.

'Sorry to have to tell you, but Mr. Doyle's been hit.'

He watched Wyndham's jaw drop. Then: 'He's alright, like, but they've sent him down the line. Major O'Donnell sent you this.'

It was a couple of pages from an official message pad, brusquely apprising Lieutenant Wyndham of the situation, with an appended sketch map.

'And this as well.'

Wyndham looked at Casey's impertinent smirk. Then he looked at the whiskey bottle that Casey had pulled from a satchel.

'The seal was broken on it already. Honest to God.'

Wyndham waited until Casey was gone before he raised the bottle to his mouth and began the day. *Might as well*, he thought. *Might be my last*.

74

He was not drunk. In fact, he felt surprisingly well. Hardly tired at all. Certainly not so jittery. He could see clearly what needed to be done, and if that meant crawling back and forth along the trench, then that's what he would do.

This was command. Just make your decisions and live by them.

He decided that the rum ration should be doled out as soon as possible. If an attack were ordered, there simply wouldn't be time. As the morning lengthened he ordered another issue. Might as well. He had two whole gallons of the stuff to get through and an ever-dwindling number of men. The bursting whizz-bangs were thus made more bearable and the wounded more comfortable.

He could even dare to peer over the parapet from time to time. There was no trench periscope, but he reckoned that with all the metal flying around, the Germans had to keep their heads down too. A battle was going full blast, he supposed, but it made for a disappointing spectacle. A few moving figures in the distance. A lot of bursting shells. A whole lot of smoke.

Private Higgins, the maker of tea, was slightly wounded. He wouldn't even countenance being sent back. He was still good enough to fight, he insisted. No one argued, but he was relieved of the great responsibility of looking after the tea. With a shrapnel bullet in his forearm he might botch the job. Private Foley stepped into replace him. Wyndham was glad of that. He knew every one of his men, but Foley was the only one who'd been part of his lamented machine-gun section back in Ireland. Foley was the last of those happy ramblers with their profusion of short-lived corporal's stripes, and, here in this trench at least, the last link with those carefree days. Wyndham thought it fitting to have him close by, here at the end.

In early afternoon Casey came back. It was remarkable to see a man move freely in daylight. He came sprinting in almost before they knew he was there, with the German machine-gun bullets beating the earth ineffectually behind him.

'Message from Battalion,' he said. 'And I brought your mail up and all.'

Was Casey just showing off? Even if he was, he had shot up in Wyndham's estimation, especially when he saw that the mail wasn't just a handful of letters but a good-sized parcel as well. Wyndham was almost tempted to offer the lad a drink.

He detailed Private Foley to take charge of the mail while he saw what Battalion had to say to him.

The message told him that the attack was going in that very afternoon. Good. Not much longer to wait then. He was signing a formal receipt of order to give to Casey when there was a sound like a pickaxe striking wood. He looked up into Casey's blank eyes and saw the blood streaking down the man's face from under his helmet. Casey's body crumpled.

Wyndham and Foley were silent for a long moment. Then Foley said, 'There's a cake for Finnerty.'

'What's that?'

'There's a cake sent for Finnerty. A fruit cake, I think, sir. Only Finnerty got hit there a few minutes ago. So did Corporal Quinn. Just a few minutes ago.'

'Very good, Foley. I'm promoting you corporal. Pass the word to all NCOs. We go over the top at half-past three. And share out Finnerty's cake.'

In the last hour, with everybody knowing what they were expected to do – as much as that was possible – Wyndham did his best to keep himself occupied. If this was command, it was suddenly quite an empty occupation.

He had sent a runner off to de Roche, but hadn't heard anything back, and doubted that he would now. He had supervised the distribution of stores. That wasn't difficult. Every man was already festooned with extra ammunition. Two hundred and fifty rounds per man – which seemed excessive, since their training in attack had emphasised that it was all about the bayonet. But they had brought the ammunition this far, so they might as well carry it a while longer, and take a couple of grenades in their pockets while they were at it. They should also take extra cigarettes. A crisis had been forestalled by the discovery of a stock of army-issue cigarettes the Dubliners had left behind. Horrible-tasting things, it was universally sworn, but most welcome now. It turned out they actually went well with a drop of rum.

Wyndham had the last of the rum measured out into the men's spare water bottles. There was a wealth of spare bottles now; an abundance of spare equipment of all kinds, in fact. Some of it was rather shop-soiled, but it was there for the taking.

He looked at the stack of dead men's rifles by his command post and thought of what Fitzmullen-Brophy would have done to get his hands on them a year ago. And that reminded him of other parties who'd still want them now. He could sell them round the back of the Volunteer Hall in Fermoy for ten pounds apiece. Nothing to it. Go home to America by first class.

He wasn't drunk. His hand was perfectly steady as he found a spare water bottle for himself and carefully decanted the rest of the whiskey. Plenty left, and better to carry it in a tin bottle than a glass one.

Then, in trying to find a way of incorporating the whiskey with the rest of his gear, he remembered Moriarty's big German pistol.

Because it didn't matter now, he pulled out the incriminating object and inspected it. It was an alien thing. It wasn't just because he was so used to British equipment. This thing was different in all respects, from the smooth wooden holster to the unknowable mechanical workings. The moving parts were entirely different to the revolver he carried. He fiddled with it until something jammed, and that was probably for the best, seeing as he found he was looking right down the muzzle at the time. He put it away. He'd rely on his trusty old Webley instead. Not that he had any particular trust in it. Never even used the thing. But Fitzmullen-Brophy had always carried one, and he'd never have chosen equipment he couldn't rely on.

Fitzmullen-Brophy! How could he forget? The letter! He'd had letters, but in the crisis of the moment he had merely registered that the one on top had a Tralee postmark. Now he searched his pockets and found two envelopes, somewhat sticky with blood and cake crumbs.

Dear Daniel,

I do hope that this finds you well. The papers are full of the war news and it all sounds most exciting but terribly dangerous. Mummy is awfully glad that Daddy has nothing to do with it. Daddy of course is in an awful wax to be out of it and is doing everything he can to get back in. We had him at home for a while earlier in the summer and he was out on recruiting drives but not doing very well I'm afraid. Then he found himself a job in the Army Cyclist Corps – imagine! – and managed to get himself command of some sort of Territorial or Yeomanry battalion that cycles all round the place.

He's angling for a posting back to France and knowing him he'll get it. He has grown quite wily when it comes to getting his own way in the Army these days. Of course he wants to

*get back to the Munsters, or to some Irish regiment at least,
so if you meet him you must look after him. He took some
nasty spills when learning to ride Mummy's bicycle. He says
he's much better now, but you know him as well as I do.
If he pops up again in the regiment, please take care that
he doesn't do himself any more mischiefs, and do look after
yourself.*

Mummy sends her best, and we both pray for your safety.
All my love,
Molly Fitzmullen-Brophy

*PS I am signing off with my full name because it's practically
the last time I'll be using it!*
M.

Well, that was nice. Wyndham took a long swig on his spare water bottle, even though he'd just decided he'd had quite enough
for the time being.

He peeled the second letter off the back of Molly's and his
heart skipped as he recognised the firm round handwriting.

Dear Dan,
*Just a quick note to say that I have volunteered for a transfer
to France and am now working in No. 4 General Hospital in
Rouen. Please do come and visit if you find yourself in the
vicinity. We can have that tea you invited me to in Basingstoke.*
Your friend,
Nora Maxfield.

Wyndham's mind overheated.

Tea! The stern girl who had so neatly rebuffed him was now
inviting him. To tea! He'd never thought the drink could awaken
such flagrantly sexual associations.

Rouen! Hospital! Base Hospital! My God! Doyle was wounded! Doyle was on his way to hospital! But wait. They said Doyle wasn't badly hurt. Didn't that mean field hospital and not base hospital? He wasn't sure. And there were lots of hospitals anyway. It wasn't just Rouen.

Oh please let Doyle be alright!

He thought about the peck on the cheek she'd given him. In his memory it became less like a perfunctory head-butt and more of a lingering kiss.

He shook himself before something unseemly happened in his breeches and he checked his watch again. Fifteen minutes. He jammed the cork firmly into the bottle, put it out of the way, and crawled purposely off to his duties.

75

'The time so long wished for by you and by me is at length arrived;
you have now an opportunity of distinguishing yourselves.
Be cool, be steady, but above all, pay attention to my word of
command.'

—Colonel Wallace, 88th Foot, Busaco 1810

Major de Roche checked the time again. Fifteen minutes to go.
Exactly. His watch had been synchronised. For the first time in
this war he knew the precise time, and that was a satisfaction.
Less satisfactory was the enforced idleness. Absurd that he, a
graduate of Staff College and an officer commanding a company,
should have so little to do at a time like this.

But the telephones lines were all cut. The plans were all set.
What could be seen to had been seen to. All there was now was
to wait. Major O'Donnell was busy, and everyone else was either
junior or senior to him, so he could hardly speak to them.

He had time to think, and he rather wished he hadn't.

He thought that when this was over he would marry. They'd
almost certainly confirm him in his majority now, and he was a
firm believer in the adage that while captains may marry, majors
should and colonels must. He hadn't the faintest idea whom he
might marry, but that would no doubt sort itself out. He came
of good family and was reasonably well off. Besides, it rather
looked like there wouldn't be very many eligible men for a lady
to choose from after all this.

No. That was an ugly thought. Especially at a time like this.

His collar felt tight and grubby. He wanted to loosen his tie. Unthinkable.

His hands were sweating heavily inside his gloves. Such nonsense. He'd endured field days in India without such discomfort, he was sure.

Nerves. It could only be nerves.

The younger chaps joked about it. You could do that, apparently, if you'd done any time at the front. It wasn't cowardice. Cowardice was still a disgraceful thing. Men were shot for it, and rightly so. No – the word the younger men bandied about was 'windy'. Windiness, he gathered, was the inevitable companion to life in the trenches. The studied unconcern, the stoicism that de Roche had striven to cultivate, was out of fashion. An officer who did not deign to duck his head or hurry past a known place of danger tended not to last long. A windy fellow, on the other hand, lasted longer. Not that being windy was something to be admired. It was just one of the darkly comic features of the war. Like an attack of diarrhoea, it was an embarrassment and a joke at the same time.

De Roche was not windy. He would not be windy. His rank and station would not allow it.

But for a man of his rank and station there was something else to be feared. It was another new word that was being heard in the mess, but this time from the more senior men.

Sticky.

A sticky officer was one who displayed too much caution. He remained stuck in place when he should be pushing forward. De Roche, even though this was his first battle, would most certainly not – *not* – be sticky.

He looked at the men, pale, pulling on cigarettes, fiddling endlessly with their equipment. He would lead them forward. He would not stick. This was his first battle, but he would be equal to the moment. Others might see him, fastidious and reserved, and might think him a cold fish. Might even think him sticky. Even windy. But he was a Connaught Ranger, and had been for ten years, and the deeds of the Connaught Rangers of a hundred years and more were his heritage.

These Dublin men and Munster men were good enough in their way, but in 1812 when the men of Bombay and Madras and Bengal were seeking the shade, the men of the 88th Foot – the men of Connacht who barely knew English – were forming up for an attack on the terrible Spanish fortress of Badajoz. Every Ranger knew the tale, and whether dressed in elegant scarlet in Galway or under a sun helmet in the Punjab, every Ranger knew he was kin to the wild men who'd stormed the broken walls that fearful night.

> *...soldiers, unencumbered with their knapsacks—their stocks off—their shirt-collars unbuttoned—their trousers tucked up to the knee—their tattered jackets, so worn out as to render the regiment they belonged to barely recognisable—their huge whiskers and bronzed faces, which several hard-fought campaigns had changed from their natural hue—but, above all, their self-confidence, devoid of boast or bravado, gave them the appearance of what they in reality were—an invincible host.*

That had been on Good Friday, and when the sun rose through the smoke on Holy Saturday a third of them were cold and dead, the fortress was taken, the city sacked, and the 88th Foot would forever after be known as the Devil's Own Regiment.

Somewhere on this field there was a new battalion of Rangers, but could Kitchener's men match up to the brutal heroes of elder days? Would they be spoken of with awe a hundred years hence? Would these Munsters of his? His men were keen, but the dead of three divisions, littering the ground in front, mocked any notion of an invincible host. The few officers he had left would undoubtedly do their best, but where were their several hard-fought campaigns? Only Wyndham, alone out there on the right flank, had done anything like this before. He hoped he could rely on Wyndham. (An odd sort. Foreign.) He knew, though, that he could rely on himself.

The day was hot and dry, but recent rain had made clinging mud of the bottom of this trench. De Roche watched the minute hand of his watch creep onward. It wasn't the watch he saw or the mud he felt. The blood-slick stones of Badajoz were under his feet.

He patted his face with a monogrammed handkerchief – his last clean one. He settled his whistle between his lips and pulled his pistol from its holster. Less than a minute left now.

Rangers of Connaught! It is not my intention to expend any powder this evening: we will do this business with the cold iron.

The second hand reached its apex. The whistles blew.

Major Esmonde de Roche *p.s.c.*, devoid of boast or bravado, neither windy nor sticky, led his men over the top.

It was time. Wyndham's watch might be a little off, but he'd know the starting signal when he saw it. He peered over the parapet, trying to see some way that wasn't covered by German fire. Johnston, Something and O'Brien – *O'Brien! Not O'Bannion!* – had the ground well swept from all angles. Over there under the ruins of Ginchy there would be a German officer with a telephone, waiting to put through the urgent call to the supporting artillery. Or, more likely, his telephone lines were cut too, and he waited with a flare pistol. The coloured lights would go up – up above the dust and smoke – and down would come the shells, and nowhere to hide from them.

He had come up with a plan of sorts. With no one to tell him not to, he was going to angle right rather than going straight ahead. The ground seemed not so deadly over there, and the indirect advance might confuse the Germans. It was more useful to deem the plan an indirect advance rather than a skedaddle for the sidelines.

But there was no evident path to victory, no sure route to salvation. Go far enough to the right and you're in Lousy Wood, and he'd been there, and he hardly considered it safe.

Still, he had to get off his knees and out of this hellish trench. Better to do it when he was supposed to.

But his stomach was suddenly a knot now. He was cold and hot at the same time and the smell of corruption was making his head spin sickeningly.

Whistles blew faintly over on the left.

'Sir?'

He had to stand up now.

'Sir?'

I will make my doings be spoken of among the great doings of heroes in their strength.

A coloured light climbed up from the British side of the line. That was the signal, a moment or two too late.

What would Fitzmullen-Brophy do? Ask if anyone needed the lavatory?

He got to his feet, dizzy. The battlefield opened up to him.

What would Fitzmullen-Brophy do?

He drew a deep breath.

'*Stand up, Dirty Shirts!*'

76

Confusion is apt to occur in any assault. It is specially to be expected when attacking a maze of carefully prepared positions, and is the most frequent cause of failure.

—*Notes for Infantry Officers on Trench Warfare*, War Office, 1916

They were going pretty well for men who didn't really know where they were going. Not all of them were pushing on, of course. The trail of Wyndham's men was dotted with shell holes in which, if they were lucky, the severely wounded were being tended by the lightly wounded, but compared to other attacks mounted in the Battle of the Somme so far – compared to attacks that were going forward on Ginchy at that very moment – this one band of Munsters at least was going pretty well.

Luck had everything to do with it. As soon as they'd climbed out of their trench and Wyndham had stood there, getting his bearings, making sure everyone was with him, Foley urgently drew his attention to a small white cloud that had puffed up somewhere to their front. Foley, the one-time trainee machine-gunner, recognised it for what it was. It was steam.

'Mooney!' he shouted, and Wyndham had no idea what he meant, but after a moment he saw what Foley was seeing. Like the Vickers guns that Wyndham's men should have been training with back in Cork, the German guns were water-cooled. When they started to emit gouts of steam it meant that they were overheating or malfunctioning. Whichever – it meant that the gunners were obliged to do something technical with the apparatus that didn't involve firing. Clever Foley. He'd read the manual.

The Munsters might perhaps have rushed the German position, but that wasn't part of the plan. The plan was to move to the right and, they hoped, out of danger. They saw in the silenced German gun not an opportunity for victory to exploit but a chance of survival to be grabbed at. Wyndham waved at them frantically and they went haring off across what had, just seconds before, been a German field of fire. Rifle shots were still zipping by, and the ever-present shrapnel was bursting here and there, but most of them made it to cover of sorts.

And that's how it went on. The only reason their advance didn't stall was that, wherever they went, the available cover was hopeless. They'd come to a jumbled halt, hug the ground as they caught their breath, and then make a panicked rush across another twenty or thirty yards, leaving a few more casualties behind each time.

To go forward meant advancing into the face of German fire, so they continued to slip sideways. Old soldiers liked to say that there was nothing on the battlefield more dangerous than a second lieutenant with a map and a compass. Wyndham didn't know about that. He hadn't been finding much use for either. He wondered how much farther they could go before his oblique approach technically became desertion in the face of the enemy.

This was no good.

A storm of fire burst upon some distant point. If those were British shells then that was most likely Ginchy, and that was where he should be heading. There was no obvious way forward. It was a great pity, seeing as they'd been doing so well up till now.

It was blind luck again that led them to a gap that had been blasted in the wire. If they hadn't come across it they might have shuttled to and fro in desperation and dwindling numbers looking for it. The wire here was not the linear barrier they'd expected, and the gap was just a space between the heaped-up coils and twisted pickets. There was random fire coming from all directions, and the view was perilous and revealed little, but Wyndham was convinced – almost convinced – pretty sure anyway – that the closest German trench was *that* way. Would fifty-odd Munsters be enough to take it? He took a swig of his water bottle. Soon find out, anyway.

Every man already had his bayonet fixed and his magazine charged. Their jaws were clenched and their faces pale. They had plenty of fight in them yet. This is what they'd come for, after all. He composed himself for a moment, and flexed his fingers on the grip of his pistol.

'Right,' he said.

On his word they got up and ran, slipping on the loose earth and tripping on strands of wire, but maintaining their momentum somehow.

There was a trench. Wyndham could see it clearly now. Not quite where he supposed, but pretty much in front of them. No one was firing from it. He felt a moment of elation, but only a moment. He'd imagined standing on the parapet shooting German after German, while all around him his men surged in with the bayonet. But there were no Germans to be seen. There was no one to shoot at.

And there was no one shooting at him because the trench was British. Maybe it had been German quarter an hour ago, but it was British now. Wyndham didn't jump down into it because it was full of British soldiers. For as far as he could see they crammed the trench, slumped or prone, all of them wounded or dead.

He might have stood there quite a while if random German fire hadn't reminded him that it was unsafe. Unable to find his voice, he waved his men on. Over on his left he could see a few figures moving in the open. They reminded him of how lonely he was. Instinctively he led his men in that direction.

They fetched up in some shell holes that marked the high-tide mark of an earlier attack, and, again, they could see no way forward. They might have been in trouble if the German position right opposite hadn't been equally wretched. The Munsters were few enough indeed by now, and had grown steadily less reckless since first they'd gone over the top. Rather than try and rush the Germans they threw grenades, with the Germans replying in kind until both sides ran out. After that the two sides sniped at each other, with casualties inflicted and suffered but neither side gaining the upper hand.

Drifting smoke, combined with the stink of high explosive and the ever-present odour of sundered corpses, prompted Wyndham to order gas helmets donned. After all the lectures and pamphlets he still had never knowingly smelled poison gas.

And so the duel went on, with each man fighting his battle through two fogged-in eyepieces, his breathing laboured, hot and close. One man, driven to distraction by his constricting mask, pulled it off. He couldn't see any of the Germans wearing theirs so he chanced it, and then thumped his mate and shouted to him that it was safe. And then Wyndham was pushing his way over to tell them both to keep their damn gas helmets on, but he had to take his own off to make himself heard.

The stupid frustration of it all was brought to an end by the instigator getting hit by a bullet, so Wyndham felt he could order gas helmets off without losing face. And then he tripped over a Lewis Gun that must have been left behind from the earlier attack.

Wyndham's platoon hadn't been issued with any such guns. Training on them had amounted to a Dublin officer, more proud of his proficiency than he was concerned with his educational technique, stripping one down and reassembling it for Wyndham, briskly naming the parts as he snapped them together. It had all been lost on Wyndham, except for the rather useless piece of information that the magazine carried forty-seven rounds. It had struck him as a most unmilitary number. Why not fifty? Why not forty-five? It was the only thing he remembered, and it wasn't likely to do him much good now.

But here was Foley, mechanically minded and brimming with initiative. Between the two of them they got the gun mounted on the lip of a crater, with Foley experimentally working the cocking handle and saying that he thought he might have the hang of it. But then they were both knocked down by a terrific bang that was probably a grenade. Foley had taken most of it, but it didn't look fatal. Wyndham busied himself with field dressings while he waited for his hearing to return. Dressing a wound was much easier once you accepted that there wasn't much you could do to make things worse.

He was still shaking when he'd finished with Foley, but there was whiskey for that.

The Lewis Gun still seemed to be serviceable – if it had been serviceable to begin with. Wyndham optimistically tried to copy what Foley had been doing, and surprised himself by using uncharacteristically strong language with regard to the makers of this weapon and why they should design something so different to the Vickers Gun, the manual for which he'd studied.

And then another pair of hands was there, and something moved and something clicked, and it all felt right. Wyndham looked into the wide eyes of Private Dineen, who looked like a frightened rabbit, but he was still doing his duty. Private Dineen had studied the manual too, perhaps. The teacher's pet, with his school certificate, paying attention even when it wasn't his business.

Wyndham couldn't hear what Dineen was saying, but he nodded in reassurance anyway. Then he took a deep breath, pushed himself and the gun forward, and brought it to bear on the German trench.

He hadn't fired a rifle since that day at St. Yvon, way back in the war's primeval days, but he remembered the first lesson his musketry instructor had shouted until he was blue in the face.

'Hug it tight in, lads! Tight! Or it'll kick you hard enough to break your shoulder.'

For Wyndham the lesson had been reinforced one time by a blow on the chin that nearly cost him a tooth. He'd been properly wary of recoil ever since.

Now he hugged the stock of the gun, muttering, '*Tight, lads, tight!*' without hearing himself. There'd be no time for more than a single burst. Push the gun up, acquire a target, fire and drop out of sight again. Dineen was at his elbow, steadying him, and probably praying, although Wyndham couldn't hear that either. He heaved himself a little further up, caught a glimpse of a grey steel helmet, and squeezed the trigger.

He kept squeezing when he really ought to have stopped. He was afraid to. The gun was an angry live thing in his grasp. If he let go it might have turned on him. It kicked into his shoulder forty-seven times in less than five seconds, at the end of which he was slid all the way back to the bottom of the shell hole and the smoking gun was pointing at the sky.

It appeared to have done its job, though, because someone shouted that the Germans were abandoning their position.

The Munsters fired after them and then moved forward. Wyndham surrendered the gun to Dineen and another volunteer, and tried to assess what had been gained. It wasn't much at all, but did appear at least to be a way into the crumbling German defences.

The German trenches proved every bit as bad as the British front line had been. They were broken down and half filled-in, with no real continuous stretches. This made it possible for Wyndham's men to infiltrate forward, and while they had a few heart-stopping moments in the course of their tentative advance, it transpired that the Germans were withdrawing. Only their dead were left to hold the line.

The village of Ginchy had been taken by determined Irish assault, but that did not mark the end of the battle. All the Irish had gained was another bite of blasted ground. Beyond the ruined houses was another German position, every bit as strong: a box of wired-in trenches and mutually supporting machine-gun emplacements. And the Germans, having held Ginchy for so long, had every inch of it marked on their maps, so now the German shelling of the village was more accurate than the British had been. But whatever units had to form up under that fire for an attack on the dreaded Quadrilateral would not be Irish. The 16th Division had done all it could. Between Guillemont and Ginchy they had battered themselves to ruin.

For now, all there was to do was hold on until nightfall before handing over to the relieving troops.

Wyndham found the rest of the Munsters with difficulty. Moving about freely was still impossible. There were Dublins and Munsters mixed together all over, but they were strangers to him.

He finally came upon de Roche at the mouth of a dugout, or perhaps it was the cellar of a house that had been obliterated. He'd have passed by except that he recognised de Roche's voice.

'We are taking prisoners, man! I forbid you to throw that bomb until the Germans have had a chance to come up!'

'Sir?' Wyndham still wasn't sure. Major de Roche was filthy. His tie was undone. Worse than that; his tunic was torn open to the waist, as was his shirt beneath. A field dressing precariously applied to a wide but shallow wound had been augmented, it appeared, with a monogrammed pocket handkerchief.

'Wyndham? Is that you? Wherever did you get to?'

'Wyndham waved a heavy arm in the vague direction of where he thought he'd been.

'Well, I must say I'm glad to see you,' said de Roche, all business. 'Precious few officers left.'

Wyndham nodded. He was sore all over and unbearably thirsty. He took a deep drink from his water bottle before realising that it was his whiskey bottle. Oh well. He found somewhere to sit down and watched as a dirty white rag flapped at the mouth of the dugout, warily followed by a man in baggy grey uniform, looking worse than Wyndham felt. More followed, with their hands up.

'Wyndham, if you're not doing anything useful would you kindly come here and take an account of these prisoners?'

'Of course, sir.'

The Germans had been holding out here all week. The British artillery hadn't just pounded on them night and day: it had kept the rations from coming up, the reinforcements from getting through and the wounded from being evacuated. The ones now coming up from underground moved like old men, week-old beards grey with dust, hands palsied with fear of what their captors meant for them.

For the moment, thankfully, their captors seemed content with souvenirs. In gratitude at being deprived only of his cap, one prisoner was unbuckling the strap of his wristwatch to give to a grinning Irishman. But not all of them were so subservient. The man with the wristwatch received a slap and a stern word from a tall man with braid on his collar. Wyndham didn't know the German rank badges, but he knew he was looking at an NCO. He didn't know the badges, but something was familiar. He was suddenly sure of it.

He stood up unsteadily and walked towards the prisoners. He pulled the big man by the sleeve.

He couldn't speak German. He tried to say it in French, but the words were jumbled in his head. The German looked at him, confused but not frightened. He might be a prisoner, but he was still a sergeant in the German army and wasn't going to be cowed by a pipsqueak of an English officer.

Wyndham was shaking the man now, his certainty so great as to make him tongue-tied.

'St. Yvon!' he managed at last. The man looked at him in angry incomprehension.

'You were at St. Yvon! *Vous étiez à St. Yvon! Hiver avant-dernier!*'

The German sergeant shook his head and shook Wyndham off his arm. The English officer was mocking him. No – he was mad. The shells had made him crazy. What was this St. Yvon he was raving about?

'Wyndham! What the devil are you playing at? Leave that prisoner alone!'

And Wyndham apologised to de Roche, in laughing embarrassment, and patted the German's arm.

'I'm so glad to see you're alright,' he said, and he turned away from the prisoners, wiping his eyes on his sleeve.

'Wyndham! I say, Wyndham!' shouted de Roche, and his exasperation was so great that he was moved to follow the errant lieutenant and take him to task. This would never have happened in the old army.

Wyndham turned a dreamy look upon the major, and for the first time de Roche saw the blood on Wyndham's tunic.

'You've been hit,' he said. 'You really should have said something, you know.' He helped Wyndham to sit down and pulled at his collar, scolding all the while. 'Doesn't look like anything much. Just a scratch. But still. I mean, really. Now hold that in place. Wyndham? I say, Wyndham! Do pay attention when I'm speaking.'

Wyndham could hardly feel the grenade splinter in his neck. He could hardly feel anything. His head was spinning. He started muttering a place name again, but now it wasn't that hamlet in the Ypres Salient where he had once seen a distant German NCO in the sights of his rifle.

'What's that? Speak clearly, man.'

'Rouen,' Wyndham was saying. 'Send me to Rouen.'

Dirty Shirt

by John Ware

When unassuming American tourist Daniel Wyndham arrived in Tralee, he was searching for whatever strain of Irish mysticism inspired W.B. Yeats and Lady Gregory.

But instead of a Celtic Twilight he found the hard-drinking redcoats of the Royal Munster Fusiliers – the Dirty Shirts.

Ireland was on the brink of civil war, Europe was on the brink of world war, and Wyndham was about to find out what the heroes and fighting men of Irish legend looked like in the twentieth century.

* * * * *

"…a fascinating tale – **fun, fast and furious** – and it shows an aspect of the Great War in a way never attempted before."

— *Irish Examiner*

"… **a distinguished first novel** … written so well that the military historical instruction it affords is a pleasure to absorb."

— *The Irish Sword* (journal of the Military History Society of Ireland)

"**Ware has an unerring eye for detail**, telling his story not from the point of view of strategy and troop movements, but compassionately and humanely from that of the soldier right there in the trench …"

— *Historical Novel Review*